One man stood out in the crowd...

He was tall and well built, but didn't walk with that muscle-bound swing several of the others had. He didn't have any visible tattoos and he carried himself easily. His gaze moved from side to side as if he was drawing his new surroundings in his head for future reference.

He looked straight at Eleanor. She caught her breath. So much anger, so much bitterness, so much grief. It was as though in that one glance she'd been able to see inside him.

"Move." The CO dug the man in the kidneys with his baton.

A second later he dropped his eyes and became simply another con, shuffling along with the others.

Eleanor didn't like that moment of recognition. She hoped he wouldn't wind up on her team.

In fact, she hoped she'd never see him again!

Dear Reader,

Most of us believe that if we are honest, hardworking and treat others with compassion and dignity, we'll get the same treatment in return.

This is the story of two people who found out the hard way that's not always true. Dr. Eleanor Grayson, large-animal veterinarian and part-time employee of Creature Comfort Veterinary Clinic, lost her husband, her practice and her self-confidence. After two years she's finally back up to speed, professionally and emotionally. Steve Chadwick lost his wife, his business, his freedom and his good name. For the past three years he's known only bitterness and grief.

Now Eleanor has taken a job building a prize cattle herd for the newly reopened prison farm. She wants to save the money to buy a partnership at Creature Comfort, but she also wants to teach her "team" a skill they can use on the outside. She's been warned against prisoners who prey on gullible women. She knows that almost all convicted criminals swear they're innocent. But Steve seems different. When he says he's innocent, she wants to believe him.

Until now, Steve hasn't cared whether anyone believed him or not. He's spent his time planning the perfect murder, and refuses to allow his growing attraction to Eleanor to deter him from his goal. He can't become a part of her life. She must not become a part of his. Yet neither feels alive except when they're together.

I hope you enjoy reading Steve and Eleanor's story.

Carolyn McSparren

Previous book by Carolyn McSparren in the Creature Comfort series

HARLEQUIN SUPERROMANCE
996—THE MONEY MAN

The Payback Man
Carolyn McSparren

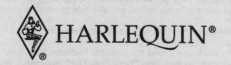

TORONTO • NEW YORK • LONDON
AMSTERDAM • PARIS • SYDNEY • HAMBURG
STOCKHOLM • ATHENS • TOKYO • MILAN • MADRID
PRAGUE • WARSAW • BUDAPEST • AUCKLAND

ISBN 0-373-71011-9

THE PAYBACK MAN

Visit us at www.eHarlequin.com

Printed in U.S.A.

To all the veterinarians, their families and their staffs who lent me books, let me watch procedures and answered a million questions. And to all the cowmen who regaled me with tales of cows, bulls, buffalo and their idiosyncrasies.

Especially for everyone at the Bowling Animal Clinic, for Bobby Billingsley who warned me I wouldn't be able to stay on a cutting horse thirty seconds (he was right) and for Sam Garner, who gave me chapter and verse on buffalo and beefalos alike.

If I've gotten anything wrong, it's my fault. Whatever is right is because of the good people who helped me.

PROLOGUE

"GUILTY."

Stephen Chadwick stood at attention behind the defense table. He was too stunned to react. Behind him, the spectators erupted into noise. He heard doors open and close as reporters ran to report to their editors. He thought he heard his sister wail.

This couldn't be happening. His lawyer, Leslie Vickers, leaned over to whisper to him, "Don't worry, boy, we'll get you out on appeal."

Appeal? How long would that take? Months? Years? Meanwhile, what would happen to him?

The hollow thud of the judge's gavel struck through his consciousness. He gripped the edge of the table and willed himself to keep standing straight. Until this moment, he'd believed Vickers. An innocent man is never convicted. There was no real evidence against him. "Piece of cake," Vickers had told him.

Most of all he'd believed in the system.

"Stephen Chadwick." How could the judge's baritone sound so casual? This was Stephen's life he was talking about! "You have been found guilty of manslaughter by a jury of your peers. The penalty phase of this trial will commence after lunch."

Now Stephen knew why all those prisoners he'd watched being sentenced on television never showed emotion. None of this felt real, but it was nothing like a nightmare. He knew he was awake. He knew this was the end of his life as he'd known it. He simply couldn't take it in.

He wanted to scream, but that would do no good. At this point, why should his precious dignity mean anything?

It was all he had.

How could the jury believe he'd killed his beautiful, clever, funny wife? His Chelsea, his friend, companion and support in all his crazy schemes?

As he was led away to the holding area and the bologna sandwich, already curling at the corners, that awaited him as it had every day from the start of the trial a week earlier, he kept his eyes straight ahead.

ALL AFTERNOON character witness after character witness testified to his value to the community, his kindness, his honorable business dealings. Even his sister spoke for him through her tears. Their father the Colonel would make her pay for that.

Stephen glanced around the courtroom, not really expecting to see his father. Yet he hoped that somehow the Colonel would support him in this way if in no other.

It was as though the witnesses were speaking of some other man. How do you prove you're a good man when you've just been convicted of killing your wife?

Most who spoke up for him were business acquaintances or men he played polo with, women he knew casually from the committees his wife had sat on.

How trivial his life sounded. He hadn't been a great philanthropist, hadn't adopted orphans or even coached Little League. He'd worked eighty hours a week building his company, and when he played, which was seldom, he played polo.

Vickers had told him after lunch that it was the polo that had convicted him. In the eyes of the jury, a man who plays polo is perfectly capable of killing his wife. But even they weren't certain enough of his guilt to convict him of murder. How could they be? Dammit, he was innocent!

He sat up when Neil Waters took the stand on his behalf. Neil was his only true friend, and as his brother-in-law, he must have endured hell from his wife, Chelsea's sister, to come forward like this. He said he still believed in Stephen's innocence, just as he had as a hostile witness for the prosecution during the trial.

Then it was over. He stood to hear his sentence.

"Stephen Chadwick, I have heard a great deal about what a fine man you are, but a fine man does not kill his wife. Granted, the jury only found you guilty of manslaughter, but I can hardly sentence you to community service. I therefore sentence you to not less than six years nor more than twelve years in prison." Again the gavel sounded.

Stephen couldn't meet anyone's eyes. From behind his shoulder, Neil said, "Don't worry, old buddy, you can handle it."

The judge gaveled the room to silence, and Leslie Vickers went up to the bench. "Your Honor, we request continuance of bail until such time as an appeal can be heard."

The prosecution broke in hurriedly. "Your Honor, the defendant is a wealthy man with many ties worldwide. He is a substantial flight risk. We request that bail be denied."

The judge looked at Stephen with something like compassion. Then he said, "Bail is denied. The defendant will begin serving his sentence immediately pending appeal."

Again the sound of wood on wood. He'd never forget that sound. It would doom him again and again in his dreams.

He felt the heavy hand of his jailer on his shoulder and barely heard Leslie Vickers's words of encouragement. As he was led away, the voice of the prosecutor cut through his consciousness. "Leslie, old son, you give me a hostile witness like that Waters guy and I'll whip your ass every time."

Stephen stopped and turned to look at the prosecutor. Despite his appearance—big, heavy, florid, in a suit too tight across the shoulders—he was a formidable lawyer. His laugh was as big as he was, and it boomed out as he

clapped Vickers on the shoulder. "Talk about your damning with faint praise."

Stunned, Stephen turned to look into the courtroom. Neil
Waters was just walking out. No, not walking. Swaggering. The way he swaggered in the plant when he'd just
pulled off a really great marketing ploy.

Neil Waters was happy.

CHAPTER ONE

"Is RICK CRAZY to recommend you to that place? Are you crazy for even considering the job?" Dr. John McIntyre Thorn looked up momentarily from resectioning the flipped intestine of the young Great Dane who lay on the surgical table in front of him.

"Probably." Dr. Eleanor Grayson watched carefully. Her specialty was large animals, but she never missed an opportunity to observe Mac Thorn's surgical expertise with small animals. Not that the Great Dane was small—except in relation to a thousand-pound horse. Amazing that such a large man as Mac Thorn could work so delicately. She'd once watched him successfully pin the tiny broken bones of a sugar glider's leg.

"So why are you applying for the blasted job?" Mac continued speaking but went back to his careful cutting. "Those men are dangerous. Oh, damn and bloody hell!" He picked up a section of intestine that had been hidden behind the original necrosis. As he worked to remove the necrotic tissue, he kept up a string of epithets aimed not at the dog but at the owners who had allowed the dog to suffer for twenty-four hours before bringing him into Creature Comfort Veterinary Clinic for treatment.

His longtime surgical assistant, Nancy Mayfield, raised her eyebrows at Eleanor. There was probably a smile to go with the eyebrows, but it was hidden behind her surgical mask.

Eleanor kept silent until Mac finally relaxed, allowed

Nancy to irrigate and tossed the dead tissue into the waste barrel beside him.

"Well," he asked, "why *are* you applying for the job?"

Eleanor sighed. "First, if I get the job, I can keep working part-time here at Creature Comfort. With Sarah Scott three months' pregnant, you're going to need another large-animal vet for as many hours as I can manage. Second, it's a minimum-security prison, so probably most of the inmates are in for nonviolent crimes. Third, they're starting their beef herd from scratch as a show herd for the prison farm. I've never done that before, and it ought to be a real challenge. Fourth, the stipend includes a three-bedroom staff cottage on the grounds, so I'll have no rent to pay, and fifth, the pay is fantastic for part-time work. I can probably save enough in a couple of years to buy into a decent vet practice somewhere in East Tennessee."

"Or here?" Mac glanced up over his magnifying glasses. "If Sarah wants to cut down on her hours after the baby is born, we'll have room for another full-time partner. Sponge, Nancy, dammit!"

Nancy, whose hand had already been poised over the intestine with the sponge, didn't bother to nod. At least Mac was an equal-opportunity offender. He cussed everybody—everybody human, that was. Never an animal.

"Okay. Let's close this sucker."

"Will he live?" Nancy asked.

Mac shrugged. "Lot of dead tissue, but with luck, he's got enough gut left."

The intercom beside the door crackled. "Eleanor?" The strangled voice of the head of the large-animal section of Creature Comfort, Eleanor's immediate boss, Dr. Sarah Scott, came over the intercom.

"Yes, Sarah?"

"We've got a bloated cow over at the Circle B ranch. You mind taking it? I'm tossing my cookies every five minutes. Oh, blast!" The intercom switched off.

Eleanor began stripping off her gloves and scrubs.

"Poor Sarah. I don't think she planned on having morning sickness quite so badly."

She went directly to her truck in the staff parking area at the back of the Creature Comfort main building. Sarah was probably in the bathroom. She'd confessed to Eleanor that she and her new husband, Mark Scott, vice president of operations for Buchanan Enterprises, Ltd., and financial manager of Creature Comfort, hadn't planned to get pregnant quite so soon after their marriage six months earlier. Now the pair couldn't be happier. Except for Sarah's morning sickness. Everyone kept saying it would pass after three months, but so far she still spent at least an hour a day in the bathroom.

That put a strain on the large-animal staff of Creature Comfort, which consisted of Jack Renfro, a Cockney ex-jockey who knew everything that could be known about horses, their part-time assistant, Kenny, a senior in high school, and part-timers hired on an as-needed basis. Eleanor worked three nights a week and most weekends, and was on call when someone was needed to fill in.

Eleanor sped out the gates to the clinic, past the brass sign that read Creature Comfort Veterinary Clinic—Aard-varks to Zebras, and turned right toward the Circle B.

She drove as fast as possible along the back roads under big old oaks still not bare of leaves, although it was October. In West Tennessee, this close to the Mississippi River and the Mississippi border, the area usually stayed warm through Thanksgiving.

Indian summer would be a blessing if she did get the job at the prison farm. There'd be a great deal of work to clean up the old cattle barn and make it usable, as well as fences to be mended, pastures to be trimmed—a dozen major tasks that were easier in good weather. Once the cold rains came in November, working outside could be miserable.

Eleanor had one final interview at two o'clock for the

position of veterinarian-in-residence at the new prison. Well, not new. That was part of the problem.

The prison had been run as a penal farm in the forties and fifties, then allowed to deteriorate while the prisoners were hired out as road crews.

Now that the farm was being reopened and recommissioned, the county was putting a significant amount of money into making it a model operation.

A real opportunity for a veterinarian. But so far, getting the job had been an uphill fight. Eleanor could not afford to be late for her interview. She knew that she was not the unanimous choice of the board, but despite the problems, she wanted the job badly.

She turned into the gates of the Circle B Limousin farm and prayed that the bloated cow would deflate fast and without complications so she'd have time to change from her coveralls and rubber boots before her interview.

"YOU DO SEE OUR PROBLEM, Dr. Grayson," Warden Ernest Portree said.

"Absolutely. I don't agree it's a problem." Eleanor sat across the conference table from the five male members of the prison governing board that had the power to hire her or not. She adjusted her body language, hoping she looked comfortable, open, at ease.

She felt miserable, hot, tired and exasperated. The bloat had taken longer than she'd hoped, and she felt thrown together and unkempt.

The small dapper man at the far end of the table chimed in. "When Dr. Hazard, who is, I believe, the managing partner in Creature Comfort, recommended you for this post, he said that you were an excellent veterinarian. He did not, however, mention your other attributes."

Eleanor gave him a smile and tried to remember his name. "What other attributes?"

"You are a young and, may I say, attractive woman."

She didn't acknowledge the compliment. Actually it sounded more like an indictment.

The warden frowned down the table at his colleague. "Gender wasn't in the job description, Leo. You wouldn't want to get us in trouble with the EEOC, now would you?" His voice was tight.

"She will be working closely with a crew of convicts, some of whom have histories of violence."

"But you have female guards," Sarah answered. Violence? She'd been assuming these guys were behind on their child-support payments or heisted cars.

Leo What's-His-Name said, "We call them correctional officers, Dr. Grayson."

"COs for short," Warden Portree added.

"I stand corrected. But you do have women. Young women. Several I saw on my way over here could be considered attractive."

"They are trained for their positions, Doctor. You are not."

"I am trained for the position of veterinarian. The job description said nothing about having experience as a correctional officer. Frankly, it didn't say I had to look like a boot, either. It did say that I would be protected by your COs whenever I was working with the inmates. Was I mistaken about that?"

"No, no, that's correct."

"Also, I thought this was a minimum-security facility. Doesn't that mean that the level of violent offenders is pretty low?"

"Not necessarily," Warden Portree said. "When we're completely full, we'll have a good many low-level dope dealers and white-collar criminals, but even a murderer with a good attitude and a clean record in prison can be accepted if he is not considered a flight risk."

"Oh." Eleanor took a deep breath and sat up straighter. The seat of the wooden chair hit the backs of her legs midthigh. She tried to wiggle her ankles so that her legs would hold her when she stood up. "I still don't think my age or gender is a problem." She leaned forward. "Gentlemen, you are looking for a veterinarian who can set up and oversee this new beef cattle operation. You are also considering bringing in other kinds of feed animals in the future, and a rescue-dog program. Correct?"

"Yes, but—"

"I will be maintaining my present position as a part-time staff veterinarian at Creature Comfort. That gives you access to the top veterinary facility and staff in four states as my backup. It also gives you a ready source for jobs for inmates who are eligible for work release and have shown themselves capable and willing to learn."

A fortyish man with thinning hair and gentle brown eyes leaned forward. The others wore jackets and ties. He wore jeans and a V-necked sweater. "We were introduced earlier, Doc, but you probably don't remember all the names. I'm a doctor, too, psychologist and psychiatrist. Raoul Torres."

Sarah nodded. "I remember you, Dr. Torres."

"Most convicts are master manipulators. A majority of them have conned their way through life. They'll fawn all over you and tell you you're wonderful, and before you know it you're smuggling in cigarettes for them and calling their lawyers to discuss early parole."

"I'm not that naive, Doctor."

"Don't believe it. Some may even convince you they're innocent. A lot of these guys can't read and write. We try to teach them that skill at least while they're here. A few are geniuses, but many have below average IQs. That doesn't mean they don't have street smarts, but nearly all of them have rotten impulse control. If they didn't, they wouldn't have committed robbery or stolen cars or even taken drugs. Just remember they see nothing wrong in using you to get what they want."

"That's a pretty grim picture, Doctor. Why on earth are you working with them at all if that's the way you feel?"

"How can I help anyone I can't diagnose properly? Many of these guys are close to being released back into society. If we can teach them impulse control, break the cycle of poverty, addiction and anger, and give them a skill needed on the outside, then maybe we'll give them a chance for a decent life. Believe me, buying into the games doesn't help anybody."

"And in the meantime, we put them to hard work and help pay the expenses of keeping them," Portree said. "Prison farms everywhere used to support themselves with market gardening and livestock. Then that theory went out of favor, but what goes around comes around. Several states now have very successful prison farm programs. Angola—about the toughest prison around—even has an inmate rodeo once a year to show the general populace what they've accomplished."

"You want a *rodeo?*"

"Not immediately of course, and it probably wouldn't be under your jurisdiction in any case," Portree said.

"Mr. Portree, gentlemen, I can do this job. I am not going to get caught up in inmate intrigues. I will teach them to be cattlemen and horsemen—"

"Horsemen?" the man named Leo said. "Nobody said anything about horsemen."

Eleanor sighed. "You have a choice. Either work your cattle from horseback or from four-wheelers or motorcycles. I don't imagine you want your inmates to have access to motor vehicles. Horses are smarter, think faster than either men or cows, and go places four-wheelers can't go. You can teach cows to come in on their own to eat, but if you have to move them any distance, you'll need horses. I'd also recommend a couple of good herding dogs eventually."

"She's right." This came from J. K. Sanders, a big, rawboned man with graying hair who sat beside Portree. "I got three or four old cutting horses out at my place I'll let you have. They're pretty much retired now, but you won't be working them hard, and I think they'd enjoy the excitement.'' He smiled at Eleanor, who nodded in return.

"This is getting complicated," Portree said.

"It's going to get worse," Eleanor continued. "A commercial cattle operation looks fairly simple, but you want a prize herd, don't you? Even a small herd of fine cattle gets complicated if done right."

"We don't want a large herd, Doctor," Leo clarified.

Eleanor suddenly remembered that his last name was Hamilton—Leo Hamilton.

He went on. "We want an exceptional pedigreed herd that wins prizes at fairs, brings good prices at auction and shows off what a good job we're doing. It's to be as much a public-relations project as anything. We don't expect to provide beef for an entire prison population. At least not initially, and perhaps never."

"Then you need a few exceptional cows, preferably with calves at foot and pregnant again, and a really superb bull that will win prizes for you quickly. You can make money from selling his semen, as well as using it yourselves. You'll have to change bulls every two to three years, otherwise you'll have an inbred herd."

"You know how to buy cattle?" The question came Sanders. Eleanor suspected he had probably bought and sold a few in his day.

"I haven't done it in a while, and I'd be grateful for your assistance, Mr. Sanders."

"Sure thing, little lady."

Her mother had taught her that the way to make a friend or ally was not to do something for them, but to ask them to do something for you. This time it seemed to have worked. "If you agree, I'll also enlist the help of the large-animal partner at the clinic, Dr. Sarah Scott. She's an expert in breeds and breeding. Have you decided the breed you want?" Eleanor asked.

"We're open to suggestions," J. K. Sanders replied, "but my choice would be Beefmaster. I know a couple of excellent local breeders who'd let us have some stock at affordable prices.'' He shrugged. ''Might even donate 'em for the write-off on their income taxes, but we'll have to pay a pretty penny for a good bull.''

''You do know they're the largest breed of domestic cow,'' Eleanor said.

''And one of the showiest,'' Portree said.

''Your inexperienced men will be handling over a ton of bull.''

''Doctor, some of those guys could throw a bull over their shoulders and walk off with it. Besides, you've got the experience.''

''Even I cannot pick up a three-thousand-pound bull.''

''So you can't handle it?''

''I didn't say that. There's not that much difference between a three-thousand-pound Beefmaster and a two-thousand-pound Brahma, except that the Brahma is probably a whole lot meaner.''

''Those are details we can discuss later if and when we decide to employ you,'' Portree said.

''There is one thing that bothers me. Animals don't work business hours. They often require care twenty-four hours a day, and most cows decide to calve at night. I know your prisoners sleep in dormitories in an inner compound. Will I be allowed to keep them at the barn when I need them? Nights, weekends?''

Leo Hamilton spoke up again. ''The bakery begins work at three o'clock in the morning outside the compound. The mess-hall staff works weekends. We have a number of men who leave the prison each day for work release and return each evening. The men who are already here and the ones who'll continue to arrive until we reach capacity are considered trusties. They are well aware that if they try to escape, they will be returned to maximum-security prisons and lose the good time that they have accrued.''

''So nobody tries to escape?''

''Occasionally,'' Warden Portree said, ''but not often,

and we invariably catch them. The general rule among prison professionals is 'three and three.' Escapees are caught within three hours and within three miles of the prison.''

"So the men on my team will be able to work overtime?"

"When absolutely necessary," Hamilton said. "They can be signed out by you or a CO and signed in again when they return."

"I won't abuse the privilege."

"That's all we ask," Portree said. "Now, on to another subject. You know that a cottage on the grounds comes as part of the stipend?"

Eleanor nodded.

"It's one in a row of overseers' bungalows, built sometime in the forties. We've brought it up to code, but it's not fancy."

"I don't need fancy." She felt her spirits lift. Surely they wouldn't be talking about housing if they weren't going to offer her the job.

"You mind living inside the prison gates?" Torres asked.

"But outside the internal compound, right?"

"Yes. Just inside the perimeter fences."

"There are five or six other cottages, aren't there?"

"Yes, but not all occupied yet. We hope to have the work done—by inmates—by the middle of February. Then we'll put the remainder up for bids to our top staff."

"Good idea."

"At the moment," Torres continued, "it's pretty lonely—only three or four others occupied."

"I'm used to being alone. And I like being close to my charges. Besides, Creature Comfort is only ten minutes away by car, so it works out well."

"All right, Doctor, what say we call you in a couple of days with our answer?" Portree asked.

Eleanor nodded and stood to shake hands all around.

Raoul Torres winked at her and gave her a small thumbs-up.

She felt their eyes on her back as she walked out. The moment the door to the conference room closed behind her on their murmurs, she leaned against the wall and let out a deep breath.

"Did you get it?"

Eleanor felt Precious Simpson's hand on her arm. Precious, principal of the general education program at the prison, had called her boss at the clinic, Rick Hazard, about the job posting in the first place.

"I have no idea." She thought a minute. "Maybe."

"Great. We'll be neighbors. Those bungalows aren't much, but it'll be fun having another woman close by. Right now all I've got is a couple of crotchety old COs who don't have any family."

Precious was the warm, golden brown of a ripe peach, and wore her hair in tiny braids that hung down to her shoulders.

"I think Leo Hamilton really hates that I'm a woman and what he calls 'attractive.'" Eleanor wrinkled her nose. "You're a beautiful woman. How come he doesn't worry about you?"

"Leo probably doesn't consider my type beautiful."

"Does being inside scare you?"

"Sometimes. A lot of the inmates they're bringing in are huge. Most prisoners pump iron constantly. Sometimes when I'm walking in a group of them past the mess hall or into class, I realize I'm one woman among a bunch of convicted criminals who haven't had a woman since they were sentenced."

"How do you handle it?"

"Keep my eyes front, walk like I know where I'm going and don't stop to chat. Then I duck into the staff common room, have a cup of coffee and shake for a while."

"But you keep coming back."

"Hey, the pay is great, the rent is free. But what keeps

me here is the occasional success—like when some tattooed crack dealer reads *Crime and Punishment* and actually *gets* it.''

Precious walked Eleanor out to the staff parking area. As they stood beside Eleanor's truck with Creature Comfort emblazoned on its side, a yellow school bus pulled through the gates and stopped by the administration building, a battered two-story brick building left over from the Second World War. The bus door opened, and a corrections officer stepped down and shouted to the passengers.

Their hands were cuffed in front of them, but they weren't wearing leg or waist irons. They wore identical blue work shirts under jean jackets, jeans and running shoes.

"You're right," Eleanor whispered. "Most of them are enormous. My Lord, look at that one."

A gigantic man, probably close to seven feet tall, who weighed at least three hundred pounds and all of it muscle, stepped from the bus and stood blinking in the sun. His skin was almost pure white—prison pallor. His white-blond hair was cropped so short it looked like peach fuzz.

"Move," the CO shouted.

The big man shuffled forward obediently. From under his brows he noticed the women watching and smiled at them shyly. His eyes were pale blue. Eleanor thought he had the sweetest smile she'd ever seen.

Then she glanced at the man behind him. He, too, was tall and well built, but didn't walk with that muscle-bound swing several of the others had. He didn't have any visible tattoos and he carried himself easily. His gaze moved from side to side as though he was drawing his new surroundings in his head for future reference.

He looked straight at Eleanor. She caught her breath. So much anger, so much bitterness, so much grief. It was as though in that one glance she'd been able to see inside him. A second later he dropped his eyes and became simply another con shuffling along with the others.

"Move, you." The CO dug the man in the kidneys with his baton.

She didn't like that moment of recognition. She hoped he wouldn't wind up on her team. With luck, she'd never see him again.

CHAPTER TWO

PLANNING WAYS TO KILL Neil Waters had kept Steve Chadwick sane during his three years in prison.

At first he'd sought advice from the murderers he met inside, but they were obviously incompetent. After all, they were in *prison*. They'd been caught. Amateurs, all of them. Apparently professional killers didn't often wind up behind bars.

He lay back on his bunk with his hands locked behind his head. Minimum security. At last.

One step closer to freedom.

He'd have to settle on the way to kill Neil soon.

The bunk beside him was occupied by an elderly con named Joseph Jasper, known as "Slow Rise." He told the other cons he got his name two ways. He was usually easygoing, slow to anger, but his wife had finally pushed him too far. He'd caught her in bed with her lover and was now serving twenty-five to life because he'd picked up his shotgun and "caught him on the rise, like a damn fat mallard." He said it was a satisfying experience, but not worth spending the rest of his life in prison over.

Slow Rise said the only truly successful murders were listed either as accidents or natural deaths and never investigated at all. He had great respect for the skill and doggedness of homicide detectives once they were alerted that a killing had taken place. He suggested Steve kill Neil with poison, and even mentioned a few varities that could handle the job. Born and bred in the country, Slow Rise knew a dozen ways to turn common weeds into deadly potions.

"If you don't do it but once and don't do anything stupid right after like marry his woman or buy a yacht with his money, chances are it'll be put down to a heart attack," Slow Rise had advised.

Steve couldn't use poison. That was the sort of sneaky method Neil might try. Besides, he wanted Neil to know he was being killed, by whom and for what. He wanted Neil to be afraid, to beg for his life.

Steve had expected to have to wait until he was paroled in two years or less to kill Neil, but if he kept his nose clean at the penal farm, he'd probably be sent out on work release soon—maybe in a few weeks if he was lucky. He could easily escape from work release.

To outsiders, two years to serve until parole might seem like no time at all, but Steve didn't think he could stay sane another two years, assuming he was still sane now. Killing Neil seemed perfectly reasonable. Did sane men think that way?

"Hey." The man on the other bunk sat up and poked Steve's shoulder.

Steve ignored him. He loathed Sweet Daddy, a small-time pimp imprisoned for cutting one of his ladies—his "bottom bitch"—when she tried to leave his employ to start her own business. Steve had inadvertently protected Sweet Daddy in the yard at Big Mountain Prison one day when a motorcycle freak had threatened to break him in two for stealing cigarettes. From that moment on, Sweet Daddy had stuck to Steve like a limpet.

Steve couldn't imagine any woman being attracted to Sweet Daddy's ferrety face and scrawny body, but apparently he'd run a large and generally loyal stable of beautiful and expensive ladies. Guess he could be charming when it behooved him.

Steve forced himself to stay calm, to keep his eyes closed, to feign patience. The trick was to seem relaxed, uncaring. If they thought you cared about anything, they took it away from you. Prison taught patience.

But now he had resources. He had the contacts to obtain false identity papers that would pass the closest inspection, and he could sign Neil's signature so well that Neil himself couldn't detect the forgery. Prison did teach a few useful skills.

Steve would have preferred to see Neil brought to trial for Chelsea's murder, convicted, sentenced to prison, see his good name, his wealth, his family stripped from him as Steve's had been.

Steve knew that wasn't possible. He'd have to be content with exacting his revenge personally. He'd have to spend the rest of his life in Brazil, which had no extradition treaty with the United States. A small price to pay.

Prison had also taught him there were no completely satisfactory endings.

Before he was convicted, he had believed in the United States criminal-justice system, that being an honorable, moral man was all the protection he would ever need. No more.

Everybody *expected* Brazil to be corrupt. There would be no nasty surprises. He'd be one more crook among many. Bribery would work every time.

His only worry was that actually killing Neil wouldn't be nearly as enjoyable as the hours spent planning it.

"I THOUGHT I GOT TO PICK my own workers," Eleanor Grayson said to Ernest Portree. She had been formally hired as resident veterinarian at the farm one week earlier. Up to now she'd been filling out reams of paperwork, going over the old cattle barn and the pastures to see what needed fixing and moving her few possessions into her new bungalow.

This was her first real meeting with the warden since she'd been hired. She looked at the list of six names. These men were unknown quantities and would be her "team."

All had only recently been moved into the facility from Big Mountain Prison in East Tennessee.

"Seniority and good time are inflexible criteria in prisons, Eleanor, or at least this prison. These men have shown good conduct or they wouldn't have been moved here in the first place. We want the inmates to see a carrot, as well as a stick, in this assignment."

"They think setting up a cattle operation is a carrot?"

"Better than working all day in the hot sun tending chili peppers."

"But chili peppers and tomatoes and whatever else you're growing die in the winter. Not much to do except prepare the land for planting in the spring."

"We already have two hydroponic facilities set up under canvas and expect to have a couple of temporary hothouses before our first heavy frost, so there'll be even more to do this winter. It would seem there's a mystique about working with animals, especially large animals, that attracts the men. Better than digging in dirt or wading in muddy water."

Eleanor sat across from Ernest Portree at his desk—a broad slab of walnut that had been made in a prison woodworking shop. At least she supposed it had—everything else had. If so, the men who built it were craftsmen who should have no problem finding honest jobs on the outside.

"I've been doing some reading, Ernest. What Raoul Torres calls his 'dummy's guide to psychopaths.' He's been a real godsend. He told me I can call him any hour of the day or night if I have a problem. Okay, with those criteria you mentioned, I'm willing to work with the men selected, with a couple of stipulations. First, no arsonists."

Portree nodded.

"Second, no one with a record of animal abuse."

"Of course. Why no arsonists?"

"Because they often progress to violence toward animals. Besides, barns are full of inflammable material. I'd rather not have prisoners who like to start fires."

"You have been doing your homework. How do you feel about murderers?"

"I read that several of the governors used to staff their mansions exclusively with murderers. They were the least likely to commit another crime—unless, I guess, the circumstances of the first one were duplicated. Anyway, I won't know."

"I beg your pardon?"

"Raoul suggested that I not read their charge sheets or their prison records so I won't be looking for trouble. I won't know the drug dealers and pimps from the guys who embezzled from the mortgage company. They'll all start with a clean slate. I also want to be able to toss anyone off my team for cause, but I won't do it without reviewing my reasons with you first."

"Agreed. All moved into your new cottage?"

Eleanor rolled her eyes. "I'm still unpacking, and a good deal of my stuff will have to stay in storage, but at least I can sleep there tonight."

"Keep your pager beside your bed."

"Oh, *that* makes me feel really safe."

"You're probably safer in that cottage than you are anywhere in town. But do it, anyway."

Eleanor stood. "So when do I meet my guys?"

"Tomorrow morning okay?"

"Fine. Early. Right after breakfast. That old barn is going to have to be dug out to the clay and rebedded before we can bring in any stock. It's knee-deep in rotted manure from twenty years ago when the penal farm shut down. The first day I'll stick with the guys. Then, until they're finished, I'll delegate that to the CO in charge and check on their progress as often and for as long as I can. That way I can still work at the clinic part-time. Once the cows arrive, I may need space to do classroom instruction, as well as the hands-on stuff. Is that possible?"

"Yes, if you don't think the office in the barn is large

enough. I've assigned a CO to you. He should be able to keep the men working.''

"But not drive them into the ground?"

"That's entirely up to you. The guards take orders from you, and it'll be up to you to monitor them."

"Fine."

"J. K. Sanders going to help you pick out the cows?"

"Monday. We should have our first cows in our pasture that afternoon."

"Good luck. Keep me abreast of your progress."

"Thanks, Ernest, I will." She hesitated. "I need one more thing. I don't know how many changes of uniform the men have, but each man needs a spare set from underwear out that will be kept in the office at the barn."

"Why? They normally have three. One dirty, one clean and one they're wearing. You want a fourth?"

"I'm afraid so. There are going to be times when they'll be in the barn all night without being able to leave. If someone falls in the pond, say, or we have to mend a fence in a driving rainstorm, they've got to have a change of clothes available. I, personally, carry two sets in my truck, along with a spare pair of boots and a set of surgical greens for emergencies."

Ernest rubbed his chin. "I don't know. That's an extra expense that's not in the budget."

"It's a very minor expense when you put it against the hospital costs of caring for a prisoner with pneumonia."

"I'll see what I can do."

"Thanks."

"In exchange, we get all that rotted manure for our hydroponics." He grinned. "Unless you have a better use for it."

She smiled back "Agreed. We'll pile it, you move it out."

She left him working through a stack of paperwork inches high. She nodded cheerfully at his secretary,

Yvonne Linden, as she went by. If they knew how terrified she was, they'd fire her before she even got started.

DR. RICK HAZARD CAUGHT ELEANOR on her way into the large-animal area of the clinic late that afternoon and pulled her into his office for one of his "chats." Eleanor hoped this one wouldn't take long.

"I've heard prisoners can scent fear," Rick said. "You sure you want to take this job? I'm having second thoughts about recommending you."

"Not you, too?"

"Come on, Eleanor. You're finally completely back to top-notch form professionally. I'd hate to see you get too stressed-out."

"Don't worry, I'll still be available to take up the slack here at the clinic. And as to scenting fear, well, so can an angry terrier."

"The terrier can do a real number on your ankles. A 250-pound man can do a number on your *life,* just like a lion or tiger. Better make sure you carry your whip and chair."

As managing partner and the man whose wife and father-in-law had invested a large part of the money to open Creature Comfort, Rick Hazard's priorities were his clinic first and the remainder of the world a distant second. "I worry that you won't have time to spend here once your program at the farm gets into gear."

"I should have guessed that was the real problem. Come on, Rick, how much time can a small herd take once it's up and going? I've never let you or Sarah down yet, have I? I owe you, Rick. If it weren't for you, I'd never have gotten my nerve back after Jerry died. A year ago I couldn't have faced all the responsibility alone. I couldn't decide what shirt to wear."

Rick slumped in his desk chair and propped his knee on his desk. "You were just worn out."

"I was exhausted all right. I just didn't know how badly.

Two years of watching Jerry getting sicker and sicker, trying to keep the practice going with interns, arguing with
the pharmaceutical companies, losing client after client.
I'm a good vet, but Jerry was the shining light in the practice. He was the guy all the old ladies wanted when Muffy
had a sore throat or their stallion needed a blood test.

"After he died, I was stupid enough to think it was all
over. It took a whole year of fighting with the IRS, the
insurance companies, the hospitals about the bills for
Jerry's treatment, and finally losing everything we'd
dreamed of in a bankruptcy auction. I suppose it's no wonder I lost my nerve. It was as if everything I touched went
wrong. I've been a widow two years, Rick. Sometimes it
seems like a lifetime, and others it seems like a heartbeat."
She flashed him a smile. "Anyway, thanks for having
enough faith in my professional comeback to recommend
me for this job."

"No good deed goes unpunished as someone once
said."

Rick was not as tall as Mac Thorn nor as handsome, but
despite his reputation as being something of a fussbudget
about the clinic, he was a formidable administrator and
manager when faced with a crisis. He was also a darned
good veterinarian, though he also preferred small animals
to cows and horses.

"What does Sarah say?" he asked.

"She's all for it. She's going with J. K. Sanders and me
Monday to pick our herd. She's promised to help me get
set up. And, Rick, remember the clinic will get *all* the
business from the farm as long as I'm there. Plus a ready
source of semitrained brawn on work release. Think of it
as a win-win situation."

"Yeah. If you say so." He didn't sound convinced.
"You planning to take drugs with you? I'll bet a bunch of
those guys would just love to get their hands on some
Ketamine or Winstrol."

"I'll only carry the bare essentials for emergencies dou-

ble-locked in my vet cabinet in the back of my truck. They
won't even know I have them. My truck should be in view
at the barn nearly all the time—either I'll be able to see it
or one of the COs will.''

"How many of those guys you think can pop a car lock
and pick the lock on your cabinet within twenty seconds?''

"Probably all of them. The COs are supposed to keep
that from happening.''

"Is the anxiety worth the money you'll be making?
Don't try to tell me you're not anxious.''

"Of course I'm anxious, but I'm also excited. It's the
first time since Jerry died that I've had the guts to try
something new on my own. I don't expect to do it for
more than a couple of years. By that time I should have
enough money to buy a partnership in a good practice
somewhere, maybe even here, if you have room and I can
afford the cost. I can't go on working part-time forever. I
have to build some sort of a life.''

"You picked one hell of a way to do it.'' He closed his
eyes for a moment. "Okay, but if I see a problem, I'll let
you know.''

"I would expect that. Thanks. You won't be sorry.''

He stood up and pulled the top of his surgical greens
down over his stomach. "Man, I've got to go on a diet.
Margot feeds me too well. You have time to help me in
surgery?''

"A couple of hours. What've you got?''

"Skin graft on that silky terrier that got burned. Floor
furnaces should be outlawed.''

She followed him out of his office and down the hall,
stopping at the storage cabinet to pick up a set of greens.
Nancy Mayfield would have everything else ready, including the surgical packs. As she caught up to him at the door
of the surgical theater, he asked, "What breed of cattle
you getting?''

"Beefmaster.''

"Good God, woman, you pick the biggest breed of beef cattle in the world?"

"They want publicity, as well as a prize herd. J. K. Sanders and I figured Beefmaster would give them that."

"You're crazy."

"You said that before."

So far nobody except Sarah Scott's new husband, Mark, who looked after the financial end of the clinic as part of his duties as CFO of Buchanan Enterprises, had encouraged her. He alone saw the financial gains she could make in a short time.

Anyone who thought bankruptcy was a quick and easy way to get out of paying bills had never tried it, but after Jerry's death, there had been no other way out for Eleanor. Their practice had been liquidated to cover the cost of Jerry's medical bills, but she had still felt like Sisyphus, sentenced to push a heavy rock to the top of a hill, only to have it slide back to the bottom again and again.

With the help of her friends at the clinic, she could pull off this new job. With Sarah pregnant, she'd have to shoulder more of the inevitable responsibilities at Creature Comfort. Good thing she'd gotten used to making do with little sleep during Jerry's illness and after.

"MAN, I DIDN'T TAKE THIS JOB to shovel cow manure. I already broke two nails," Sweet Daddy grumbled. Sweet Daddy worked hard to keep his small hands smooth, his fingernails long. One day shoveling aged cow manure from the old barn, unused for more than twenty years, would destroy his manicure and leave him with blisters.

"Shut up and shovel," said Mike Newman, known to the inmates and the other COs as "Lard Ass Newman." He was a bully and a sadist. If his authority was questioned or he felt any personal slight, payback was vicious. Steve had only come into contact with him a couple of times before today, but he'd been warned to avoid even a hint of arrogance.

"When's this bitch coming?" Sweet Daddy asked.

"Use that word near her and you'll be walking around with those pretty hands in casts," Newman snarled.

"Might be worth it," Sweet Daddy whispered. "Oooh-eee, what have we here? Yo, mama." He grinned at something over Steve's shoulder.

"Good morning, gentlemen. I am Dr. Eleanor Grayson. We're going to be working together."

Steve hadn't been called a gentleman in years, and probably nobody had ever called any of the others gentlemen. He rested on the handle of his pitchfork and turned toward the voice. The others had stopped work, as well.

It was that woman he'd seen with the other one—the beautiful black woman who worked with the GED program—the day he arrived at the farm.

This woman was taller, with brown hair pulled back severely, revealing her strong bone structure. Almost no makeup. Oversize sweater and jeans.

Bet she thought that sweater would hide her womanly charms. Not from these guys. Three years without a woman gave a guy X-ray vision and one hell of a fantasy life.

Steve glanced at Sweet Daddy. The little man's eyes were burning into her, stripping her in his mind with professional skill. From the way he licked his lips, Steve knew that he was assessing Dr. Grayson as if she were one of his women.

Steve loathed Sweet Daddy's attitude toward women. He longed to smash the pimp's face, but that would give Newman a chance to smash his in return, probably kick him off this team and maybe out of this facility. He concealed his anger and kept his face blank.

"At the moment there are only six of you on my team. I know you feel as though you are getting the dirty end, having to clean out this place, but I'll be driving a tractor with a front loader and scraper blade for you. That should make things go smoother and faster. Also, when we do need additional personnel, those of you who make the grade will remain as supervisors of the new people. You're getting in on the ground floor, no pun intended. Tomorrow we're bringing in painters and carpenters to repair everything that needs repairing. The plumbing and electricity have already been done, or redone. There's hot water in the shower room and on the wash racks. Monday of next week I'm bringing in our first cows. Any questions so far?''

"Yeah." Sweet Daddy raised his hand. Steve could already see the blisters on his palms beginning to pucker.

"Yes, *Doctor,*" Newman said with menace.

"Right, yeah. So, *Doctor,* do we get first choice on the steaks?''

Everybody but Newman laughed. He snarled and started to move forward. The vet stopped him.

"Good question. Not for a long time. It takes time to build a herd, especially a show herd like this one. But I promise you if you're still here when we slaughter our first cow, you guys will definitely get steaks.''

Everybody cheered.

"Anybody here know how to ride a horse?''

Steve raised his hand. So did a couple of other men whose names he didn't know.

"What kind?''

"Just horses,'' Steve said. "Nothing special.'' The last thing he wanted was for these guys to know he'd played polo.

One of the others admitted to riding horses as a child, and another had ridden occasionally many years earlier.

"Okay. The horses you will be riding—'' she waited until they'd settled down "—are cutting horses. I guarantee they are smarter and can move faster on a cow than you can think. You *will* fall off. A lot. You'll also learn how to take care of horses. That should give you a skill that will be readily usable in this area, given the number of horses we have and the lack of knowledgeable stable help. You won't be doing much riding until we get set up, and then just straightforward riding, and not much herding. Learning to stay on a cutting horse when he starts ducking from side to side to work a cow will take some time.''

She rubbed her hands together. ''Now, how about we go over names? I have a list, but if I go strictly by that, I'll never keep you straight. If you introduce yourselves, I probably won't remember your name right away, but I'll try. Let's start with you.'' She pointed to the giant. Steve had sat behind him on the bus and beside him at meals, but he had never heard him speak.

The big man hunched his shoulders and shook his head.

''I'll start,'' Steve said. The giant gave him a grateful look. ''Steve Chadwick. I'm here for—''

''No. Don't tell me. I don't want to know what you did. I only care what you do from this point on. Clear?''

He raised an eyebrow. ''Clear.''

She nodded and pointed to the man at Steve's left, instead of back to the giant, who stood at Steve's right.

''Elroy Long, at your service. Call me Sweet Daddy.'' The wiry little black man sketched a deep bow and grinned at her and then at the others. They snickered.

She moved on.

''Joseph Jasper, ma'am—uh, Doctor. They call me Slow Rise. I ain't young, but I'm strong. Grew up on a farm. Worked cattle most of my life. Rode some years ago. Had my own place.''

''Wonderful.''

The fourth man was completely bald. Like the rest of them, he wore jeans and a work shirt, but all the visible skin, pate included, was covered with elaborate tattoos. Most were prison tattoos. Steve could tell from the black and blue ink and the lack of skill. Some, however, were colorful and beautifully done. A red-and-yellow dragon curled from the back of his right hand all the way up his arm, or at least as far as the rolled-up sleeve of his shirt allowed Steve to see.

"Gil Jones," he said.

Steve thought he'd look more at home on a motorcycle. Dr. Grayson waited, but Jones said nothing more.

Next to him stood a very young black man in a stocking cap. He was as tall as a basketball center but scrawny, as though the bone growth had outstripped his muscles. "Robert Dalrymple," the boy said. His tone and expression were sulky.

She inclined her head and smiled at him. Newman growled in the background. "You rode horses?"

"My granddaddy had a couple of racking horses," the kid said. "Ain't been on no horse since."

"Let's hope the skill stayed with you."

Finally she'd come back around to the giant. "You're our last man," she said with surprising gentleness. "What should I call you?"

He raised his head and glanced around at the others. "My name is Bigelow Little, ma'am." He sighed. "See, folks call me Big."

Sweet Daddy guffawed. "Big Little? Look at the size of him. Word up, man, you a freak."

Big hunched his broad shoulders again and ducked his head between them like a turtle.

"That's enough!" Dr. Grayson snapped. "Big, I'm glad to have you on this team. May I call you Big, too?"

"Uh-huh."

"Yes, ma'am!" Newman snapped.

"It's okay. When you work as hard as we're going to work, we can't stand on ceremony. Now, gentlemen, I'm going to go get the tractor, and we are going to clean out as much of this barn as we can manage before quitting time."

For a civilian and a woman, Steve thought, she handled herself extremely well. She hadn't allowed Newman to walk over her, and she'd shown real compassion toward Big Little, who was obviously used to being taunted. There hadn't been a lot of kindness in Steve's life these past years, and he realized how much he missed it. And from a beautiful woman...

Allowing Dr. Grayson to become a distraction would be a mistake. He'd have to watch himself.

ELEANOR WAS MILDLY ANNOYED when she found that the men had to march all the way back to the mess hall for lunch. She decided to ask the warden if they could bring their lunches with them in future. Although the cows wouldn't require a great deal of coddling, she'd need the men on site for as many hours as possible during the day if she was to teach them.

She drove to her cottage for a quick lunch, looked at the pile of packing boxes and the small empty rooms with dismay, and wound up eating her salami-and-cheese sandwich standing at the counter in the galley kitchen before she drove back to the barn.

The men had returned before her. Like soldiers detailed to dig latrines, they didn't seem anxious to start without her. They lounged on the grass, enjoying the late-October weather. She heard Sweet Daddy groan as she got out of her truck, and she motioned him over to her. He smirked at the others and sauntered toward her truck.

"Move it!" the CO snapped. She knew from Precious that Newman had a reputation for sadism, and that his nickname was Lard Ass. She doubted he'd be pleased if she called him that.

Sweet Daddy's saunter changed to a lope.

"Hold out your hands," Eleanor said when he reached her.

"Yes, ma'am."

"I noticed you seemed to be having difficulty earlier. I don't know how you've managed to avoid manual labor thus far in your sentence, but at the moment you're courting a bad infection in those blisters. Possibly some of the rest of you are, as well. Mr. Newman, I believe I asked that these men be issued heavy leather work gloves."

Every head turned toward the guard. For a moment he said nothing, simply glared at Eleanor with angry, piggy eyes. "Yeah. Some kind of mix-up."

Eleanor inclined her head. "You don't by any chance have the gloves with you, do you? It would certainly be easy to forget to give them out."

Newman glared at her.

"Oh, well, I can call the supply office on my cell phone. No doubt they'll issue the gloves in the morning," Eleanor said. She kept her voice mild, but she could see Newman knew a threat when he heard one. She was furious with herself for not checking on the gloves earlier.

She also didn't know why she guessed that Newman might have the gloves, but one look at his enraged face told her she was right. She had to fight to keep her eyes on his. He looked away first. Good thing. She was starting to shake.

"Yeah. Maybe I forgot I had 'em."

"Perfectly understandable. But I'd appreciate your distributing them now. Elroy, let me clean those hands and put some bandages on them."

"And I get to sit down, right?"

"No. You'll be fine with gloves."

She heard the snickers from the other men. Sweet Daddy curled his lip and threw her a glance of such malevolence that she stepped back a pace.

She treated his hands and watched as Newman gave him a pair of heavy gloves, which he pulled on with a grimace.

"Anybody else have bad blisters?" she asked. No one answered.

"Fine, then put on your gloves and let's go back to work. I think we can finish cleaning out this muck before quitting time if we really try." She knew she sounded like a schoolmarm with a bunch of kindergartners, but she couldn't seem to strike the right note with them.

The way they watched her and moved around her reminded her of Rick Hazard's remark about her whip and chair. It was like being in the midst of a pride of lions. She had no way of knowing whether they'd had their fill of prey or not.

Newman couldn't have forgotten he had those gloves. He had withheld them out of pure meanness. And for half the day he'd gotten away with it. She'd be more careful in the future.

She squared her shoulders and walked ahead of the men toward the tractor, which sat on the concrete pad in front of the barn. They followed.

Without warning, she felt a pair of muscular arms around her waist. She was lifted off her feet and swung violently away from the tractor.

"Hey!" Newman yelled.

She was hoisted across Steve Chadwick's chest. His cheek brushed hers. She could feel the stubble and smell the musky scent of his sweat.

"Snake!" Big screamed.

From her position on Steve's hip she looked back at the concrete. In the shadow cast by the tractor curled the largest copperhead she'd ever seen. One pace more and she'd have stepped on it. It had been sleeping, but now it lifted its triangular head and prepared to defend itself.

"Damn!" Newman hauled out his gun.

Steve said quietly, "If you plan to shoot at that concrete, I'm sure the doctor and the rest of us would appreciate the chance to take cover from the ricochet behind one of the posts."

"How else we gonna kill it, smart ass?" the CO hissed.

Gil Jones, as though his dragon tattoo conferred immunity from copperhead venom, took one step to the side, reached down, grasped the copperhead right behind its skull, hefted it one-handed while with the other he kept the writhing tail from wrapping itself around his arm. He took a couple of steps toward the open meadow and hurled the snake end over end the length of a football field into the tall weeds.

He threw an arrogant glance at Newman and returned to his place in the group.

"Thanks. You can put me down now," Eleanor gasped.

"Right," Steve said, and let her slide down his body.

She could feel her pulse thrumming in her throat. Her skin tingled where his hands had touched her. Fear. The residue of fear. That was all it was.

To cover her nervousness, she went to Gil. "Thanks. How on earth did you learn to handle snakes? I have to work with them from time to time, but I'm still terrified of the poisonous ones."

For a moment she thought he wouldn't answer. Then he looked across the meadow to the general area where the snake had fallen and said so softly that she could barely hear him, "My people's into snake handling. They say that if you got enough faith, you can drink poison and handle snakes and not be hurt."

"Have you been bitten often?"

"Hell, no. I had faith, all right, faith that if they sank those fangs into me I was dead. I can throw a rattler clear to the Mississippi River. First chance I got, I run away, and I ain't never been back."

He smiled. Eleanor thought it was even more chilling than his normal stony expression.

"I was a great disappointment to my daddy," he finished.

Not for the first time, Eleanor wondered if she was doing the right thing by not finding out what the members of her "team" had done to wind up in prison. Maybe imagining was worse than reality. Even if Gil looked like an ax murderer, he might be inside for nothing more sinister than stealing motorcycles.

She realized that Big hadn't moved since the snake was spotted, and his face was ashen. If such a man could cower, that was what he was doing. "Big?"

He made an inchoate sound deep in his throat. He was petrified.

"Big man, scared of a little ol' snake," Sweet Daddy crooned.

"Hush, Elroy," Eleanor said. "I didn't notice you stepping forward to deal with it." She touched Big's shoulder. "It's all right, he's gone."

"He's out there someplace. He could come back."

"Unlikely. And hey, we've got Gil to protect us, right, Gil?"

Gil shrugged.

"What if there's more of them in there?"

"Too late in the season for a nest," Gil answered. "We need us some big ol' king snakes—keep the bad ones down."

Until now, Robert Dalrymple had stood silent at the edge of the group. Now he took a step toward Gil. "Snake is snake. I see me another one, I'm gonna chop it in bits."

"Yeah." Newman said. "Hey, Jones, why the Sam Hill didn't you kill the thing when you had it?"

"Got a right to live same as us. Just trying to find someplace warm before dark. This late in the year they get sluggish, can't run away from you."

Eleanor hesitated, then turned to Steve. She couldn't hold his eyes. "Thank you again."

"My pleasure."

That deep voice as much as the words sent a jolt of heat through her. The others sounded as though they came either from the country or the "mean streets," but Steve spoke like an educated man. He must be one of those white-collar criminals. He didn't seem to belong with the others.

"So, barring unforeseen critters, let's get back to work," Eleanor said. She looked carefully around and in the tractor before she climbed aboard.

"I can run a tractor, ma'am," Slow Rise said. "No call for you to have to do it."

"Thanks, Slow Rise, you can take over tomorrow or

when I'm not here. Today I'd rather have you on the ground directing where to drive and how deep to dig.''

"Yes'm."

They worked through the warm afternoon without further incident. Sweet Daddy kept up a litany of complaints, but the others worked in near silence. At one point she looked around for Newman and found him propped against the side of the barn in the sun sound asleep. Great protection. Any of the men could have overpowered him. She didn't wake him. She'd already made an enemy of him.

Maybe she could get another CO assigned to her. Preferably one that wasn't vicious or ill-tempered—and one that didn't sleep on the job.

She was beginning to feel more comfortable with the inmates—at least some of them—than she did with the guard.

ELEANOR LOOKED DOWN at her grimy arm and brushed the dirt off the face of her wristwatch. Four-thirty. The men were supposed to work from eight in the morning until five in the afternoon—later if she needed them for something special.

Since Warden Portree agreed to let the men work nights and weekends when necessary—the animals would have to be fed and watered Saturdays, Sundays and holidays—she had to agree to see that they were properly checked in and out of their dormitories. And to have a CO with them. "I'll set up a roster," she'd told him.

Today the men must be completely exhausted. They weren't yet used to the hard physical labor they'd been doing for hours. With the exception of Sweet Daddy, who she was pretty sure goofed off every time her eyes weren't on him, the inmates had worked harder and longer than she would have believed possible.

Tomorrow she'd have a private talk with Sweet Daddy. He'd either do his share of the work or she'd find someone else who would. This evening she wanted to give them all a break.

Everybody was filthy and sweating. She was certain her own face was streaked with grime. All she wanted was a shower. No doubt so did the men.

But could they have showers? They might only be allowed to shower on certain days of the week. If so, she'd have to get Warden Portree to make an exception for her crew. Tonight she'd request an exception from Newman. He'd better not refuse, or she'd see that Ernest knew how he'd slept on the job.

The pile of rotted manure and shavings that they'd dug out of the barn was as tall as Big, and looked rich enough to nourish the weakest vegetables. Portree should be pleased about that. He could never buy fertilizer one-tenth as rich for his hydroponic vegetable gardens.

But he could darn well have somebody else move it from the back rear of the barn to his gardens.

"Okay, guys, let's knock off." She leaned back in the tractor seat and pulled the kill switch for the engine. "I've got a cooler full of soft drinks in my truck if you're interested."

"Got beer?" asked Gil. "I could go for a brew."

She shook her head. "You know better than that."

Newman grumbled. "You got no call to supply sodas."

"Sure I do. Big, how about you help me bring over the cooler, then we can all sit in the shade."

He ducked his head and followed obediently. The cooler was large and full of semi-melted ice and soft drinks, but Big hefted it as though it were a roll of paper towels and carried it back to the concrete pad in front of the barn.

The shed roof over the pad projected ten feet or so beyond the walls so that trucks and stock could be unloaded in bad weather. At the moment that side of the barn was in shade, and the evening was already cooling, but the concrete still radiated warmth. She considered suggesting they bring the cooler inside. The men, however, seemed to prefer being outside—anywhere outside—to being within walls.

She handed out drinks, then realized as she took one herself that she'd have to sit beside someone. Even so small an action could be misconstrued. She sat on the cooler, instead.

"Plenty more."

The men had simply opened their throats and poured the soda down. She stood, bent over, and realized all they could see was her upended denim-covered rear. She straightened quickly. "Big, why don't you hand them out?"

He seemed grateful to be chosen and shuffled over.

When she sat again, she said, "Here's the plan for to-morrow." Groans. "The worst part is over. Tomorrow you'll be helping the painters, setting up the office and the storeroom, and rebuilding the fences that divide the pastures. The old barbed-wire fences are twenty years old but still in fairly good shape in most places. The posts are concrete and broken ones have been replaced during the years. We'll still have to walk the fence lines, mark the few posts that may need to be replaced, restring wire and enclose the bull's stall and paddock in electric fencing to keep him in."

"Just like us," Robert said.

She caught her breath. He was right, but what could she say to that? "This electric fence will simply give him a jolt when he touches it."

"Yeah, up at Big Mountain, we touch the fence, we get a lot more than a jolt."

"Will it stay on all the time, ma'am?" Slow Rise asked.

"Good question. Depends on the bull we get, as I'm sure you know, since you raised cattle."

"Yes'm."

She turned to the others. "Bulls are as individual as people. Some of them will test the electric fence a couple of times and never go near it again. Others will try it every time they go out to pasture. Still others will take the jolt and keep right on going—straight through.''

"And some jump over." Slow Rise grinned at her.

"If we get one like that, we send him back where he came from. Once a bull learns to jump out, there's no way to keep him in.''

Robert again. "Come on, man. Bulls can't jump.''

"Hell, they can't," Slow Rise said. "Why, I've seen a bull jump a five-foot fence soon as look at you.''

"Nah, old man, you're crazy.''

Slow Rise surged to his feet with blinding speed for a man who had to be over sixty. In an instant he stood over Robert, his fists clenched, his face dangerously red. "You take that back.''

The kid raised his hands in front of him. "Hey, man, chill, okay?''

"Sit down." Newman's voice was dangerously hard and flat.

The moment passed, but Eleanor realized how close to the surface violence flowed among these men. She glanced over at Steve, who hadn't moved, his knees drawn up, his fine-boned hands dangling between them.

He was watching her, possibly had been watching her throughout the exchange. She felt her skin flush and looked away quickly. The connection between them had been— was—visceral. As though they were alone. She shivered and knew he'd seen her reaction.

"Okay, guys, drop the empties into the cooler, and, Big, would you put it back in my truck for me? Thanks.''

"Up." Newman prodded Sweet Daddy with the end of his baton.

"Ow, man, ain't you got nothin' better to do with that thing?''

"Don't you sass me, little man.''

The men stood and formed a ragged line.

"Oh, La—Mr. Newman—the men will be allowed to

shower and change into fresh clothes when they get back to the compound, won't they?''

''Huh?''

''Let me rephrase that. They—we—all smell like goats. We're filthy. They should shower and change before they come in contact with any of the other inmates, not only for comfort but for health reasons.''

''Yeah, I guess.''

Steve caught her eye. He raised one eyebrow and nodded almost imperceptibly. She raised her chin. Apparently she'd done something right, and though she shouldn't give a darn what Steve thought of her or her decisions, she felt a glow from his approval.

She climbed wearily into her truck and watched as the men trudged up the hill toward the compound.

She'd expected them to turn from mere inmates into people to her, but not this soon and, in one case especially, not so personally.

''YOU BASTARDS THINK you gonna have it easy 'cause she's a civilian and a female. You ain't, not with me around,'' Mike Newman said. ''Showers! Shee-ut.''

''But she said we—'' Robert clamped his mouth shut as Steve's hand fell hard on his forearm.

''She said, she said. What she said don't mean squat. What I say's what counts.''

''If we show up dirty in the morning, she's gonna be pissed.'' Slow Rise's voice was plaintive.

''Shut your yap, old man. Or you gonna find out what this here stick's for.''

''He's right, you know,'' Steve said mildly, and knew the moment the words left his mouth that he shouldn't have spoken.

Newman already disliked him. He'd recognized that immediately. Steve tried to be just one of the cons, but he'd never managed to get the shuffle down quite right. Newman saw attitude and arrogance in him and hated both.

He was also looking for revenge after Dr. Grayson called him about the gloves. Someone had been almost certain to take a beating over that. Steve had just broken the cardinal rule of prisoners the world over. He'd called attention to himself.

"You saying I'm wrong? Huh? Yeah, you saying ol' Mike Newman is wrong. My, my. Well, I do apologize. Sure wouldn't want to trample on no civil rights of any of you *gentlemen,* now would I?"

The last rays of sunshine had given way to twilight. Steve knew the blow was coming, but not where or with how much force. He tried to brace himself, but he wasn't fast enough. The steel baton slashed across the backs of his knees and dropped him. As he fell forward and gritted his teeth to keep from howling, the baton slammed across his kidneys.

Now he couldn't howl. He couldn't even breathe. The pain was electric, as though he'd been hit with a cattle prod rather than a baton. He tried to gather strength to roll over, to resist somehow, or at least to present a smaller target, but Newman was nothing if not expert in delivering pain.

Newman could crack his spine with that baton, and there was nothing, not a damn thing, that Steve could do to stop him.

"Enough." The voice was Gil's.

God, Steve thought, now Newman would go for Gil. Although Steve barely knew the man, he didn't want to be responsible for another man's pain. He groaned and tried to struggle to his hands and knees.

He expected to hear the whish of the baton, to feel it across his shoulders or his hips.

Instead, Newman said with the kind of bluster that usually covers fear, "Ain't nobody tellin' me I'm wrong."

Steve felt hands under his armpits. Sweet Daddy on one side and Slow Rise on the other barely managed to hold him up. His back felt as though it had been broken, but he could still feel his legs, so he supposed it hadn't.

Newman tried to laugh, but the sound came out strangled. "Hell, even when I'm wrong, I'm right. You remember that. You go on, git, and take your damned showers."

Steve didn't turn around. He didn't think he could move without help, but after a couple of steps he managed to keep his legs straight, to put one foot in front of the other. He gulped in air with every step. He felt like an old man who'd had a stroke.

"Man, you stupid." Sweet Daddy sounded put out. "Man hates yo' ass, fool. Next time he gonna kill you."

Steve turned to Gil. "Thanks," he managed to choke out.

Gil shrugged. "Hey, man, the bastard kills you, we gonna be up to our asses with Internal Affairs and union reps. I'm not lying for Newman. Easier to keep you alive."

"Yeah." Steve managed a faint grin. They reached the door of their dormitory.

Originally an old army barracks, the room now held cots for twenty men. So far only fifteen had been assigned. A two-drawer chest with a lock sat at the end of each cot, and beside it, a single bedside table with a lamp. No posters on the walls, no personal possessions in the open where they could be stolen, nothing to enliven the drab green of the walls or cover up the scars on the old wooden floors. At the far end of the room were latrines and a gang shower that could hold ten men at a time.

The men who were already lounging on their bunks waiting for the call to dinner looked up curiously, then quickly dropped their heads back to their books or porn magazines. Something had obviously happened. Nobody wanted to know what.

"Can you get your clothes off without help?" Slow Rise asked.

Steve nodded. "I think so. I'll be better after I stand in the shower awhile."

And he was. He managed to carry his own tray through the chow line and sit down at one of the long tables to eat. As usual, he didn't speak, and afterward walked slowly and hesitantly to his bunk, lay down and prayed his kidney damage wasn't permanent. He knew he was leaching blood, probably would be for several days.

Work tomorrow would be difficult if not impossible, but he didn't dare go to the infirmary. He'd have to explain what had happened or make something up. He suspected the people at the infirmary would take one look at his bruises and recognize precisely what had happened to him.

That would not be a good thing. Either Newman would make up some excuse to deprive him of the good time he'd accrued, or Newman would be brought in and disciplined. Then he'd really be out to get Steve. Either way Steve would lose.

He couldn't tell Eleanor, either—he already thought of her as Eleanor. She'd tear into Newman with the same effect. Newman would take out any dressing-down he got on the men.

Most of them could fend for themselves. Sweet Daddy was small, but he was wiry and fast. He was also cagey. He usually talked his way out of trouble, or whined his way out, if need be.

Obviously Newman had decided not to mess with Gil Jones. Steve had no idea what Gil had done to land behind bars, but he suspected this wasn't his first trip. From the tattoos, Steve guessed he was well allied with others in the prison. Newman apparently knew it, too. Together Gil's people could take on Newman or any of the other guards, take them out if necessary, and nobody would ever know who did the actual killing. Best to keep on Gil's good side.

Slow Rise was simply a decent man who had a bad temper. Prison had made it worse. He was also an aging con among young men. He had to seem invulnerable to survive.

Robert was an unknown quantity. He could be a kid who

went for joy rides in other people's cars, or a gang member who had gunned down someone on an opposing gang. Steve was fairly certain drugs played some part in his sentence, but whether Robert was a consumer or a supplier, Steve had no way of knowing.

And Big? Despite his size he seemed like a shy, frightened child. Forrest Gump in extra, extra large. If so, why was he in prison?

Steve had taught reading at Big Mountain. He'd written letters for illiterate cons, helped with their business problems. Many knew they owed him. If and when he got a chance to talk to any of them, he'd try to get some information about the team members he did not know. Inside the fences, knowledge was definitely power.

He'd been offered a job teaching here, as well, but working inside the compound all day didn't serve his purposes. He had to seem trustworthy on his own, away from the group, even if that meant passing up chances to escape in favor of better chances down the road.

He had always worked out and, besides polo, had played handball, tennis and golf. He'd run in charity races. He was already in shape. When he discovered the weight room at Big Mountain, he put on twenty pounds in six months—all of it muscle.

One con had tried to attack him with a knife, but Steve had countered him successfully and won grudging respect. His knowledge of business eventually won him some measure of protection, as well. As long as he kept his mouth shut, he was moderately safe at Big Mountain.

The prison farm, however, was a new environment. He didn't understand the rules or know many of the people, and they didn't know him. He'd met sadistic guards before, but not one who had an unreasoning personal grudge against him.

Eleanor had to be the catalyst. She was the outsider, the female among males. A peahen for a Lard Ass Peacock to preen in front of. Newman's ego had taken a beating from her. Maybe he'd picked Steve for his scapegoat because he and Eleanor seemed to have an affinity.

The CO was right. Steve and Eleanor did have a connection. Steve had felt it the moment his eyes met hers in that parking lot. Nothing that happened since had changed his mind. Today, when he'd snatched her away from the snake, he'd felt her in his marrow. Newman had punished him tonight not so much for touching Eleanor as for Eleanor's response. He'd nearly forgotten what a woman's soft voice sounded like, how she thought, the way she felt.

He'd have to be more careful.

The problem was that he wasn't certain he could be. It wasn't simply that she was an attractive woman, someone with the same kind of background as his. Not even that she was the first woman he'd touched in three years.

No, not even that.

If he had met her at a cocktail party or a polo game before...well, before, he knew he would have felt the same pull. She stirred his blood, yes, but more than that, she stirred his imagination. He could hear her voice in his head, see the gentle smile she'd given Big. Wished that smile had been for him.

He couldn't afford to lose his objectivity, his separateness, his focus.

He was going to escape and kill a man. He needed to husband his anger, hone his bitterness, remember his grief.

He did not want to feel anything but hatred.

CHAPTER THREE

"SO HOW DID YOUR FIRST DAY GO?" Precious stretched out her long legs and propped them on the nearest cardboard box in Eleanor's small living room. The white walls were devoid of pictures. Except for an old leather couch and matching chair, a couple of end tables and a rolled-up rug in the corner, the room was furnished with cardboard boxes.

Eleanor handed her a glass of white wine, then took her own and sat on the chair across from her. "Weird."

"How weird?"

"On the one hand, they seem like people you'd meet anywhere, might even like, and then some tiny thing sets them off and, bang, it's World War III." She shuddered. "Slow Rise, this country boy over sixty, nearly came to blows with Robert Dalrymple, a lanky black kid, when the kid said he was crazy. I don't think Robert meant anything by it—just a casual remark."

"I know Slow Rise," Precious said, watching the wine swirl in her glass. "He's usually very gentle, but he's inside for killing his wife's lover in a fit of rage."

"My God! Now I'm terrified."

"Don't be. Most of the time he's the soul of kindness. He's got another ten years to serve before he can even think of applying for parole."

"He probably won't live that long."

"No, he'll likely die in prison."

"Lord, how sad."

"Don't let the sad stories get to you, Eleanor. Remember he did kill a man."

Eleanor leaned her head back against the chair. "You're right. I had no idea I was this tired. Do you mind if we skip the unpacking tonight? I'm grateful for your help, but I really think I just want to go to bed. Tomorrow I've got the men in the morning, and then I'm working a full shift at the clinic in the afternoon and evening."

Precious finished her wine and stood. "Girl, you are going to burn out at that rate."

Eleanor didn't bother to get up. She was sure her legs would be too weak to hold her.

"Want me to fix you some soup or a sandwich?"

"No thanks, Precious. I'm sorry to be such a poop."

"Forgedaboudit, as they say in the gangster movies. We'll do it this weekend."

"You have things to do."

Precious laughed. "Right. A couple of rich radiologists are just breaking down my door trying to take me away from all this. Girl, I *so* have nothing to do this Saturday except unpack your stuff. Now, go get some sleep."

She moved to the door. "I'll let myself out."

Eleanor listened for the closing door without opening her eyes.

Not since the long nights and days nursing Jerry had she felt this completely depleted nor this close to despair. She roused herself long enough to call Raoul Torres. When he answered, she said, "Raoul, were you serious when you offered to give me some help understanding this place if I needed it?"

"Absolutely. You feeling overwhelmed on your first day? Want me to come over? I can be there in five minutes."

"Thanks, but it's not that urgent." In the background, Eleanor heard the sound of at least two children, one of whom was screaming something in Spanish.

"Pipe down!" Raoul shouted. "Lupe, tell my children

I will chain them to the whipping post and flog them as soon as I'm off the telephone.''

A woman's voice said something indistinguishable, and the screaming children began to laugh.

"Okay, if not tonight, when would you like to get together? Tomorrow sometime?''

"What?'' Eleanor had lost track of the conversation momentarily. "Oh, how about I buy you lunch tomorrow? Someplace close to the farm. I shouldn't be as dirty as I was today.''

"You got it. I'll pick you up at the barn about eleven-thirty.''

"Thanks, Raoul. I really need to talk about the men. If I'm going to work with them, I need to understand them.''

"Don't worry about everything so much. It will work out.''

"I hope God's listening to you on that one.''

She crawled into bed certain that she'd fall asleep instantly, but found she was too tired and ached in too many places to get comfortable.

How many nights after Jerry died had she slept rolled in a comforter in his old leather recliner, hoping to capture a fleeting scent of the man he had been before he got sick? How many days did she try to remember his face, his smile, the way his laughter crinkled the corners of his eyes?

Since his death no other man had stirred her blood. Her friends told her she was still young, still attractive. She didn't feel either young or attractive. Until today she'd have sworn that the juices had all dried up. Until today when she'd felt Steve Chadwick's strong arms around her waist.

Raoul would undoubtedly tell her she was attracted to Steve because he was completely out of her reach and therefore safe. But there was nothing safe about him. It was insane to feel attracted to him. He was a *criminal*, for

God's sake. A man who had done something dishonorable, and that made him unworthy to be Jerry's successor.

That sounded priggish even to Eleanor, but it was true. Jerry had been the kindest, the most generous and honorable of men. He had devoted his relatively short life to saving the lives of animals, even though he could have gone to medical school and possibly made a lot more money.

Even more important, after Jerry died she'd sworn never to invest herself so completely again in any man or any relationship. No one should have to endure losing a true love even once, much less twice. She didn't dare love that way again.

She would devote herself to her goal—saving enough money to buy a decent veterinary partnership. She had enough problems without Steve Chadwick.

Getting even slightly involved with any of the men she worked with would be a fatal error. Whatever crime Steve Chadwick committed probably had to do either with drugs or with money. He could never be considered a love interest.

She'd been wrong not to check her team members out. She *did* need to know what these men had done to land in prison. If it colored her opinion of them, so be it. She'd discovered that not knowing was much worse than knowing.

"MORNING, EVERYBODY," Eleanor said with a cheeriness that made her want to throw up. So obviously phony, but then, no matter what she said or did outside of actual work seemed to sound phony. She climbed out of her truck, locked the doors and pocketed the keys, although the only people around were her crew and the new guard.

"Where's La—uh—Mr. Newman?"

The new CO, a fiftyish woman who could probably have held her own in a fight with Big or Gil, grinned at her. "Mr. Newman is off today. I'm Officer Selma Maddox."

She turned to the men standing in a ragged line behind her. "And I do not want to hear one word about my ass or any other part of my anatomy, you got that?" No response. "I said," Selma repeated patiently, "you got that?"

Heads nodded.

"Good, we understand each other. Now, Doc, what say we put these lazy bums to work? What you got for 'em to do?"

Eleanor motioned for Selma to follow her as she moved out of earshot. She didn't want to put Selma on the spot, particularly since, unlike Mike Newman, she seemed to be a reasonable person.

"The painting crew should be here any minute," Eleanor told her. "They have their own team leader, and I've already discussed with him what they need to do. I have a suspicion you don't want my guys spreading out to check fence lines alone, do you?"

Selma laughed. "This may be minimum security, but it's still a prison. Outside the compound the fences are intended only to keep the herd animals we're going to be raising in separate pastures. Four-foot-high barbed wire will not keep your average inmate from climbing over and taking off. Then we have to go after them with bloodhounds. The bloodhounds enjoy it, but I don't."

"I take it that's a no?"

"Right."

"Okay, so we'll put them to work helping the painters. They can start painting the one-by-six pine boards for the stall enclosures—they're easier to paint flat before they're nailed up. Tomorrow we can go do the fence lines as a group. I doubt anyone but Slow Rise knows how to tension a wire fence, so he can teach the others. It'll be slow going, but we'll get it done." She leaned against the building. "Will you be back tomorrow?"

Selma snickered. "Maybe. I think Mike Newman is an-

gling for a cushy job indoors. He's not much into the great
outdoors, 'specially when it's still so warm.''

"I'll ask the warden if we can keep you. You seem
pretty relaxed around the men. They don't tense up around
you the way they did with Newman.''

"That's because even the nastiest con usually has a soft
spot for his mother. In some cases I can't understand why
they would, but they do. Anyway, that's how they see me.
I have kids and grandkids, and I try to keep my temper.
But a couple of them already know I can come down on
them hard if I have to.''

Eleanor raised her eyes as a truck labored up the rise
toward the barn. In the back were a dozen prisoners. "The
painters have arrived. Let's get started.''

She walked back to her own team and told them what
they'd be doing. She met the painters' team leader, asked
him to give her guys paint and brushes, and followed them
to the piles of wood.

She knew immediately that something was wrong with
Steve. He moved like an old man, carefully keeping his
torso erect and shuffling his feet slowly, keeping his knees
straight with obvious effort. She started to say something
to him, then shut her mouth. She watched the men set up
makeshift sawhorses and saw him bend to pick up one end
of the first board.

He nearly fell on his face. Slow Rise caught the end of
the board, hefted it easily and put a hand in the center of
Steve's back to help him straighten up. Something was
very wrong, but the men apparently didn't want anyone to
know.

She went back to her truck, unlocked it, picked up her
laptop computer and carried it back with her.

"Hey, Chadwick,'' she called.

He turned pained eyes her way.

She'd better make this good. "You know anything
about computers?''

He nodded.

"Good, then I've got some extra work for you. The rest of you keep on with what you're doing. Chadwick, let's go into the office."

She turned on her heel and marched away through the barn as though oblivious to anything behind her.

The government-issue steel desk, two desk chairs, a table and a couple of file cabinets sat in a jumble in the middle of what would eventually be the cattle-operation office. An equally utilitarian steel credenza sat against the wall beside the door. She walked in, waited for Steve to pass her, then shut the door and set the computer on the credenza.

"Can you sit?"

"I'm not supposed to sit unless you do."

"That wasn't my question. *Can* you sit?"

"I don't know what you mean."

"Of course you do. How badly are you hurt?"

The lines around his mouth tightened, his jaw clenched, his eyes narrowed. "I'm not hurt."

"Bull. Turn around."

He didn't move.

"I said, turn around."

"Against the rules to be alone without a guard and the door closed."

"Then we'll leave the door ajar." She opened the door a dozen inches and called to Selma, "This shouldn't take but a couple of minutes. Okay with you?"

"Whatever," Selma replied. "It's your show, Doc, within limits."

"Thanks. Now," she said to Steve, "do as I asked, please."

He turned around carefully.

"Assume the position if you can. Hands flat on the desk."

He managed not to groan, but she heard the sharp intake of breath. She hadn't wanted to ask him to do that, but it was the only way she knew to make certain he wouldn't interfere with her examination.

She reached for his shirt and began to tug it out of the waistband of his jeans, pulling slowly and with infinite care.

"Stop that."

"Shut up. I want to find out what's wrong with you."

His shirt came free and she lifted it as high as she could. She caught her breath. "Oh, my God, who did this to you?"

"I fell over a curb."

"Newman. How many times did he hit you?"

"He didn't."

"Steve——" She couldn't conceal the anguish in her voice. "*Please* sit down. Let me help you."

She slipped under his armpit, put her arm across his back to his shoulder and lifted to take the weight off his hands. She felt the tension in his muscles, heard his breath sough in his chest. She tried to turn him so that she could slide one of the desk chairs under him.

"No. Forwards."

She caught the chair with her left foot and pulled it across in front of him, then lowered him so that he straddled it. She sat in the other chair, knee to knee with him. He closed his eyes.

"I'll get you to the infirmary, then I'll go straight to the warden. I'll have that bastard fired."

Steve shook his head. "He's civil service and union with high seniority. You can't touch him."

"But if the others saw it…"

"They didn't see anything."

Eleanor was certain he was lying.

"Why did he do it?"

"He doesn't need a reason."

"It's because I humiliated him in front of the men, isn't it? He took it out on you."

He looked up and into her eyes. He wasn't certain she

recognized the connection between them. Newman had certainly picked up on it. He guessed the others were aware of it, as well.

He nodded. "Yeah, I think that was his reason."

He had rested his hands on the back of the chair he sat in. She covered them with hers. They were warm and strong, and yet gentle. The touch flashed along his nerve endings.

"I'm so sorry," she said, and snatched her hands away as though she had only that moment recognized the intimacy of the gesture. She stood up and moved to the back of the office to look out the single dirty window. "I wanted to make things better, not worse."

He was so used to hearing only commands from his captors that the pain in her voice caught him off guard.

He longed to stand, go to her, tell her he'd survive, that it wasn't her fault, that he'd had worse, but he didn't think he could manage to stand without help. "Newman was looking for an excuse. You were only the trigger. It's personal with him."

"Because you're not like the others."

"I'm exactly like the others. Don't ever forget that."

"No, you're not. I don't know what you did that brought you here, but I know that Newman is a redneck who resents you because you've managed to keep your dignity even in this place. He can't endure it."

"Then *I'm* the one who has to endure it. If I make trouble, he'll find some way to send me back to Big Mountain. I can't—I don't want that."

He could see from her expression that she thought she understood that he didn't want the soul-numbing life behind steel bars, that he preferred to serve his time in the open air. He let her think that was what he meant. He wasn't certain whether she would be a help or a hindrance in his flight plan. She was already a distraction.

She sighed deeply, then said, "I'll have to respect your wishes this time. You understand the dynamics of the place better than I do.'' She squared her shoulders and became all business. "I wasn't kidding about needing some computer help. I hope you weren't kidding about knowing how to work the things.''

"I've had experience." More experience than anyone within ten miles, probably.

"I need a database to keep track of the cattle program, start to finish. I know the basic information I need to be able to track—vaccinations, insemination and calving dates, that sort of thing. I know some of the ways it should be cross-referenced, but I have no idea how to set up the program. Can you do something like that?''

"Doesn't sound too difficult.''

She nodded. "That's a legitimate way of keeping you in here and sitting down for a couple of days. Since Lard Ass isn't here, at least he won't know about today.''

"He'll know, all right.''

"It will still be my choice, not yours. I'm going to request that we keep Selma and find another job for Newman. If he does come back, I'll put the fear of God and the warden into him.''

He caught her hand. She drew in her breath sharply, braced against him.

"You will not.'' It was the voice of command. He hadn't used it in three years. Amazing how quickly it came back.

"Let go of me," she said softly.

"Sorry.'' He released her and struggled to his feet.

He could see from her eyes that she was suddenly uncomfortable with him, perhaps even a little afraid. He dropped his hands. "I apologize. But I've got to make you see that you can't interfere with Newman on my behalf or the behalf of any of the other men.''

"Of course I can. He's a stupid man.''

"He's a sadistic bastard, but he's clever at that, if nothing else. He's also dangerous, and not only to me and the

other men. If you cross him, he'll find some way to hurt
us. And he may hurt you, too.''

''Hurt me?'' She laughed and walked to the computer.
''He wouldn't dare use his baton on me. What's he going
to do, get me fired? I don't think so.''

Steve shook his head. ''Not fired and not hit with a
baton. And not by him directly. Probably not even on
prison property, but hurt, nonetheless.''

''You're serious.'' She wrapped her arms around herself
and hunched her shoulders.

He longed to pull her close, feel the warmth of her body
against him. The very thought shredded his nerve endings.
He didn't dare allow her warmth to seep into his soul. He
might begin to question his goals.

He had to teach her how to be careful. She was more
vulnerable than she knew. ''This place has its own un-
written rules. A man like Newman has power that reaches
outside the prison gates, to men who owe him, who know
they may be under his control again someday.''

She raised her eyes. They were hazel, the color of the
last leaves of autumn. She leaned toward him and, without
the consent of his body, his hands reached for her arms.

''Hey, Doc, you okay in there?''

They jumped apart like a couple of guilty adolescents
caught in the hayloft.

''Absolutely.'' Eleanor opened the door the rest of the
way. ''Come in, Selma. You need to know what's been
going on and what we're planning.''

Steve shook his head. He knew she saw the gesture, but
whether she'd keep her mouth shut about Newman's attack, he had no idea.

She shut the door behind Selma and leaned against it.
''Okay, here's the deal. Chadwick, here, knows enough
about computers to set me up a database to track the cow
program. It's fairly complicated, and heaven knows we
can't afford to pay one of the computer geeks at the uni-
versity to do it. Any problem with that?''

Selma looked from one to the other. "Nope. He's working for you. You want him to dig a hole to China, he starts digging."

"Will the others resent it?"

"Sure. Not much we can do about that."

"I can handle the others," Steve said quietly.

"Good. Then let's get started," Eleanor said. "What's happening with the painters?"

"I am going to kick Sweet Daddy all the way to the mess hall at lunch," Selma replied. "Other than that, we're okay."

"I thought the men were brown-bagging it."

"Not until tomorrow. You know changes take time when you work for the state."

"Okay. Tomorrow. Today, I'm the one going out for lunch. Raoul Torres is picking me up here at eleven-thirty. I'll get Steve—Chadwick—started with what I want and leave him with it."

"Fine." Selma turned to leave.

"Leave the door open all the way, will you?" Eleanor said.

"Sure thing."

The moment the CO left, Eleanor said to Steve in a businesslike tone, "I spent last night making notes about what I want in the database, but they're very rough. I'm not precisely certain what should connect with what."

"I'll take a look at what you're proposing, then I can make suggestions about changes and additions. Okay with you?" He kept his voice as businesslike as hers. No one overhearing them would think they'd had any sort of personal encounter.

"Be my guest." She pulled a folded-up sheaf of lined yellow pages out of her jacket pocket and dropped it on the desk. "Can I bring you some lunch? The walk up to the cafeteria is going to be painful."

He shook his head. "Cheeseburgers alone down here?

Against the rules. Don't worry. I'll make it. I'm already feeling better.''

"I'm only an animal doctor, so I can't prescribe for human beings, but I can offer some horse liniment that might help, so long as it's our little secret. I use it myself for aches.''

"Thanks.''

She picked up the computer and placed it on the desk. "Good luck.''

"Right.''

He sat behind the desk and watched her walk out of the room, back straight, hair swinging. Sweet Daddy would call her "fine''—if he called her anything printable. Fine she was, and not only her sleek body. There was a directness, an honesty about her that he found disarming even as it worried him. That very directness might be her downfall. He wouldn't be able to watch his back and hers, too, not if he got out of here safely.

Somebody had to look out for her, that was for certain.

At the door she turned. "You said not to forget you're just like them. I can't believe that.''

As she turned and walked out of sight, he said softly, "One difference. I'm innocent.''

ELEANOR HAD NO IDEA whether Steve had intended her to hear his comment or not. But she *had* heard, and now she wondered....

At eleven-thirty Raoul Torres's dusty white minivan pulled up by the barn. She hurried toward it and opened the passenger-side door.

"Oh, sorry,'' he said. "Just dump that stuff in the back.''

She scooped up a stuffed bear, a plastic dinosaur, six CDs for children, and a stack of books and papers and laid them on the seat behind, next to a pink child's seat. She climbed in and fastened her seat belt.

"Where to?''

"Anywhere as long as it's out of here," Eleanor said as they headed down the driveway toward the open gates at the front of the farm.

"Rough morning?"

She ran a hand over her hair and leaned back against the headrest. "You might say that. Lard Ass Newman beat up on one of my guys last night, and the victim won't let me say anything."

"He's right."

"Why?" She turned in her seat so that she could see Raoul's profile. "Why is everybody so afraid of rocking the boat? There are rules against that sort of thing."

"You ever have a really bad teacher?"

"Of course. Most people have at least one."

"But they go on teaching every year because the rules and regulations they serve under require such meticulous documentation to do anything about them, and they have such power to pass or fail you that you just endure it."

She shrugged. "Yeah. I guess."

"Ratchet that power up to about a million, and that's how much power the COs have. The pay is lousy, the hours suck, certainly the ambiance, if you can call it that, is one step lower than the sewers of New York, and the people they are supposed to guard are dangerous. They have to have leeway to protect themselves. They have to be able to count on the support of the warden and administrators. Most of the people who work here are decent people trying to do a decent job. But sometimes even the good ones can be corrupted."

"Power corrupts, I know."

"Yeah, and these guys have almost absolute power. It's a battle between good and evil, and mostly evil wins."

"Can I avoid corruption?"

He grinned at her. "I don't know. Can you?" He pulled into a second-rate strip mall and parked. "You like Tex-Mex?"

She nodded.

"Then let's go stuff ourselves."

When they were settled in Texas Pete's and busily scooping up salsa on tortilla chips, she said, "I think I need to know the criminal records of my team."

"Not a good idea."

"I already know about Slow Rise. I can't believe it, but I know it. And what could a sweety like Big possibly do to wind up in prison? Somebody must have led him astray."

"I warned you."

"And this morning one of them said he's innocent."

Raoul laughed so loud he choked on a tortilla chip and had to wave her away while he gulped down half a glass of iced tea. When he finally got his breathing back to normal, his eyes were tearing and his nose was red. "Didn't think it would happen so quick, that's all. I warned you in that first interview that most of the people in prison say they're innocent."

"But—"

"Certainly there are miscarriages of justice. DNA testing has freed a lot of convicted rapists and murderers who turned out to have been innocent. But the odds are still very high in favor of the justice system. Confessions, plea bargains and smoking-gun evidence are the order of the day. Take it from me, if he's in for it, he did it."

"That's the thing—I think I need to know what 'it' is."

"Okay. Your choice. I can copy your team's records. I still think it's a mistake, but I'll do it for you. I can drop them by your place on my way home tonight."

"Thanks. Actually, Raoul, I may decide not to look at them after I have them. I just want the chance to make that choice."

"Good. Ever hear of Pandora's box? Or Bluebeard's chamber? Open the box or the door, and you can't ever shut it again."

"What if I find that there *has* been a miscarriage of justice?"

He leaned back as the waiter set a steaming platter in front of him. "Ah, I hate to think of what these fajitas will do for my arteries, but I can't resist."

She looked down at the taco salad in front of her and wished she had ordered the fajitas, as well.

Raoul began wrapping fajitas in tortillas. "Don't even go down that road. These guys have lawyers and families to handle their appeals or fight for new trials. You do not have a vested interest. You have no standing with the courts. Remember the rules. Keep your distance. Do not get involved. If you do, you'll get hurt."

"St—one of the team members intimated that if I rock the boat about Newman, I could get hurt—physically hurt."

Raoul stopped with his fork in midair and set the unfinished tortilla down in front of him. "He could be right."

Eleanor banged her fist on the table. "I hate this."

"Do your job, follow the rules, stay out of the way of prison politics, and you'll do fine."

"And if not, I wind up in cement shoes?"

The only thing that kept Raoul from choking a second time was the fact that he had his tortilla only halfway to his mouth. "I doubt it. And he won't rake your car with submachine gun fire, either." His tone turned more serious. "But you could be mugged coming out of a department store, or carjacked at a fast-food drive-through. Totally random, no connection with Mike. Do you carry a gun?"

"Of course not!"

"Do you have a permit?"

"I had to go through the course and get a permit before they'd hire me at the farm, but I certainly don't carry one. For one thing, it's illegal inside the gates."

"It's not illegal in your house, and there are lockers outside the gates for you to store stuff in while you're inside."

"That's such a bother."

"Think about it, that's all I'm saying. And I would definitely keep one beside your bed at night."

"I'm beginning to wish I'd never taken this job."

"Actually, you're safer inside than outside."

"That's what Ernest Portree says. I'm starting to disagree."

By common consent, they spent the remainder of their lunch talking about Raoul's two children, on whom he obviously doted, and his wife, a speech pathologist, whom he adored. They were silent on the way back to the farm.

As he parked in front of the barn to let her out, he said, "There's an old New Jersey saying—don't mix in. So don't."

She nodded. "I'll try."

She had beaten the men back to the barn by ten minutes or so. The place was completely deserted. She walked into the now completely open barn, half-painted in white enamel.

She found her laptop still sitting plugged in on her desk. The screen saver flashed scenes of green fields and mountains.

She heard conversation outside, and a moment later Selma stuck her head in the door, saw the computer and said, "Damn. Didn't think. You need to requisition a safe to lock that computer up when you're not here."

"The credenza locks."

"I could open it with a paper clip. Besides, you'll need to store paper and things, won't you?"

"Why would they steal the computer? They couldn't use it."

Selma came in and leaned against the doorjamb, easing her back against the angle of the door like a bear. "God, that feels good. Listen, they snatch the computer, they stash it somewhere outside, call a buddy, and shazaam, that night it's picked up and sold before morning. The men aren't moving around much on their own yet, but they will be when they start working the cows, won't they?"

"Yes."

"So requisition a safe."

Eleanor nodded. "Right. Okay. And the warden finally agreed to issue an extra set of clothing to each man to keep here for emergencies. I thought we could put each set into a grocery sack with each man's name on it. Think that would do?"

"You'll have to lock the clothes up, too," Selma said. "Won't be room in the safe or the credenza."

Eleanor thought for a minute. "Okay. I've got an old footlocker at my place I used to pack books. It's a little musty, but it's got a good padlock. How about I bring that down tomorrow?"

"Sure." Selma grinned. "The least I can do is contribute the grocery sacks. My family hoards them."

Eleanor looked at her watch. "I'm leaving for my regular shift at the clinic in about fifteen minutes," she said. "Will you take the laptop home with you for tonight?"

"Sure."

"You will be back tomorrow, won't you?"

"I think so. Will *you?*"

"I beg your pardon?" Eleanor asked.

"Pretty obvious this isn't what you thought it was going to be. So, are you going to pack it in or stick it out?"

Eleanor didn't answer her right away. Instead, she headed out to her truck, Selma right behind her. Part of her wanted to leave this place and never come back, even though it meant finding another place to live. At least she wouldn't be faced with Steve Chadwick every day. She wouldn't have feelings she didn't want to admit to herself, nor would she have to worry whether he was innocent or guilty. And if he really *was* innocent, what on earth could she do about it?

She slid into the front seat of her truck. Selma stood outside the door, hands on her ample hips. Finally Eleanor leaned out the window. ''I'll be here tomorrow and the next day and the next. I'm not quitting.''

''Good,'' Selma said, then laid her hand on Eleanor's arm. ''Remember, if you want to keep your peace of mind, keep your distance from the men—*all* the men.''

CHAPTER FOUR

ELEANOR FELT HER FACE FLAME as she drove out through the farm gates toward Creature Comfort. She should have realized Selma would know that something out of the ordinary had happened between her and Steve.

He was plausible, good-looking, charming and intelligent. Of course, he might also be a sociopath and a liar. He probably had a dozen women writing him fan letters and coming to see him on visiting days. She sure did not intend to be one of them.

When she drove into the Creature Comfort staff parking lot, Jack Renfro, the ex-jockey and veterinary technician, and her boss, Sarah Scott, met her before she had a chance to climb out of her truck.

"Guess what you're going to do this afternoon?" Sarah said. "You like sheep?"

"Not one of my favorite of God's creatures."

"I'm sure you'll learn to love them before the afternoon's out. You've got to vaccinate a herd of about thirty and oversee dipping them."

Eleanor stared at Sarah. "You're not going with us, are you? The last thing a pregnant woman needs is to be around all those chemicals."

"Nope, you and Jack are on your own. You've got coveralls and rubber boots in the truck, haven't you?"

"Of course."

"Took time to persuade her to stay out of it," Jack grumbled. "Sheep kick and butt like goats. I'll not have you putting my godson in danger."

"I do miss going out on calls," Sarah said wistfully. "My stomach's finally settling. I'm only three months pregnant, and I'm already starting to get cabin fever." She looked down at the top of Jack's head. "And your godchild is a she, not a he."

"Not certain yet, are you? I'll spot you eight to five on a boy." Despite his years of riding racehorses in the United States and Canada, and his wife from Marion, Arkansas, Jack had traces of his Cockney accent, although overlaid with an Arkansas drawl and an occasional "y'all."

"You're just bored, Sarah," Eleanor said. "Go help Bill Chumley with his exotics or Rick with the cats and dogs. Come on, Jack. Ah, the odor of sheep-dip on the balmy October air—my favorite perfume."

They drove out before Sarah could change her mind.

"Jack, I have a very strange and terribly personal question to ask you," Eleanor said after a few minutes on the road. "Tell me to stuff it if you like. I won't take offense."

"Takes a lot to offend me, Eleanor. Go ahead and ask."

"Did you ever know anybody in prison?"

Jack sat up. "This side of the pond or the other?"

"Either."

"Couple of what I believe are called 'domestic disputes,' a couple of public drunkenness cases among my friends when I was riding. Jockeys can come all over bad-tempered when they've had a drop too much or too many losses in a row. Small men, you know."

"Not some overnight thing in the county jail. Real prison. For a long stretch."

"Oh. Then, no."

"Darn. I was hoping you could give me some advice. I don't seem to be handling my new job very well."

"Can't get them to work for you?"

"Everybody but one works hard. That's not a bad average. The problem is that I seem to be getting involved in their lives, listening to them as though they were telling me the plain unvarnished truth. I was warned ahead of time how plausible they can be, but I thought I'd be able to tell the difference. I can't.''

"Listen, my girl, don't you turn into one of those loonies who fall in love with killers and marry them in prison. We'll none of us have it.''

"That won't happen.'' She turned down a narrow lane and began checking mailboxes. "But what if I find that one of them actually is innocent? Then what do I do?''

"Run like hell.''

She dropped the subject and turned at the entrance to the sheep farm.

Two hours later, both she and Jack were dripping with sweat and soaked to the knees with sheep-dip. The pungent aroma made her eyes water and her nose run.

She watched as Jack and the owner of the sheep, a retired engineer from New Jersey who'd moved south, wrestled the ram to the edge of the dipping pool and shoved him in.

"Bloody stupid animals, and mean with it,'' Jack snarled. "Ewes are bad enough, but yon tup's a devil.''

"Tup?'' Eleanor asked.

"What the Highlanders call 'em.'' He grinned at her and waggled his eyebrows. "Why they calling it tupping.''

"Call what tupping?''

"Don't be dense, girl. Tumbling a lass in the clover.''

"Oh.''

The farmer, Salvatore Montano, a burly man with gray hair as curly as one of his sheep's, poked the backside of the ram as he catapulted out of the dip pond and ran to his ewes. "I only bought these animals to keep me from going crazy after I retired. And I couldn't get decent pecorino cheese down south. Decided to make my own. More fool I.''

"No cheese?''

"Ever milk a sheep? I don't recommend it. Now I sell a few lambs, and the ewes are almost like pets.''

"Yon tup's no pet."

"That's for sure. He'll knock you down and stomp on you while he's butting you with those horns of his." Montano started toward the gate. "So, Doc, I'll see you in lambing season."

In the truck on the way back to the clinic, Jack groaned and complained about his aches and pains. Eleanor took about five minutes of it, then said, "So how would you like some help?"

"What kind?"

"What if I could bring you a man who could pick that ram up, swing him around his head and dump him head-first in the sheep-dip, then turn right around and do the same thing with a two-year-old bull calf?"

"Even I've heard of Paul Bunyan. He's a myth."

"Big Little is no myth."

"Big Little? You're having me on."

"Not at all. His name is Bigelow Little. He doesn't have much education and may even be a little slow, but he's a kind man who tries very hard to do what I ask of him."

"One of your criminals?"

Eleanor wanted to say that Big was in for something minor and nonviolent, but she didn't know. "He's serving time, yes, but I've been told he's eligible for work release, and if I request him, he might be able to work three days a week."

"I'm no Igor playing no benighted flute for Franken-stein's monster."

"He's not like that. Meet him, see what you think."

Jack grumbled some more, but in the end he agreed. Now all Eleanor had to do was figure out how to spring Big for work release so soon in the program. And not only Big. Steve Chadwick was too smart and well educated to be doing the job he was doing. But she didn't think Jack Renfro would like giving him orders, and if Jack had any inkling of the feelings Steve engendered in her, Jack would

flay him alive. She'd have to find—or make—another job
for him at the clinic.

As soon as the evening meal was finished, Steve
dragged himself back to the dormitory and stood under a
hot shower for ten minutes before he pulled on fresh underwear and slid into bed. It was much too early for most
of the men to sleep, but he'd learned to tune out the con-
versations, the television set, the card games, the yelling
and, deep in the night, the snoring, the sobbing and the
screams when someone had a nightmare.

Tonight, however, he couldn't sleep. He told himself it
was because his body still ached so badly that he couldn't
find a comfortable position to lie in, but he knew that
wasn't it. He couldn't get Eleanor off his mind. When he
closed his eyes, he could smell her light, airy fragrance,
which was probably only soap or makeup, but still lingered
in his nostrils.

Eleanor wasn't classically beautiful, but her face had
strength and character. Above all, he liked the kindness
and concern she showed to all the men. And there was
something about her eyes that spoke of sadness and loss.
Maybe loss was the thing they had in common.

Steve's wife, Chelsea, had come from a wealthy family.
She'd been socially prominent, with the right education,
the right connections. She rode to hounds, played scratch
golf and a good game of tennis. She was also very beautiful with a knockout body, and spent more than a thousand
dollars a month keeping herself that way.

He'd never begrudged the money. They could afford it,
and besides, the major capital in the marriage was hers,
not his. He'd loved having her on his arm at parties, watching other men staring at her, seeing the lust in their eyes.

Maybe if they'd had children, they might have kept the
magic alive. By the time he lost her, they were good
friends, but seldom lovers.

He suspected she'd had affairs from time to time. If so, she was discreet.

He should have made more time for her—for them. As the business grew ever more successful, he spent more and more time away. He forgot how closely they'd worked when they were getting it off the ground, how much he'd relied on her judgment.

No wonder she became a shopaholic, one of the "ladies who lunch."

But the last few months before she died, they'd been beginning to rediscover each other. He'd expected her to hate the idea of using some of the profits from the business to invest in inexpensive water-purification systems that could be used in Third World villages. The potential for profit was there, all right, but his "dream" was just as likely to bankrupt them. She'd listened grudgingly at first, then with mounting enthusiasm.

Maybe she realized that their marriage, their partnership, needed a challenge they could share together.

All he'd known was that they were happier together than they'd been for several years.

She'd been the one who suggested he keep his plans secret even from Neil, his best friend, his brother-in-law, his business partner. She'd known instinctively that Neil and her sister, Posey, would feel threatened by any change in the status quo.

How threatened neither of them had any way to guess.

The grief Steve felt when she died stunned him. He was no longer a whole person without her.

Then he'd had to endure the horror of accusation, trial, conviction…

How could anyone who knew him think he'd kill Chelsea?

Yet a jury had believed he was that kind of man. Even his lawyer thought he was guilty. At first.

So he'd gone from relative wealth and power, to earning

a dollar a day working in the library at Big Mountain prison.

That's where he'd learned to value small things. A new toothbrush or a current paperback novel gave him as much pleasure now as a new polo pony had in the old days.

But Neil would return the wealth to him before he died, if only to try to save his life. In Brazil, Steve would find ways to make that wealth count toward the public good. Prison had taught him that, as well. Each man was responsible for his own actions, but living in poverty, illiteracy and despair made many people easy prey for evil. Somehow Steve would use Chelsea's wealth to help at least some of them get an honest job and a decent life.

But first he had to bring Neil to justice. And Steve couldn't count on the legal system.

Steve hadn't thought he'd miss anything in this country that had falsely condemned him, but suddenly the image of Eleanor popped into his mind.

Why should he care about the opinion of a woman he'd known only a couple of days? Yet, he did. Even on such short acquaintance he knew in his heart that she wouldn't want him to do what he was planning to do to Neil.

Obviously she mustn't find out until it was too late to stop him.

He had thought there was nothing about his old life he would miss. Now he had to admit that he'd miss Eleanor Grayson. And that was crazy.

He was on the edge of sleep when he felt a hand on his shoulder. "Hey, man, you awake?"

Steve groaned and rolled over. Sweet Daddy leaned above him in the semidarkness. "I am now."

"What you got goin' with that sweet mama?"

Steve shook his head. "What are you talking about?"

"Man, we all seen. She took you off to that office and shut the door. Next thing we know Selma's gone to find out what you two been doing."

"Working on a computer program to track the cattle operation." Steve sat up.

"Riiight. I want me one of them sweet office jobs, man."

"What do you know about computers?"

"Computers, my skinny butt. It ain't your computer skills she likes."

"Elroy," Steve said, keeping his temper with difficulty, "a computer program is what she wants and what she's getting. I'm going to be digging manure right beside you most of the time. Now go to bed and let me get some sleep."

"Ain't I helped you when Lard Ass cracked your kidneys?" Sweet Daddy whined. "You don't know nothin' about treating a lady right."

"And you do?"

"Indeed, I do. My ladies visit me every Saturday now that we come down to Memphis from Big Mountain. Way they cry, I know they miss Sweet Daddy, just prayin' for me to get out."

"I'll bet." Steve rolled over. "Go to sleep, Elroy."

For a moment Elroy didn't move, then muttering some curse under his breath, he slid off Steve's bed and padded to his own. "Friends help friends, sucka."

Steve lay still with his eyes closed, his breathing slow and even. But Sweet Daddy's visit had his mind churning furiously again. He rolled over and lay on his back, stared up at the cracks in the ceiling and did what he always did at times like these. He fantasized about killing Neil.

For the first time, he couldn't focus. And for the first time, the idea made him uneasy.

ELEANOR FOUND a fat envelope of file folders on her front steps when she got home. She stooped to pick it up.

"Well, hello, neighbor," said a voice from the darkness. Eleanor jumped. She knew that voice. "Mr. Newman. I had no idea you lived in this compound." *I wouldn't have taken the house if I had.*

"On the other side of Miz Precious. Didn't know that? We're neighbors."

He came out of the darkness and walked to the foot of her front steps. "Heard you mentioned my name to the warden." His grin was a leer. "I don't think you were trying to do old Mickey a favor, but you did. Got me a cushy inside job."

She hunted for her house key in her pocket and clutched the folders to her chest like a shield.

"Once it gets cold, we can roast us some neighborly marshmallows in front of a roaring fire. Maybe pop us some popcorn. And have us some good barbecues next summer."

She found the key, turned to dig it into the lock, then twisted it. She had to get away from him. If he tried to come in, she didn't know she'd do. Scream? Something told her that he fed on fear, female fear especially. She opened her front door and over her shoulder said coldly, "Unfortunately, we're all rather busy at the moment, aren't we? Now, if you'll excuse me, I have work to do."

She didn't wait, but slipped inside, shut the door behind her and leaned against it. From the other side, she heard him chuckling—no, cackling. Her hands were shaking. She threw the deadbolt, fastened the chain and switched on a light.

She never felt this uncomfortable around the men on her team, not even Gil. Thank heaven the cottage windows came with heavy drapes. She called Precious, but got only her answering machine. She said, "Why didn't you warn me Mike Newman lived on the other side of you? Call when you get home."

She set the files on the kitchen table, poured herself a glass of white wine and drank most of it in one gulp, something she never did. *How on earth did he find out I told the warden I didn't like him?* she wondered. *I can't let him get to me.* She wasn't hungry any longer, but she found a hunk of cheddar cheese and sat down with it, a box of crackers and another glass of wine.

"Haute cuisine in a prison compound." She lifted her glass and opened the envelope.

There was a note from Raoul Torres on top. "Here are the prison files you requested. This is only the bare bones. The real story you'll have to get from them, if they'll tell you. Even if they've talked to me, I can't share that information with you. Doctor-patient privilege and all that. Call me if you need me. Raoul."

She spread them out on the table and sorted through them. The one on top read Steve Chadwick. She carefully slipped it under the pile. She would read that one last. Wondering what he'd done was infinitely preferable to discovering he was guilty of something sordid.

She reached for the file on Gil Jones.

"Gilford Jones, aka Gil Jones, aka John Gilbert, aka Gil Johnson."

Gilford? No wonder he kept changing it.

She was stunned at the length of his rap sheet. Any juvenile record he'd had was closed to her, but from the day he'd hit his eighteenth birthday he'd been boosting cars and motorcycles, and finally, after spending several years in another jail for illegal possession of firearms and incendiary devices—*bombs?*— he had been busted for running a chop shop.

He had a wife, and a daughter who would now be about eleven. What kind of father would risk going to jail and not being around to raise his daughter?

But he had never been arrested for actually *doing* anything violent, even with the guns and bombs. He'd never even been picked up in a barroom brawl. There was a note that he had tie-ins with several motorcycle gangs. He was a career criminal. Unless he had converted to honesty very recently, the chances were good that he'd get out on parole and be back in prison again before the term of his parole was up.

He seemed like such a nice guy.

She slapped the folder closed and slid it back into the envelope. Then she took her dishes to the kitchen and stacked them in the dishwasher, staying to scrub the countertops and straighten the refrigerator.

She was putting off reading the other folders—Steve's in particular.

As she started back to the dining room, her telephone rang. She jumped at the shrill sound, then snatched up the receiver.

"Hello?"

"Hey, you okay? You sound jumpy."

Eleanor relaxed, leaned against the wall beside the kitchen telephone. "Hi, Precious. I'm not used to the silence, so when the phone rang... I'm jumpy. And for good reason. Why on earth didn't you tell me Newman lived on the other side of you?"

"Would the name have meant anything to you when you moved in?"

"I guess not. I hadn't started the job yet."

"Then what's the big deal? I mean, he's creepy, but he's never there except for his poker nights."

"He was there tonight. Or rather, he was here. He loomed up at me out of the darkness as I was opening the front door."

"He say anything?"

"Not a lot—just some stuff about being neighborly— but it was the *way* he said it."

"Shoot, he's a bully. He'll back off. He never even speaks to me, but then I'm the wrong color to interest him."

"Lucky you."

Precious laughed. "Oh, right. Listen, you want me to come over?"

"No. I'm being silly. Sorry. We still on for Saturday?"

"Absolutely. Noonish? I'll bring lunch. Now get some sleep."

"I've got work to do tonight."

"Not tonight, girl. You climb into bed and get some sleep. No wonder you're on edge, much as you been working. Promise."

"But—"

"Promise, or I'll come over there and stand over you until you do."

Eleanor laughed. Actually, she felt relief. She had a good excuse not to look at Steve's file until tomorrow night. One more day of blissful ignorance. "I promise."

Raoul was both right and wrong, she thought as she dragged her weary bones into the bathroom to brush her teeth, wash her face and get ready for bed. At least she now knew that Gil wasn't violent and that he could probably fix anything that went wrong on the tractor or any other equipment.

She dreaded reading Steve's file. How could she equate the picture she was building of him in her mind—decent, intelligent, even sensitive—with a man who embezzled money or conned elderly pensioners out of their savings—or worse?

She had to know sometime. Just not tonight.

"TODAY WE MEND FENCES," Eleanor announced to her assembled crew. "Any of you know how to handle a fencing tool or a wire tensioner?"

As usual, Slow Rise raised his hand. "Good," she said. "Selma will pass the tools out. Make certain you wear your heavy gloves. Barbed wire can cut you to the bone. You'll notice we have a new four-wheeler. I'll drive, and Selma will ride shotgun. We can carry the rolls of wire on the back of the four wheeler and roll it out as we need it. Now, Slow Rise, would you like to give us all a lesson in fence mending?"

He was a capable teacher. Even Robert roused himself

from his perpetual lethargy long enough to practice splicing and tensioning the barbed wire.

"Good job," Eleanor said to Robert. He actually grinned at her briefly, then went back to his blank-eyed stare.

After an hour of practice, the group moved out. As Eleanor started to put the four-wheeler in gear, Selma stopped her. Eyes on the men, she said loudly, "Listen up. I do not like to run. If any of you bozos is considering taking off for parts unknown because you're away from the barn and the compound, I promise you I will shoot first and ask questions later. A load of buckshot in your rear can be real hard on your gittalong. Are we clear?"

Gil was lounging against a fence post with a piece of grass between his teeth. "Hey, Madam CO, what's to keep us from rushing you, ripping that sucker right out of your hands and taking off on the four-wheeler?"

His voice was light. He was smiling. Still, Eleanor felt a frisson of disquiet. His question was relevant. She and Selma were women, and only Selma was armed.

The CO smiled back at Gil and slowly climbed down from the four-wheeler. She held the shotgun one-handed, butt against her right hip, short barrel pointed skyward.

Then so quickly that the movement was a blur, she pulled down the shotgun, racked one into the chamber and blew the top off a pine sapling six feet from where Gil stood. Before anyone moved, she had racked another shell and was aiming the gun directly at Gil's feet. "Any more questions?"

"No, *ma'am.*"

Eleanor's ears were ringing. She could smell the acrid smoke from the shotgun shell, and her eyes stung. She was always uncomfortable around guns, but obviously Selma wasn't. She tried to get her breath moving in her chest again. Selma touched her arm. "Sorry, Doc." She pulled another shell from her belt and reloaded.

"Won't all the COs come flying?"

"Probably." Selma flicked the radio on her collar. "Just making a point. All clear." Eleanor heard a string of curses followed by a command to make points without alerting the whole prison in future.

"Right." Selma rolled her eyes. "Come on, Doc, let's get to work."

Eleanor watched Steve carefully as he moved along with the column of men. He looked a bit more comfortable today, his walk close to normal. She must remember to pick up that horse liniment for him when she went to the clinic. She pulled up beside him and said, "Steve, how much did you get done on the database program yesterday?"

He looked at her without breaking stride. "Most of what you asked for, but you need a good deal more. I can probably finish up tomorrow."

"No work tomorrow," Selma said. "Saturday's visiting day, remember?"

"Yeah, Doc," Sweet Daddy said. "Thass right. My ladies all comin' to see me. They can come every week now we this close to Memphis. Why don't you stop in while they here and see how a real lady dresses?"

"What a kind suggestion," Eleanor said. She saw Steve's lip curl. She pulled to a stop beside a ragged stretch of sagging wire. "This looks like a good place to start. Slow Rise, you're the crew chief on this one."

"I ain't taking no orders from no old man," Robert said sulkily.

Eleanor saw Steve stiffen, then lay his hand on Slow Rise's shoulder. His long fingers bit into the muscle as he shook his head very slightly. Slow Rise visibly relaxed.

"You take orders from who the doc says you do!" Selma snapped. "Otherwise I guaran-damn-tee you won't see any visitors tomorrow."

"Aw, hell."

Once they'd established a rhythm, the men stretched and spliced with a fair amount of expertise and only the occasional yelp as somebody got a strip of barbed wire across exposed flesh. Most of the fences were still in adequate shape and only required tensioning.

"How come we got to use these old saggy fences?" Robert asked.

"If we make a success of the pilot program, the prison board has promised we can replace them next spring. In the meantime, cows don't know whether fences are pretty or not, just so long as they're tough and tight."

"Damn!" Gil Jones exclaimed. "Wouldn't know it was October, hot as it is!" He looked at Eleanor. "Boss lady, you mind if we take off our shirts?"

"Go right ahead, but remember that's more skin to get ripped open."

"I'll take my chances. I been cut before." He unbuttoned his prison blue work shirt and hung it on the nearest fencepost.

Eleanor snapped her mouth shut before he could catch her gaping. His whole body was a canvas. The dragon that wound up from his hand sported a red forked tail that encircled his shoulders, and another even larger and more ferocious dragon flew up his back, scarlet wings extended, talons grasping across his lats. His whole torso was wound around with vines and flowers. The effect was, well, stunning. Some people might think it was beautiful. Eleanor could only think of the hours of pain he must have endured. She tore her eyes away from him in time to see Steve strip off his shirt.

This time she didn't gape, but she caught her breath. She already knew most of the men lifted weights, and from the breadth of Steve's shoulders and the ropy muscles to his arms, she'd assumed he worked out, but she didn't expect the sheer beauty of his body. A mat of curling dark hair ran across his chest and in a line down to disappear under the waist of his jeans. He wasn't muscle-bound like Gil, but each muscle stood out perfectly formed. She could count the six-pack on his abdomen. She gulped. If he was as beautifully built under those jeans—

Selma caught Eleanor's eye. Her expression said, "Nice."

The only one who kept his shirt on was Big. He seemed embarrassed and hunched his big shoulders more than usual. Even Slow Rise was in good condition for his age, and Robert, despite his skinny frame, was well muscled. Only Sweet Daddy was scrawny. Not an ounce of fat on him, but not much muscle, either. Probably too much trouble to work out.

They stopped at noon. This time there were lunch bags for everybody, and Eleanor drove to her truck for her cooler of drinks. Nobody bothered putting shirts back on, but hunkered down against the trees.

Steve sat with his arms on his raised knees, his head against the trunk of a honey locust. Several times she caught him looking at her through almost closed lids, and each time she felt that stirring in her belly. She tried to ignore him, but every fiber of her was aware of him. She longed to run her fingers over his shoulders, curl her fingers in that hair—

"Ma'am?"

She started. Realizing she'd been daydreaming—about a convict, no less—she blinked and looked up into Big's concerned eyes. "Yes?"

"Ma'am, could I work tomorrow?"

"Tomorrow's Saturday, and we're off then. You heard Selma. It's visiting day."

He hunkered down further. "Don't nobody visit me."

"Is your family too far away?"

"Mama died last year. Wish they'd have let me out for her funeral."

Eleanor was aghast. "Aren't they supposed to? Why didn't they?"

"Said they couldn't. First thing I get out I'm putting

flowers on her grave, if I can find it. Don't have no head-stone. Couldn't afford one.''

"I'm sure she'll love the flowers. As for this Saturday, I don't think so. We'll have to run a roster to work week-ends once we get the herd started, but this week we don't really have anything that can't wait until Monday. Most of the COs will be off, and I'm working at the clinic in the morning.''

"I'd like to work as well," Steve said. "Get that pro-gram finished and tested before we actually input any data.''

"Surely you have visitors. Wife? Parents?''

"My wife is dead. I have no other visitors.''

Eleanor found herself at a loss for words. Robert, how-ever, came to the rescue.

"I got visitors. My mama comes, and my woman and my little boy.'' His voice and face softened when he men-tioned his child.

Eleanor was surprised. He didn't seem old enough to have a wife and child.

"How old's your little boy?''

His face lit with more animation than she'd yet seen. "Tyrell's going on two.''

"You have any pictures?''

"Yeah.'' He reached into the pocket of his jeans and pulled out a grimy and much-folded envelope. He handed it across to Eleanor. She carefully pulled out a faded shot of a very young, pretty woman holding a fat, grinning little boy.

"He's very handsome.''

"Hey, he gonna be a doctor or a lawyer or something,'' Robert said.

"Sure he is.'' Sweet Daddy snorted and rolled his eyes. "You gonna deal enough crystal meth to pay for Hah-vad?''

Robert surged to his feet, fists clenched, face contorted in anger. Selma surged to hers, shotgun at her hip.

"Relax, Robert!" she commanded. "And you, Elroy, you apologize, you hear me?"

"Hey, man, chill. I didn't mean nothing."

Robert hunkered down again and was once more his sulky self.

Eleanor sat, too stunned to move. For the second time she'd experienced the sudden flare-up between the men. She kept forgetting how dangerous they were. And that in itself was dangerous to her.

To try to cool the moment down, she asked Gil, "How about you, Gil? You got visitors?"

She knew from his file that he had a wife and a daughter, but he had no way of knowing she knew.

"Yeah. I got a family. My wife visits. She don't let the kid come. Don't want her to see me like this. Hey, how about you, Doc? We told you about our families. What about yours?"

Eleanor was aware that Steve raised his head and was watching her intently. She avoided his eyes and kept hers directly on Gil. "Fair enough. I've been a widow for two years. No children. My husband was a veterinarian, too. Since his death I've been working part-time at a large veterinary clinic in the suburbs, and I hope I can place at least some of you there on work release when and if you work out."

"Hey, cool," Robert said.

"And this Saturday, I'm spending the afternoon unpacking. I'm still not completely moved into my house."

"You got one of them bungalows?" Sweet Daddy asked.

Eleanor wished she'd kept her mouth shut. Now they all knew she lived on the place. She definitely did not want uninvited guests, especially Sweet Daddy. She ignored the question. "How about we get back to work?"

On her way out that afternoon, she stopped at Ernest Portree's office. The warden's secretary, Yvonne, said he was terribly busy, but when she buzzed him, he called Eleanor in.

She walked in and shut the door behind her. "Why wasn't Bigelow Little allowed to go to his mother's funeral?"

Portree looked up from the stack of folders on his desk that never seemed to grow shorter. "I have no idea. He was at Big Mountain at the time. Maybe it was too far to go. You'd have to check with them."

"They're supposed to take them, aren't they? Close relatives? Parents?"

"Generally, unless the prisoner is a flight risk or has committed so heinous a crime that he has life in prison without parole and has nothing to lose by trying to run."

"Bigelow doesn't fall in that category, certainly."

"Take a look at the man. My guess would be that the warden decided that if Big Little wanted to take off, nothing short of an elephant gun would stop him, and that he couldn't afford to send half a dozen COs along with him to see that he didn't."

"That's cruel."

"That's good sense. I'm sorry he didn't get to go to his mother's funeral, but I'm busy, Eleanor. Go away."

"I want him for work release."

Ernest Portree blinked and sat back, his broad hand on the four-inch stack of file folders on his desk. "What brought this on? You've been working with him less than a week."

She slipped into the uncomfortable chair across from him. She suspected he used that chair so nobody would stay long. "Raoul said he's close enough to his parole hearing to be eligible, and he's the type of person we can really use at the clinic."

"You read his file?"

"Not yet."

"You go read it, then you tell me whether you want him for work release. Besides, don't you need him here?"

"Of course. We're talking work release two days a week to start, then working up to three if I can spare him here. Maybe a job when he gets out."

"If you still want him after you've read his file, I'll look into it." He looked down at his hands. "Anything else?"

Eleanor took a deep breath. "I want the same thing for Steve Chadwick."

"No."

"Ernest? Why on earth not?"

"No."

"I think I deserve an explanation."

He sighed and shoved the folders to the edge of his desk. "You don't deserve anything, Eleanor. You think I don't hear about the preferential treatment you've given Chadwick?"

"That's not true. I asked him to do a computer program for me because he's good with computers. That's why I want him at the clinic. We desperately need someone to back up our business manager, Mark Scott, who's having to spend more and more time at his regular job. Steve's good, and frankly, he'd work cheap."

"You may think this is an ivory tower, but it's not. I hear all the gossip. He's a good-looking man with an education. You speak the same language. You're a young widow. Not surprising you should be attracted."

"I am not attracted!"

"Have you read his jacket?"

Eleanor blushed. "No. Raoul gave me copies of all my team members' files. I knew about Slow Rise, but so far the only file I've read is Gil Jones's."

"You don't want Jones for work release?"

"Not at the clinic. Come on, Ernest. If he works anywhere, it ought to be in a garage or someplace he can fix motorcycles or cars. He doesn't seem like an animal lover, and I don't think all those tattoos would endear him to our clients. Steve Chadwick is at least presentable."

"You go read his jacket, Eleanor. Tonight. I've seen it

too many times—guards, teachers, administrators get involved with prisoners and they get hurt. Steve Chadwick is not like the men you meet on the outside.''

"I already checked his status. He's eligible for parole in just under two years—maybe less than a year with his good time. He could certainly be released a couple of days a week under my supervision. He'd be crazy to try to run with only a couple of years on his sentence. Whatever he is, he's not crazy.''

"I've had cons run when they had a week to serve. He's definitely a flight risk. He has more resources than the others, and his family lives in town.''

"He told me he didn't have any family.''

Portree leaned back and templed his fingers. "Oh, he's got family, all right. His old man probably disowned him the day the gates at Big Mountain closed behind him. I don't blame him.''

"By the way, don't pay any attention to anything Mike Newman says.''

"Why's that?''

"I shouldn't have mentioned it.''

"Yes, you should.''

"All right. I told you I didn't think Newman was the best CO to look after my team. He found out about it, by the way, and made a really nasty comment about my speaking to you.''

"Sorry, but I warned you that very little in this place is private.''

"I didn't tell you that Newman beat Chadwick with his baton the night we started because I called Newman on his neglect to provide the men the gloves I'd requested. He's a sadistic bastard and he ought to be fired.''

"Wait just a minute. Mike's just tough.''

"He's vicious. None of the other COs has the nerve to tell you.''

"What did Steve do to provoke him?''

"Nothing.''

"As far as you know."

"As far as the rest of my guys know. Please forget I said anything about Newman. I'd prefer that he not get any more angry at me than he already is. In the meantime, I think Steve would do fine on the outside. I'd personally guarantee he wouldn't run."

"You can't do that."

"Maybe not legally."

"Go home, read Little's file and Chadwick's, then call me and tell me you still recommend they should be allowed outside."

"No problem." She got up to leave.

Ernest's voice caught her at the door. "The last woman who loved Steve Chadwick died for it."

"What?" She spun and stared at him.

"Prosecution could only make the case for manslaughter. He ought to be on death row. He murdered his wife."

"I don't believe you."

"Believe it."

"Then it was like Slow Rise—he caught her with a lover. A crime of passion."

"It was passion, all right. Passion for the two million dollars he planned to inherit. Your fancy man, Eleanor, offed his wife for money."

CHAPTER FIVE

ELEANOR WENT STRAIGHT FROM Ernest Portree's office to her house to pick up the remaining prisoner files Raoul Torres had brought her, then drove to Creature Comfort for her shift. She kept glancing at the files on the seat beside her as though they might rear up like that copperhead snake and strike at her.

She couldn't have been so wrong about Steve! A killer? There must have been extenuating circumstances. Could it have been an accident? Ernest said it was over money. That made it worse, somehow.

If Steve's wife had been having an affair, had betrayed him some terrible way…

No. There was no betrayal terrible enough to warrant killing someone. She simply couldn't put herself into the mind of anyone who would conceive of the death of another human being as any kind of solution to even the worst problem.

She remembered his softly spoken *I'm innocent.* Could he really be innocent?

Raoul Torres thought he was taking advantage of her naiveté. Maybe. If Steve Chadwick were all that Raoul and Ernest said he was, then she'd lost every instinct she'd ever had to read people.

Maybe the pain, the grief, the loneliness of those months after Jerry died had screwed up her perceptions.

Was there a possibility that her instincts about Steve were right and everyone else was wrong?

She'd like to believe that, but she wouldn't, not until

and unless she had a lot more facts. She pulled into the staff parking lot at Creature Comfort and sat in her truck for several minutes. At the first sign of unhappiness she showed, the clinic staff would be all over her, worrying about her. They didn't need that added burden, nor did she.

She put a ridiculously perky expression on her face and went to find her boss.

Usually Sarah Scott and Jack Renfro spent a half hour with Eleanor at the start of her shift to bring her up to speed on her current patients. Most large-animal calls took place during daylight—pre-purchase exams for horses, routine vaccinations for herds of cows. Only real or perceived emergency calls came in at night, and many nights were quiet.

Eleanor floated among all three sections, large and small animals and exotics, throughout her shift. She usually spent most of her time with sick pets that clients brought in after their own work hours.

Initially, after Jerry's death, the quiet time had been a godsend. Eleanor's spirit was so frazzled, her body so exhausted by not only Jerry's sickness and death, but the bankruptcy and closing of the practice, that she was simply emotionally incapable of handling too much pressure. But with the help of the staff at Creature Comfort, she'd made it back to full strength.

Now the quiet hours were often *too* quiet, especially after ten o'clock. A colicky horse or a cow having trouble calving were becoming welcome breaks. She didn't like seeing animals in pain or trouble, of course, but she did like being able to cure them.

Tonight, however, she looked forward to her quiet time so that she could read the rest of the prison files.

As she walked into the reception room at the front of the clinic to check in with Mabel Haliburton, the night receptionist and clinic earth mother, she literally ran into Nancy Mayfield, the small-animal vet technician.

"Eleanor, thank God! Sarah had to go home sick and Mac's left for the day."

"What's the problem?"

"The cops just busted a dogfighting operation in Tipton County. Mabel says they're bringing in some badly wounded pit bulls."

"Oh, my Lord!" Eleanor crossed quickly to Mabel. "What do you know about the situation?"

"Nothing, except that they're in a pretty bad way. I've called Mac. He's coming back in, but it'll take him at least forty-five minutes. I tried to call Rick, but he's at some kind of fancy dinner party with his pager off, and Bill Chumley's giving that paper on rehabilitating bald eagles in Cincinnati. Should I call Sarah?"

Eleanor shook her head. "Don't you dare. She and Mark have little enough time together as it is, and I know she's still woozy from morning sickness. Is Kenny here?"

"In the back. I've got him setting up some additional cages."

"Good. How are you at triage?"

"I know blood when I see it," Mabel said grimly.

"Okay." Eleanor checked the waiting room, where half a dozen clients had listened avidly with their own pets either in their arms, in cages or at their feet. She walked over. "Folks, I'm so sorry. We've got a real emergency situation here as you heard."

"Are any of those horrible animals rabid?" One very large lady asked. Her hairless Chinese crested female shivered in her arms.

"Highly unlikely. There hasn't been any rabies in West Tennessee in fifteen years, Mrs. Milligan, not even among bats."

"Will these pit bulls be under restraint?"

Eleanor turned to the small man next to Mrs. Milligan. He held a leather leash attached to the collar of the Great Dane whose bowel Mac had resectioned. The dog lay quietly on the tile floor, his large brown eyes following Eleanor.

"I'm sure they will, Mr. Bass. How's Ernest T. doing? Any fever?"

"Nope. Seems to be doing fine, but he's awfully quiet. Dr. Mac told me to bring him in tonight so he could check the incision."

Eleanor stooped and rubbed the Dane's ears, then coaxed him gently onto his back. The incision looked perfect, but then, she had expected it to. Mac did not sew ragged incisions. There seemed to be no heat, no sign of infection. The Dane's ears were uncropped in the continental way and flopped endearingly against his broad forehead. "He eating?"

"Baby food."

"Pooping?"

"Yes."

"Good. Then I suggest you take him home, watch him tonight and bring him back tomorrow morning. Mrs. Milligan, can you wait until tomorrow for us to look at Wang Chun?"

She nodded. "Absolutely. I want her out of here before those ruffians arrive."

Still on her knees, Eleanor turned to the three other clients. "Any emergencies, folks?"

Three heads shook.

"I know it's terribly inconvenient to have to come back, but the police say this is a pretty bad scene. If you want to wait, we'll see you after we've taken care of the worst injuries, but if you want to come back tomorrow—" She called to Mabel over her shoulder, "Mabel, leave Alva Jean a note not to bill these folks for their next office visit. They're going out of their way to be accommodating, aren't you, folks?"

She caught a glare from the man at the end who was holding a struggling Persian cat, but at the offer of a free visit, even he relaxed.

Eleanor stood. So did everybody else.

"Thanks so much for your forbearance."

She could hear sirens in the distance. Mrs. Milligan grabbed her Chinese crested and bolted for the door. "I want to have Wang Chun safely locked in my car before they arrive. I suggest you all do the same."

As the double glass doors leading from the reception room to the clients' parking lot closed behind the last patron, Mabel raised her eyebrows at Eleanor. "I sure hope you know what you're doing."

"I made a decision. A free visit is a small price to pay to keep from losing a client, am I right?"

"I hope Rick sees it that way."

The sirens were louder, and the first flashing lights could be seen turning into the parking lot from the road in front of the clinic.

"Mabel, buzz Kenny. Tell him to get to OR and suit up. He's about to become a surgical assistant. And keep trying to get Rick. If you know where he's having dinner, page him."

"Margot won't like it. They're having dinner with her father and his new girlfriend."

"I don't care if Margot doesn't like it."

Mabel grinned. "Go. I'll handle this end."

By the time Mac Thorn barreled into the small-animal OR ready to do surgery, Eleanor had already stitched up some of the nastiest wounds she had ever seen in animals that were so pitifully thin they broke her heart.

One of the pit bulls had died of blood loss in the animal control van.

"Well?" Mac snarled.

Eleanor knew that once he saw what she was working with, he'd use language she'd probably never even heard before, but at this point, all Mac could see was the sheet draped over the ripped shoulder of an emaciated dog.

"We've lost one, and we'll be lucky not to lose at least one or two more," Eleanor said. "At the moment Nancy's the only surgical technician. She was still here when the call came in, and she stayed, bless her. So did Kenny."

"Kenny?" Mac shouted. "Hell and damnation, the kid's still in high school!"

"He's doing fine. Hush, Mac. You take Nancy, I'll take Kenny. Second table's already set up for you."

"Who's bringing in the patients?"

"The Humane Society people stayed and so did a couple of the animal-control guys. Just stick your head out the door and yell for Mabel to send you another dog."

The OR doors swung open and two men from animal control carried in a litter on which a wounded dog was strapped. Sure enough, Mac Thorn began to curse. Not his usual full-throated snarls of rage, but low in his throat as though his very anger choked him.

Eleanor had no time even to look at the state of Mac's patient. She had her hands full with her own.

Kenny was willing but inexperienced. She thanked God that now that Mac was here, Mabel would send the most difficult cases to him as a matter of course. In the meantime, she and Kenny had to insert IVs, airways, collars to keep the dogs from biting at their wounds when they awoke, and disinfect the skin and tissue surrounding the wounds and shave the hair away.

The dogs were half starved, covered with their own excrement and jumping with fleas, but there was no time to clean more than the affected areas until their wounds were closed. Tonight they'd have to be kept separated from the other animals in the ICU, and those that lived could be cleaned up tomorrow. Assuming they could be handled.

"They catch the bastards who set up the fights?" Mac snapped.

"No idea."

"I say shoot 'em. Just stand 'em up against a wall and mow the SOBs down with machine guns. No—better yet, hang 'em up and flay 'em. I'll be happy to do it myself.

Anybody who'd do this to an animal..." The sound he made was in itself more animal than human.

"Shut up, Mac, and work. You're distracting me," Eleanor said. A year ago she'd never have spoken to him like that. He'd terrified her. But then everything and everyone had terrified her then.

Behind her she heard the doors to the operating room open. "We're not ready for another dog yet," she said without looking up from her needle. "We'll let you know."

"I'm not a dog," Rick Hazard said. "What do you need me to do?"

Eleanor gave a sigh of relief. "Help Kenny move the cages he set up into an isolation area at the end of the large-animal area—probably in the cattle pen, since we don't have any cows in residence at the moment. Then come back here and help out."

"Got ya. Come on, Kenny, let's move us some houn' dawg cages."

As always, Rick was in his element in an emergency. He might seem laconic in day-to-day operations, but he thrived on crises that would make the average person huddle in a corner and suck his thumb.

"Can I help you until he gets back?" Nancy said from across the room.

"Don't you move, woman!" Mac snapped. "Hold that hemostat still, dammit!"

"I'm fine, thanks, Nancy. I'm only stitching."

"God, we have got to get some more help around here at night!" Nancy said.

"Tell Rick."

"I have."

"Tell him again."

The team worked for what seemed like hours before all the dogs were lying sedated in recovery cages in the ICU. Eleanor looked at her watch. Nearly midnight.

"Kenny, you ought to be home in bed," she said.

He clicked the cage door shut on their final patient, a brindle female missing most of one ear and with a laceration on her flank that was already infected when she was brought in. "Tomorrow's Saturday. I can sleep all day." He nodded at the dog. "She's had puppies. She's still got milk. Wonder what happened to them."

"Sold, probably. Pray they went to somebody who only wanted house pets. Even as guard dogs, they would be better off than this. Somebody who'll feed them and socialize them."

"Yeah." He pulled himself up. Obviously he was exhausted.

"Go home," Eleanor repeated.

He shook his head. "No way. You need somebody to stay here tonight, watch the dogs."

"Your dad will have a fit."

"I already called him and told him I might stay. He's okay with it. He'd rather I was here than out with my friends."

"Where would *you* rather be?"

"Here." He glanced at the cages. "Like these guys *are* my friends, you know?"

Eleanor smiled and squeezed his arm. In six months Kenny had gone from being a kid in trouble to a committed assistant at the clinic. His dad said his grades had improved, along with his attitude.

Eleanor hoped his enthusiasm would last. The boy was a born veterinarian. He had the same healing touch Mac Thorn had, the same empathy for the animals, and yet he didn't allow his emotions to cloud his judgment.

"Okay. Bed down in one of the equine recovery stalls," Eleanor said. "I'll be in Sarah's office with my feet up. Call me if you need me."

"You staying, too? Don't you get off at midnight?"

"I can sleep in tomorrow, too, at least until noon. Of course I'm staying."

She waited until she saw him curled under a horse blanket in one of the padded recovery stalls. He fell asleep and began to snore the moment his body was prone.

Had she ever been that young? Tomorrow she'd feel as though she'd been beaten with a two-by-four. Her hands would ache for a week from her careful needlework. She grabbed a bottle of horse liniment off the supply shelf and used it like hand lotion, then dropped it into her purse. She'd promised Steve Chadwick she'd bring him some. This was the best. The liniment immediately began to warm her skin. The stuff might not be approved for human beings, but it certainly did the trick for her.

The prisoner's files sat like a fat brown toad in the center of Sarah's desk, daring her to read them.

Not tonight. She simply could not face any more stirring of her emotions. She slid them into her bag, leaned back in Sarah's comfortable chair, clicked off the desk lamp and composed herself for sleep, hoping the telephone wouldn't ring.

If not for the dogs, she would have been forced to read the files tonight.

Why had she ever promised Ernest Portree she would?

WHEN SHE CHECKED THE DOGS at dawn, she found Mac Thorn crouched beside the brindle female. She put a hand on his shoulder. "Prognosis?"

"Touch and go." Mac stood. "If the antibiotics kill the infection, she's got a chance. Want a cup of coffee?"

"No thanks. I'm off home and to bed for a few hours. Did you get any sleep?"

"Yeah, but I woke up early."

Eleanor looked at the cages. Several of the less-injured animals were already standing in their cages and wagging their tails. She fought tears. Even after the horrors that had been inflicted on them by human beings, still they forgave. Still they offered affection.

"You know there's never been a case of attack on a human being by a purebred Staffordshire bull terrier or an

American bull terrier from a reputable breeder?'' Mac said. He worked his index finger through the bars of the nearest cage and was rewarded not with an angry bite, but with a gentle lick.

Eleanor nodded. It was almost more than she could bear.

"Before they got popular," Mac continued, "reputable breeders culled any puppy that showed aggression toward human beings. Then, God help them, they got 'discovered.' Now trash and criminals breed crazy half-breeds to even crazier half-breeds, cage 'em, starve 'em, mistreat 'em, and then they're surprised when the dogs act crazy."

"You think these poor things can be rehabilitated?"

"Some of them." He pulled himself up and leaned against the pipe fence that surrounded the cattle pen. "You said the prison wanted to start a rehabilitation program for dogs. Why not start with these?"

"Oh, no." Eleanor shook her head vehemently. "I think the warden and the board were talking about abused dogs, or abandoned ones."

"What do you call what's been done to these if not abuse?"

"Can you see the publicity if we turned over a bunch of pit bulls trained to fight to a bunch of convicts? Get real, Mac."

"Look at them, Eleanor. They have an infinite capacity to forgive the human race, which I, for one, neither understand nor agree with. It'll be a while before any of them is healthy enough to release. I'd prefer not to save their lives only to have to euthanize them later. Let's see how they progress."

"Okay. But I don't think sending them to the prison is the way to go."

She left Mac sitting in the wood shavings in the cattle pen outside the cages and talking to the dogs as though they could understand him.

Maybe they could.

SHE SLEPT UNTIL NEARLY NOON, then put on fresh jeans.

Precious brought over lunch, and together she and Eleanor unpacked boxes, hung pictures, put books on bookshelves and china in cupboards all afternoon.

At four o'clock Precious shut the kitchen cabinet on the last of the glassware. ''There. Looks like somebody lives here now.''

''I'm whipped and I know you are. I can't thank you enough. What say I take you out and buy you a steak?''

''How about tomorrow night?'' Precious slid her rump onto the bar stool in front of the breakfast bar and began to rub her calves. ''I actually have a kind of date tonight. Just a movie with one of the COs. Want to come along?''

''On your date? Good grief, no! I'm going to soak in a hot tub, call in to check on the dogs and go to bed early. I'm working at the clinic all day tomorrow.''

''Woman, do you never take a whole day off?''

''I'd rather work. Keeps my mind occupied.''

Eleanor said goodbye to Precious, fixed a sandwich, called the clinic, watched the news on television and ignored the file folders on the dining-room table every time she walked past them.

Finally she could think of no more excuses. ''Oh, heck,'' she said. ''Can't be all that bad.''

She opened Big's file expecting to find out he'd been caught drunk and disorderly or joyriding in somebody's car.

He was serving three to five years for assault with the intention to create grievous bodily harm.

Big? Bodily harm? No way!

She read on. He'd gotten into a fight in the parking lot of a roadhouse outside of Mission, Tennessee, at two o'clock in the morning. He'd broken the other guy's arm in four places. Not simple fractures. Compound with bone displacement. And dislocated the shoulder as well.

Eleanor sat back in her chair. Big must have been so drunk he didn't know what he was doing. He'd been ar-

rested at his mother's house two days later "without incident." That meant he hadn't resisted. He was probably
ashamed of himself at that point and horrified at the damage he'd done.

She'd get his side of the story. He would tell the truth
as he knew it. He didn't seem capable of lying.

She slid Steve's file to the bottom once more and picked
up the file on Sweet Daddy—Elroy Long.

There were no photos in any of the files, and from what
Eleanor read in Sweet Daddy's file, she was grateful. Elroy
Long had taken a switchblade to one Tanitha Smith. She
had spent six weeks in the hospital, had required more than
a hundred stitches and had undergone five reconstructive
surgeries to repair the damage to her face.

Eleanor shivered and went to get herself a cup of hot
chocolate. She'd seen the flash of anger in Elroy's eyes
when she'd forced him to go back to work with bandaged
hands. Not a man she'd ever want to be alone with. She
wondered again whether she should dump him from her
team.

It wasn't that simple. He could make life hell for the
remaining members if he were culled. And she might get
somebody worse in his place.

For the moment she'd keep an eye on him and endure
him. But if he ever raised a hand to Selma, to her or even
to one of the other team members, she'd throw him off the
team in a heartbeat. Perhaps she should tell him that pri-
vately.

She opened Robert Dalrymple's file with trepidation. At
this point she wouldn't have been surprised to find he'd
blown up a building or massacred an entire gang.

But Robert was strictly small-time. Raised in the country
in North Mississippi, apparently he'd come to the big city
and gotten mixed up with some lower-level gang wanna-
bes, dealt a little dope and been sentenced under the man-
datory drug-sentencing laws. He'd never been accused of
violence. Raoul Torres had stapled a handwritten note on

the top of the file. "This guy is salvageable. He really loves his family, and they are there for him."

The only file left was the one on Steve Chadwick.

He'd been sentenced to a minimum of six and a maximum of twelve years for voluntary manslaughter in the death of his wife, Chelsea Wadsworth Chadwick. According to the file, she had died of a single stab wound to the chest that penetrated her aorta and caused almost instant death. There was no struggle, no defense wounds.

Why only voluntary manslaughter? Why wasn't Steve sitting on death row? No doubt the prosecution had settled for voluntary manslaughter only because they couldn't make a case for first-degree murder. Why couldn't they?

Her hands shook so hard she couldn't close the folder. Ernest Portree hadn't been lying. Steve was a convicted killer. And a single stab wound didn't seem like an accident.

She couldn't conceive of Steve's using a knife to kill. He was no Sweet Daddy. He might hit someone his own size who threatened him or someone close to him. He wouldn't hit a woman. Certainly not his wife.

Or could he? How much did she really know about him? How certain was she that her instincts were correct and not governed by her hormones?

Raoul Torres had warned her. Everybody had warned her. Even Steve himself had warned her that he was just like the others.

The files contained only facts, not the reality behind them. She could ask Big Little to tell her why he had broken a man's arm.

Did she dare ask Steve Chadwick why he had killed his wife?

CHAPTER SIX

BY THE TIME Eleanor got home from Creature Comfort at around four Sunday afternoon, the work she'd done that day was a blur. Frightening to think that she'd treated animals on autopilot, but obviously she had.

The brindle female was improving. Miraculously so far none of the other wounded dogs had died.

Rick had been annoyed when he'd discovered she'd offered the clients a free visit to the clinic. "Listen, we're making money now, but we're not out of the woods yet, not by a long shot," he'd grumbled. "And who exactly is going to pick up the tab for those dogs in the holding pens? Not the jackasses who trained them, that's for sure. Last I heard, they hadn't even been caught."

"Mac says the Humane Society is picking up the tab, but it's probably going to take them a couple of months to pay. He says we ought to cut them a little slack. After all, they only brought us the worst cases. The others went straight to animal control."

"And God knows where after that." Rick knew his position was weakened, because everyone, Eleanor included, understood perfectly well that he would never have turned those dogs away, even if nobody ever paid a cent for their care.

Most were still too sick to be bathed. Tomorrow would tell the tale.

Eleanor wouldn't be there. Monday was C day at the prison—cattle buying and transporting. Since Sarah Scott would be too busy at the clinic to be spared, Eleanor would be buying the stock with only J. K. Sanders, the prison board member who had offered to help.

She prayed she wouldn't make a total idiot of herself.

She was completely preoccupied when she climbed out of her truck in her driveway. It was twilight, and she'd left the porch light on in case she didn't make it home before dark. As she walked up her porch stairs, a voice behind her called, "Hey, sweet cheeks, how's about you and me share a little cold beer?"

Her immediate reaction was to check next door for Precious Simpson's car. It wasn't there. Nor were any lights showing in the two cottages past Mike Newman's.

She slowed her breathing and wished she had that whip and chair. She pasted the coolest possible look on her face—her duchess face—and turned around. "I wish you'd stop jumping out at me, Mr. Newman."

"Why, you gonna shoot me?" Snicker. He had taken a couple of paces toward her. The long-necked bottle in his hand was obviously not his first. "Would that be neighborly?"

"No, but it might happen nonetheless. I prefer that even neighbors call first before they drop by. Tonight I am extremely busy and very tired. Now, if you'll excuse me, I have to go in." She didn't want to turn her back on him. The stupid grin was still pasted on his face, but there was no smile in his eyes.

He glanced around. He obviously knew they were alone. Suddenly the mask dropped. "Listen, you arrogant bitch—"

"No, you listen. I've alerted Warden Portree and several other members of the administration about you. You come around here again uninvited, and I'll have you up on harassment charges so fast your union rep won't have time to get there before they fire you. Now please leave."

She reached into her pocket and saw that he jumped, startled, as though she might pull out a gun. Unfortunately, it was only her cell phone, but for the first time in her life she wished she was carrying a weapon.

She had no idea whether he would have carried things any further, because headlights turned into the lane in front of the cottages. Mike blinked, turned, shielded his eyes with his free hand.

"Go home," she said coldly. "Don't come back."

"I'll have plenty of time to see you, sweet cheeks, when I'm back guarding you and your fancy-assed cow-herders."

He swaggered off toward the big blue SUV that turned into a driveway two doors down from his cottage.

"Over my dead body," Eleanor whispered. She was shaking, wet with perspiration, and frankly scared out of her wits. All she could think of was that Steve would have made short work of the man if he'd been there. So, for that matter, would Gil and Big. Things had come to a pretty pass when the inmates had to protect her from the people that were assigned to protect her from *them*.

She had planned to finish unpacking, break down the boxes and take them out to the back of her truck so that she could put them in the Dumpster on her way to the barn in the morning. But now she didn't want to leave the house. Lard Ass Newman was turning her into a prisoner in her own house.

"GOD A'MIGHTY, they're the biggest dad-blasted cows I ever saw," Slow Rise said.

The rest of Eleanor's team stood outside the stock trailer in which J. K. Sanders's friend had brought the cows. A dozen of the finest Beefmaster cows, four with calves at foot, three heavily pregnant, and five ready to be bred.

"Wait'll you see Marcus Aurelius IV of Duntreith," Eleanor said with a smile.

"Who's that?" Gil asked.

"Our new bull. He's still young and needs to fill out

some, but we already weighed him in at twenty-two hundred pounds.''

Gil whistled.

''You ain't gettin' me in the same county with no bull that size, no, sir you ain't,'' Sweet Daddy said, shaking his head back and forth.

Eleanor turned to him. ''Unfortunately Duntreith farms has kindly offered us a bonus.''

''Why unfortunately?'' Steve asked. He had climbed onto the side of the trailer to get a better view, and now hung one-handed to look down at Eleanor.

''It's like an ad I once saw advertising one pony for fifty dollars and two ponies for twenty-five dollars,'' Eleanor said.

Slow Rise chuckled. ''I've had me a couple of ponies like that—damn near had to pay somebody to take 'em off you.''

''Well, since Mr. Duntreith kindly donated both the stock trailer and half of the cows, and gave us a real break on Marcus Aurelius, we couldn't very well refuse to accept his gift.'' She waited a beat. ''We are going to be the proud recipients of three female buffalo and one longhorn steer.''

Slow Rise sneered at Sweet Daddy. ''You think these things is big, wait'll you see them buffalo. How the hell we gonna keep 'em in a pasture, Doc?''

''We spend the next two days reinforcing the fencing in the side paddock and pray,'' Eleanor said. ''I managed to persuade him we couldn't possibly handle them until next week.''

J. K. Sanders swung out and stood with one immaculately booted foot on the bottom step of the truck. ''Can't look a gift horse, and all that stuff, Doc. Larry Duntreith ought to get here middle of the afternoon with Marcus. I won't be bringing you my horses until tomorrow. You got stalls for 'em?''

''Three, right?'' Eleanor asked.

"Yeah. And tack. The saddles are pretty old, but they're still serviceable."

"We'll have everything ready tomorrow when you come, including space for the tack in my office."

"Door got a lock on it?"

"A very good one."

"Yeah," Gil said dryly. "We installed it ourselves, didn't we, boys? Cut the keys, too."

J.K. looked at Gil narrowly and scowled. He apparently didn't enjoy jokes at his expense.

"It's secure," Eleanor said, and shook her head at Gil. He raised his eyebrows in a "Who, me?" gesture.

"If y'all are through funning, how about we unload these ladies into the pasture?" J.K. said.

Big and Robert stood silent and wide-eyed. Eleanor noticed that Selma stayed as far back as she could.

"Okay, J.K., back 'er up into the pasture so we can open the gates. Chadwick, can you and Slow Rise handle unloading?" Eleanor asked.

He nodded and gave her a quirky smile as he dropped to the ground from his perch. He moved with the easy grace of a man who was comfortable in his body. Unfortunately, Eleanor wasn't comfortable watching him, not with the connection that seemed to hold even when they weren't speaking directly to each other, or even when they weren't *looking* at each other.

She was constantly physically aware of his presence, knew the compass point at which he stood, and like a needle that pointed north, she found herself gravitating toward that point automatically.

She had to try consciously not to address every remark to him. As a matter of fact, she was trying not to say anything to him that wasn't a direct order. Let Ernest Portree make something of *that*.

The others hung over the newly mended pasture fence while Steve and Slow Rise opened the gates and prodded the cows and their calves down the ramp and into their new home. There was much lowing, some bellowing, and a great deal of jostling before they were all on firm ground.

Slow Rise stood back with his hands on his hips. "My, my, but ain't they pretty things. When we gonna start taking 'em to some stock shows, Doc? Winning a few prizes?"

"When we're ready." And when the prison establishment decided it could trust prisoners to take care of their cows at a county fair and not run off to drink and gamble—or try to escape. That might not be for a while, if ever.

Steve propped himself easily against the side of the trailer and watched the cows wander off to investigate their new home. The autumn sun stroked his brown hair with red-gold, and his face and arms had lost the prison pallor already after less than a week in the sun. He looked as comfortable among the animals as Slow Rise and J.K.

He's a murderer. Eleanor tried to repeat the words in her mind like a mantra, but they didn't stick. Not when he smiled that gentle lopsided smile at her, not when his eyes crinkled at the corners that way.

"Man has a great butt," Selma whispered.

Eleanor jumped. "I hadn't noticed."

"Baloney. Woman would have to be dead not to appreciate those buns, not to mention the bulge on the front..."

Eleanor felt her face flame.

"Look all you like, Doc. Just don't let him get close enough to touch—not your body, and definitely not your heart. You could get hurt real bad. I'd hate to see that happen to a nice lady like you."

Eleanor felt her anger flare, then subside just as quickly. "You're right, Selma."

"You need to find somebody decent, honey, not some con."

"I had somebody decent, Selma. I guess that's all I'm entitled to this go-around. The last thing I want is to get mixed up in something that'd cause me more heartache."

"Or headaches, and that man is a migraine waiting to happen, if you get my drift. He's not like the others."

"How so?"

"Most of them fight being in prison at first, then they kind of relax. Even if they swear they're innocent, they act like 'okay, you got me.' Not Chadwick. He never gives any trouble, does what he's told, but part of him isn't really here."

"Doc?"

"Yes, Big?" Eleanor turned from Selma, but had trouble tearing her mind away from Selma's words.

"Can I go into the pasture with the little calves?"

"Of course. Just don't leave the gate open."

"No, ma'am."

Robert followed him, sticking as close to Big as possible—using the huge man body as a shield, Eleanor thought—and after him trudged Gil. The only person who didn't want to be enclosed with large bovines was Sweet Daddy. He was obviously terrified, but swaggering around as though he had more important things to do than play with calves.

The moment Big shut the gate, she asked Selma, "What does it mean? Steve's attitude?"

"No idea. Makes him more dangerous, I guess. Too smart. Shoot, those calves are cute little devils, aren't they?"

"Oh, heck, Selma, let's go in, too," Eleanor said. "Just don't fall over that shotgun."

Despite her mantra, Eleanor gravitated at once to where Steve still leaned against the side of the stock trailer with his arms folded across his chest.

"Watch Big," he said. "I think he has a gift with animals."

"I think so, too. There's something about people like Big that animals tune in to."

"I had a groom like that," Steve said absently. "He'd had a bad fall as a child. The horses watched out for him like a mother bear with a cub. But me—they'd just as soon run over me as not.''

Eleanor looked up at him. This was the first bit of personal information he'd given out. Horses? Plural? And a groom? She felt her hair rise at the back of her neck. Was that why he needed the two million dollars Ernest Portree said he'd killed for? So he could maintain a lifestyle that included horses?

"What? What did I say?''

Eleanor could have sworn she hadn't moved or shown any change in her body language, but Steve apparently knew instantly that the emotional distance between them had increased. She shook her head. "Nothing. You must have done a considerable amount more riding than you intimated. Quarter horses? Jumpers?''

"Polo ponies. Please don't mention it to the others.'' He walked off with his hands in the pockets of his jeans, his back straighter than she had seen it.

MARCUS AURELIUS IV of Duntreith came out of his trailer like a sleek red tank—a diesel that smoked and tried to mow down everything in its path. The trailer had been unloaded on the far side of the barn in the bull paddock, far enough away from the cows that Marcus could neither see nor smell them in anything less than a southerly gale. He was bellowing when he arrived and continued to bellow as he trotted around his paddock.

At the first touch of the electric fence he jumped back, snorted twice, stuck his nose against it a second time, repeated the snorts, then regarded it with a baleful brown eye. In succession he tried another side of his enclosure to see if it too would shock him. When it did, he moved around to the next until he'd circumnavigated the enclosure. Apparently satisfied he wasn't going anywhere he trotted off to the center, put his head down and began to graze.

"Good bull," Eleanor said approvingly. "Very sensible. Thinks on his feet."

"Probably smarter than most of *us*," Slow Rise said. "When we gonna start collectin' him?"

"Collectin'? Whaddaya mean?" Robert asked. He couldn't take his eyes off the bull.

"Well, son, it's like this. See, a bull don't have to go to the ladies no more. That's old-fashioned. His sperm gets *collected* coupla of times a week, and each time he makes about a hundred of what they call *straws*. One straw will take care of getting one cow pregnant. Freeze it, it's good for years. Sell a good bull at ten bucks or more a straw."

"Twice a week? Two hundred at ten bucks a pop?" Robert looked at the bull with wide eyes. "Man, that's more'n I get for a rock." He glanced at Eleanor. "'Course I never did sell no cocaine. The cops planted it on me."

"The only difference is that someone has to do the collecting," Eleanor said sweetly. "Any takers?"

Robert's eyes grew huge. "No, ma'am!"

She laughed. "Don't worry. We won't start collecting him until spring, and by then I hope he'll have at least a couple of blue ribbons from stock shows."

"Whew."

"We feed morning and night and top off the water troughs every morning," Eleanor said. "The same for Marcus Aurelius, but nobody, and I mean nobody, is to go into that enclosure with him until we know how he reacts around people. Everybody got that?"

"Don't have to tell Sweet Daddy twice," Sweet Daddy said.

"He may be a perfect gentleman, but nobody's ever demanded anything of him in his young life. If he resents our attentions, he could stomp any one of us through to China. Okay, everybody, evening chores, and a soft drink, then you're off for the night. See you tomorrow early. We have to start getting that second pasture ready for the buffalo and finish bedding the stalls for J.K.'s quarter horses."

The soft drinks every evening had become a tradition in just the short time that Eleanor had worked with the men. She could afford the minor expense, and the public relations value with her team was well worth it. Now without Mike Newman, everyone could relax, although Selma still kept the shotgun at hand.

Eleanor was leaning against the door of the barn when Steve came over to her.

"May I speak to you?"

"Sure."

"Can we go into the office? I need some clarification on some of the fields you want in your database."

"Of course." She called to Selma, "Chadwick has some questions about the database. We'll be in the office, but we'll leave the door open. Is that all right?"

"With the door open? Yeah, fine." But her mouth twisted in a tiny grin, which Eleanor pretended not to notice.

Eleanor entered the office with Steve right behind her.

She took a deep breath and thrust her hands into the pockets of her jeans. "So, what problems are you having?"

"With the computer program? None."

"Then why—"

"I had to speak to you. You know why I'm here, don't you?"

"What?"

"You've read my file. I saw it in your face when I mentioned the polo ponies. Don't ever play poker. You'll lose."

"We shouldn't be having this conversation." She stared past him.

"I swear to you I did not kill my wife."

"Steve—"

"I haven't bothered to try to convince anybody I'm innocent for a long time. I told myself it was enough that *I* knew. Now it matters that *you* believe me. It shouldn't, but it does.''

"A jury didn't believe you. Why should I?"

"Chelsea was my best friend, as well as my wife. I could never have harmed her.'' His voice had grown louder.

Eleanor touched his mouth with her fingertips. "Shh. They'll hear you.''

He grasped her hand and held it to his lips.

She shivered, but not with fear. "Please. You mustn't.''

She pulled away from him, but he held her gaze. "Do you know what it's like to spend years convincing yourself you don't need the warmth of a touch, a kind word, someone who actually looks into your eyes and sees a human being and not just a number?''

"Steve, please, Selma could come in at any minute.''

"All the more reason to tell you now. I may not have another chance. The day the jury convicted me, I knew I could survive in prison only if I stayed cold and shut myself off emotionally from everything that was going to happen to me.''

His voice now was low and urgent. "Dammit, until now I thought it had worked. I was handling it. Then one day you climb out of that truck. From that moment you never treated us like numbers, like criminals. The way you've looked after Big, the way you touched me and worried about me when I was hurt... You've awakened memories of a world of peace and love and honor where you don't have to watch your back every moment or look for ulterior motives in every conversation. It hurts to remember, because I know I can never be a part of that world again.''

"Come on, people, time to go home.'' Selma's voice was louder than necessary.

Steve walked back to the waiting men without a backward glance.

Eleanor leaned against the wall beside the open door and tried to breathe. She was afraid. Afraid of believing him, afraid of caring what happened to him, of being caught up in everything Raoul Torres warned her about, and most of all, afraid that she no longer had the ability to tell truth from fiction, right from wrong, and simple loneliness from the blossoming of affection.

She hadn't been emotionally touched by any man since Jerry died. Not even Mac Thorn had stirred her, yet this...this killer heated her blood, left her shaken, confused and frightened.

Jerry had not been the first man in her life. She understood the game, or thought she did.

But nothing had prepared her to feel such a pull of heart against brain as she felt now. This was a looking-glass world in which no one was what he seemed. Raoul had warned her that sociopaths tended to be expert at reading the needs of the people they came in contact with and reflecting them back. But they couldn't keep up the pretense for long. Sooner or later the true personality emerged.

Had Steve recognized how lonely she was, how she longed to sink into a strong man's arms? Did he understand how much she ached to feel the body of a man she loved moving inside her?

Did he understand her fear that she would never make love again? That no man would ever want her as Jerry had? Worst of all, that she would never be able to feel that complex mixture of passion and trust that she'd known with him?

Even if she were to trust Steve, they could never be alone together. Even the few sentences they'd spoken had been watched. All the men knew. Selma knew. Ernest Portree and the entire staff of the prison farm probably knew. And laughed at her, even pitied her.

All she knew was that her body and her spirit were hungry for his touch. She longed to feel his lips on hers, feel his body hard against her, see his face above her.

She suddenly realized she was completely alone in the

twilight—Selma and the man had left. She walked through the barn and out to Marcus Aurelius's paddock. The moment he scented her, he swung his great head toward her, snuffled and sauntered slowly over to where she stood beside the electric fence.

God, he was arrogant. So sure of his maleness, his superiority, his dominance over any female, even a human one.

"Not me, buddy," she said. "I'm the wrong species."

She could have sworn he shrugged. She reached carefully across the fence and touched his nose. Without warning he wrapped his tongue around her finger. She scratched the knot of curls in the center of his broad forehead. He sighed.

A moment later he pawed, spun and raced off to the center of the paddock again, for all the world like a fighting bull ready to charge.

"And they say females are changeable," she said. "This particular female had better get her act together, or she's going to get her booty bounced out of here before she's even finished unpacking."

ELEANOR WAS SCHEDULED for a short shift at the clinic—only four hours, five to nine. She walked into the clinic from the staff parking lot in back, passing the cattle holding pen that held the wounded pit bulls in their cages, but in the low light, couldn't see much. The dogs set up a chorus of barking, but there were no growls.

Up front Mabel presided over an empty waiting room.

"Nobody waiting?" Eleanor asked.

"Dinnertime. Wang Chun just left. Every time I think about how much a lot of our owners look like their pets I think of how Mrs. Milligan and Wang Chun don't. You think she wanted a Chinese crested because it's so fragile and dainty and Mrs. Milligan could play linebacker?"

"Tacky, Mabel, tacky. How're the pit bulls?"

Mabel sighed. "Lost another one today. Too starved to fight the infection."

"Not the little female? She's the one I worked on."

"No, one of the male dogs. We got them all bathed and cleaned up today. Talk about your three-ring circus!"

"Did anybody get bitten?"

"I think they were too scared to bite. A couple of the Humane Society volunteers came in to help, thank heaven. I don't think any of those poor mutts had ever felt warm water before, much less soap. Had to bathe most of them at least twice, and a couple three times. You should have seen the water—filthy. And then two of them we had to hand-bathe because we didn't want to get their incisions wet. According to Dr. Rick, most of them are pretty young—under a year old."

"Most of them don't survive much beyond that."

"Terrible to think so, but you're probably right. That female had no more business having puppies that young than I do."

Eleanor patted Mabel's shoulder. "The mind boggles at the thought of you having puppies."

"Oh, go on back to Dr. Sarah's office and read your charts. I'll call you when the clients start coming in after supper. You've got a couple of notes from Dr. Sarah. She's finally stopped throwing up."

"Any large animals staying overnight?"

"Here." Mabel handed Eleanor a stack of charts. "Megan Cormack's Welsh pony is in the founder stall with his front hooves bandaged. He needs a shot of bute every four hours for the pain. Dr. Sarah says watch him, he bites."

"Ponies usually do."

"And one of Mr. Montano's ewes is down at the far end. She had a run-in with a barbed-wire fence and tore her udder. Dr. Sarah stitched her up and says just to watch her, too. She's had antibiotics in her feed, so she doesn't need a shot."

"Thanks, Mabel."

"Can I say something?"

"Since when do you ask permission?"

"This new job—are you sure you haven't taken on too much?"

"Why?"

"Well, frankly, you've got circles under your eyes so dark they look like tar pits."

"I haven't been sleeping all that well in my new house. I'm not used to the peace and quiet after my little apartment."

"Those cons, or whatever they're called in these politically correct days, are they giving you problems?"

"Not the way you mean."

"Then how?"

Eleanor would dearly have loved to dump all her feelings about Steve onto Mabel's shoulders, but she knew darned well what Mabel would say and she didn't want to hear it. Everybody said the same thing. Everybody's advice was probably right-on. So why couldn't she accept it? "It's a long story, Mabel. I can't really talk about it. I'm handling it."

She took the folders and walked through the door back to the examining rooms before Mabel had a chance to reply, but she did catch a decided "humph" as the door shut behind her.

The dogs began to bark again the moment they spotted her walking up to the cow enclosure. As soon as tomorrow some of them would be well enough to be exercised in the parking lot and paddocks behind the clinic. Could they be trusted? Did they have any idea how to walk on a leash?

She sat cross-legged in front of their cages and talked quietly to them until they settled down. Several of them seemed downright cheerful, and grinned at her. Maybe it wasn't such a crazy idea to send them to the prison for rehabilitation. She'd have to work out the details. They wouldn't be able to share quarters with the men; there wasn't enough room in the dormitory. But there was plenty of room in the barn to construct kennels, even large kennels with runs, and if they were found to be trustworthy and trainable, they could accompany the men on their duties.

They might harass the stock, which wouldn't be acceptable. But if they were still puppies under a year old, or even a little older, their minds might not have been irreparably harmed.

She longed to open the cage of the brindle female, but she knew Mac would kill her if he wasn't with her, so she had to be satisfied with scratching the dog's one remaining ear through the wire mesh. "Did you have a name, I wonder? Probably something sweet like Killer. We'll have to fix that."

She checked the other patients, gave the pony another shot of Butezalodine for pain, narrowly avoided having a chunk removed from her forearm by his incredibly fast teeth and finally went to Sarah's office to read the charts.

Tonight, when she didn't want time to think, there were no emergencies and only a few cases of sniffles among the dogs and cats brought in by their owner. She tried to concentrate on reading up on the diseases of beef cattle, but the words ran together.

She had to make up her own mind about Steve, and to do that, she needed more facts. Why had a jury convicted him? And why only of voluntary manslaughter?

She remembered that the lawyer listed on his case file was Leslie Vickers. She didn't know the man, but she knew his reputation. He seldom lost a case. Very high priced, high profile. His services must have cost Steve a great deal of money.

She looked up his office number in the telephone book and called, leaving a message on his answering machine for him to call her. Would he? When she was dealing with the aftermath of Jerry's death, she'd found getting in touch with her lawyer next to impossible. She ended by mentioning that she was calling about Steve Chadwick. That could work for or against her.

If he didn't call back, how could she find out more?

What about Steve's family? If, as the file said, they still lived in the area, then perhaps they'd talk to her. He said nobody ever came to visit him. Did that mean that, they too, thought he was guilty?

She looked up as Mabel walked into the office and stood on the other side of the desk with her hands planted on her ample hips.

"Hey," Eleanor said. "Who's minding the store?"

"Up front? Nobody at the moment. I left a note on the registration desk that says 'Buzz if you need assistance.' So either we talk here and leave the desk unattended, or you come up front with me and talk there. Your choice."

Eleanor sighed in exasperation. "How about you go back to work and we don't talk anywhere?"

"Mind my own business, you mean? Uh-uh. Anything that affects the doctors in this practice *is* my business."

"Don't mother-hen me, Mabel, I'm a grown woman. And I'm fine."

"You're acting like Juliet just before she took the poison. Now come up front with me. You have two minutes to decide or I come right back here." Without waiting to see whether Eleanor would follow, Mabel turned around and walked out of the office.

Two minutes. Sarah's office combined the familiar scents of disinfectant, clean wood shavings and just the slightest hint of manure. The equipment that Sarah had fought Mark Scott so hard to get lined the walls, waiting to be taken out to calls or used on their large patients. For Eleanor this office had become her refuge, her den, her nest. She felt safe here, certain of her skills, sure that she could do the job asked of her.

She did not allow emotion to color her professional decisions. Pity she couldn't say the same about her private life.

Without the support of this clinic, these doctors, this staff, she'd still be a grieving widow in her studio apartment watching daytime television, eating take-out pizza when she remembered to eat at all and sleeping eighteen hours a day.

She'd been so certain she was back at full strength. How wrong could one person be?

Eleanor told herself she deserved a pleasant uncomplicated life. She'd had about all the emotional upheaval one person should have to endure.

She and Jerry had thought they were going to work side by side in their practice in Franklin, treating the suburban horses and pets. They'd been together since veterinary school. She knew people who said they could never work with their spouses, but she and Jerry had loved every minute of it.

Until the cancer. Even now she couldn't bear to think of her beautiful, funny, big handsome husband wasting away while she had to treat him like a baby. She knew how much he hated it.

Not as much as she did. She knew she was supposed to go from anger to acceptance, but she'd never made it that far.

And after Jerry's death, her world kept collapsing until there was simply nothing left.

Eleanor had nothing left either by that time—emotionally or physically. If not for Rick Hazard and Mac Thorn, who came up to Franklin to buy some of the equipment at the bankruptcy sale, she might well be homeless now.

But Rick, ever the organizer, had simply dragged her up and away to Memphis, pressured her to work part-time at night in one of the local emergency clinics, and harassed and cajoled her until she could go a whole afternoon without bursting into tears.

But thanks to Creature Comfort and Rick Hazard, professionally at least, she was back at full strength. However, there weren't any reserves. She didn't know how to deal with the deluge of feelings she had for Steve.

The intercom buzzed. "You have thirty seconds. And we still have no clients, so we can talk in private."

"Coming, Mother."

She stopped in the staff conference room, picked up a couple of diet sodas out of the machine and carried them up front. She slid her rear onto the second bar stool behind the high reception counter and handed a can to Mabel.

"I think I'm going to quit."

"The clinic?" Mabel sounded horrified.

"The prison."

"You'll lose your new cottage. You haven't even had a housewarming yet."

"Everybody is going to say I told you so."

"The work's too much?"

"Not the work. The people, the rules, the atmosphere. You know what cognitive dissonance is?"

"Isn't that where you know what you're supposed to be seeing and hearing isn't what's really going on, but you're not certain you can trust yourself?"

"Couldn't have put it better myself. The thing is, I *like* the members of my team, except for Sweet Daddy, and even he makes me laugh sometimes."

"Sweet Daddy?"

"Most of them have nicknames. The only person I've met I truly dislike and am scared to death of is a certain CO."

"What's that?"

"Corrections Officer. Guard. One of them is a sadistic monster named Mike Newman who beats up prisoners who can't fight back and has come pretty close to stalking me."

"So report him."

"I have. My word against his, and he's been there far longer and has a lot more seniority. After the first day, managed to get him off my team, but I think that was more his choice than because the warden believed me."

"You want to quit because of a guard? I don't believe you. There's more to it than that. I heard you even want to bring a couple of those guys over here on work release a couple of days a week. I probably wouldn't feel any more comfortable around them than you do."

"I made a big mistake, Mabel. I wasn't going to read their prison files so I wouldn't know what they were in prison for. But my curiosity got the better of me."

"Sounds like simple self-protection to me."

"Maybe. But I found out things I don't want to know about what they did to wind up in jail. One man in particular. I can't believe he did what they say he did."

"Uh-huh. And what does this guy look like?"

"He's just a man, all right?"

"Whoa! Did I ever touch a nerve!" Mabel looked at her through narrowed eyes.

Eleanor knew she was blushing. She also knew she was stammering. "He's…he's fairly attractive."

"Do not get involved with a prisoner. I read the advice columns just like you do—these guys prey on unattached women, get them to send money to them, romance them, write them poetry. A couple of years ago one guy even convinced his lawyer—his *lawyer,*—to help him in a prison escape. Now she's in prison, too."

Eleanor dropped her eyes. "He swears he's innocent."

"I'll bet he does."

"But what if he *is* innocent? What if I believe him? What do I do then?"

"Not a damn thing."

"There's got to be some way to find out for myself."

"A prosecution team and a jury thought he was guilty. It's over and done with."

"But people do investigate, don't they? I see you here behind the registration desk reading all these true-crime books when there aren't any clients. Where do those reporters come up with their facts? The police do make mistakes. Look at all the rapists that were wrongly convicted."

"Good grief! Don't tell me he was convicted of rape?"

"Certainly not." She couldn't bear to tell Mabel that his crime was even worse. "Just tell me. How do I find out the facts for myself?"

"I thought you said you'd read his file."

"The prison file. That just tells me what he was convicted of, how long he has to serve before he can be paroled, and what kind of a prisoner he's been—solitary, detention for breaking rules, things like that. It assumes he's guilty. I need to make up my own mind."

"Well, I suppose you could go down to the courthouse and request a copy of the arrest reports. They're a matter of public record. I think they charge a small fee for copying."

"That will still only give me one side—the side of the people who arrested him."

"So talk to his lawyer."

"Right. Like Leslie Vickers is going to talk to me in any sort of depth."

Mabel took a deep breath. "There is one way you can find out."

"Tell me. Why are you so hesitant?"

"Because it's expensive. You can request a copy of the trial transcript. It costs two or three hundred dollars and can run to seven or eight hundred pages—more, if it's a high-profile case."

"How do I request one?" Eleanor felt a rising tide of excitement. At least with a transcript she'd see what the jury saw—the evidence that made them believe he was guilty. Then she could see if she agreed with their decision.

What she'd do about Steve after that she had no idea, but it was better than wringing her hands and worrying. Even in vet school her professors had said she was decisive, quick to make a diagnosis. That could have caused problems if she'd just shot off her mouth, but she always garnered all the facts first.

Maybe it was time for the old Eleanor to reassert herself

once and for all, whatever the consequences. Her heart would mend a lot more quickly now than it would if she allowed herself to fall in love with Steve, then was forced to agree that he was a murderer.

"Do those true-crime books of yours really tell you how much a transcript costs?" Eleanor asked.

"That I know firsthand. I have a nephew who got busted for dealing drugs. The family chipped in and bought a transcript in case there was something his public defender missed."

"And did he?"

"She. No, it was pretty much open-and-shut. The idiot was guilty. He's out now and straight, but he nearly broke his mother's heart."

"Oh." Eleanor's shoulders slumped. Suddenly the enthusiasm she'd felt drained away and left her exhausted again.

Mabel leaned over and rubbed her shoulder. "Honey, don't quit your new job over this. No man's worth it. Why not get rid of *him,* instead? Get him assigned to some other team?"

Eleanor's stomach lurched. Send him away? Miss seeing him even at a distance? Eleanor dropped her head into her arms on the desk. "I thought this job would be exciting, that I might actually make a difference. Now I don't think I've got the strength or the stamina to cope. I wanted a quiet simple life without complications, without aggravation, without..."

"Without love?"

She raised her head. "I loved Jerry, and his death wore me out."

"You can't possibly love this guy. You've known him a week. You've never even been alone with him." Mabel looked at her with suspicion. "You haven't, have you?"

"Not the way you mean. And no, I don't love him. Or at least I don't think I do. But it's there all right, the same feeling in the gut I got every time I looked at Jerry's big blue eyes or heard his laugh or watched him walk into a room. Except Jerry was fun. Steve Chadwick is not fun. He's sad and angry. He scares me and he attracts me and, God help me, Mabel, I want him so badly I can taste it.''

"Honey." Mabel covered Eleanor's hand with hers. "You need to get laid, but not by some jailbird."

Eleanor began to laugh. At least it started out as laughter, but after a moment she couldn't tell whether she was laughing or crying. And she couldn't stop.

"How about you let me and Ernest T. in on the joke?" Mr. Bass strode into the clinic with Ernest T., the Great Dane, padding along behind him with his head low. "We could use a laugh."

CHAPTER SEVEN

WHILE THE MEN WERE WORKING to increase the height and strength of the fence that Eleanor hoped would keep the buffalo in their pasture, Eleanor strolled over to Big. When she touched his arm, he jumped and stammered, "Ma'am, Doc, am I doing it wrong?"

"Not at all, Big. I just need to talk to you a few minutes." The day had dawned gray with a hint of the kind of cold fog that chilled worse than a driving rain. Now that the sun was fully up, however, it promised to be another perfect Indian-summer day. "Come on, let's go sit in my truck."

Selma shook her head. "Against the rules."

"Even with you watching? It's okay, Selma, Big and I need a few minutes. I promise he won't drive off in my truck, will you, Big?" She grinned at him, and after a moment of confusion, he smiled shyly back.

"Don't know as I'd fit in your truck, Doc. Not with you in it, too."

Eleanor drove a big 350 with an extended cab, but looking at it and at Big, she considered that he might be right. In any case, there'd be no way he could be comfortable. "So let's go sit under the pine trees. That against the rules, Selma?"

"Nope. Better take one of the tarpaulins or you'll come back with a wet rear end."

As they strolled over to the clump of pines that grew beside the front pasture, Eleanor asked, "You really ought to wear a baseball cap, Big. I'm surprised as fair as you are, you don't burn to a crisp.''

Big ran his palm across the stubble of his white-blond hair and grinned at her. ''Must be that touch of Cherokee blood my mama used to talk about.''

''How on earth do you manage to sleep in the dormitory? Do you have a longer bed?''

''No ma'am. I scrunch up. I been doing it most of my life.''

Eleanor tossed the tarpaulin out onto the pine straw, sat cross-legged and invited Big to sit. He sank onto his haunches with surprising grace for such a large man.

''I done something wrong, ma'am?''

''Not at all. That's not why I wanted to talk to you. I know I said when we started working together that I didn't want to know what any of you did before you came here, but then I felt obliged to change my mind.''

Big hunched his huge shoulders and moaned softly, ''Oh, Lordy.''

''There are some things in the works that made it imperative—things that might be good for you. But I really have to hear your side of the story. Don't worry about sounding bad. Just tell me the plain truth.''

Big sighed. His huge chest rose and fell as though his lungs were an industrial-strength bellows. He wouldn't look at Eleanor. Instead, his frightened eyes sought the men by the fence.

''Please, Big. Tell me what happened. Trust me. I won't betray you.''

For a long moment he still didn't speak, and when he did, his voice was barely above a whisper.

''My mama told me us Littles dassen't ever get mad.'' He looked at Eleanor under long, soft lashes. He reminded her of the Great Dane Ernest T., whose ungainly body and sore tummy had never once made him grumpy or angry at the people who worked with him.

''See, all us Littles is big. My mama was tall as Steve

and a lot wider, and my daddy could pull stumps without a mule. Mama said if she'd a'known I was gonna be as big as I am, she'd a never let Daddy name me Bigelow Little, Jr.—but she woulda, 'cause my daddy could be right mean when he was crossed and when he'd been drinking. By the time he got killed logging when I was eight, it was too late to change.''

Eleanor nodded. She wasn't certain what Big's life story had to do with his crime, but now that he'd started talking, she wasn't about to cut him off.

''I'm not real smart, Doc, and I pure D hated school. Run off whenever I could until Mama stopped whupping me and just let me help with the farm and help folks stack wood and stuff.''

''The report said you got in a fight in the parking lot of a roadhouse. Were you like your daddy? Did you drink, too?''

''Lordy, no!'' Big turned horrified eyes to her. ''My mama woulda killed me if I ever touched a drop. My daddy used to run 'shine sometimes, and he always had a couple of bottles stashed, but the day he died Mama poured every one onto the hydrangeas. Took 'em two years to bloom. No, ma'am. I was in that parking lot 'cause I had a job.''

''A job?''

''Yes, ma'am. See, Mr. Dacus, the owner, hired me to wash dishes.''

He picked up a dozen strands of pine straw and began to twiddle it in his fingers.

At first Eleanor assumed he was keeping his hands busy so he wouldn't have to meet her eyes, but when she looked closely, she realized he'd begun to weave the straw into a small tight circle. ''Can you weave pine baskets?''

His fingers stopped and he dropped the straw.

She picked it up. ''This is beautiful, Big. It's almost a lost art. How'd you learn to do that?''

''Mama taught me. Her grandmamma taught her. Daddy

said it was sissy, but I always kind of liked doing it. Holds real well once you get it started. My mama's would hold water more'n an hour, longer if I varnished it."

She handed him his perfect circle. "Keep on doing it. Even small baskets like this one sell for a great deal of money."

"They do? Seems kinda silly, little old thing like this."

His huge, clumsy fingers didn't seem so big and clumsy working with the flimsy straw. She encouraged him to go on with his story.

"Yes ma'am. I washed the dishes, and sometimes if the customers got rowdy, Mr. Dacus would get me to ask them to leave." He shrugged. "They mostly did."

"I'll bet they did."

His fingers began to move faster and faster. "See, there was this bunch of boys home from college for Thanksgiving, at least that's what Mama told me later. They'd been causin' a real ruckus, and Mr. Dacus told me to ask 'em to leave. They did, but then a couple of them come back. They was in the parking lot when I come out to walk home."

"Did they have guns?"

"Yes'm." He looked up. "But they didn't go to use 'em. *Everybody's* got guns."

Too true, Eleanor thought.

"They found somebody's coon hound down the road." He looked straight at her as though he was the teacher and she the student. "When folks hunt over coon hounds, like as not a couple of 'em'll get lost. Folks look a while, then they take the rest of the hounds on home and hope the lost one'll either find his way, or somebody'll pick him up, see his collar and take him home. This ole boy, he was runnin' a while. Lost his collar somewheres. You could tell he was a fine hound, though, just skinny.

"I know'd both them boys, and I knowed they was bad, and they was still drunk and mad at getting thrown out. One of 'em, he had that ol' dog by the scruff of the neck."

Big was becoming agitated. His shoulders hunched, his fingers clutched at the straw and began tearing apart the careful weaving. "The other'n, he said that ol' hound had so many fleas, wadn't but one way to get rid of 'em. He had some kind of can in his hands, and he poured it all over that poor dog. I could smell it. Kerosene. What Mama and me used in the winter. That hound started howling and jumping around. Then the first one, he took out this fancy lighter, and he flicked it. He said if I didn't get down on my hands and knees and apologize, they was gonna set that poor dog on fire."

Now it was Eleanor's turn to shudder. She didn't want to hear the rest of the story. Tears were flowing from Big's eyes, streaming down his dusty cheeks.

"See, I knowed them boys. Didn't matter what I did, they was gonna burn that ol' dog and make me watch it." He dropped his head. "Ma'am, I'm sorry to say, I got mad. Kinda lost track of time."

"Good for you."

"Next thing I know I'm running through the woods with that ol' hound over my shoulder, and there's all this crashing around and yelling behind me."

"What'd you do?" Eleanor whispered.

"First, I washed that ole dog clean in the creek, then I went on home so Mama could give him a meal. Didn't know noplace else to go."

"And you're in jail for that? They should have pinned a medal on you."

"No ma'am, they shouldn't. Folks said them boys was just funning. I had no call to break Dewayne's shoulder and his arm in four places when I took that lighter away from him, said I was a danger to the community and had to be locked up to keep me from killing somebody. Said I was like Frank somebody's monster."

"Frankenstein." Eleanor could barely hear her own voice.

"Yes, ma'am. I told Dewayne I was sorry." He raised

his head and his jaw set. "But I'm not. Not a bit. I'll do my time, but I'd probably do the same thing again. See, they're right. I *am* a danger to the community."

"What happened to the hound?"

"Mama found the man owned him. He gave her a reward for finding him. He testified at my trial, said he woulda done the same thing or worse. But nobody believed me about the fire. See, I washed the dog off real good, and one of those boys—he's the mayor's boy."

"I see. Thank you for telling me, Big. Oh, and would you give me a lesson on how to weave those baskets sometime?"

He smiled. "Sure, Doc."

At lunch she went home and called the number listed for the sheriff's office in Marlton County, of which Mission was the county seat. Even if she believed Big, Ernest Portree would want confirmation. If anybody could tell her the circumstances of Big's arrest, it should be the sheriff listed as the arresting officer. But she found out he'd retired.

It took her some time to convince the young deputy to give her the sheriff's home number, but eventually he did, and when she called, she found him at home having lunch. She explained the reason for her call. "Do you remember Bigelow Little's case?"

"Yes, ma'am. That's one I am embarrassed to have on my record."

"Oh?"

"See, the sheriff is an elected official, and I'd just won a real tough fight. The mayor backed me, so I owed him. But now I'm retired I don't owe that fool or that scumsucking hooligan son of his the time of day. Shoulda given Big a medal for what he did, not throwed him in jail for three years."

"So he told me the truth about saving the dog?"

"Big Little can't lie. Now, I'll grant you that he broke that kid's arm in four places—damned near tore it off at the shoulder. Don't think the boy's got the full use of it back yet, but given Big's size and the way he feels about animals, it's a miracle he didn't tear his head off. People said his mama was a witch, but she was just a poor, un-educated hill woman who kept to herself. I used to see her in town sometimes selling those baskets of hers. Damn near tall as Big, with white hair she could sit on, and those blue eyes… No wonder folks gave her a wide berth. I've heard she taught Big how to walk up on a wild doe with a fawn and pet her, but I doubt it. One of those country legends.''

"So he'd be a good candidate for work release at a veterinary clinic?"

"Perfect. When's he due out?"

"About six months, if he's paroled."

"Tell the boy not to come back here for his own good."

"What about his mother's place?"

"She only rented the house and the land, too. After she died, everything got sold to pay for the funeral. Preacher saved a couple of boxes of family pictures and things up in his attic for Big, but they didn't have much to start with. Mostly lived on social security after Big's daddy's death—until Big got to be eighteen."

"He wants to come home to visit his mother's grave."

"Then let me know ahead of time, and somebody im-portant better come with him. I'd hate to see him get hurt."

"That's some town you got there, Sheriff."

"I know. Why I retired." He sighed.

The moment she'd hung up from speaking to the sheriff, she called Ernest Portree. He picked up his own phone. Eating at his desk as usual. She told him about the sheriff's assessment and asked again to have Big on work release.

"Give me twenty-four hours to assemble the paperwork. You get your people to fill out the forms, and we'll let him go."

"I'd like to take him over there tomorrow to meet the staff, see if they approve of him. Would that be possible?"

"Sure. Check him out and check him in. I'll leave word."

"Now about Steve Chadwick…"

"I said no, Eleanor. Drop it."

"No way. He's eligible, we need him, and the next time I ask, I'll have my ducks in a row."

STEVE WATCHED Eleanor surreptitiously all morning while he worked on the fences, saw her talk with Big and wondered what it was about. Big would tell him if he asked, but then the other men would know, as well. Better wait until they could be private.

Eleanor had stayed well away from him, had refused to make eye contact, or even to speak to him.

Last night he'd come close to having a panic attack for the first time since he'd moved from Big Mountain. He'd tried to focus on his escape and how great it would feel to kill Neil.

This morning on the fence line he was closer to being truly alone with his thoughts than he'd been in three years. There had always been someone else in his cell, the yard, the showers, the latrines, the mess hall, even in his classes. He'd been constantly aware, always on the alert for trouble.

But as the chill wind whipped his face, as his fingers mechanically tensioned and twisted and hammered, there were no distractions. He thought about his revenge. Once he'd worked out that Neil had killed Chelsea, had framed him for murder, had stolen the company, he'd hated the man with an all-consuming passion. And until now, when he visualized his revenge, he'd always focused on Neil's terror as he faced death.

Now instead he saw Neil's dead body and Posey's grief. She loved the man. Even if she knew for certain he'd murdered Chelsea, she'd still love him.

Steve understood grief. God knows he faced it every

day. Until now he'd never allowed himself to think of the aftermath of Neil's death.

Worst of all, Steve finally acknowledged that he would grieve for Neil, too.

From the day Neil had walked into Steve's dorm room his sophomore year, they'd shared pizza and beer, double-dated, played soccer and softball, married sisters, started a company together. Neil was the brother he'd never had.

Steve had shared his hopes and his dreams, his inner-most thoughts. He'd thought Neil had shared his. If he could be wrong about Neil, could he ever trust his judgment again?

Facing that was hard. Letting go of his hatred was impossible.

Or was it?

If somehow Eleanor could believe in him, maybe he could find a way to live again as the man he'd thought he was. Maybe he could endure the rest of his sentence with equanimity. Maybe he could even let go of his need to avenge Chelsea.

As Eleanor walked along the fence line behind him, he took his chance. "When do you want me to finish the computer program, Doc?" He kept his voice neutral and businesslike.

For a moment he thought she wouldn't stop or reply, but then she came over to him. He drank in the scent of her perfume—a barely detectable musky odor.

"I've got my laptop locked in my vet chest in back of the truck. It's fully charged, so you should be able to work outside the barn where Selma can see you for at least a couple of hours after lunch."

Selma wouldn't detect any warmth in their exchange, but Steve realized he'd have relished the sound of her voice if she'd been reading the telephone book.

"Hey, Doc, how come he's the only one gets to play with your little *computer?*" Sweet Daddy leered at her.

Selma snapped to attention. "Shut your face, little man."

"You got no call to diss me."

"You keep up that smart mouth, *little man,*" Selma replied, "and you're gonna be on the next bus back to Big Mountain."

The moment Sweet Daddy had started to speak, Eleanor grabbed Steve's arm and dug her fingers into the muscle. "Don't say anything," she whispered. "Let me handle it."

"What's more to the point, Elroy," Eleanor added, "if you don't shape up and start pulling your load of the work, you're going to be off this team."

It was like looking into the eyes of a wolverine. For a moment Steve thought Sweet Daddy was actually going to lunge at Eleanor, and he thrust her behind him. Then Sweet Daddy stepped back, pasted a stupid grin on his face and raised his hands in front of his chest. "Riiight. Sweet Daddy just havin' a little fun. Ya'll need to loosen up and take a joke." He picked up his fencing tool and marched back to his place in the fence, where he began to twist wire fiercely.

Both Eleanor and Selma blew out their breaths.

That was the second time women had forced Sweet Daddy to back down in front of the others. He was used to controlling women, not being under their command. Steve didn't think Eleanor had any idea how serious a breach of Sweet Daddy's rules of etiquette she'd just committed, but Selma should. It was Selma's job to know.

He'd have to convince Eleanor to carry out her threat and toss Sweet Daddy off her team, but in such a way that Sweet Daddy thought the summons came from someone outside the group. That way there would be no reprisals either against the team members or the staff.

He caught Gil's eye. Gil nodded, barely moving his head. Gil was an old con. He didn't want any trouble, either.

After lunch, Eleanor brought Steve her laptop.

"Easier to work in the office," he said. "I can spread your notes out on the desk."

"All right. I'll simply tell Selma that I choose to have you work in the office. She won't like it, but she'll agree."

ELEANOR SLIPPED IN half an hour later, closed the door behind her and stood in front of the desk with her hands behind her. She didn't want him to know that she'd intertwined her fingers to keep them from shaking. Being alone in this small room with him gave her gooseflesh. "How's your back?" At least she could keep their exchanges casual.

He looked up at her with those fine sad eyes of his. "The liniment you brought really helped."

"I'm glad." She hadn't noticed the touches of silver along his temples before, but now under the single lightbulb, she could see what the cropped prison haircut had disguised. Had the pressures of prison life accelerated the process?

"When do you think you'll be finished with the program?" she asked. "We should start entering data."

He eased his shoulders and leaned back in the rickety desk chair. "All I'm lacking now is a few neat touches like buttons to make the program more user-friendly. It should be simple for anyone to update or change if you decide you need additional data in the future when I'm not here."

She came around the desk, so eager to see what he'd done that she forgot to keep her distance until she was practically leaning over him. She felt her heart speed up, but her voice sounded normal. Good. "I hope you made it idiot-proof."

"You know what they say—whenever you make something idiot-proof, God makes a better idiot."

"Show me."

He shoved back and stood with difficulty, hands on either side of the computer. The liniment hadn't been completely successful, then. He was still sore.

Eleanor kept forgetting how tall he was. She backed away quickly while he moved out of her way in the other direction.

"Sit down," he said.

"I'd rather see a demonstration."

"Consider yourself the test idiot."

He actually smiled. One corner of his mouth turned up and his eyes danced for a moment before going flat again.

"I may be a better idiot than you planned."

"We'll see." He held the back of the desk chair.

She slipped into it. "I'm okay with straight word processing, but I've never used a database."

"Time to learn." He leaned over so that he could see the screen. He'd braced his right hand on the desk, while his left arm lay across the back of the desk chair.

Eleanor kept her eyes fixed on the screen, but she had no idea what he was saying. Her senses were filled by him, the slight scent of perspiration that lingered on his skin, his breath warm and close to her ear, his shoulder almost touching hers.

"What?" she asked, and turned her face toward his.

Big mistake.

He looked down at her, his eyes warmed to gold by the harsh light above their heads.

And his mouth…

HE COULDN'T TAKE HIS EYES off her lips. All he could hear was the roaring of blood in his ears. He might have been speaking pig Latin, for all he knew. The room was suddenly too hot. She was too close. And those full, soft lips…

He caressed her cheek, her throat, the nape of her neck where her hair cascaded over his hand. He tilted her face so that he could touch those lips with his own—only touch, only taste, a moment only, a gentle memory to cherish in the darkness.

The moment his lips touched hers, he knew one taste would never be enough. Her lips parted beneath his, her tongue met his, hunger for hunger.

He'd thought prison had long extinguished the fire in his loins, but the instant he kissed her, his senses flared, caught. The blaze engulfed him.

He wrapped his other arm around her, lifted her and turned her toward him so that her body met his breast to thigh.

She made only a tiny sound as her arms slid around his neck, while his slid down to cup her hips against him.

She broke the kiss and leaned away from him. ''Selma...''

''All I care about is you.''

CHAPTER EIGHT

ELEANOR CAME INTO HIS ARMS willingly, even eagerly. Steve had promised himself a taste, a gentle taste. Instead, he crushed her against him and kissed her fiercely. She opened to him, met him as though they could devour each other in an instant.

She broke away first. "I can't...we can't..."

"We can." He leaned his cheek against her hair, let it fall over his face so that he could breathe her in one more moment.

"Let me go. Please, Steve."

He released her then and leaned against the wall to catch his breath.

She let out a ragged gasp, swayed and caught herself on the desk.

Steve wrapped his arms around her from behind, felt her body melt against him, her fingers cover his. He wanted to hold her forever, to let all the goodness he saw in her seep into him, wash away that cold, hard center he'd developed. She was everything beautiful about the world that he'd forgotten. He desired her, yes, but he also longed for the peace of falling asleep in her arms, safe from the evil that surrounded him.

She gave him back his humanity without even realizing it. She was—

"This is madness. Please, we've got to open the door before Selma comes in and finds us."

He came closer at that moment to screaming his curses at what his life had become than he had since he'd been convicted. He longed to grab Eleanor's hand and run—just run and keep on running until he could taste freedom, if only for a moment. To be free! Free to make love to her, to watch her blossom with desire under him, to fall asleep entwined, satiated. At peace.

What did he have to give her in return? Nothing good. Prison had eaten away all his goodness. He moved in a world where the traits that Eleanor possessed in such quantity weren't valued. He should tell her to run back to her safe little world, never come to this place again, never look into his eyes, touch him…

He let her go and backed into the far corner, as far away as the little office would allow.

She stood before the closed door, raked her fingers through her hair, straightened her shoulders and opened the door wide. "Sorry, Selma," Eleanor called. "Wind caught the door."

"Yeah. Right. Better prop it open with something so it doesn't *accidentally* shut again." Selma turned away to watch the men who were still in the far pasture.

It was like that first stolen kiss under the bleachers in high school, except that the consequences were much more serious than a trip to the principal's office.

Eleanor didn't look at him. "I should never have allowed that to happen."

He could almost reach out and touch her shoulder, but he didn't think he could bear it if she flinched.

"You didn't allow anything. It happened. I'm trying to feel sorry, but I can't."

Still with her back to him she wrapped her arms around her self as though she was cold. "I can't trust myself anymore."

"Trust what you felt just now. I told you I'm just like the others, but I'm not lying when I say I care about you. I wish I was strong enough to tell you to get the hell out of this place before you get hurt by me or somebody else. I'm too damned selfish to give up seeing you every day, even if I can never touch you. I want to keep hearing your voice, even if you're not speaking to me. I have nothing to offer you in return except to tell you I'm not a killer, that the system made a serious mistake. On that one thing alone, believe me.''

"How can I?'' She sounded anguished. This time she did look at him and he could see the glint of tears on her lashes. ''And why should you care what I think unless you've decided I can do something for you.''

His jaw clenched. ''That's Raoul Torres talking. He's indoctrinated you well about the manipulative inmates. If you can't see why I care what you think of me, I won't try to convince you.''

"Hey, Doc, J.K.'s here with the horses,'' Selma called.

"Coming. You better come, too, Steve. You know how to handle a horse.''

"Right.'' He forced himself to sound casual. ''Let me shut down the computer. I can show you the database program later. I'll be right behind you.''

He sat down and stared at the computer screen, then brought up the first instruction screen for the database. In the first line he typed, ''Please talk to my sister and my lawyer.'' Then he shut the computer down, unplugged it and put it back into its case. He left it on the front seat of her truck.

Now he could only hope that she'd try the program herself before she turned it over to some secretary.

ELEANOR CAUGHT Rick Hazard at the clinic as he was getting ready to go home. She told him about Big and got his reluctant permission to bring him with her tomorrow afternoon so that the staff could check him out.

"He's pretty remarkable to look at,'' Eleanor warned him. ''And not very well educated, but he's gentle and willing and has great instincts. I think he'd be perfect for us. Heaven knows we need somebody. Kenny can't work but three nights a week, and then only until ten. Kenny's

a real find, but tough as he is, he couldn't possibly handle
a rank stallion with a bad allergic reaction or a cow with
a fever.''

"The Minnesota Twins couldn't handle a cow with a
fever,'' Sarah Scott said from the doorway. "What's the
latest on the other guy, the computer whiz? When do we
get him?''

"I'm not certain we do,'' Eleanor said.

"Mark met him once or twice before...'' Sarah said.
"He didn't really know him, but at the time it was a very
big deal in the newspapers. Prominent businessman, rich
wife. Not the usual Saturday-night drug shooting.''

Eleanor started to say something, but Rick beat her to
it. "Margot knows his sister, Mary Beth, and served on a
couple of committees with his wife. Said they seemed like
a nice couple. She couldn't believe it when he was accused
of killing her. I mean, why not just divorce her? She says
it must have been some kind of domestic thing that got
out of hand. The jury must have thought so, too, otherwise,
why'd he get such a short sentence?''

Eleanor realized that to Rick and Sarah, the story of
Chelsea's murder was no more than gossip about strangers,
something they might see on a television show. The cast
of characters wasn't real to them, as it was to her. "Would
Steve's working here create problems?'' she asked Rick.

"People forget fast. He probably doesn't even look like
the same guy. Might be a good idea, though, for him to
stay in the back most of the time.''

"If Mark has his way, Steve won't ever leave Mark's
office,'' Sarah said. "At this point I think he'd welcome
Jack the Ripper if he could figure out a way to handle the
paperwork more efficiently. Mark's about to pull his hair
out by the roots with all he's got to do, and now that
Buchanan Enterprises is really getting into out of town
development bigtime, I'm beginning to be thankful I've
got Piglet here.'' She stroked her small belly. "We may
never get a chance to make another one.''

Rick blushed. He could talk breeding all day long with his clients, but anything remotely sexual in human beings made him uncomfortable.

Both Eleanor and Sarah laughed at him. He managed a sheepish grin.

"I'm having a tussle with the prison administration about Chadwick," Eleanor continued. "He's officially eligible for work release, but they're dragging their feet. Still, I'm making headway. In the meantime, I can probably arrange for Mark to visit him and bring him piecework."

"Please, for the sake of my unborn children and my unfulfilled libido, hurry up," Sarah said. "Now, I'm going home possibly to fulfill said libido. If you get a problem, call me." She waved and shut the door behind her. A moment later Eleanor and Rick followed.

"Bill Chumley's back from giving his paper on eagle rehabilitation," Rick said. "He's left you some notes. There's a mama possum that lost an eye. She has to be checked to make certain all her babies are getting into her pouch for dinner. He's got a pet European hedgehog with some kind of mangelike fungus he's not sure about. Poor old hedgehog's losing his quills."

"I'll take a look, although I don't know much about hedgehogs."

"If you have some free time, check the textbooks. This hedgehog thing may be perfectly normal where hedgehogs are found in the wild. And this afternoon somebody brought in a peregrine falcon some fool actually shot off a high-rise building in downtown Memphis. The nerve of some people. Here the city spends thousands of bucks and five years to get the peregrines to nest downtown, then some idiot brings his little air rifle to work with him so he can do a bit of hunting at lunch."

"Did they catch the guy?"

"Caught, charged and will probably pay a five-thousand-dollar fine. Plus get his name and picture in the paper as being a total horse's ass, which he is.''

''Will the peregrine live?''

''Mac helped Bill pin his wing before he left for the day. He's royally pissed off—the falcon, that is. If you want to look at him closely, wear Bill's gauntlets or he'll tear the hide off you. He's little but he's mean.''

First she checked the possum. Her babies were all snuggled safely in her pouch. The poor thing would probably wind up in the local wildlife facility's teaching program for schoolchildren as soon as her babies were weaned. They could be released into the wild. She couldn't.

The instant Eleanor removed the cover from the falcon's cage he began to scream at her in pure rage.

''How can such a little guy have such a mean mouth?'' she said. He seemed particularly annoyed at the collar Mac and Bill had fashioned so that he couldn't reach his wing and tear off the bandages. ''I know, it's undignified, but you'll have to put up with it.''

He shrieked at her and drove his bill against the wire. ''Boy, you are a tough critter, aren't you?'' She chuckled. ''How about we name you Sweet Daddy? Okay, lights out.'' She lowered the cover. The falcon grumbled, then went quiet. ''Wish I could quiet Sweet Daddy down that easily.''

She went back to Sarah's office and settled down to read Bill's copy of *Diseases of Small Mammals Indigenous to Europe and the British Isles*. Nothing helpful on hedgehogs.

''Okay, next step the Internet.''

She logged on, saw that she had several e-mail messages waiting, and ignored them while she went to the Net. After a half-hour search she had reached the conclusion that the hedgehog was suffering from a bacterial infection that wouldn't have thrived in the wild, but had perfect conditions when the little animal was caged. She wrote notes for herself and for Bill as to treatment. The treatment was simple, but would take several weeks to complete, during which time the poor hedgehog would probably turn semi-nude as more quills dropped off.

The good news was that the quills should grow back again healthier than before.

Before she logged off, she checked her e-mail, read and answered four messages from colleagues either simply keeping in touch or with professional questions they thought she could answer. She deleted, without reading, another four messages forwarded from people whose chat groups she had inadvertently landed in. She was in no mood for blonde jokes.

She was about to shut down for the night when she decided she should at least try to get into Steve's new database program. If *she* couldn't figure it out, it was probably too esoteric for anyone else on her team to use.

If he had actually made it user-friendly, even for such an amateur user as she was, then she could show it to Ernest Portree and the people at the clinic. It would be another reason to release Steve for work.

She double-clicked the program icon and waited a second until the first instructional screen popped up.

The hair at the nape of her neck rose. The message "Please talk to my sister and my lawyer," no salutation and no signature, stood out boldly at the top of the screen.

Did his sister and his lawyer believe he was innocent? Or that there were extenuating circumstances that had made a decent man into a killer?

Before this afternoon she'd have sworn she owed Steve nothing. But now she had to know what kind of a man he truly was, what he had done and why, for her own peace of mind.

She looked up Chadwick in the telephone book, and found an M. B. Chadwick listed off of Houston Levee Parkway in a very ritzy section of Germantown. An S. Chadwick, col., ret., was listed at the same address, although the numbers were different.

She called, heard the soft Southern voice of Mary Beth Chadwick asking her to leave a message, left her name and number, hung up and stared at the phone as though it might explode at any moment.

She dug out the latest issue of the local livestock news from under a pile of clients' reports on Sarah's desk and tried to focus on the list of winners at the last all-breed cattle show in Somerville.

Would Mary Beth Chadwick call her back?

Marcus Aurelius III of Duntreith had won his class, so Marcus Aurelius IV did indeed come from prize stock. She needed to ask J. K. Sanders to give a class on preparing livestock to show. The cows were a lot bigger than a standard poodle, but before a show, they were prettied up at least as much. She hadn't presented a heifer for show since Four H when she was eight. No doubt the tips and tricks had changed considerably.

Was Mary Beth out for the evening?

They'd have to start handling Marcus Aurelius. At the moment the only person who could safely enter the pen with him was Big.

The bull loathed Sweet Daddy. Once Eleanor had caught Sweet Daddy teasing Marcus with a pitchfork and trying to get him to bump the electric fence. She'd warned him that if it came to a contest with Marcus, Sweet Daddy would come in a far second, and would probably spend time in the prison infirmary, if he didn't go straight to the graveyard.

Bulls, like elephants, had prodigious memories. Just as Marcus remembered that Big was kind, he would hate Sweet Daddy his whole life.

The telephone on her desk rang, and she picked it up on the second ring.

A female voice asked tentatively, "Are you Dr. Eleanor Grayson?"

"Yes. Thank you for calling back so promptly, Miss Chadwick."

"Do I know you, Doctor?"

"We've never met. Your brother asked me to call you."

Eleanor heard the indrawn breath. Mary Beth whispered, "My brother? Stephen?"

"Mary Beth, who is that on the telephone?" The voice in the background was gruff, older. The voice of command.

"Somebody about the symphony ball, Daddy."

"Expensive foolishness. Don't know why you bother."

"It's for a good cause."

Eleanor thought Mary Beth must have a lifetime of lying to her father behind her to do it so glibly.

"Steve asked if I might call you."

"What for?"

Oh, great. Because his kiss set me on fire and I'd rather not fall for a murderer?

Suddenly the answer came to her.

"He's being considered for a work release program with which I'm associated. He gave you as a character reference." Whew. "I wonder if you might join me for lunch tomorrow? For Steve's sake."

Eleanor heard the sudden intake of breath followed by silence. She had opened her mouth to ask again when she heard Mary Beth's breathy whisper. "Someplace in Bartlett? Daddy never goes there and doesn't know anybody who could see us."

Why should Mary Beth care if her father knew they were meeting for lunch tomorrow? Eleanor named a chain restaurant and a time.

"Yes." Mary Beth hung up without another word.

Next Eleanor called Leslie Vickers's office and left another message on *his* answering machine, but this time included that Steve asked him to speak to her about the work release program. She hadn't expected the lawyer to answer his phone at nine in the evening, but at least he could call her back during business hours.

She would make it clear that Steve Chadwick was responsible for any bills. At least that way she wouldn't have to admit to anyone that she'd spent money on him. She already knew what they'd say if they found out she'd kissed him.

ELEANOR REALIZED on her way to meet Mary Beth Chadwick on Wednesday that they had no way to identify each other. Eleanor hadn't told Mary Beth she was a veterinarian rather than a medical doctor, so she wouldn't recognize the Creature Comfort logo on her truck, and Eleanor didn't know how to identify Steve's sister.

When she pulled into the parking lot at the restaurant, she noticed an attractive young woman climbing out of a Mercedes. The woman looked so much like Steve that Eleanor was certain this could be no one but Mary Beth.

Eleanor went to her with outstretched hand. "Mary Beth? Hi. I'm Eleanor Grayson."

"You said *Dr.* Grayson. Is my brother sick?"

"No. I should have told you. I'm a veterinarian. We're setting up a herd of prize show cattle. Steve is helping with the computer programming."

Mary Beth let out a breath. "I'm glad he's well. Let's go inside."

When they were seated in the darkest booth in the far corner of the restaurant, Mary Beth asked, "Why are you in Memphis if you work with my brother?"

"You don't know? He's been moved from Big Mountain. He's here at the new West Tennessee Prison Farm."

Mary Beth grasped Eleanor's wrist. "Here? How long has he been here? Why did they move him? Is he all right? How does he look? Is he terribly thin?"

"Whoa. One question at a time. Me first. Didn't he notify you about the move? Didn't somebody from the prison system?"

Mary Beth shook her head so hard that her hair swung around her face. "No. You have to register with the prison before they inform you about anything like a move, and

Daddy said having the Chadwick name on prison rolls was bad enough without letting the authorities know our address.'' She dropped her gaze. ''I sent him cards on his birthday and for Christmas, though.''

''I see.'' Eleanor didn't see at all, but then, she didn't know these people. ''He is doing well for somebody who has spent three years in prison.''

Mary Beth covered her mouth with her hand.

''I don't know how he looked before, but at the moment he's lean and muscular. There's some gray in his hair, but it makes him look distinguished, although prison haircuts aren't done for looks.''

''His hair is gray?''

''Only around the edges. Listen, Mary Beth, it's none of my business, but why on earth have you let your father force you to abandon a brother you obviously care about?''

''You wouldn't understand.''

''Try me.''

Mary Beth drew herself up. ''I don't even know you. I have no intention of speaking of family business with a total stranger. I only met you because you said you wanted some information about Steve.''

''You're right, it's none of my business. I can see why you might not have the time to drive to Big Mountain to see him. But now that he's here, why don't you visit? There are visiting hours every Saturday afternoon.''

''The Colonel wouldn't like it.''

''Steve is his son.''

''As far as the Colonel is concerned, Steve besmirched the family honor.'' She wrinkled her nose. Her tone changed. Suddenly she sounded more friendly, even eager to impart information. ''That's a crock, of course, but the Colonel won't let me mention his name in the house.''

''What about you? Do you think he betrayed the family honor?''

''I don't know, and frankly, I don't care. He's still my brother and I love him.''

"Does he deserve to be in prison? That's what I'm asking you."

Mary Beth's reserve returned. "He was convicted."

"So you do think he was guilty." Eleanor's heart sank.

"I think he's the dearest, kindest, most completely honest man I've ever known." Mary Beth's voice had risen. "If he did kill Chelsea, he had a good reason."

There was definitely something strange about Mary Beth. One moment she sounded in control, the next, her words spilled out as though she were an adolescent school girl. Eleanor couldn't fathom the woman. "What reason could possibly be good enough to kill somebody over?"

"Maybe it was a stupid accident. Maybe she attacked him, and he hit her back and she hit her head or something." Mary Beth began to shred her paper napkin. "He shouldn't have married her. She resented anyone else in his life, even me. He could have gotten the money someplace else."

"The money?"

"Chelsea inherited a bundle. Her father owned a string of hotels and sold out just before he died. She gave Steve the seed money to start his company."

"What was his company, exactly?"

"Some kind of thing computers use to make games move faster or look better or something. I don't understand all that stuff. They weren't rich, but they were doing really well financially. Not many people worked for Steve's company, but apparently you don't need many. When Steve had to have money to pay for his defense, his partner bought him out. Now *he's* in the process of selling out to some humongous company for a gazillion dollars." Her eyes turned angry. "It's not fair. He's going to retire to Phoenix and play golf all day while Steve sits in jail. No matter what anyone says, I'll always blame Chelsea."

Eleanor felt lost in the conversation. Following Mary Beth's arguments was extremely difficult. She saw no sense in arguing, so she simply nodded and changed the subject.

She knew that Mary Beth and Margot Hazard, Rick's wife, sat on several boards together, and kept the conversation light for the rest of the meal.

She made a mental note to ask Margot Hazard for a rundown on Mary Beth the next time she saw her. It wasn't only that she led a sheltered life, although apparently it was one driver's license short of a cloistered nunnery. There was something slightly off about Mary Beth, but Eleanor couldn't put her finger on what.

Margot didn't have a paying job, but she ran half the charities in West Tennessee with an iron hand and an alligator charm, and meddled in the clinic every chance Rick gave her. Mary Beth, on the other hand, didn't seem capable of running a bath.

When the two women headed to the parking lot after lunch, Mary Beth opened her driver's side door, then turned back. "You wouldn't like to read the trial transcript, would you? I've got a copy in the trunk you could borrow."

Eleanor felt a surge of adrenaline, but tried to keep her voice casual. "I'd be glad to, if you think that would help."

"Great." Mary Beth popped the trunk, rummaged among fancy gym bags, moved an elegant leather golf bag, and came up with a bedraggled package wrapped in brown paper. "There."

"Thank you. I'll return it."

"No! At least not when the Colonel could find out. He doesn't know I bought it. He'd have a conniption."

"So you keep it in your car?"

"I couldn't keep it in the house. Daddy might see it. He never looks in my trunk." She laughed shortly. "He says it's a rat's nest. Most unmilitary."

Suddenly Eleanor felt sorry for Mary Beth. There must

be some reason she didn't simply rebel and move out of her father's house.

At least Eleanor now had the trial transcript, which was much more than she'd expected. She'd read it tonight and call Leslie Vickers again in the morning. This time she'd demand an appointment whatever the cost.

Was Mary Beth right? Had Chelsea's death been an accident? Or had Steve done it in self-defense?

Eleanor drove at once to the prison farm to check on the men's progress with the buffalo-field fencing. Actually, she wanted to see Steve, if only for a moment and under Selma's watchful eye.

Impossible. One of the hydraulic lines that lifted the front loader had broken. Rather than take it to the prison motor pool and wait while it took its turn after other vehicles in need of repair, Gil Jones had convinced Selma to requisition the parts over the lunch break. Now, Gil and Slow Rise were working on the tractor, while Sweet Daddy, Steve, Robert and Big finished the fencing.

Sweet Daddy kept up a litany of grumbles.

Robert moved in his usual trance, but kept pace with Steve and Big most of the time.

Big and Steve worked side by side in perfect harmony. The manual dexterity that Big had shown in weaving the pine straw showed here, too.

Eleanor greeted everyone and noticed that all the cows and calves in the pasture were lying down. That meant rain before too long. Old wives' tale it might be, but she found it to be an excellent indicator. The cows always recognized a drop in barometric pressure even before instruments picked it up. They got as much rest, chewed as much cud as they could, before they were faced with standing tail on a cold wind.

Eleanor walked through the barn to check on Marcus Aurelius. He was also lying in his paddock, nose to tail, his short horns across his broad back.

She turned off the electric fence and opened the gate to

his paddock, then carefully closed it behind her. She'd stuck a cattle prod in the back pocket of her jeans, but she doubted she'd have to use it. Besides, she suspected that a jolt of electricity would only annoy Marcus Aurelius, not drive him away from her. She was used to bulls. They were unpredictable, but usually laid-back—as long as there wasn't a cow in season or another bull on the horizon. Marcus had already showed himself to be good-natured.

With only a lone woman sharing his space—a creature he apparently did not consider a threat—he barely raised his head when she entered. She moved toward him, keeping her demeanor subservient and her pace slow. She also kept an eye on the gate in case she had to get out in a hurry. When she was ten feet away he heaved himself up with a groan, but didn't approach. The last rays of the afternoon sun turned his coat to molten copper. He looked more like one of the cattle from an Egyptian tomb painting than a modern bull.

"Hey, sweetie," she said as she stepped up to him. He looked at her with liquid eyes, lowered his head and swiped his huge tongue across the toe of her boot. She scratched the soft brown pelt between his eyes and was rewarded with a gentle sigh, and a moment later, her other boot was wiped clean. "Is this a hidden talent? Can we rent you out as a bootblack if you don't make nice babies?"

He sighed and leaned his left shoulder against her. He nearly knocked her off her feet. It wasn't a hostile gesture—more like a friendly dog asking to have its ears scratched—but Eleanor decided she'd gone far enough for one day. He was still young. There was plenty of time to accustom him to being groomed and handled. She scratched the hair at the base of his horns and began to step backward in retreat.

It took him a moment to realize he'd lost his masseuse. He followed her step for step. If she turned her back and he decided to give her a friendly head butt to get her attention, he could very well launch her into the next county. If she sprinted for the gate, he might decide they'd started a nice game of soccer in which she was the ball.

She reached the gate, felt behind her, unlatched it and squeezed through the opening, then latched it behind her. Marcus Aurelius looked at her reproachfully, so she gave him one more horn scratch before she turned the electric current back on, shooing him away before she did. She did not want him to think of her in the same terms he thought of Sweet Daddy.

"Are you crazy going in there by yourself?"

It was Steve.

"Not especially. I've got a cattle prod in my back pocket. I knew I could yell for help if I needed it."

"One of the first things I learned about bulls was never to get close to them without backup handy."

"Maybe on open range. He's in a stall, and he's already proved that he's quiet and intelligent. I'm a professional, remember?" She was getting annoyed. "I do this all the time."

"I do remember you're a professional. You still shouldn't take chances."

"Chance is unavoidable in this job. I thought I'd be safe and I was right. What are you doing up here, anyway? You and Big were mending fence."

"Selma said it's quitting time. I volunteered to come tell you."

"Marcus wants his dinner."

"I got it right here, ma'am," Big called. "Y'all go get drinks. I'll be there in a minute."

Eleanor started past Steve, but he stopped her.

"I wanted to see you."

She turned and met his gaze. "I had lunch with your sister."

"You did?" His eyes lit. "How is she?"

Eleanor opened her mouth to form a reply, then said,

"Come on, we'd better get my cooler or Selma will start looking for us."

He followed her.

She spoke over her shoulder and just above a whisper. "She jumps around from one subject to the next. She's very much on edge. Why on earth doesn't she tell your dad to take a short leap off a tall building? Or at least move out of his house?"

Steve stopped with his hands on the cooler, then picked it up without a word and carried it to the shelter of the barn where the men pounced on it.

He took a soda and moved over closer to the pine trees. They were in full view of Selma, so the CO had to be content with giving them a sour look.

"She didn't even know you'd been moved from Big Mountain," Eleanor continued.

"I guess she wouldn't."

"She wants to come to see you, but she's afraid to upset your father."

"Did she tell you how the Colonel is doing? He's not young."

"Other than that he won't allow your name to be spoken in his house or his presence, I have no idea."

"Don't be too hard on him. As far as he's concerned, I let down the whole family."

"Not if you're innocent."

"He doesn't believe that."

"Did you try to tell him?"

"Again and again before the trial. I haven't spoken to him since."

"You're his son, Steve. Nothing you did can change that."

"Drop it, please."

"As you wish. It might help if I knew what areas of your life are taboo and which you want me to dig into."

"I'm sorry. I'll tell you about Mary Beth when we have more time."

"Mary Beth also told me that your business partner is selling out to some big company and retiring to Phoenix."

Steve spun around to stare at her. "What? When?"

"I don't know. Does it matter?"

"Damn right it matters."

Eleanor glanced over his shoulder to where Selma stood looking at them. "Keep your voice down."

"Okay, boys. Time for dinner," Selma said. "Come on, let's go, let's go." She approached Steve and unnecessarily prodded him with the barrel of her shotgun. He winced, and Eleanor realized that his bruises were not yet completely healed. She started to say something, then caught the slight shake of his head.

She watched them march off toward the inner compound as she sat in her truck. Darkness was beginning to fall. The cattle were all clustered around the feed troughs close to the fence.

No calves were expected to be born for at least two weeks, but if the size of the mamas was any indication, they might come sooner. She made a mental note to have Jack Renfro check the calf emergency equipment she carried in case she had to pull a breach calf.

A band of sullen gray clouds blotted out the last remaining rays of autumn sunshine on the horizon. The temperature had dropped twenty degrees in as many minutes, and a chill wind from the northwest had risen just as quickly. If there should be a bad storm in the next few of days, one of those cows would probably calve right in the middle of it.

"Please, Lord," Eleanor said, "let her not need my help to do it."

ELEANOR CHECKED for Mike Newman's car before she got out of her truck in her driveway. She didn't see his car or Precious's. She microwaved a frozen dinner, pledged to have a decent meal in a decent restaurant this weekend, even if she had to go alone, and settled down in front of the fireplace with the transcript of Steve's trial.

She woke up at nine-thirty with a crick in her neck from the chair she'd fallen asleep in. She'd felt she had to read every word, but she'd found most of the legal preliminaries both confusing and mind-numbingly dull. Maybe she ought to skip straight to opening arguments and witnesses. She fixed herself a cup of tea with caffeine, and moved to the dining-room table, where the chairs were less comfortable.

The opening arguments simply stated that Steve had stabbed his wife to death because he was angry at her, tired of being beholden to her for money and wanted her million-dollar life-insurance policy of which he was the beneficiary. He was also sole beneficiary of her estate, which was large. And the life-insurance policy paid double indemnity because she had been murdered.

He thus had motive.

The knife came from a matched set of carving knives that were kept in a drawer in his own kitchen—not in plain sight. There were, however, other sharp knives that *had* been in plain sight and would have been closer at hand for a stranger.

He had means.

He and his wife had returned home together from a dinner party with his business partner and his wife. The business partner, Neil Waters, was married to Steve's wife's sister, so was not only his partner, but his brother-in-law. No forensic evidence was found to suggest the presence of a third party at the Chadwick house either before, during or after the murder.

Steve had opportunity.

Eleanor tried to think of "the defendant" as a nameless, faceless person, but she kept seeing Steve. The longer she read, the more damning the evidence seemed.

The defense stated in its opening argument that Steve Chadwick had loved his wife, that they had been happily married, that he was making plenty of money from his company and did not need hers, and that if he had needed money she would have given it to him without strings.

They had come home together, but Steve had been tired, so had gone right to sleep upstairs, while his wife stayed downstairs to watch television. He said when he woke up in the morning and found she had still not come to bed, he thought she had fallen asleep in front of the television set and had stayed downstairs so as not to disturb him.

He had gone through his usual morning routine of shaving, bathing and dressing, and had even called downstairs to see whether she was making coffee. When he received no answer, he assumed she was in the kitchen and couldn't hear him.

He had called police immediately upon finding her body, had been completely distraught at her death. He swore an intruder must have entered the house during the night to rob it, discovered Chelsea, killed her to keep her from being able to identify him, stolen the jewelry she was wearing and run away. The missing jewelry—necklace, bracelet and ring—had never been found. The knife could have been out on the drain board or the kitchen counter— Steve didn't remember. He had heard nothing and slept deeply all night long.

Then came the evidence. The first witness was the medical examiner.

Chelsea Chadwick had been sitting upright in her recliner in the den, possibly dozing in front of the television set, when her killer had crept up behind her and stabbed downward with such force that the sternum was split and the heart punctured. There was been little blood because the knife had been left in the wound and death had been instantaneous. The killer probably did not have bloodstains on his person or his clothing.

There were no defense wounds. She died within seconds, and probably never realized what was happening to her.

Then came the detectives.

Steve, who said he was asleep upstairs, said he did not awaken. No one made any attempt to hurt him and no evidence was found on the stairs that anyone else had been to the second floor.

Although the expensive jewelry that Chelsea had been wearing had not been found, nor pawned, nothing else of value in the house had been taken.

Glass had been broken out of a pane in the French doors, but most of the glass had fallen outside on the deck rather than inside on the carpet. This showed that the door had been broken from inside. Since breaking glass would have made noise, if Chelsea had still been alive when it was broken, she'd have gotten up to go see what had happened. She did not. The latch had been lifted, but the door had been shut. There was no other evidence of a break-in, nor evidence that she had let anyone in the front or back doors.

No forensic evidence from a third party had been discovered—no shoe tracks, hair, bits of fabric or unknown fingerprints. No unusual cars had been seen in the secluded neighborhood, which had a roving neighborhood patrol.

The house had not had a burglar alarm, supposedly because Mrs. Chadwick did not want one in case she forgot the code to disarm it.

Eleanor laid down the transcript. She couldn't take any more tonight. She was glad she was on a full day shift at the clinic tomorrow, because she didn't think she could have looked Steve in the face.

Why had he asked her to read it? She'd never read anything so damning in her whole life. No wonder they'd convicted him.

CHAPTER NINE

ELEANOR DREADED running into Steve in the prison compound, but she managed to pick Big up for his interview at Creature Comfort on Saturday morning without meeting any of her team. Most of them were probably inside waiting for visitors.

She wondered whether Mary Beth Chadwick would get up enough courage to visit her brother.

Big had stuck two small pieces of toilet tissue on his chin where he had cut himself shaving, and his face shone from the scrubbing he had given it. He'd ironed his jeans so that the crease would cut butter, and his shirt was fresh, starched, the sleeves rolled down to a single cuff. Probably no prison shirt had sleeves that would reach his wrists, but he'd tried.

Big crammed himself into the front seat of her truck like Alice in the White Rabbit's house, with one elbow out the window and his head scrunched against the roof.

On the way to the clinic she told him about the staff, the clients, what they did and what they expected from him.

At one point she looked over at him to see if he was listening. He was, avidly, but he was also staring wide-eyed at the passing suburban landscape, with its manicured lawns and immense houses.

"Here we are," she said as she pulled around to the back of the clinic and parked.

"Ma'am," he whispered, "a grown man oughtn't to say

this. I'm scared. What if I break something or hurt some-body?''

''You won't. Now, the man you'll be working with most closely is Jack Renfro. He's even smaller than Sweet Daddy, but much nicer. Even when he sounds grumpy, he's only acting. Come on. It's going to be all right. Remember you said you swing a great mop?''

Big smiled gently. ''Yes'm.''

Big nearly filled the door into the large-animal area. Across the way, Jack Renfro knelt beside Megan Cormack's foundered pony, which was securely cross-tied on the wash rack. He was carefully unwrapping the bandages that protected the pony's sore front feet and ankles.

The four remaining pit bulls had been moved to the regular kennel area at the back of the small-animal portion of the clinic. Someone had removed their temporary quarters from the cow paddock.

''Morning, Jack,'' Eleanor said brightly. ''Awfully quiet around here without the dogs barking every time I open the door.''

Jack looked up, saw Big and gaped.

''This is Big Little. He's going to be helping out here a couple of days a week.''

''Gawd'' was Jack's only comment.

Eleanor knocked on the door to Sarah's office, leaned in and repeated her introduction. Sarah came out with her hand outstretched and barely missed a step or changed expression when she saw Big. He took her hand as though it were a hummingbird's wing, dropped his eyes and gave her a flash of his angelic smile.

Sarah was captivated.

''You don't look like you're gonna have a baby,'' Big said, then ducked his head and blushed furiously.

''Not for a while yet.''

''Dr. Eleanor says we have to take care of you.''

''Oh, she does, does she?'' Sarah swung her gaze to

Eleanor. ''I'm sure you'll do an excellent job. Now, I have to get to work.''

''Any problems?'' Eleanor asked.

''The farrier's coming to trim and pad the pony's hooves. If his temperature is normal, we can send him home this afternoon.''

''Good. He's lucky they caught that laminitis as soon as they did.''

''Bill's having some real problems with that Pere David deer. It's getting too big to keep inside and badly needs exercise, but every time he and Jack try to move it out to one of the paddocks, it tries to kill them. They may have to sedate it, and you know how deer react to sedation.''

''How?'' Big asked, too interested to be shy.

Sarah said, ''They tend to go into shock and die. That's why they want to move it without drugs if they can.''

Eleanor glanced at Big. ''Come on, Big, let's find Dr. Chumley and give him a hand.''

Tubby, balding Bill Chumley sat at his cluttered desk in the exotic-animal area with one hairy leg propped on the desk while he dabbed at it with a Betadine-soaked cloth. ''Ow, Ow, Ow,'' he whimpered as he wiped.

''Hey, Bill,'' Eleanor said. ''What got you?''

''I have never really approved of deer hunting before,'' Bill said without looking up, ''and I realize the Pere David is an endangered species, but if that little dickens keeps kicking the stew out of me with those pointed hooves, I may change my mind. He's got to get out to exercise that shoulder, but…'' He caught sight of Big in the doorway behind Eleanor. ''My word.''

''This is Big Little. We've come to help. Big, can you handle a fawn?''

''Depends how old. I carried a couple of yearlings.''

''Yearlings?'' Bill sounded strangled.

Big smiled sheepishly. ''One of 'em caught me right in the crutch with one of them little hooves. Put him down right fast.''

''Let's see how large he is.'' Eleanor said. She was so used to Big now that she was surprised at her colleagues' reaction to him.

She followed Bill and Big to the cages where the larger exotics were kept during treatment.

The fawn could barely turn around in his cage, which had been ideal while his wound was fresh, but now he obviously needed his own paddock and lots of exercise.

''We'll have to get Jack to help us lash his legs. He's got to weigh close to 150 pounds, and every bit of it flashing hooves.''

Big crouched in front of the cage. ''Never saw no young deer this big. He's got real funny eyes, too. Kind of tilt up at the ends.''

''Pere David deer all have eyes like that,'' Eleanor said. ''This one belongs to a farmer in Atoka who keeps his own menagerie. He got cut playing with a Scimitar-horned Oryx.''

''Nice little feller,'' Big crooned. ''Bet you'd like to go out and play, wouldn't you?'' He flattened his hand against the cage wire. After a moment the deer stretched out its velvet nose and touched the big fingers, then whuffled softly. Big started to undo the fastener on the door of the cage.

''Don't do that!'' Chumley snapped. ''If he gets loose in here, he could destroy himself and half the clinic.''

''I won't let him loose.'' Big didn't take his eyes from the fawn's. He opened the cage, then spread his arms. The deer snorted, then stepped delicately over the lip of the cage. Even Bill froze.

Big gathered the ungainly body into his arms, pressed him against his chest and stood up as easily as though the fawn were a house cat. It struggled a moment, then laid its head against Big's shoulder and relaxed.

''Now, Doc, where you want him?''

After Big let the fawn loose in its paddock, it began to nibble at the sere grass at Big's feet.

Big walked to the gate of the paddock while the young deer limped along behind. At the gate Big looked down. "You go on, now. Doc says you got a shoulder needs exercise."

A moment later the fawn limped away, and Big joined Bill and Eleanor.

"My word," Bill said again. "Can he always do things like that?"

"He can answer your questions himself."

"Big, or whatever your name is, can you always do that?"

"Mostly."

"Would you like to meet Sweet Daddy?" Eleanor asked Big.

Bill stared at her. "Who?"

"That's what I named that peregrine. He's little but he's mean."

Big laughed. The instant the cover was removed, the little falcon launched itself at the wire of its cage and began to scream. "He's a lot prettier than *our* Sweet Daddy."

The peregrine stopped screaming and cocked his head. Big poked a finger through the wire and scratched the falcon's head.

"Would you look at that," Chumley whispered.

"Now that we've made a believer out of Dr. Chumley, how about we meet the other people at the clinic and see the other areas?"

Big was a hit with everyone. Even Mac Thorn liked him, and he never liked anybody.

Mabel Haliburton simpered and promised to bake him cookies.

Rick Hazard tried to be very businesslike, but then asked Big if he'd ever played football or baseball, and if not, why not. Then he whispered to Eleanor that he could hardly wait to field the Creature Comfort football team next fall so he could run Big in on a couple of those self-styled tough guys from the animal shelter.

When Eleanor took him all the way back to Dr. Sol Weincroft's new research wing off the end of the exotic-animal area, she found Sol moving boxes of loose-leaf notebooks from his SUV into the empty room that would be his research library.

"Sol, you shouldn't be doing that all by yourself!" She took one of the boxes out of his hands, and Big immediately took it from hers.

"Want me to help?" he asked Eleanor.

"Sol," she said, "this is Big Little. He's going to be helping out here a couple of days a week. Big, Dr. Weincroft is moving his equine research facility into the new wing that's just been finished."

Sol Weincroft was older than Slow Rise, about the same size as Sweet Daddy and only about half as irascible as Mac Thorn when he was operating. He frowned at Eleanor. "Young woman, I am not in my dotage yet. I am perfectly capable of moving boxes."

"But you shouldn't have to, Sol. Don't you have any research assistants to do this for you?"

He grimaced. "I am at the moment, um, between assistants."

That meant he'd fired the last one.

"I do not intend to waste a research assistant on furniture moving. By the time he arrives, I shall be moved, organized and ready to begin work."

"Or in the hospital with a slipped disk and a myocardial infarction," Eleanor answered. "At least let Big move the boxes inside, Sol. Then you can spend the afternoon happily puttering around shoving everything onto shelves all by yourself."

"I do not putter." He looked up at Big. "However, I see your point. Young man, can you give me half an hour's physical labor?"

Eleanor winked at Big, who smiled back.

When Big found Eleanor to report that the boxes were all moved, she took him to the kennels.

"You'll probably be doing a lot of mopping, Big," she told him on the way. "All the droppings have to be picked up every day, and the kennels and cages cleaned and sanitized."

The dogs began to bark the minute the kennel door was opened.

Big dropped to his haunches in front of the brindle female's cage. "Who done this to her?"

"Some people running a game for fighting dogs."

"They catch 'em?"

"Not yet."

"Huh. I'd like to catch 'em."

The sound Big made deep in his throat reminded her of Mac Thorn's growl when he'd first seen the wounded dogs. She put her hand on his shoulder. "We have to go back to the farm now, Big."

"I'd like to stay some longer."

"You'll be back."

On the drive to the farm, Eleanor said, "I'll straighten out your schedule with Warden Portree. The prison van can deliver you and pick you up when I'm not going to the clinic at the same time as you."

"I'll try not to do nothing bad."

"You won't."

"Just you be like my mama and keep telling me I don't get mad."

As Eleanor drove away from the compound after dropping Big, she prayed there would never be a situation that made Big angry, because nobody would be able to stop him once he was.

ELEANOR DRAGGED OUT Steve's transcript after dinner, not because she wanted to finish it—she didn't. But she'd promised Steve. Then she'd have to find some way to tell him that she, too, agreed with the jury that he was guilty.

The prosecution designated the next witness as hostile and asked for latitude in questioning him. Neil Waters, Steve's business partner and brother-in-law, made it clear that he was testifying under duress, and that despite even his own wife's opinion, he didn't believe Steve could ever be guilty of murder.

The prosecutor needed all the latitude he could get, because Neil fought hard to show that his partner was innocent. Eleanor thought what a good friend he must be to go against his wife's wishes.

She read through Neil's testimony once. Then as she reread it, her scalp began to tingle and her palms began to sweat.

With every statement that was dragged out of him, every seemingly innocent answer, Neil Waters drove the nails deeper and deeper into Steve's coffin. He was either extremely dull witted and had no idea how his answers sounded to the jury. Or he was extremely intelligent and knew exactly what impression he was leaving.

Eleanor didn't think she'd have picked up on it if she had been sitting in the courtroom, had heard his voice. It was only when the written word was divorced from the person speaking that the subtle condemnation showed. Even Steve, who expected help from his friend, probably thought at the time he was getting it.

Once you overlooked Neil's protestations that he was certain none of this meant anything damning, the "facts" he presented added to the impression of Steve's guilt.

First, he mentioned that Steve and Chelsea had argued at the restaurant because Neil—not Steve—had wanted to expand the company once more. Steve had merely agreed that Neil's plan was a good one. Neil swore *he* had brought up the subject of a loan from Chelsea—as the older sister, she had inherited the bulk of her father's estate. Her sister, his wife, had a trust fund, but it was managed by lawyers and not liquid.

He swore that Steve and Chelsea "seemed" to have

made up before they left the restaurant, and said that the two couples parted "more or less" on good terms. He said Steve had told him not to worry about the money, that he had other ways of getting it.

Good Lord! Steve's lawyers had asked that the jury be directed to disregard the comment. Oh, right. As if they could un-think something.

He said that Chelsea drove home because Steve said he was too drunk to drive, although he hadn't drunk a great deal at dinner. Neil "thought he might" have been drinking earlier at home. At any rate, he seemed half-sloshed when he climbed into the passenger seat of their car. Neil said that Chelsea seemed a "bit put out" that she had to drive home, but it "didn't amount to anything."

He knew nothing else until Steve had called him the following morning to tell him that Chelsea had been stabbed to death by an intruder. He said he arrived at the same time as the homicide detectives and found Steve not so much upset as stunned.

He admitted he'd always found Steve to be a light sleeper when they'd traveled together.

He also admitted that he recognized the murder weapon as belonging to a set in Steve's kitchen drawer. When pressed, he said that he recognized the knives because he and Steve had bought two sets exactly the same in Germany the year before to give to their respective wives.

He realized that there was no evidence of an intruder, but he maintained that Steve was innocent. If Steve said there was an intruder, then there must have been, even if there wasn't any evidence of one. Why he hadn't reported one during the night, Neil did not know. Why he had not discovered his wife's corpse before he bathed and dressed for the day, Neil did not know. Nor why Steve hadn't realized Chelsea had not been to bed.

Neil's testimony had turned out to be damaging—because he had seemed to say one thing while in fact he'd said another. Leslie Vickers should have seen, noted and gone after the man on cross-examination. Why hadn't he set forth the possibility that Neil himself might be guilty?

That was answered during cross-examination. Neil had an alibi. He had been home asleep with his wife. They had gotten ready for bed together the previous night, and had even made love. He had come over to Steve's house in the morning still unshaven, and dressed in his pajamas and robe.

Posey Waters was his wife. Would she lie for him? Probably. To protect her sister's killer? Who knew? Maybe. At any rate, there was no other trace evidence linking him or anyone else to the crime scene.

The two sisters probably had keys to each other's house. If not, who better than Neil to know where a spare key might be kept outside for emergencies?

Maybe Steve wasn't drunk, but drugged. And who better to drug him than one of the people he'd had dinner with?

Eleanor didn't know this Neil person. He might be a saint, but reading the transcript had given her a powerful gut feeling that he was anything but.

She was beginning to believe Steve. He'd been framed. But by whom? Neil? His wife, Posey? A real intruder? A hired killer?

Leslie Vickers hadn't put Steve on the stand. He apparently didn't want to open him up to cross-examination. As a matter of fact, he'd put on no case at all, saying that the case against Steve had no merit and had not been proved. In his summation he'd hit on the lack of real evidence again and again, and told the jury that unless they were positive in their own minds there had been no intruder, they had to acquit Steve.

They didn't. The jury members weren't certain enough to convict him of first- or second-degree murder, but they weren't certain enough of his innocence to let him off free, either.

The punishment portion of the trial started immediately after Steve's conviction. Now that it was too late to do anything but mitigate against a long sentence, Vickers paraded witness after witness to testify what a fine decent man Steve was, what an excellent boss, a man of integrity, an honorable man who always played by the rules. Vickers had even put a couple of members of his polo team on the stand to talk about what an honest player he was. That had probably done more harm than good.

Reading the testimony, Eleanor became more and more uncomfortable. Either all these witnesses were right about his character, or he was an incredible actor. But didn't Raoul say that even the smartest sociopaths couldn't keep up the act for long? Apparently everybody, including Steve's high-school history teacher, thought he was a wonderful human being.

One character witness was absent. Steve's father, the Colonel, did not testify for his son during the penalty phase.

Even fine men can snap. But do they lie about it afterward? Everyone agreed that Steve was extremely intelligent with a computer maven's logical mind. If he was going to make up a story to cover killing his wife, surely he could have done a better job of it. A two-year-old could see through that intruder story.

So what now? Steve would be up for parole in a little less than two years, unless Neil and his wife opposed it. Would they take the chance? Would Neil simply move to Phoenix with his millions?

Could Steve let it go and rebuild his life from scratch?

Eleanor desperately wanted to talk to Leslie Vickers, Steve's lawyer.

She longed to talk to Steve even more.

CHAPTER TEN

SUNDAY MORNING DAWNED dull and even colder. The weather report spoke of the first real cold snap of the year at some point during the week, possibly accompanied by sleet. The first two weeks of November were usually the most beautiful of the year in Memphis, with the fall foliage at its peak. This year, however, the trees were already losing their leaves.

She went to the barn to make certain that Gil Jones and Robert Dalrymple, the two men detailed to feed and water the stock this weekend, had done their jobs properly. Everything seemed in good shape. She let the three horses out into the far paddock, and despite their age, they raced around like yearlings. She left them out when she went to the clinic. She could bring them in on her way home.

Creature Comfort didn't keep regular hours on Sunday, but was available for emergencies. Eleanor found Liz Carlyle, the night vet, sitting at the registration desk studying a heavy textbook on diseases of the eye.

"I didn't know you were on call," Eleanor said.

"I'm not. I left the kids with my dear old hubby. I hope he can keep his eyes off football long enough to prevent major disaster. This is the only quiet place I could think of to study. I'm headed to Mississippi State for a week of hands-on eye surgery tomorrow morning."

"Who's looking after the children?"

"They're in day care full-time this week, then home at night. I hope everybody survives." She pointedly looked back at her book.

Eleanor left her. In the kennel, the brindle pit bull female greeted her joyfully. The dog now wore a mesh collar, as did the other three pit bulls who were still under the care of the clinic. "Who cares what Mac Thorn thinks. *I* think it's time we started teaching you to be a lady."

She found a training lead and collar, opened the cage and slipped the collar over the female's head. "Come on, sweetie, let's take a walk."

The dog hunched and sat back, pulling toward the back of the cage. She began to shiver.

Eleanor dropped to her knees. "It's all right, baby." The dog stared at her in terror. The cage had become her refuge. Since she'd been at the clinic she'd only come out to have her wound cleaned or get a shot, both painful.

And before, out of her cage must have meant a fight for her life.

Eleanor pulled over the pad that was used as a recovery area for big dogs that had undergone surgery. She made herself comfortable and began to talk softly.

"First, you need a name, don't you? All ladies have pretty names. How about Rose Petal? Peony? You're yellow, so we might call you Goldenrod."

The dog watched her from the back of her cage.

Eleanor kept talking in the same quiet, singsong voice. She recited nursery rhymes, sang old Broadway show tunes, cajoled, and cussed but always in the same soft voice.

Little by little the dog relaxed until she lay on her mat with her one and a half ears relaxed and her eyes on Eleanor. But she made no move to come out. Finally Eleanor gave up, pulled the collar off, stroked the dog's head, and shut her in once more. "You know what, dog? I think you need a dose of Big Little. Tomorrow afternoon I'll make sure you get one."

The rest of the day passed with the usual crises that were not really crises, except in the minds of frightened owners.

By the time Eleanor got home, she was ready for a diet microwave dinner and bed. At nine-thirty the phone rang.

"Hope I didn't call too late. J. K. Sanders here."

"No, it's okay. What can I do for you?"

"Larry Duntreith wants to bring his buffalo over tomorrow afternoon."

"That's almost a week early!"

"Fences mended?"

"Well, yes, but none of the men has even attempted to ride the horses yet, and we really need some mounted wranglers when we turn them loose, don't you think?"

"Yeah. I'll stall Larry until Tuesday. I'll be over tomorrow morning to work with your men, show 'em a few techniques to stay on their horses when they start cutting. That's all I can do."

"They shouldn't need much more unless the buffalo turn loony."

He laughed. "Now, that I cannot promise. 'Bye."

J.K. RODE WITH THE EASE of a man to whom a horse is an extension of himself. His demonstration of cutting techniques was awesome. No matter how quickly his horse moved from side to side, or how deeply he sucked out from under J.K. when he did it, the man never bobbled. He made the whole process look easy.

Robert Dalrymple and Steve, the members of the team who'd claimed they had riding experience, were chosen to attempt to ride the other two horses.

Robert was the first to take a lesson. Old Will, his quarter horse, had been a champion before he'd retired.

"What that horse doesn't know about cows, the cows don't know themselves," J.K. told Robert.

Robert's limber frame gave him a natural balance. All he needed was to remember what it had been like to ride as a child. In ten minutes he was loping happily around the pasture. J.K. pronounced him ready to try sitting the horse while it cut out a cow.

"You don't do nothing. The horse knows his job. He'll do it whether you're up there or not—he *hates* cows. Now brace your feet in front of you in the stirrups, tuck that elbow hard into your side and hang on for dear life."

J.K. trotted into the pasture where the cows watched warily. Robert followed. "Whoa! I don't like this," he said, as his horse perked up.

J.K. sidled quietly in among the cows and began to move one cow away from her calf. She went quietly at first. J.K. took care not to spook her. "Soon as she realizes she's all alone, she'll break back. That's when Old Will will start to work. Whichever way she runs, he'll be there before she even thinks about it, so you hang on to that saddle horn."

The instant the cow broke to go back to the herd, J.K.'s horse began to move from side to side like a pendulum. A second later Robert's horse did the same thing. Robert, however, did not. He landed hard on his bottom in the dirt.

All the men hanging over the fence started to clap and hoot with laughter.

Robert stood up, brushed himself off, and yelled, "You think you so smart, you try it!" He began to walk off.

"Not too bad for a first try, young man," J.K. said. "Get back on that horse. You can do it. Now listen to me."

After an hour Robert was wringing wet and so was the horse. The cows were extremely annoyed, but Robert could stay on. He was even beginning to enjoy himself, and when he finally drove a calf into the imaginary pen set up at the end of the field, everyone applauded.

J.K. nodded. "Fine. Walk him out. You're a long ways from a finished cowboy, but you got some talent. Maybe I got a job for you when you get out of here, you keep this up."

Robert scowled, but it was obvious he was pleased.

Steve rode as easily as J.K. He took just two minutes to pen a calf.

"Where'd you learn that, boy?" J.K. asked.

"Spent a couple of summers on a ranch," Steve said. "Guess I remembered more than I thought I had." Steve wasn't about to mention that the ranch had belonged to one of his father's old army buddies on Kauai. That was where he'd learned to play polo—not among the south-Florida rich, but with a bunch of hard-bitten cowboys.

"I'll tell Duntreith we'll take his dad-gum buffalo tomorrow afternoon, then," J.K. said. "Set up one of them big round rolls of hay in that pasture. Maybe they'll eat, instead of running."

"Good idea," Eleanor said. "About the only thing good about this whole situation. Slow Rise, can you and Gil and Sweet Daddy get that bale moved?"

"Sure thing, Doc." Slow Rise swung onto the tractor, and Sweet Daddy and Gil jumped up and hung beside him. He drove to the far end of the enclosure where the big round bales of winter hay were stored. The prongs with which they had to be moved were quickly attached to the tractor, and all three men were positioning the bale ten minutes later. When set on end in the metal holder in the center of the buffalo pasture, it stood six feet tall and at least seven feet in circumference.

"That ought to keep even them buffalo eating for a while," Slow rise said.

"Then let's knock off," Eleanor said. "Steve, Robert, look after the horses. Thanks, J.K. We'll see you tomorrow."

J.K. took her arm and walked her to his truck. "That Chadwick guy. I know his daddy. Fine man, the Colonel. Terrible thing that boy of his turning out like he did."

Eleanor nearly defended him, but managed to keep her mouth shut.

"He was supposed to go to West Point until his sister got so bad hurt. I guess he just went downhill from there." He shook his head. "I wasn't kidding about maybe giving that black kid a job. What'd he do?"

"Drugs, I think. Talk to Raoul Torres about him. He could use a job when he gets out."

"Can't do much, but I try to help out where I can. See you tomorrow."

THE BLACK-AND-WHITE longhorn steer came out of Larry Duntreith's stock trailer first. Eleanor had forgotten that the steer was part of the deal. He was small, and from the way he tore down the ramp and into the pasture, he seemed to be fleeing from his companions.

When the three female buffalo erupted from the trailer and jumped off the ramp, Steve could see why the steer was so intimidated.

"Easy, girl," he whispered to his mare. She had begun to wriggle from side to side the moment the longhorn came off the trailer. He could feel the pull on his reins, and set himself in case she decided to go herding on her own without his instructions.

On his right, J. K. Sanders sat easy on his horse, as well, but one glance told Steve he also was set for trouble. Robert, on his left, was the unknown quantity. He'd done remarkably well yesterday learning to stick with the horse when it dodged from side to side under him, but one day penning calves was a far cry from herding buffalo.

"Hold on, Robert," Steve said softly. "Don't ask for trouble."

"No way, man. Damn! Those mothers are *large*."

Perhaps they'd worried for nothing. The longhorn and the buffalo looked at the roll of hay with interest, then circled it as though searching for the best place to start tearing into it.

The other members of the team, plus Selma on her four-wheeler and Eleanor on the tractor, sat absolutely still outside the pasture. Except for Sweet Daddy's gasp, no one had made a sound since the trailer gates had opened.

Larry Duntreith grinned at Steve, gave J.K. a thumbs-up, and slammed the metal doors of the stock trailer.

The sound reverberated like Big Ben at midnight. In an instant the buffalo exploded into flight. A moment later the longhorn joined them.

And a second after that, all three horses decided it was time to go to work.

Steve had been prepared. So had J.K.

Robert yelped as Old Will dropped low on his hind legs and thrust himself to the left. Robert slid right, his spidery legs riding up in the stirrups, his hands gripping the saddle horn.

"Stay with him, boy!" J.K. yelled.

There was no way. Old Will slid left a good six feet. Robert slued right the same distance.

"Help!" he screamed as he hit the ground.

Old Will, stirrups flapping, reins flying around his ankles, decided he'd waited for his incompetent rider long enough. He had a job to do—herd those hump-backed creatures that were flying around the pasture at a dead gallop.

And right at Robert.

Steve drove his horse forward. He could hear the hooves of J.K.'s horse right behind him. Somehow they had to turn those buffalo.

Steve's horse had guts for an old guy. He skidded to a stop in front of the buffalo and began to dance from side to side. Steve held on and moved with the horse. His body remembered what to do without instruction from him.

The buffalo snorted and thrashed.

"Get him out of there!" Eleanor shouted.

Steve glanced behind him. Robert was on his feet. A little dazed, but apparently unhurt.

In the nanosecond he'd taken his eyes off the buffalo, they'd done a one-eighty and were now flying around the pasture in the other direction.

"I'll handle this," J.K. yelled as he galloped by. "Get the boy."

Robert's riderless horse's reins had broken just above

ground level—a good thing, since now he wouldn't trip on them. He galloped behind J.K. A true professional, even if Robert wasn't.

Steve wheeled his horse. The buffalo were incredibly fast for such heavy beasts. He measured distances and shouted, "Go for the hay roll. Climb on top. I'll pick you up."

Robert just stared at him.

"Move, man! Look behind you!"

Robert looked and took off at a dead run.

It would be close. Steve had no idea what would happen if there were a dead heat—Robert, buffalo and Steve's horse.

Then he saw nothing but Robert. Time slowed.

He heard his heart and his breathing, and somewhere way in the background hoofbeats. He knew he was in the zone. He hadn't been so focused since his last polo match. God, it felt good, as though he'd suddenly come alive, if only for a few seconds. All the time in the world.

Robert scrambled up the hay.

The buffalo were close. Would they swerve if Steve cut across their path? Or run right over him?

He drove his heels deeper into his horse's flanks.

Out the corner of his eye he saw a monumental brown creature almost crash into him.

Then he was past.

He pulled his horse to a stop beside the roll and reached out for Robert.

"Jump on behind me. We're outta here."

The instant he felt Robert's arms lock around his waist, he spun his horse and drove for the pasture gate.

Gil Jones held it open long enough to step in and haul Robert off the back of Steve's horse.

Steve wheeled and galloped back to help J.K.

In the end, they gave up and pulled their horses in close to the hay roll to let the buffalo run themselves out.

The longhorn gave up first. He cut away and trotted over

to the shelter of the hay roll. Robert's horse snorted, but J.K. held him by the remaining length of rein.

Little by little the buffalo slackened their pace, until at last they broke into a trot and then slowed to a walk.

When the last buffalo dropped her head and began to graze, an eerie calm settled over the pasture. Steve looked at the little group assembled on the other side of the fence. Even Eleanor looked stunned. Robert sat on the back of the four-wheeler with his head in his hands.

J.K. raised an eyebrow at Steve. "Didn't think you'd make it—get the boy, I mean. Should have known. I've seen you play polo. More guts than sense, if I remember. Lost, but you shoulda won."

"I'd rather none of the men knew. I'd never live it down," Steve said.

"You got my word on it. Now, if you'll excuse me, I got a mite of dressing-down to do."

He moved off, the riderless horse trailing him quietly.

He walked to the cab of the truck where Larry Duntreith huddled. "Larry, you like to have got somebody killed slamming that door like that."

"I'm sorry, Mr. J.K.," Duntreith said. "I never thought it'd set 'em off the way it did. They're usually real quiet when that longhorn Rowdy's in with 'em."

"You owe us one. All of us. Mostly you owe that young man there," J.K. pointed at Steve, "And the one that near got smashed to smithereens."

"Yessir. What can I do to make it right?"

"We'll work something out." J.K. turned his horse and ambled to the gate. Robert's horse followed meekly. Steve followed both.

"Larry, you better not set those fools off running when you fire up that diesel, you hear me?"

"Nossir, I'll try not to."

"OKAY, ERNEST," Eleanor said as she perched carefully on her tailbone in the kitchen chair on the far side of the warden's desk. "I told you I'd be back to argue my case. Steve Chadwick is the hero of the prison. Robert Dalrymple would have been killed if Chadwick hadn't rescued him from those buffalo."

"Uh-huh."

"Don't look at me like that. You say you know everything around here."

"What's that got to do with letting him off the leash on work release?"

"Chadwick and Big Little can be dropped off and picked up at the clinic together. The place is always full of people—staff, clients, doctors. It's also at least five miles away from the nearest bus line, and the neighborhood is so upscale that anybody who's not wearing a fancy track suit and three-hundred-dollar running shoes gets stopped by the cops before he's run a block."

"He could hijack one of your clients' fancy SUVs."

"Ernest, come on, you're grasping at straws. A stolen car wouldn't get out of the area before it was stopped. And don't talk to me about taxis. They don't run out that far."

"Doctor, you do not play fair."

"Nope." She smiled.

He didn't smile back.

"What?"

He took a deep breath and leaned back in his chair, which groaned under his weight. "I thought the prison gossip system was fast. That clinic of yours beats all. So far this morning I have had calls from a Dr. Hazard, a Dr. Scott, and a Mr. Mark Scott, all three begging me to put Chadwick on work release. Apparently you've convinced them that he's the answer to all their logistical problems. Scott wants him to design a computer program to handle their inventory, purchasing and patients' records. Don't forget, Eleanor, Steve Chadwick is a killer."

"Didn't you tell me once that killers are the least likely repeat offenders? Unless they're mobsters or hit men or something."

"Now you're throwing my words back in my face. I knew we shouldn't have hired you. Women don't ever let go."

"We also squeeze from time to time."

"I've noticed. I'll give you this much. I'll interview Chadwick myself, and I'll allow him to ride the prison bus one time so that your people can interview him."

"I can take him to the clinic. I took Big."

"He rides the bus. Take it or leave it."

She stood and extended her hand. "It's a deal. You won't regret it."

"I already do."

CHAPTER ELEVEN

STEVE LAY ON HIS COT with his hands locked behind his head. He hadn't planned to be a hero. Hadn't planned at all. He simply saw that Robert was in trouble and did what he could to save him. No thinking required. He'd have done the same for anyone, even Sweet Daddy.

Work release. Steve couldn't believe that Eleanor had actually arranged for him to leave the prison. He would be able to use a telephone without calling collect and leaving a record of the people he called.

He might even be able to arrange to see Mary Beth. He knew his father had forbidden her to visit him in prison. Of course, she didn't have a pet to use as a reason to come to the clinic. The Colonel had never allowed them. His excuse was that an army family moved too frequently to assume the added responsibility.

Most important, he'd see Eleanor without Selma and the others looking over his shoulder. He kept telling himself that he was complicating her life when all he wanted was to be with her. He had nothing to offer but heartache.

Before he'd met Eleanor, being assigned to work release had been the first step in his escape plan. Being picked up from the prison, dropped at the clinic, then returned via the prison van might present a small problem, but not an insurmountable one.

Then again, Eleanor, even though she still might not believe he was innocent of Chelsea's murder, had gone to bat for him anyway. How could he justify using her as a means to escape or expose her to the repercussions?

He had an obligation to see that whatever path he chose, she would not be blamed. Whatever the jury said, he'd never yet betrayed anyone's trust. Not yet.

Maybe he ought to sit out his remaining sentence, take his parole and try to build a new life. He could come to Eleanor a free man. And in her eyes at least, an honorable one.

But he wouldn't be whole.

Neil would have gotten away with murder. He'd be sitting in Phoenix with his millions, married to the sister of the woman he killed. Chelsea deserved better. Hell, Posey deserved better than to spend her life with a man like Neil.

Until now he'd never considered that he had a choice. He could never convince anyone that Neil had killed Chelsea. So it was up to him to avenge her death.

Now that he had met Eleanor, had started to think like a normal human being outside the prison walls, he knew he could choose to let Neil go and try to build a life after he was paroled. Eleanor had already awakened emotions he'd ignored. With her his angry spirit found at least momentary peace. With her he could relearn what it meant to feel tender, protective....

But he hadn't protected Chelsea. Chelsea had never trusted Neil, hadn't thought he was good enough for her sister. Steve had been the one to plead Neil's case to Chelsea. In a sense he was the one who brought the snake into the house. His guilt wouldn't simply vanish, no matter how he longed to find peace.

No, he would never be free, never be whole, until he had paid his debt to Chelsea by avenging her death. He would have liked to see Neil standing in front of that judge while sentence was passed on *him*. That would never happen. Chelsea had no other champion but Steve. Until he had righted that wrong, he could never simply go on with his life, never open himself fully to another love. Only when the wound was purged of infection could it begin to heal.

Whether he punished Neil or not, Steve knew he was already branded as a murderer.

He'd have to leave town. He couldn't live where everyone remembered him. No matter how he longed to stay, to try to build a future with Eleanor, he'd have to go away, start fresh with a new identity, a new name.

Big had seen her at Creature Comfort, said she was real happy there. He had no right to ask her to uproot her life for him, a man she barely knew.

That was the problem. How could they learn to know each other fully, build a relationship, while Steve was locked away so that they couldn't even speak together without someone trying to listen in?

For three years he'd kept a tight lid on his libido, but he was a man, not a eunuch. Being around Eleanor made him happy, but it also drove him crazy. He loved watching her, talking to her, but he wanted more, and he thought she did, too.

It was his bad luck that the first attractive woman he'd met in three years stirred more than lust. After he met Chelsea, he'd never looked at another woman, although he was the reason their marriage had become merely comfortable. He'd taken her for granted, assumed she'd always be there, beautiful, willing, when they both took time out of their busy lives to affirm the bond that they had made.

Her death had taught him not to take love for granted. He would never be casual again. Each day was too important, too short and too fragile.

And if he did move away, make a new life, manage to become successful again, how long before some enterprising competitor discovered his true identity? How long before Neil himself traced him and blew the whistle on him? Neil wouldn't simply let him be. He'd come after him again and again, if only to satisfy Posey. She'd want Steve hounded for the rest of his life for killing her sister. If Neil refused, Posey might begin to wonder why.

No. For Neil crime had paid handsomely. Loving wife,

wealth and the good name Steve had once possessed. He had to be stopped. And there didn't seem any other way to do that except by killing him.

Steve had known from the beginning that Eleanor was trouble. Now his feelings for her were the biggest roadblock to his plans. Either he'd have to harden his heart or he'd have to let Neil go.

He worried at the problem like a dog with a particularly nasty piece of roadkill until he fell into a troubled sleep.

"Hey, Steve, wake up boy," the voice whispered.

Steve fought his way to the surface to stare up into the concerned face of Slow Rise.

"I ain't never heard you moan and groan like that. Your back hurting you?"

Steve shook his head. He was dripping with sweat. The sheet was soaked and the blanket damp. "I'm okay. Thanks for waking me."

"Some of these boys get right nasty when they get their beauty sleep interrupted." Slow Rise smiled at him, gave his shoulder a perfunctory pat and climbed back into his cot on the other side of Steve. Steve rolled over and tried to find a dry spot to keep the chill out. The least his mind could do was to allow him to deal with his problems when he was awake, not trouble what little sleep he got.

By morning winter had made its first appearance. The skies were the gray of dirty gym socks, and frost lay heavy in the hollows.

Steve and Big huddled in the heavy jackets that had been issued to the men as they waited to enter the prison van along with the other prisoners on work release.

Steve knew several of them by sight. Some, he knew, were working as painters or construction laborers for contractors. In this area, construction didn't shut down when winter came.

Others prisoners worked behind the counters of fast-food restaurants. He wondered how many customers knew

that the men who served them their burgers and fries returned at night to sleep behind razor-wire fences.

He and Big sat across from each other. Nobody sat beside Big. He needed both seats to accommodate his bulk.

"I can't hardly wait, Steve," Big said. "You gotta see.
They got puppies and kitties and deer with funny eyes and
possums and raccoons and I don't know what all."

"What about the people?" Steve asked.

"They're real nice. Even the doctors. Dr. Mac, he
sounds real gruff, but he don't mean nothing by it. And
Dr. Sol, he's this little bitty old guy who's working on
some kind of important research." Big chuckled. "He
fusses all the time, but he's real nice, too. In the springtime
Dr. Rick, he's the head doctor, he wants me to play on the
football team. I ain't played football since I was a kid."
He looked over at Steve with concern. "You think I can
play football?"

"Absolutely."

"I'm gonna be cleaning and keeping everything neat.
But maybe they'll let me pet some of the animals."

By now, the other prisoners had been dropped off and
only Big and Steve remained on the bus. Big was almost
bouncing in his seat, for all the world like a child on his
way to the circus.

The area was familiar to Steve. His house hadn't been
more than three miles away from this subdivision, although
in a much more secluded location and on a larger lot. He
and Chelsea had loved all the trees and the wild area that
separated his place from Neil and Posey's. Posey had
worked to turn her backyard into a garden, but Chelsea
and Steve had let theirs go wild, except for a small rock
garden beyond the deck.

Maybe if they'd had open manicured lawns and a swim-
ming pool like Neil and Posey did, someone might have
seen something the night Chelsea died.

Seen Neil slipping through the trees on his way to commit a murder.

"We're here!" Big jumped up from his seat and banged the top of his head against the ceiling. "Shoot." He rubbed his head. "Come on, Steve. I'll introduce you."

Steve climbed out of the van and stood looking at the outside of the clinic. Architecturally designed—not some contractor off-the-peg generic office structure. Handsome. The entire place, which looked to be at least four or five acres, possibly more, was surrounded by a dark brown four-board fence, very much like a Kentucky horse farm.

A pair of tall wrought-iron gates separated the driveway from the road. He could see a keypad and electronic control beside them. Radio operated, then. Could probably be opened and closed from inside. At the moment the gates stood wide open in expectation of clients. Probably only closed at night to prevent any of the large animals from escaping.

The fence would not keep in a dog or cat. Or a man. Even if the gates were closed, he could vault that fence easily. There was no electric wire running across the top of it.

The landscaping was elaborate, but low to the ground and pretty much maintenance-free, although they might add flowers in the spring. Big would enjoy gardening. From things he had said about his small farm in East Tennessee, he seemed to like plants almost as well as he liked animals, and probably had the same talent for making them flourish.

A broad brick path led from the double glass doors into the front of the clinic from an asphalt parking area. The driveway continued around the side of the building. Probably to an area where large-animal vans could be unloaded.

He'd go exploring the first chance he got. He needed to know how far back the land went and what lay behind the clinic's land. From the territory they'd driven across to get here, he suspected that at least part of the clinic land backed up to the Wolf River bottoms, a federally protected wetlands area.

In spring and summer, the river would be too high and swift to cross without a boat of some kind, and the bottoms were crawling with both cottonmouth moccasins and copperheads. Possibly even rattlesnakes. At the moment, however, the snakes would be hibernating, although the water would be both too cold and too swift to swim. If he decided to make his escape that way, he might drown, but he wouldn't be bitten by a snake.

"Come *on*, Steve!" Big took his arm and half dragged him to the front door and inside.

Straight ahead sat a high reception desk. Behind it, a pretty blonde of twenty-five or so presided over a bank of telephones, a computer terminal and a bank of file cabinets. She wore a telephone headset so that her hands remained free to write down appointments while she spoke on the telephone.

The moment she saw Big, she gave him a broad smile and waved. Her gaze moved to Steve, then looked away shyly. Big was already accepted; Steve was an unknown commodity. To his left a comfortable waiting room sat empty. Big had told him the clinic didn't open for business until eight-thirty, twenty minutes from now. To his right another set of double doors. Must be the way to the examining rooms and the working part of the clinic.

The receptionist punched the button on her phone to break the connection.

"Hey, Big."

"Hey, Alva Jean. This here's Steve. He's gonna be working here, too."

"Hey, Mr. Steve."

"Just Steve. Steve Chadwick."

The phone rang once more. "Oh, darn. Big, y'all go on back. Dr. Rick's waiting for you."

Big shoved through the double doors, turned a corner and led Steve down a hall with doors on either side. He stopped at the first door, which was ajar, and stuck his head in. "Hey, Dr. Rick. I got Steve with me."

Rick came out and shook hands warmly. "Heard what you did with those buffalo. Man, I hate those things. Can't ever trust them. Good thing they didn't go straight through that fence and keep going all the way to the river."

"I was lucky."

"Eleanor says you're great with a horse, but that's not why we need you." He turned to Big. "Big, why don't you go find Nancy Mayfield? She's got a list of things for you to do long as your arm."

"Yessir, Dr. Rick." Big lumbered off, whistling under his breath.

"Sit," Rick said, and pointed to the chair across from his desk. "Eleanor vouches for you, says you've got experience in running a business. And my wife Margot is on several committees with your sister. Doesn't quite make you a member of the family, but when Margot tells me someone is competent, I generally believe her."

Steve inclined his head, acknowledging the compliment. He knew that Margot Hazard had been on committees with Chelsea, too. Better not bring that up. If Dr. Hazard chose to ignore the fact that he was a convicted criminal and act as though they were simply business colleagues, let him. It certainly made their dealings much simpler.

"So I'm going to be up-front with you," Rick Hazard continued. "Creature Comfort is in a bind. We're making money, but the margin is slim. Every penny counts. We can't afford to waste anything or to lose track of what we have. We need to have what we need when we reach for it. There are packaged computer programs out there that are supposed to do inventory and such like for veterinary clinics, but Mark Scott, who at present is handling the business end of the clinic, says none of them is adequate for our needs."

Steve nodded. "Usually they are either too simple or too complex. That's why it's better to either start from scratch or tailor an existing program."

"Precisely." Rick rubbed his hands together. "I don't

mind telling you that if we can get somebody of your caliber working on our computer inventory and setting up our records on a more efficient database at what amounts to minimum wage, well, it's tough on you, but great for us.''

"It gets me out of the farm, Doctor, and back to what I know best.''

"Call me Rick. Everybody's pretty much on a first-name basis here. Mark Scott's main job is Vice President of Operations for Buchanan Enterprises, Ltd., which just happens to be owned by my father-in-law, Coy Buchanan. Mark has done a magnificent job helping us, but he can't go on doing it forever. Our evening receptionist, Mabel Haliburton, has been trying to keep up with the data entry at night, but we're getting more and more clients at night, so she's falling behind on everything except billing.''

"I'd like to take a look at what you're currently doing so that I can see where I can make improvements.''

"Be my guest. I've got you set up in Mark's office. It's not much, but the computer is a real screamer. Mark's in California for a few days, possibly longer, so if you run into questions, save them up.''

"Can I e-mail him?''

"We've got e-mail, but we're not really properly networked, either. First it was a matter of money. Now, it's a matter of time to decide what to do and find somebody to do it.''

"Do you have a web site?''

Rick eyes lit. "Now, you see! I've been telling everybody we need one. But we can't afford a good design or anyone to update it. Do you know how to do that sort of stuff?''

"That's what I'm here for.''

"So, let me show you the office. It's not much. We still stack stuff wherever we can find space.'' He hesitated and dropped his gaze. "Uh, Steve, I don't know quite how to say this....''

Steve waited. Whatever was coming obviously wasn't good.

"You see, this is a very upscale facility. Lots of new rich, but lots of old families, too. It might be a good idea if you kind of, you know, kept a low profile."

"You don't want me running into anyone who recognizes me." It wasn't a question.

"I know that sounds bad. I'm sorry."

"Frankly, I'd prefer not to run into old friends, either." He glanced down at his prison shirt and jeans. "Embarrassing for everyone concerned."

Rick smiled. "Okay. Glad you understand! So let's get cracking, how about it?"

Twenty minutes later Steve began going through Mark's computer. The man had done a good job, but it was obvious that he was used to working with existing computer programs, not designing them. In five minutes Steve could already see half a dozen places to make improvements, increase ease of use. Make things, as Eleanor said, idiotproof.

He leaned back and glanced at the clock on the wall beside the door to Mark's office. He couldn't believe he'd been working nonstop for two hours.

He felt better than he had in months—years. It was as though he'd suddenly begun to struggle back to life. His mind had spent three years with no challenge except to plan the perfect murder. No wonder he'd gone a little nuts.

Eleanor had done this for him.

"MAN, I HATES THIS, know what I mean?" Sweet Daddy stamped his feet and swung his arms from side to side in an effort to keep warm. "How come we couldn't wait till springtime to start this stupid herd?"

"Good question," Gil answered.

"How come Steve and Big gets to go off and we gets to shovel manure?" Robert asked as he threw a couple of flakes of hay over Marcus Aurelius's enclosure.

"You gotta ask?" Sweet Daddy said with a leer. "You and me don't got no *computer* skills."

"Knock it off," Gil said quietly. Sweet Daddy gave him a sullen glance, but he shut up.

"We gonna get some more help?" Robert asked.

"Ask her."

"Ask me what?" Eleanor stuck her head out of the office door.

"Big and Steve, they not gonna be around so much. Who gonna do their jobs?"

Eleanor came out and lounged against the doorjamb. "They're not gone that often, and until spring with calving and show season, we won't have much to do except keep this place clean and get Marcus Aurelius used to being groomed. Once calving starts, we may sometimes be here around the clock, especially if we have to hand-feed any of the calves."

"Some of those cows look like they could drop them calves any minute now," Slow Rise said. He leaned on his pitchfork. "Real bad weather's coming, Doc. That always means trouble."

"As of today, we'll not only have hot water for the shower and sinks in the rest room, but heaters for the water troughs in the pasture and in Marcus's stall. If anyone gets cold and wet, you can warm up without going back to the dormitory."

"Better than having somebody wind up in the hospital with pneumonia," Gil said mildly.

"I'm bringing over a coffeepot and picking up an allotment of coffee and fixings from the mess hall," Eleanor told them. "Anybody want to volunteer to make the coffee? Or should we run a roster?"

"A roster would be good," Robert said.

"You want to count on Sweet Daddy to make your coffee?" Slow Rise asked.

"Hey, man, you got no call to say something like that," Sweet Daddy said.

"Can't count on him for nothing else. How 'bout I make the coffee?" Robert said. "My woman says I make good coffee. Hot and strong."

"Deal," Eleanor said. "I'll drop the pot by late this afternoon on my way back from the clinic. Any more questions? Looks like we've got some work to do. Robert, how about you and Slow Rise take the horses out for some practice?"

"You don't want to wait for Steve to do it?" Slow Rise asked.

"He doesn't need the practice. The rest of you do. How about you, Elroy? You ever been on a horse?"

"No way. You not getting me on one of those things. I don't like riding nothing bigger than me." He swaggered off, pitchfork in hand. The pitchfork, Eleanor noted, was suspiciously shiny.

"Gil," she said, "you're in charge of the inside crew." The others had their backs to her, so she moved her head toward Sweet Daddy and rolled her eyes.

The edges of Gil's mouth quirked and he nodded. "You gonna be in the office?"

"Actually, I'm going to try entering some data on the computer, then after I screw that up, I'll be in with Marcus Aurelius, and then I'm going to check the herd for signs of impending motherhood. I won't be here after lunch. I'll be at the clinic. I will be back this evening before you knock off, however, and I may keep Big and Steve a little later to bring them up-to-date on what we've been doing."

"Better be sure I check them out," Selma said. "Don't want anybody thinking they've escaped."

"I promise. We're going to have to start working more closely with Marcus Aurelius. Big seems to have better rapport with him than anyone else, so if he's not too tired, maybe he and I can start grooming him while Steve takes care of the evening feeding."

Gil nodded and started down the barn toward the men.

"Oh, Gil," Eleanor said, "before you get started, can I speak to you?"

"Sure." He followed her into her office.

"Sit."

He sat.

"I need your advice."

Gil's eyes widened. "Me? Advice?"

"I'll come right to the point. Should I have Sweet Daddy taken off the team and replace him with someone else?"

Gil took a deep breath and leaned back in his chair. "Me and Steve been talking about that. He's lazy and sure doesn't pull his weight around here. He's also mean as that copperhead. I'd like to toss him across the pasture the way I did that snake, but we've got to be careful how we do it."

"All I have to do is go to the warden."

"Yeah, but you'd be buying trouble. You kick him off the team, and we'd all be watching our backs, starting with Steve, and followed by you."

"Me? He can't get to me."

"Haven't you learned anything about this place yet? If it's not the guards, it's the inmates. Everybody's got outside connections, Sweet Daddy more than most. You think his girls come to visit him on Saturdays because they love him?" Gil laughed shortly. "Hell, no, they're reporting on the status of his business and how well his lieutenants are running things, as well as proving they're still loyal to him for when he gets out. There's a whole other world out there you don't know about, ma'am. There's streets in this town I wouldn't drive down at noon on a sunny day in an armored personnel carrier."

"What about *your* connections on the outside?" Eleanor asked quietly.

"I have friends. But I can't protect you outside. Steve doesn't have any connections. Big and Slow Rise don't, either. Robert's so small-time he doesn't count. Sweet

Daddy likes being on the team, even if he has to work sometimes. Makes him a big man inside. But if he gets mad, then somebody's going to wind up hurt or dead, and it's most likely going to be Steve. Or you.''

"Why, Gil? That's what I don't understand. Why would a man like you who obviously has some education and certainly a multitude of talent when it comes to anything mechanical…''

"What's a nice boy like me doing in a nasty place like this?''

"Yes.''

"I'm not a nice boy. Or I wasn't. Smoking and drinking and wild wild women. I was planning to be dead before I hit thirty. Then all a sudden here I am damn near forty and I ain't dead yet. And I got a decent woman and a daughter I'm crazy about and a body covered with tattoos and the only people I know on the outside are the other bad boys that managed to survive past thirty.''

"You've spent more time in jail than out of it since you turned eighteen.''

"So you did check the records.''

"I'm afraid I did. I don't know how much money you made on the outside, but if you amortize it…'' She raised her eyebrows to see whether or not he understood the word. He nodded. "If you amortize it over the years you've spent in prison, I imagine you've been working for less than minimum wage.''

"Probably.''

"So when you get out this time, what then?''

He shook his head wearily. "Doc, Doc, you are a nice lady, but I don't think you're ever going to learn the way the real world works. Who's going to hire me for an honest job? And if somebody should take a chance on me, how long will it be before my biker buddies are pulling into my driveway at midnight and threatening my old lady and my kid unless I go in with 'em on something that's going to land me back in prison?''

"So you'll go along with them?"

"I don't know. I'm damn tired of sleeping alone and not seeing my little girl play soccer. My wife says she's fast and tough."

"If you had somebody to take a chance on you, how hard would you fight to stay straight?"

"I don't know that, either. I'm being straight with you, Doc. It would be easy to say 'oh, no, ma'am, I'll never do a bad thing again.'" His voice sounded as phony as his all-too-innocent eyes. "Can't say that. All I can say is I'm going to try. One day at a time, isn't that what the drunks say?"

"Fair enough. In the meantime, please keep an eye on Sweet Daddy for me. I'll talk to Steve about him, as well, but this is one case where you're a whole lot smarter than I am. I'll be guided by you and the rest of the team."

Gil walked to the door. He turned with his hand on the knob. "Trust is a damned dangerous thing, Doc."

After he left, Eleanor leaned back in her chair. She had a headache starting behind her right eye. That meant the weather was changing more quickly than she'd thought. The barometric pressure must be plummeting like a runaway elevator.

She massaged her temples and shut her eyes against the glare of the single hanging bulb.

Gil was honest about his dishonesty. She wished there were something she could do for him—for all of them, except possibly Sweet Daddy. That little creep liked his life of crime. He needed simply to be removed permanently, but no doubt there were a dozen others as bad or worse ready to take his place.

She felt dreadfully sorry for Slow Rise, who had little hope of ever seeing the outside again, but she knew Warden Portree would never allow him on work release.

As for Robert, maybe he had a chance if J. K. Sanders really did give him a job. J.K.'s farm was large, there was housing on the place for families, and it was far enough away from the housing projects that Robert might be able to break his old pattern. But drugs were everywhere, and no village or hamlet was immune any longer. The more poverty, the fewer jobs there were in the poor counties, the worse the problem became.

And Steve? Was he innocent? Had he simply accepted his fate? She didn't think so. But what could he do? Even his lawyer had deserted him. The man had never returned her calls.

The headache had turned from ache to throb. She took a couple of painkillers. She couldn't face the computer. The dull light of the laptop's screen pulsated when her head felt this way. Maybe the cold air would help.

She locked the office behind her, picked up a bucket of horse brushes from beside Old Will's stall and walked over to Marcus Aurelius's stall.

The bull was no fool. He'd come indoors to shelter from the wind. If she shut the double doors behind him, he'd be effectively closed into his twenty-by-twenty-foot stall. She wasn't certain how he'd take the restriction. Time to find out.

She could reach the sliding door to his outside paddock by leaning over the stall fence. First she shut off the electric wire, then gave the door a hefty shove. It slid closed. Marcus grunted and stared at it. She tossed him a large flake of hay, and the minute he dropped his head and began to eat, she eased into the stall, then closed the gate into the barn behind her.

He didn't have long horns, but he didn't need them. A swipe of that heavy head followed by a pounding of those cloven hooves would effectively dispatch anyone who couldn't get away from him fast.

She picked up a currycomb, ran her fingers lightly across his forehead and began to groom him, starting with his shoulder. He was covered with dried mud where he'd lain in the damp pasture.

The moment he felt the curry, he grunted once more,

lifted his head and swung it to stare at her a moment, then went back to his hay.

"Good boy," she whispered.

Ten minutes later she'd decided that Marcus Aurelius was like most of the men she'd known—he didn't seem to care what she did to him as long as it felt good. "You are some spoiled bovine," she said as she worked over his beefy rump. When he stamped his back foot right beside her head, she jumped.

He relaxed again and let her work around to the other side.

She was using the soft brush on his curly forehead and trying to avoid his tongue when the team walked by on its way to take a break.

Marcus ignored them until Sweet Daddy swaggered by his pen.

Without so much as a grunt, he swung his head and swept Eleanor aside as though he were swatting a fly. She stumbled over to the side of the stall and grabbed at the top rail of the fence to keep from falling.

She felt as though she'd been hit in the ribs by a baseball bat.

Marcus Aurelius began to bellow. He backed up half a dozen steps, lowered his head, pawed the ground and charged the fence.

CHAPTER TWELVE

THE HEAVY TIMBERS that made up the fence of Marcus's stall shivered and bent but didn't break.

As he backed up to take another run at them, Slow Rise yelled, "Damnation, Elroy, get the hell out of his sight before he kills you!"

Sweet Daddy seemed paralyzed. Then he raised his pitchfork in front of him like a lance.

"Fool!" Robert grabbed the pitchfork and shoved Sweet Daddy around the corner by the office.

Too late to stop Marcus's charge. Eleanor cowered in her corner, although Marcus didn't seem at all interested in this more accessible target.

She felt hands under her armpits. "Come on out of there, woman!" Slow Rise said.

"No!" Eleanor croaked. She wasn't breathing very well. "It's not me he's after." She wrenched away from Slow Rise and stood stock-still.

Marcus leaned out to see around the corner into the barn as far as he could. Eleanor could hear Sweet Daddy and Robert yelling at each other by her office. So could Marcus, but the sound didn't seem to bother him. It was only the sight of Sweet Daddy that set him off.

Marcus finally glanced Eleanor's way. She held her ground. He snorted as though to put her on notice that he could choose to stomp her or not.

Not, apparently. At least not this time. As quickly as he'd freaked, he went back to chewing his hay.

Miraculously Eleanor had kept her hold on the grooming

brush. She'd heard of getting muscle spasms from sheer terror—this would certainly qualify. She got her breathing under control and slowly walked up to the bull.

From outside the pen, Selma, Gil and Slow Rise watched.

"You want me to shoot him if he goes for you?" Selma asked.

"No!" Eleanor laughed shakily. "Anybody got a red cape?"

"Yo, Toro!" Gil whispered.

She reached down, stroked Marcus's forehead and began to brush him again. He seemed totally unconcerned. She let out a breath that she didn't realize she'd been holding.

"Okay," she said quietly as she backed toward the gate. "Now, please, somebody get me out of here and turn that electric fence back on."

The minute she was out, she went to find Sweet Daddy. He leaned nonchalantly on a bale of hay, picking his teeth with a hay straw. He refused to meet her eyes.

She didn't know whether the others had followed or not, and at this moment she didn't care.

"I warned you not to tease that bull." Her voice was low, almost cajoling, but she could hear the anger shaking in it.

"Who says I been teasing anything?"

"Marcus does." She got in his face, emphasizing that she was taller and could look down on him. He tried to back up, but the hay stopped him. "Be glad those boards held, Elroy, or you'd be a dead man."

"Shoot, I ain't done nothin'. I coulda handled him." But his eyes shifted.

"Handled him? One ton of angry bull against a man who weighs maybe 125?"

"You dissin' me!"

"Damn right I am. What have you done to deserve anyone's respect? If you ever tease him or any other animal again, I promise I will personally turn Marcus loose and let him tromp you into the dirt.'' She started to turn away. ''One more thing. As of now you are on probation with this team. You put a foot wrong, you goof off, you say or do one thing I don't like or Selma doesn't like or one of *them* doesn't like—'' she pointed behind her to the rest of the team ''—and Warden Portree will have you wading around in hydroponic muck before you can set your pitchfork down. Do I make myself clear?''

He opened his mouth, but Eleanor raised a finger. ''A simple 'yes, Doctor' is all you better say.''

He met her eyes. This time she didn't quail from the hatred she saw there.

It was about time the inmates stopped running the asylum. She'd put up with almost anything except the mistreatment of animals. He'd probably poked at Marcus and taunted him. No real damage, but enough to sour the animal on the sight of him. ''Yes, *Doctor*.'' He tried to say it with his customary swagger, but it didn't quite come off. She turned on her heel and saw the others melt away around the corner. She'd done the thing Gil had warned her against, and now in the cool light of returning reason she knew that she'd created a truly dangerous enemy, where before there had only been potential danger.

She would have to watch her back. So would the others.

''YOU DON'T LISTEN TOO GOOD,'' Gil said quietly the first time he could get out of earshot of the others.

''I'm sorry I couldn't take your advice. Not only because I can't endure having an animal mistreated or teased, but because Marcus is big enough to kill somebody if he goes rank. He might be happy to take out his temper on any one of us if Sweet Daddy isn't immediately available. At least Sweet Daddy's on notice that he'd better shape up or I'll ship him out. I'll make a report to the warden. He can alert the COs.''

''That'll do about a nickel's worth of good in a dollar

economy.'' Gil walked away from her. She could tell by
the set of his shoulders that he was annoyed.

At least her headache was better. All that adrenaline
must have cleared out whatever was causing it. She
checked her watch. She was due at the clinic in thirty
minutes.

Steve would be there. She wanted to tell him about
Sweet Daddy before he got back to the compound. It
wouldn't be fair to ask Big to watch out for him. Big could
get in serious trouble and Steve would be furious if he
found out she'd done something like that. Should she do
it anyway?

She picked up the electric coffeepot from her cottage,
stopped by the mess hall long enough to assemble the other
things she'd need to keep a steady flow of hot caffeine in
the team's veins and drove to the clinic.

Her stupid heart began to flutter at the prospect of seeing
Steve. They'd be on a totally different footing here—no
Selma to watch their every move. Steve would be doing
what he was trained to do. He'd be treated like a human
being, instead of like a prisoner.

Her car phone rang. She jumped as she always did when
she heard its nervous *brap*. She kept her hands on the
steering wheel and answered in hands-free mode.

''Dr. Grayson? Please hold for Mr. Vickers.''

''Doctor?'' The voice was low, rich, an actor's voice.
''Sorry to take so long to return your call. I've been in
court.''

''How did you get this number, Mr. Vickers?''

''What? Oh, my secretary called your clinic. They gave
it to me.''

''I see. I'm calling about Steve Chadwick. I'm working
with him at the prison farm. He's been there several weeks
now. I've read the transcript of his trial, and I've become
convinced he didn't kill his wife.''

''I see.'' Silence. ''I don't think we should have this
discussion over an open line, Doctor. Are you available

at—'' pause ''—say, ten-thirty tomorrow morning? My office?''

''I'll be there. Would you mind if I tried to bring Steve's sister Mary Beth Chadwick with me?''

''Not at all. I remember her from the trial.'' He laughed shortly. ''For God's sake, don't let the Colonel catch you. The man's a Tartar.''

''I've heard.''

''For what it's worth, I agree with you about Steve's innocence. I'm not certain there's much in law we can do about it, however.''

''We'll talk about that tomorrow. Thanks for calling, Mr. Vickers.''

That plumby voice again. ''Please, Eleanor, call me Leslie. Everybody does.''

As she hung up, she thought, *If he agrees with me that Steve is innocent, then why isn't he doing something about it? Why is there nothing to do? In law? Or in justice?*

Should she tell Steve? No. But she could call Mary Beth to tell her Steve would be at the clinic until five in the afternoon and ask her to come with her to her meeting with Mr. Vickers.

When she pulled into the staff parking lot, she saw a shiny new oversize red two-horse trailer backed up to the loading-dock doors. Good. Business.

But first she had to find Steve. She had to see him, to warn him. But mostly simply to see him.

Hoping to be able to go directly to Mark's office, she slipped in the side door beside the cattle holding pen. No doubt that was where they'd put Steve so he could work on the computer system.

''Eleanor, thank God you're here!'' Rick Hazard stood at the back door of the horse trailer. From inside came the rhythmic sounds of an angry horse fiercely trying to kick his way out.

''What's the problem?'' So much for finding Steve.

''It's that young stallion of Abel Neyland's. Abel thinks

he's broken a sesamoid from jackassing around in the pasture this morning. He went out sound and came in on three legs. Abel had to sedate him to get him loaded, but whatever he used has worn off. If he keeps on the way he's going, he'll break all four of his legs and his neck, too.''

"Where's Jack? He can handle any horse on the planet.''

"Gone home with a bad cold. Mac's operating, Sarah's off duty, Bill is down at the zoo working on a siamang gibbon, and Liz is down at Mississippi State on her opthamology course. Abel says that stallion's been in pasture. He's only two and hasn't been handled much, and he's never been in a trailer before.'' Rick listened to the metallic noise a moment. "He doesn't like it.''

Eleanor took a deep breath. Rick wasn't comfortable around bad-tempered horses. He'd go into that trailer and face the beast if he had to, but given his choice, he'd prefer to send someone with what he called "greater rapport'' to unload the horse.

"Where's Abel?''

"At the front desk filling in the forms to give us permission to operate.''

"Big?''

"Mopping the kennels, I think.''

"And Steve?''

"Last I saw of him he was hunched over Mark's computer.''

"Okay. Is there a stall ready for the stallion?''

"Abel called ahead to tell us he was coming, so we got one ready. Mac can do the surgery if you'll assist, but we've got to get that youngster out of that trailer in one piece first.''

"I'm considerably more concerned about keeping *us* in one piece. Buzz Alva Jean, tell her to send Big and Steve out here. Big's a natural with animals, and Steve knows horses. With Abel we should be able to handle whatever this two-year-old throws at us.''

Rick sighed. "Thanks. That means I can go back to work. Egg Roll has just acquired a mate."

"Judy bought another potbellied pig? Where does she keep them?"

"In the house, so she says. Anyway, she's bringing Char Shu over for shots and an exam. She's still pretty young, but Judy says she's a handful."

"As if Egg Roll weren't. What is Judy going to do when she winds up with a dozen piglets?"

"More clients for us," Rick said.

"All right, you're excused."

Rick almost ran from the room. He called over his shoulder, "I'll send Steve and Big."

Eleanor walked to the front of the trailer. It looked as though it would be large enough at the front to give her room to stand in front of the stallion and yet be out of biting range. He was only two. How bad could he be? She opened the front side door as quietly as possible, planning just to stick her head in to see what they were dealing with.

The big teeth followed by the striking left front hoof missed her face by inches. She slammed the door as the stallion began to scream with fury. "Oh, brother. He must be seventeen hands tall at least. Some two-year-old."

Two maddened male animals in one day was more than enough. She sat on the back bumper of the truck that had towed the trailer. Then she walked over to the wall phone and buzzed Rick.

"Where does Bill keep his capture pistol?"

"Huh?"

"I know that darting a horse isn't the best idea, but I might be able to get enough tranquilizer into the muscle in his rump to calm him down a little, then I can slip in and give him the real intravenous shot in his neck."

"You ever dart a horse before?" Rick sounded worried.

"Once. With Jerry, right after we'd started practicing."

"Successfully?"

"Jerry shot so many darts into his rear end that he looked like a pincushion. He still managed to stagger all over that pasture and stay just out of reach for half an hour. A cow would have keeled over and gone to sleep like a baby after the first dart."

"So maybe it's not such a good idea."

"Got any better ones? We'll try the regular way first. Here comes Abel. Talk to you later. I hope."

"He's not usually this bad," Abel said without preliminary. "He's in a lot of pain and he hates confinement, and he's so damned big he gets away with murder. My grooms are scared of him and he knows it. I'm supposed to be sending him off to my trainer next month for basic training. Or I was."

"With luck you still will. And with a lot better manners than he had when he came."

Abel laughed. "You planning on a lobotomy along with the sesamoid?"

"Trust me." She turned as Big and Steve walked into the room.

Her heart lifted at the sight of Steve. He'd been in good physical shape before, but now his shoulders looked broader, his step lighter, and his eyes were alive in a way she hadn't seen before. She longed to go throw her arms around him. He'd respond, she was sure of it.

But not now. She explained the problem.

"I know where Dr. Bill keeps his pistol," Big said. "And the dart things." He trotted off without further instruction.

"How'd you get him loaded into the trailer in the first place?" Eleanor asked Abel while they waited.

"Hit him with a small shot of tranquilizer. Should have lasted a lot longer. His metabolism must be sky-high."

"He's settling down," Steve said. The noise from the trailer had largely subsided.

"Don't trust him," Abel said. "He's saving up."

"Here's Dr. Bill's stuff." Big carefully handed Eleanor

a heavy revolver and a cardboard box with shells and darts. "I ain't supposed to touch guns." He blushed and glanced at Abel.

"I'm sorry, Big, that never occurred to me," Eleanor said. "But this one uses tranquilizer darts, not bullets."

"Dr. Bill said all you got to do is change the cylinder and it shoots real bullets."

"Oh. I don't know much about guns, I'm afraid. I hope we don't have to use this one. Big, are you game to try to hold his head long enough for me to give him a shot in his neck?"

"Yes'm."

"Somewhere we've got a horse muzzle, but I have no idea where. We really need a better control system."

"That's what I'm here for," Steve said cheerfully. "So far I haven't found any entries for 'muzzle, horse, teeth, avoidance of.'"

He was a different person. If she hadn't known better, she'd have thought he was actually happy.

"Then it's up to Big and me. Steve, will you and Abel get ready to open the back doors of the trailer and let down the butt chain when we tell you we're ready to back him out?"

"At your service."

"Stand way back," Abel said. "He's got some kind of range on those hind hooves."

Big and Eleanor opened both front doors of the trailer at the same time so that they'd have easy access to get out if things went awry. This time the youngster stared from one to the other. His coat was slick with sweat, and white foam covered his shoulders. He rolled his eyes, but he didn't snap at them.

"He's broken the tie line to the front. That's why he nearly got me the first time. I didn't realize his head was completely free. Big, I don't suppose you could hold on to his halter long enough for me to shoot him with the tranquilizer, could you? You'd have to hold him fairly still, otherwise I won't be able to hit the vein."

"Yes'm. Now, you big ol' boy, just you calm on down now. Ain't nobody gonna hurt you. Doc here's gonna fix you right up, ain't you, Doc?" He extended one of his huge arms, wrapped his hand around the side piece of the stallion's halter, and climbed in.

It took a second for the horse to realize that somebody had him. By that time it was too late to do much about it. Big talked to him and stroked his nose. Eleanor could see the horse straining against the tension with his whole body weight, but Big held on tight.

She found the vein, popped in the needle, followed it with the syringe, then backed out.

"Okay, Big. See if you can get out of there without getting yourself hurt."

"No'm. I believe I'll just stand here a while till he's quiet. Would that be okay?"

Eventually the horse settled, was unloaded and limped into a stall with no further problems. Big went with him every step of the way.

"Hey, you want to come work for me?" Abel asked after they'd closed the stall door on the stallion.

"Can't, sir."

"Not for at least six months," Eleanor said. "And we're not about to let him leave the clinic without a fight."

"Man who knows horses like that—can't find 'em much anymore."

As he drove away, Big turned to Eleanor. "I don't know much about horses. How come he thinks I do?"

"Because of the way you handled that colt," Steve said.

"Oh. That wadn't nothin'. Can I get on back to the kennel? Nancy's got me working with them pit bulls."

"How's the little brindle female?"

Big's face broke into smiles. "She's real sweet and gentle. She does just about anything I ask her."

"In or out of her cage?"

Big looked confused. "Out."

Eleanor sighed. "I should have guessed. Go on. And thank you." She turned to Steve. "And thank *you*."

Together they walked down the hall to her office.

"Wadn't nothing, as Big says. You're pretty feisty for a girl."

"Hey, I'm no girl. I'm a woman."

"I've noticed." He stopped on the threshold of her office as though unwilling to invade her space further. "You have no idea how I've noticed."

She faced him. Their eyes held.

STEVE KNEW he should go back to his computer. It was his only safe course of action.

A moment earlier they had been bantering like casual friends.

In an instant the tension became unbearable. All he could think about was that kiss—that time his lips had tasted hers, the sweetness that had so quickly flared into passion.

He had to touch her again, hold her, feel her lips against his once more, the warmth of her body as it fitted against his.

In three years he had almost forgotten the soft warmth of a woman's touch. He had been locked in an angular, unyielding universe where even his heart went armed.

The look in her eyes stripped him and left him soul-naked.

He stepped across the threshold and kicked the door shut behind him, then came to her with outstretched hands.

Her gaze still held his, but he wasn't certain what he read. Was she still afraid of him?

He took her hands and drew her forward. She sighed, closed her eyes and raised her face to his. He kissed her temple, her eyelids, and then her lips, trying this time to keep a firm grip on his passion.

Not easy. Not easy at all, as she opened to him, tasted

him as he tasted her, setting off hot flares along his nerve endings, which seemed to explode faster than he could control them.

In seconds, her kiss became demanding, fierce. Her fingers bit into the muscles of his shoulders, her hips moved against his and she whispered his name against his lips.

At the very verge of the abyss he broke the kiss, but still held her close. "Do you know the danger you're in right now?"

"I'm not afraid."

"We're finally alone, with nobody and nothing to interfere, to stop us."

"I don't want to stop."

He kissed her again, only this time the kiss was gentle, the brushing of lips that deepened slowly as their lips parted, their tongues intertwined.

As his palm swept over her breast, she sighed and whispered his name. Her voice sent shivers of desire through him. His hands slid down to her waist. He longed to touch her, stroke her until she lay warm beneath him, as hungry for him as he was for her.

His lips slid down to the open throat of her shirt, then lower.

Suddenly he clenched his fists and forced himself to turn away from her.

"Steve?" The way she whispered his name sent daggers of desire through him.

"I know what I'm doing," he said, "and I know it's dangerous for both of us. Do you?"

"Lock the door." Her voice was so low he could barely hear her.

He caught his breath and did as she asked.

She came to him, pressed her body against his. "Yes. Yes, I know."

He picked her up. She wrapped her legs around his waist and her arms around his neck. He laid her on the desk. He'd wanted moonlight and magnolias when he made love to her, but suddenly all that mattered was to be joined, to feel her warm beneath him, surrounding him, moving with and for him. His fingers sought the zipper of her jeans as hers sought his belt buckle.

"Please, please," she repeated. He could feel her palms on his naked hips, her fingernails digging into his skin.

"Wait. One danger I can save you from." Prisoners were issued condoms as a matter of course. He'd never used his, but now he was grateful for it.

When he was ready, he caressed her until he knew she was ready for him, and entered her in one great thrust.

He watched her, eyes half-open, lips parted. He felt her hips meet him thrust for thrust as though to drive him to the very center of her being. The world existed only where they were joined in a swirl of color and sensation.

He was afraid that after such a long time, he would be too fast, but Eleanor arched her back and sobbed out his name before his own climax.

When at last he lay spent on her body, waves of tenderness swept him where only a moment before waves of passion had crested.

My God! What had he done?

He looked down at her drowsy lovely face and felt waves of guilt.

How could he have allowed this to happen? The whole thing was his responsibility, and he was a man who might well be on the path to destruction.

She said she knew what she was doing.

There was no way she could know. If he were still the man he'd been three years ago, they might have had a chance, but not now. She couldn't fathom the degradation, the bitterness, the grief that had turned him into the man he was now.

What in God's name could he say to her?

They had made love. And now they were supposed to go about their business as though nothing had happened?

She touched his hand. He clasped her fingers but without

looking at her. She laughed shakily. "A good thing Sarah believes in keeping a tidy desk. At least we didn't break anything."

He wrapped his arms around her and buried his face in her hair. "I didn't mean for that to happen."

"Oh, that makes me feel grand."

She was trying to keep her tone light, to give him a way out.

He couldn't take it. "I wanted to come to you with champagne and roses. I wanted to come to you *free*."

"We can't always have what we want. Sometimes we have to settle for what we can get."

He kissed her hair. "I wanted moonlight and satin sheets and all the time in the world to explore you, taste you, touch you."

"Maybe we'll have that someday." She caressed his cheek. "In the meantime, wild spontaneous passion on top of a desk in a veterinary clinic isn't all that bad, now is it?"

He kissed her fingertips. "Not all that bad at all."

The telephone that had miraculously clung to its place on the far side of Sarah's desk rang. Eleanor closed her eyes and answered it. "Dr. Grayson. Oh, yes, Mac. Whenever you're ready. We'll have to get Big and Kenny to help get that stallion into preop." She listened. "Give me ten minutes. We still need X rays. Fine." She hung up and turned to Steve. "How do I look?"

"Relaxed."

She smacked him lightly on the shoulder. "Braggart. If you'll pick up everything and put it back on Sarah's desk, I'm going to use her bathroom to try to conceal what we've been doing." She sighed. "One good thing, my hand should be steady on that scalpel. I suspect my blood pressure's down considerably from what it was."

He began to rearrange Sarah's desk in what he hoped was a reasonable facsimile of what it had been before they'd trashed it.

Eleanor was an amazing woman. He knew she didn't take this lightly, but she'd chosen to let him think that what they'd done was no big deal if that's what he wanted. She'd been as passionate, as hungry, as demanding as he.

"Well?" Eleanor came out of the bathroom with her hair drawn tightly back, her face freshly washed, and wearing surgical greens that were baggy on her lithe body. She carried green booties, a surgical cap and a mask. "Does my skin have that extra glow?"

"Your eyes do. Eleanor—"

"Not now." She unlocked and opened the door. No one was in the hall beyond that Steve could see. Good. She started out, then stopped suddenly. "Oh, my heaven, Steve! I forgot to tell you. There was…an incident at the barn today. I had to put Sweet Daddy on probation with the team."

"What? Why?"

"Gil says I shouldn't have, but I didn't have a choice. For God's sake, Steve, be careful. Don't let him hurt you." She walked away quickly.

"Hurt *me? Me?*" He sank onto the corner of Sarah's desk. That did it. The closer she got to him, the more danger he put her in. He had to do the job he'd planned to do and get out of her life before he destroyed both of them.

CHAPTER THIRTEEN

ELEANOR DECIDED not to tell Steve about her upcoming meeting with Leslie Vickers. No sense in getting his hopes up, especially not now. But she did call Mary Beth Chadwick to tell her that she could make arrangements to see Steve the next time he came to the clinic and to invite her to her appointment with Leslie Vickers.

Mary Beth was overjoyed at the prospect of seeing her brother and seemed eager to go along to Vickers's office, as well.

The following morning, dressed in a decent pair of slacks and a blazer, as arranged, Eleanor went by the Chadwick house to pick up Mary Beth in plenty of time to find a place to park downtown close to Vickers's office.

The house was not ostentatious, but it was substantial. The yard was immaculate but boringly symmetrical, almost like the Queen of Hearts' garden in *Alice in Wonderland*.

She was about to press the doorbell when the heavy front door opened and Mary Beth pulled her inside. She wore a chic navy-blue suit over a pale blue silk blouse and looked much more sophisticated than Eleanor felt. "I just have to get my handbag."

"Sure."

As Mary Beth reached for a smart, boxy lizard handbag, Eleanor heard footsteps coming down the stairs into the entryway. Mary Beth froze.

"Mary Beth, aren't you going to introduce me to your friend?"

"Eleanor, this is my father, Colonel Sylvan Chadwick, retired. Daddy, this is Dr. Eleanor Grayson."

"How do you do, Colonel? I'd like to stay and talk, but I'm afraid Mary Beth and I are going to be late for a meeting."

He turned to his daughter. "The symphony again?"

Mary Beth nodded, but avoided her father's eyes and started toward the front door.

"Symphony, my foot. I forbid you to see that lawyer."

"Daddy—"

"I heard you make the arrangements on the telephone. Did you think I wouldn't find out?" He turned to Eleanor. "What right have you, young woman, to interfere in the business of this family?"

"It's Steve's business. And I have every right to intervene when I think there's been a miscarriage of justice."

"So you've convinced my daughter that justice was not served? You plan to rake up all the old scandal? Surely you're aware that she isn't in a position to—"

Eleanor's patience snapped. "Mary Beth and I are not going to be late for our appointment with Mr. Vickers, Colonel. She's a grown woman. You apparently think *both* your children belong in prison, even if you have to act as jailer."

"Mary Beth, go to your room."

"Daddy, please listen. You've got to stop looking for somebody to blame when anything goes wrong with your life."

Both Eleanor and the Colonel stared at Mary Beth. Tears rolled down her cheeks, but her voice was strong.

"When Mother died, you blamed the doctors. You didn't know how to grieve for her, so you cursed and yelled and threatened to sue them. And you blamed Steve and me because we were alive while she was dead. Then you went off on temporary duty for thirteen months and left us with Aunt Marge. You acted as though we'd ceased to exist. Then when I...when I was hurt, you blamed Steve for not coming to get me at that party. I've told you time and time again he did come, but I didn't wait for him. I drove off before Steve had a chance to get there. But it's not really about me, is it? Or even about Chelsea. You've never forgiven him for turning down the appointment to West Point.''

''Young woman—''

''That's right, Daddy, I'm a woman and your daughter, and the accident didn't leave me as brain-damaged as you think. You think you didn't make brigadier because you came up from the ranks and didn't go to West Point. Steve was supposed to do it for you.''

''He failed this family.''

''He failed *you,* not the family. Maybe it's time you faced facts, Daddy. You didn't make brigadier because you have an awful temper, and because the promotions board realized you had a daughter you couldn't control who did drugs and drank like a fish. Steve turned that appointment down because of *me,* Daddy, to look out for me.''

''He almost let you die in that accident.''

Eleanor stepped between them. ''That's unfair.''

The Colonel made a nasty sound.

''Even the father of the prodigal son never yelled at his kid for disgracing his family when he came home,'' Eleanor went on. ''He killed the fatted calf and welcomed his boy with open arms, whatever he'd done. You're a soldier, Colonel. You ought to thank God you have a *live* son to love. So many fathers don't. Come on, Mary Beth.'' She grabbed Mary Beth's wrist to drag her to the truck if necessary.

Mary Beth picked up her purse again. ''I'm going to see the lawyer, Daddy. Maybe we can get Steve a new trial. Then this Saturday I'm going to the prison to visit him, and I think you should come with me.''

The Colonel no longer looked angry. He looked merely stunned.

Eleanor didn't relax until they'd driven well away from

the house, then she glanced at Mary Beth. "Are you all right?"

Mary Beth nodded and rubbed her fingers along her cheekbones under her eyes. "He'll probably have the locks changed while I'm gone," she said, then laughed through her tears.

"You can sleep at my house if he does."

"Thanks, but he and I need to talk. I have to make him listen to me. He's been in so much pain ever since Mother died, and everything that's happened since he sees as a blow from God aimed directly at him."

"Heck of a selfish viewpoint."

"He's incredibly self-centered, and he always thinks he's right. I think the military makes officers that way so they'll be able to send men out to die. Until Mother died, he lived a charmed life, and then suddenly everything seemed to go bad for him. What happens when one of your animals gets really badly hurt? Do they understand you want to help them?"

Eleanor laughed. "They generally try to chew your arm off, and the worse off they are, the meaner they get."

"See? Just like the Colonel."

"Mary Beth, if you've known all this, why haven't you done anything about it before now?"

"Oh, I'm not smart enough to figure all that out. Before Steve...went away, he asked me to get some professional help. I've got money of my own Mother left me, so I could pay for my sessions without running them through Daddy's insurance. That way he wouldn't know about them. I've been working up the nerve to confront my father, but as long as I thought Steve was guilty, there didn't seem to be any point. Now, I've got something to fight for—my family. I guess Dr. Mitchum would call this a breakthrough."

"Dr. Mitchum's the psychologist you've been seeing?"

"Since about a year after Steve left. When they turned

down his appeal. I had to do something or really go crazy.''

''What happened to you, Mary Beth? I'm not certain I understand it all.''

''It was the summer Steve graduated from high school. He's four years older, so he was eighteen and I was only fourteen. And pretending to be twenty-one. I could do it, too. I mean, I'm tall and I know how to dress. I thought I just wanted to have a good time, but Dr. Mitchum says I wanted to get my father's attention by being bad, since he wouldn't pay attention to anybody but Steve. But Steve was the *best* brother. He tried to help, tried to explain to the Colonel what I needed and why I acted the way I did, but the Colonel wouldn't listen. One night I went to a frat party at the college. There was a lot of drinking, and some pot and stuff. Some of them were doing Ecstasy and coke, and things started getting really scary. I called Steve and asked him to come get me, take me home.''

''He didn't?''

''Of course he did, but the party was in midtown and we live in Germantown. Before he had time to get there, a guy I knew slightly with a new red Mustang told me he'd drive me home right then. He didn't seem drunk or stoned or anything, and there were a couple of guys hitting on me pretty hard, so I said okay. Steve pulled up just after we drove off. Steve followed us, tried to flag us down. I tried to get the guy to stop, but he wouldn't. He said he could outrun anything on the road. Thank God I had my seat belt on. He didn't. He missed a turn on Raleigh LaGrange and went off an embankment. He was thrown clear. I got smacked with the air bag. That saved me in front, but the car rolled, and my head got hurt.''

''What happened to the boy?''

''He...he never came to. I was in the hospital for six months with a broken leg, a broken arm and head injuries. I have a steel plate. Not a big one, but it's there. And I have problems with language and stuff sometimes. The

Colonel keeps telling me I'm brain-damaged. I guess I am. That's why I don't move out. I probably couldn't hold a job, and he pays the bills. He wouldn't support me anywhere else. He doesn't trust me, although I have been lily-white ever since. I guess you could say I got scared straight. That's why Steve turned down the appointment to West Point. Oh, look, there's a parking place."

LESLIE VICKERS WAS SMALLER than Eleanor would have expected, given that big baritone voice. He wore a slightly rumpled dark-blue suit, but his gray hair was thick and lustrous. He was charming, jovial, solicitous to Mary Beth and suspicious of Eleanor.

Eleanor said without preamble, "You let Steve go to prison for a crime I don't think he committed. You didn't even put on a case. Why?"

"You don't beat around the bush, do you?" He chuckled. "Because I was sure I'd get him off. The police had no real evidence."

"You relied on that intruder theory of Steve's, which didn't make a bit of sense. Didn't it occur to you that somebody close to the family killed Chelsea?"

Vickers narrowed his eyes. "Who do you think did it, then?"

"Neil Waters, of course. Why did you let him get away with that nasty stuff about Steve without suggesting he could be the killer himself? That alibi from his wife is worse than useless."

"I know juries. In this case I thought I had them completely pegged. The last thing I needed to do at the last minute was to confuse them with a completely different theory of the murder, one that had not even been suggested up to that point. And frankly, until I heard Neil's testimony, the possibility that he might be guilty hadn't occurred to me. Certainly it didn't to Steve."

"Then why didn't you appeal?"

"I did. Most laymen don't know this, but appeals are

judged solely on whether or not there were errors in legal procedure, not on new evidence. The judges look at transcripts. They do not hear new evidentiary witnesses nor consider the guilt or innocence of the party in question. So if there's an error, then there's a new trial. If not, the verdict stands. Appeals courts do not second-guess juries. That isn't their function. I even argued that I did not represent Steve properly because I did not put on a case. You have no idea how that hurt me, but I did it, because by then I believed he was truly innocent."

"Didn't you at first?" Mary Beth asked.

"I thought he was guilty as sin," Vickers said cheerfully. "I didn't give a damn. I thought I could get him off."

"Why didn't you try for a new trial?" Eleanor asked.

"That's an entirely different process and requires convincing evidence that a miscarriage of justice occurred. What new evidence did I have? My gut feeling that Neil Waters was guilty? I tried to take the appeals process higher and was turned down. They refused to hear the case—they can do that, you know."

"So Steve rots in prison and this Waters character gets away with murder?"

"It would seem so."

"No," Mary Beth said. "If money will help you get Steve a new trial, then tell me how much you need and I'll write you a check this minute."

Vickers held up his hands. "Miss Chadwick, please. If I thought I could get Steve a new trial, I would have done it and worried about the money later."

"So there's nothing we can do?" Eleanor asked.

"I didn't say that."

"Yes, you did!" Mary Beth snapped.

"Then I misled you. Money may not get a new trial, but it can pay to uncover evidence that may have been overlooked previously. There are a couple of possibilities that the police never properly followed up. I didn't consider them at the time. However, a private detective might uncover something even now.''

"What? Tell me.'' Mary Beth was becoming excited.

"I'd prefer to speak to Steve first. In any old case, the detective starts from scratch. I now employ an ex-homicide detective who happened to work on the Chadwick case at the time. He's an old-time detective, as dogged as a bloodhound.''

"But he thinks Steve is guilty,'' Mary Beth said.

"Perhaps I can convince him otherwise.''

"Do it,'' Eleanor said. "Oh, how much does he cost?'' There went her savings toward buying a partnership. And on a thousand-to-one shot, as Jack Renfro would say.

"That's not important,'' Mary Beth said. "I'll pay for everything.''

"Mary Beth—''

"Steve's my brother.'' She sounded stubborn. "He's looked after me. It's time I looked after him.''

"Will Steve see me?'' Vickers asked.

"I'll persuade him,'' Eleanor said. "Would you be willing to come to Creature Comfort Veterinary Clinic? Steve's working there two days a week on work release. It would be much more private than the prison.''

"Shoot, Dr. Grayson, I interview clients in worse places than a veterinary clinic every day of the week. If my defense got Steve convicted, then it's up to me to get him exonerated.'' He paused. "Now, if you ladies will excuse me, I have other clients to see. My assistant, Harris, will set up the details. When is Steve next at your clinic?''

"Friday.''

"Good. I'll bring my files and my detective. You prepare Steve for my visit. If anything changes, call my assistant.'' He hit an intercom. "Virginia, would you send in Harris?'' He smiled and walked out without shaking either woman's hand.

"Well, I never,'' Mary Beth said.

ELEANOR DROPPED Mary Beth at home and watched her until she unlocked the front door. The Colonel hadn't changed the locks, then. She'd offered to face the Colonel with Mary Beth, but Mary Beth had been adamant that she'd face him down alone and convince him that not only was Steve innocent, but that it was time the family rallied to his defense.

By the time Eleanor got back to the clinic, much of her initial enthusiasm had evaporated. There still wasn't much hope that Steve would get a new trial or that new evidence could be found, but he deserved to know that she and Mary Beth were trying. Even a faint hope might be enough to carry him through until his parole hearing.

He wasn't in Mark Scott's office working at the computer, or in the conference room. Alva Jean didn't know where he was, nor did Big or Nancy Mayfield in the kennel.

Eleanor felt an edge of panic. Making love had been cataclysmic for her, and she thought he'd felt the same way. Surely he wouldn't have run away. She began to search for him. With every step she grew more frightened.

STEVE LOOKED DOWN into the drawer of Bill Chumley's credenza. He'd watched Big put the gun away after the young stallion was unloaded.

Chumley didn't even bother to lock the drawer. The extra cylinder for the revolver lay beside a half-filled box of .45-caliber shells. Steve could change that cylinder in thirty seconds. Another thirty to load the gun with real bullets, and no time at all to conceal it under his jacket.

The bottom of the drawer was dusty; so was the box of shells. So was the revolver, for that matter, although it looked well oiled. It would be simple to take it on his way out of the clinic, use it and return it the following morning. Chumley would probably never even know it had been taken and returned.

And if the police should discover that the gun existed?

What if they test-fired it to compare the LANS and grooves with the bullet that he used to kill Neil? That would be very damning evidence against Steve. No one else at the clinic even knew Neil.

Perhaps it would be better if the revolver simply disappeared for good. The police might suspect it was the gun used to kill Neil, but there would be no way to prove it.

But Big might be suspected of stealing it. That risk was unacceptable. Steve would never do anything to jeopardize Big's chances for early parole. The man didn't belong in prison in the first place.

Steve had been careful about fingerprints. Boxes of disposable gloves were everywhere throughout the clinic. He'd simply slipped on a pair as he walked through the large-animal area on his way to the exotic-animal area and Bill's office.

Now he eased the drawer shut and peeled off the gloves. He'd dispose of them in one of the bins in the small-animal examining rooms. There would be no fingerprints.

He turned to leave. Eleanor stared at him from the doorway. He quickly shoved the gloves into the pocket of his jeans. "I'm trying to get a feel for the different areas of this place," he said. It sounded feeble even to him.

"You're thinking about killing him."

"Bill Chumley? Why would I kill him?"

"Not Bill." She reached across and took the gloves from his pocket. "I followed you. I saw you with the gun. Why else would you be checking it out?"

He pushed past her into the hall and said over his shoulder as he went, "I thought we'd gotten beyond the suspicion stage."

She ran after him and caught his arm. "Steve! You mustn't even think of such a thing."

"I told you…"

"You've got to hang on. There are things going on you don't know about."

"What things? There's no evidence against Neil. He's home free."

"There may be a way to get you a new trial."

"How? On evidence that doesn't exist?"

"Maybe it does. Killing Neil would be a terrible thing to do."

This time he stopped and turned to face her. His mouth was dry, and his jaw set so hard he could barely get the words out. All the old anger flared. "He killed my wife. Killed her! He can't do that and get away with it. He's destroyed my wife, my family, my company, my honor…"

"*He* hasn't destroyed your honor, but *you* will if you kill him. How much honor does a murderer have in your book? The kind of honor that will let you lie when the police question you? You didn't lie to them before."

"And look where it got me."

"What about all of us who believe in you?"

"Who believes in me? You? You *want* to, Eleanor, but even you can't. Why were you looking for me just now?"

He saw the color rise in her cheeks. "I—"

"You were afraid I'd run away. Admit it. And then when you found me in Bill's office, you immediately jumped to the conclusion that I intended to commit a murder. That could only be because you're still afraid I've already committed one."

"That's not true! I'm not the only one who believes in you. Your sister does."

"But not my father. Dammit, why did you follow me, then?"

"I couldn't find you." She sounded crushed.

He longed to reach for her, to take her in his arms again, but he couldn't. Not now when he was so deeply confused about what he should do.

"I should have walked off sooner, before anything happened between us."

She recoiled as though he'd slapped her.

He put his hands on her shoulders. Somehow he had to

make her understand. He'd lived for revenge for three terrible years. He couldn't simply drop his crusade because he was falling in love with a woman—a woman who didn't even fully believe him and definitely didn't understand him.

"Eleanor, Neil's moving to Arizona." He kept his voice level, rational. "How can I let him go? He's got to pay for what he did to my wife and my life. Nothing is as important as that."

"Oh." She turned away.

"I didn't mean—"

"Yes, you did. I actually thought this morning that maybe you and I had a real chance to build another life, a good one on the ashes of the first. If you do anything to Neil, you've chosen death, not life." She sighed sadly. "I can't fight death. I tried it once before and lost."

"I won't be the one to die."

"Yes, you will, if you pull that trigger. Even if they never catch you, never even suspect you—and they will, believe me—you'll still be dead inside. Everything that is fine and true and honorable about you will die in that instant."

"I've always known that whatever happened I'd have to leave here, go someplace where no one knows me. No matter what happens to Neil, I'll still have to do that."

She grabbed his arm. "Not if you get a new trial, not if you're exonerated."

"That won't happen. Come with me. We'll start over together."

She shook her head. "No. Don't do this thing. Let him go. Let God punish him, let the lawyers and the detectives try to catch him, but don't destroy yourself, destroy us, to avenge yourself on him. If you do, then he will truly have won. Your soul is your own. If you kill Neil, it won't be."

"Are you going to call the police?"

"What would I tell them? That I saw you looking into a drawer that had a gun in it? The choice is yours. You and me, or Neil. I can't make it for you. I can only pray you'll make the right one." Again she turned away. "I'm so tired."

He touched her arm, but she shook him off and left him standing, staring after her.

She ran all the way to the front of the clinic. She was crying, and she couldn't seem to stop the flow of tears. Had making love been of so little importance to him? She hadn't even had a chance to tell him about the meeting with Vickers that was set for Friday. Would Steve be here by then?

She brushed away the tears, squared her shoulders and walked into the reception area to meet her next patient. And straight into Colonel Sylvan Chadwick, retired.

"Colonel Chadwick?" Eleanor couldn't conceal her surprise. She looked over at Alva Jean and raised her eyebrows. If he attacked her verbally again, she'd signal Alva Jean to call Rick or Mac Thorn. She was in no mood to deal with him.

"Dr. Grayson, I owe you an apology. I do not generally berate visitors to my home."

I'll bet you don't, Eleanor thought. Maybe he really had come to apologize. "I had no right to tell you off. I'd say we're about equal in the bad-manners department."

"Is there someplace we can speak—" he glanced at Alva Jean "—in private?"

"Certainly. We can—"

"Doctor?" Alva Jean nodded at the back of the Colonel's head and looked a question at Eleanor. "You've got a rabbit over there with ear canker."

Eleanor smiled at the woman who held an enormous gray French lop-eared rabbit on her lap. "I'll be right back, Mrs. Peterson. This won't take more than a minute."

Mrs. Peterson smiled back. "That's all right, Dr. Grayson. He's already had it for four days. Another few minutes won't make a bit of difference."

"Thank you. Colonel, we can use the conference room."

Eleanor led the Colonel through the door to the hall, past Rick's and Mark's offices, and into the small conference room. "As you can see, I'm pretty busy." Then, darned if he'd outdo her in the manners department, she said, "Please have a seat, Colonel. Can I get you anything? The coffee's strong, hot and fresh."

"No, thank you." He stood until she sat, then took a seat across from her. If Hollywood had been casting a retired army colonel, they would have looked no further than Colonel Chadwick with his short silver hair, his neat mustache and even neater tweed blazer and slacks, right down to the regimental striped tie. She hadn't noticed his feet, but Eleanor would have taken a bet that his shoes were spit-shined.

"I won't take up much of your time, Doctor. I have spoken at length with my daughter about your meeting with Vickers…and other things."

He sat erect, a good six inches from the back of the chair. His eyes didn't meet hers. Eleanor nodded.

"She tells me that there is indeed some possibility that…that my son may not be guilty of the crime for which he was convicted."

"More than a possibility."

"How can that be?" This time he did meet her eyes, and his were anguished. "I attended the trial. I listened to the evidence. At first I hoped, no, I prayed, that he would be exonerated, but the evidence was damning."

"What evidence?" Eleanor asked quietly. "The only evidence against him was that there was no evidence against anyone *else*."

"And now there is?"

"Not yet, but his lawyer thinks evidence may still exist, and that there's a chance we may be able to find it—at least cause enough ruckus to get Steve a new trial."

The Colonel got up and strode around the room with his

hands behind his back. "If I thought for a moment that were true… You reminded me I am a soldier. Perhaps that makes me quick to judge, even to cut my losses when a project goes bad, but it also forces me to accept reality, no matter how unpleasant. If Steve is innocent, then I have committed a grievous injustice."

"Yes, you have."

"Mary Beth was right, blast it. I never forgave Steve for turning down that appointment to West Point. I felt incapable of handling either of my children, that they were rebelling against me personally and against the values I tried to instill. I was also aware that my inability to control my family lowered my chances for promotion. Steve's appointment to West Point was a vindication of everything my life stood for. It's what he and I had planned for his life. When he threw that appointment in my face to stay here at a second-rate commuter college, I felt as though both my children had betrayed everything I stood for. Then when he went into business…"

"He was successful. Brilliant, even."

"It isn't the same as service to one's country."

"Because he changed his mind from what *you* wanted to what *he* wanted?"

"West Point was what he had always wanted, too. I didn't force him to apply, didn't pull any strings or ask any favors. He deserved the appointment. He would have been a credit to the military."

Eleanor said quietly, "He was a credit to you whatever he did. Wasn't that enough?"

He seemed not to have heard her. It was as though he was speaking to himself, that he had forgotten she was even in the room. "I was too willing to believe that he'd changed so fundamentally that he was capable of murdering another human being. It's almost as though I wanted him to be guilty to prove my point. If so, then I have behaved unconscionably."

"I agree."

He stared at her.

"Did you think I'd let you off the hook?" she said. "Okay, so you were in a lot of pain. Okay, so your career taught you to keep a stiff upper lip. The only person who can forgive you is Steve. Go tell him what you've told me."

"I can't."

"Why on earth not?"

"Mary Beth thinks I am a hard-hearted monster who stayed away from the prison because I hated him." He sank into the chair and dropped his head. "In reality, I don't think I could bear to see him behind bars. Men do not cry in public, Doctor."

Eleanor could tell by his face that he honestly believed that. She sighed. "He's not behind bars now. See him. If you can't, then write him."

"Perhaps I will. Forgive me. I meant to do nothing but apologize for my behavior. Instead, I have aired a great deal of dirty linen. Frankly, I don't know why. In any case, thank you for your interest in my son. I still do not have the faith that his sister has that he is innocent. I am, however, willing to pursue the matter to its conclusion, whatever that may be."

He stood and extended his hand. Eleanor took it, and as she expected, his grip was one step this side of painful. For the first time, a shadow of a smile lifted his lips. "I believe you have a rabbit awaiting you. I can see myself out."

"That's okay, I have to go up front, anyway." She opened the door and was looking at him over her shoulder when she saw his expression change. She turned and stood face-to-face with Steve in his prison denims.

"Colonel," Steve said formally.

"Stephen," said the Colonel with equal formality.

For a moment Eleanor feared that the two would simply nod and walk on in opposite directions. She held her breath.

"Son." It was a whisper, but a whisper so filled with pain and longing that Eleanor felt her eyes tear up.

The Colonel reached out—a few inches only.

"Dad."

They stepped forward into each other's arms.

Eleanor pushed Steve and his father into the conference room and shut the door. So much for "men do not cry." She'd seen the Colonel's face, watched the tears spill.

She motioned to Mrs. Peterson and whispered to Alva Jean, "Would you try to keep everyone away from the conference room for a few minutes?"

"You okay? Who was that man, anyway?"

"Steve's father. I put them in the conference room so they could have a little privacy."

"Rick won't like it. Steve's supposed to be here working, not seeing visitors."

"He'll make up the time. Alva Jean, those two haven't seen each other in three years. I've got enough rules at the farm. I don't need a bunch more here."

"Sure. Okay." Alva Jean picked up the phone.

"Sorry I was short with you, Alva Jean," Eleanor said. "I guess I'm just tired."

"Sure."

Eleanor sighed and went to find Rick to tell him what was happening and that Leslie Vickers would meet Steve on Friday, if he agreed. It was, after all, Rick's clinic. She was his employee.

"I don't want to get dragged into any court cases," Rick said. "Don't they have places at the farm where prisoners meet with their lawyers?"

"This would be more private. And I promise the clinic won't be dragged into anything."

"Well, all right. But don't make a habit of it. Steve's doing a great job and so is Big, but I'm still not totally convinced this work-release thing is good."

"Thanks, Rick." She'd left Big watching the young stallion who'd had his sesamoid operated on. He was in one of the totally padded recovery stalls, but he was the sort of horse who might come out of the anesthetic fighting and ruin Mac Thorn's superb arthroscopic surgery.

"He's standing up, Doc," Big said. "He's kind of weaving, but he's got weight on all four legs."

"Good. I'll take over for a while. Thanks, Big."

She longed to listen in on Steve's conversation with his father. Would they managed to make amends, or wind up even more estranged than before?

She couldn't believe Steve would even consider killing Neil Waters. Not after what had happened between them. She thought their lovemaking had meant something to him.

Was it strong enough to stop him from throwing away his life?

She said she'd fought death once and lost. Fate had given her a second chance. This time she must not lose. She was not battling for Neil's life, but for Steve's soul.

She knew now she loved him. She couldn't lose again. Not this man. And not this way.

CHAPTER FOURTEEN

JUST BEFORE TEN-THIRTY on Friday morning, Leslie Vickers arrived at Creature Comfort in a black limousine.

The man who came to the clinic with him wore a brown suit that had seen better days several years and twenty pounds ago. Vickers carried a neat leather briefcase. The other man carried a beat-up brown briefcase that looked as though it probably held his lunch.

"Damn," Steve whispered as the man struggled to remove his bulk from the back seat of the limousine. "Schockley. What the hell is Vickers doing bringing him?"

Vickers shook Steve's hand warmly as though they were old business acquaintances who hadn't collaborated in a while. He pointedly ignored Steve's prison jeans and work shirt. "You remember Charlie Schockley?"

Their eyes met. Neither offered a hand.

"Charlie's retired from the force. He works for me now." Vickers slapped Schockley on the shoulder. "Side of the angels for a change, eh, Schockley?"

"Mostly the side of the devil, but it pays the bills."

Eleanor had commandeered the Creature Comfort conference room for their meeting. Steve didn't invite her to sit in, and she didn't attempt to invite herself. Thank God she had plenty to do.

She and Jack Renfro worked side by side as Eleanor trimmed away the extra fold of skin from beneath the eyes of a six-week-old Arabian foal. The foal had been born with entropion, a condition in which the eyelashes grew in rather than out and continually scratched the foal's eye.

"Must feel like somebody's poking you in the eye with a sharp stick," Jack said as he handed Eleanor a pad of gauze.

"Good thing we caught it early," Eleanor said as she drew the final tiny suture tight. "That ought to do it. The stitches should dissolve in a couple of weeks. Keep him on pain medication. I don't want him scraping those stitches, but I don't want to completely blindfold him, either. One eye, maybe, but not both. For a colt this young…well, let's hope we don't have to."

"I gave the mare a shot, too, just so she wouldn't holler her head off at her son while we were working on him."

"Good. Can you walk him back to her on your own? I can always get Big—"

"Since when does Jack Renfro need help with a foal? Besides, great glump of a man is outside in the back with that sorry excuse for a dog he's taken up with."

"The little female with the torn ear?"

"And a sorrier specimen I've never seen. What's going to happen when we have to turn her over to the animal-control people?" Jack looked fierce, so fierce that Eleanor knew he was worried about what the separation would do both to Big and the little dog.

"I honestly don't know. Big should be paroled in six months or so. Maybe we can provide her a temporary home until he can take her."

Jack raised his eyes. "This place is becoming a haven for stray dogs. First there's that Nasdaq, Mark Scott's little scrap of fur, and now this one."

"Maybe I can take her home with me in the meantime. I think the men on my team would enjoy having her around. That is, if Big can teach her not to bark at the cows."

"Doesn't bark, that one. Doesn't listen to anybody but him."

"I'll figure something out. We are not turning her over to animal control, whatever happens. Watch that foal—he's still kind of groggy."

Jack sniffed and walked off with the foal securely in hand.

Eleanor walked down the hall past the conference room. Not a sound could be heard through the door. Margot Hazard, Rick's wife, had insisted that every room in the clinic be soundproofed so that clients would not have to listen to the howls and barks of animals in adjoining examining rooms.

That was fine, but for once Eleanor would have liked to listen at the door. *Please God,* she prayed, *let Vickers and that fat detective convince him he can get a new trial so he won't do something stupid.*

STEVE TRIED TO HOLD HIS TONGUE and his temper while Leslie Vickers recapped the evidence that had convicted him. His eyes kept straying to Charlie Schockley, who seemed bored by the whole process.

Schockley had arrested Steve in the first place. Why he should change his mind now, Steve couldn't imagine. Except that Vickers was now paying him—probably a good deal more than the city police department ever had.

Finally he couldn't take it any longer. He turned to Schockley, cutting off Vickers in midflow.

"You still think I'm guilty? And if not, what changed your mind?"

Schockley leaned back and templed his fingers together over his paunch. The bottom button of his rumpled shirt had come undone, so that a triangle of hairy stomach bulged out over his trousers. "Wondered when we'd get around to me." He glanced at Vickers. Steve saw him nod.

Schockley took a deep breath and leaned forward so that the edge of the conference table made an indentation in his flesh. "It's like this. I was a cop for thirty years and a homicide cop for twenty of that thirty. In all that time, you know how many genuine murder mysteries I worked on? I'm talking the kind of case where you can't figure out who did it in the first thirty seconds. Exactly three.'' He held up three fingers. "When I arrested you, I didn't think your wife's killing was one of them.''

"You thought I was guilty.''

"My partner and I, the district attorney, everybody was certain. Maybe on some of those fancy television mysteries people get framed for murder, but it doesn't happen in real life. In real life, if you see a guy standing over the dead body of his wife, the chances are a thousand to one that he did it. And higher than a billion to one that somebody else did it and made it look like he did.'' He shrugged and looked away. "So maybe we didn't look hard enough, but, hey, I'll bet there were times you even wondered whether you'd done it yourself in a blackout.''

Steve started.

Schockley grinned. "Even *I* would have under the circumstances. I was a witness at your trial, so I couldn't be in court for anything except my own testimony. I never heard this Waters guy on the stand. When Vickers told me he thought you'd been framed, I told him he was crazy— stuff like that doesn't happen. Now I think he may be right.''

"Lot of good that does.''

"You'd be surprised,'' Vickers said. "Steve, did you ever read the police reports? Look at the crime-scene photos?''

"No.'' He shivered. "You didn't want me to, as I recall.''

"Well, I want you to now.'' He gestured to Schockley, who opened his beat-up briefcase and pulled out a thick manila folder that was dirty and smudged around the edges.

"Here,'' Schockley said, and spun the folder across the desk to Steve.

He sat with his hand on it, unwilling to open it. "Are there pictures of…is *she* in there?"

"Yeah. Is that a problem for you?" Schockley, always the cop, asked the question as though Steve were still very much a suspect. In Schockley's mind, perhaps he was.

"Of course it is, dammit."

"Do it, anyway," Vickers said. "There are pictures of the room, the kitchen with its drawer pulled out, the empty space where your knife was—even the murder weapon itself after the coroner removed it. There are only a few of your wife. You must do this. If there is anything, anything at all that seems out of place, anything that you remember that you didn't four years ago just after it happened, say so."

The next hour was purgatory for Steve. His palms were so sweaty that his fingers slipped on the edges of the photographs. Some of them were in color—the most horrific ones—but many were simple black-and-white shots composed for accuracy and not for style. He felt as though he was back in that interrogation room when he'd first begun to suspect the police thought he had killed Chelsea.

He had already been convicted once. Nothing worse could happen to him now. And yet he felt wave after wave of guilt. He should have awoken during the night, he should have heard the intruder, he should have come downstairs earlier in the morning, he should have, he should have…

After the first time through the files, Schockley led him back through the crime step-by-step using the pictures as a way to jog his memory.

Steve's head throbbed. He dug the heel of his hand into his right eye and looked for the fifth or sixth time at the picture of the knife that had taken Chelsea's life. This photo had been taken after the coroner had processed the weapon. There were no longer any telltale dark splotches on the long thin blade. A boning blade, the dealer in Mannheim had told him and Neil when they bought the sets.

"Who else would have known about these knives?" Schockley asked.

"Neil and his wife, Posey, of course. The housecleaning team. Any of our friends who happened to be there when one of us used it." He leaned his head back and closed his eyes against the pain. The light felt like a nail being driven through his forehead. "It's a miracle we still had it after a year. Chelsea hated to cook, and she was notorious for losing things or breaking them."

He stopped speaking and opened his eyes. "Give me that photo again, Schockley—the one of the knife."

"Sure."

He stared at it. "Is there another shot, maybe from another angle?"

Schockley glanced at Vickers.

"About six of them. Here." Schockley tossed them over. Both he and Vickers kept silent, barely breathing, while Steve went over the photos.

Finally he dropped them on the table and looked up at Vickers. "It's not my knife."

"I beg your pardon?"

"I said, it's not the knife from my kitchen. It's not my knife."

"Sure it is," Schockley said. "Neil Waters identified it at the trial. It's in the transcript. He recognized it because the two of you bought the sets in Germany at the same time. He swore you kept it in your kitchen drawer."

Steve shook his head. "I told you Chelsea hated to cook and broke things. About three months before she was killed, we had the kitchen painted. It didn't need it, of course, but Chelsea said it was too dark. She fought with the paint people for about a month, getting sample after sample of paint for the woodwork. She made them mix a dozen samples before she picked one." He shrugged.

"Neil was with us at one point, and he and I both said it was white. Just white. Looked white to us. Chelsea said it was special, with just a hint of mauve or puce or some silly color. Then the painters painted the window over the sink shut. Chelsea was furious. We didn't open the windows often because of the air-conditioning, but when Chelsea burned something—and she often did—she'd open the windows to try to clear out the smoke the exhaust fan couldn't handle before it set the smoke alarms off. She was furious when she found out about that window. She said she'd had to use a knife to pry it open. The boning knife from that set. She'd made a tiny nick in the blade doing it, and she'd gotten paint on the blade and the handle. She cleaned it, but there were still bits of that paint stuck between the blade and the hilt. This isn't my knife.''

"Then it has to be Neil's," Vickers said with wonder. "He took the knife from his set with him to your house. He couldn't take the chance that Chelsea would hear him opening your kitchen drawer and come to investigate. Killing her would have been much more difficult if she'd gotten up or turned to look at him. For one thing, she'd have screamed. Even drugged, you might have responded to a scream. No, the less noise he made in your house the better. After he killed her, all he had to do was take your knife home with him to replace the one from his set.''

"I wonder if he's still got it?" Schockley asked. "He'd be crazy to keep it.''

"Why? He wouldn't realize it was incriminating." Vickers sounded excited. "Certainly not as incriminating as if it suddenly disappeared." He rubbed his well-manicured hands together and asked Steve, "You say the paint was special? We could prove it came from your kitchen?''

"I don't know who bought the house when I sold it. They may have repainted.''

"Maybe not. In any case, the paint store would have a record of the formula. You do remember which paint store, don't you?''

"Some decorator—Décor Fashion Colors, I think.''

"I know them well. Overpriced. My wife insists on using them. We've got to get into the Waters house and get that knife." Vickers turned to Schockley. "Can you do that?"

"Probably. We can check for the nick and do a color analysis on the paint if it's still there."

"There's something else we need to find. The real clincher. The jewelry that was stolen, Steve. You remember it?"

"How could I forget? Chelsea was wearing the heirloom diamond ring she inherited from her mother. It was an old emerald cut. At least six carats. I thought it looked like an ice cube, but she loved it. She had on the pearls I gave her for our anniversary. Big and matched. Expensive. And a diamond bracelet—not a tennis bracelet, wider than that. Set in platinum. The insurance company said they were worth about fifty thousand dollars all together."

"They've never turned up, you know."

"How would I know?"

"Neil Waters is greedy," Vickers said. "A poor man who attained wealth early and married a rich wife. I don't think he could bring himself to throw fifty thousand dollars' worth of jewelry into the Mississippi River, which is what he should have done the first moment he could get free from the investigation. No, if I read our Mr. Waters correctly, he'd want those gems where he could see them occasionally. Eventually perhaps have them reset or recut.

"I doubt he'd keep them in a safety-deposit box. If anything were to happen to him, the box would be opened in the presence of the IRS. He wouldn't want his wife to know he'd killed her sister, not even after he's dead. No, I think he'll have them somewhere around that house. Someplace he could have stashed them fast when he came back from killing Chelsea. He couldn't be certain that the police wouldn't search his house, so the obvious hiding places are out. Well, Schockley, you think you can find those jewels?"

"If they're there, I'll find 'em."

"If you do," Steve asked, "can the knife and the jewels be admitted into evidence? Can't Neil say they were obtained without a search warrant?"

"Let me worry about that. The chain of evidence will be impeccable, and one nice thing about Schockley's no longer being with the police is that as a licensed private detective, he has more legal leeway."

"I can also get busted for breaking and entering," Schockley said.

"But you won't let that happen, will you?" Vickers clapped him on the shoulder.

"What happens if you do find the things?" Steve asked. "Do I get a new trial?"

"Possibly. I would prefer a confession. Neater and faster."

"From Neil? Confess? Never."

"Not even if he thought you were going to kill him?" Steve froze. Did Vickers know of his plans?

"I speak, of course, theoretically. I think it may be just possible to run a scam on your Mr. Waters. I have a personal dislike for the man that is out of proportion to this case, Steve. He put one over on me. Not many can do that. I intend to bring him to justice if at all possible."

"Why did you wait so long?"

"All I can say is that I'm busy. Things tend to be shoved to the back of my mind. I work for a living, too."

"You're saying that if Eleanor and Mary Beth hadn't come to your office and offered to pay for all this, you'd have let it go? Have let me rot?"

"That doesn't matter now. One more thing. You must not tell a living soul about this meeting. The quarry must at all costs not be alerted."

"Not even your clients?"

"The doctor and your sister? Especially not either of them. Mary Beth would tell the Colonel, the Colonel would tell others. The doctor would tell her colleagues to show that you are not a bad man. They would tell others for the same reason. No. As far as the rest of the world is concerned, we have had only a preliminary meeting this morning out of which nothing substantive arose. Do I make myself clear?''

''How long can I wait? Neil's moving his family to Arizona.''

''I am aware of that. If Schockley is successful, then we move quickly. If not, we go back to square one, and it will not matter in the least where Neil Waters lives. Now, this session has taken entirely too long. I have other appointments. Keep the faith, Steve. My own ego is involved in this now. I never let my ego down.''

Eleanor demanded a report on the meeting. He hated to lie to her, but he agreed with Vickers. The fewer people who knew, the better.

''Please, promise me, Steve, that whatever happens with us, you won't do anything that would put you back in jail.''

''I can't promise.''

She turned away. ''So I really was simply a means to an end.''

''No! Don't think that! From the first moment I saw you I've had to fight to stay focused when all I want to is to think about making love to you.''

''Then why can't you promise?''

''There are things going on I can't tell you about.''

''Good things?'' She searched his face.

''Please, just let it be.''

''I don't understand you at all.'' She turned on her heel and left him.

He barely heard Big's excited chatter about all the things he'd done during the day. He'd named the little pit bull Daisy and told Steve he wanted to find some way to keep her. Steve was afraid he was in for another disappointment. Prisons didn't allow pets.

By the time they reached the barn area, sleet dropped out of the night sky. Big had promised Eleanor he'd make certain Marcus and the horses had been fed and watered. Steve volunteered to check the pasture cows and the buffalo.

"You go on up to the compound," Steve told Big. "It'll take me longer to check the pastures. Tell whoever's on duty that I'll be up there before supper."

"Okay. Sure you don't want me to stay?"

Steve shook his head. He wanted to think. In the compound no one was ever alone. Maybe the sleet would cool his fevered brain so that he could figure out what to do about Eleanor and his feelings for her. He wished he'd never promised Vickers to keep her in the dark.

JUST AFTER DUSK, Eleanor received a call from Selma. "Steve's gone."

"I beg your pardon?"

"Listen, I've covered for you before. I hoped he was with you. If he's not, he's gone. Big left him checking the water troughs in the pasture. He should have been back fifteen minutes ago." Her voice was so low that Eleanor could barely hear her.

He'd done it, then.

She refused to believe it.

"Selma, please, please, please, give me time to find him and bring him back. The weather's foul, he didn't have any transportation unless he's driving a tractor down the highway. He can't have gotten far. I'm on my way to the farm now. He may have gotten hurt by one of the buffalo."

"I can't keep doing this. I'll lose my job."

"He hasn't run away." Eleanor hoped she sounded more certain than she felt. "Not after today. He simply wouldn't."

"Thirty minutes. That's all you have. Then I'm ringing the alarms. Damn, I told you I hate tracking. And in this weather, too."

Eleanor drove the rest of the way to the farm much faster than the speed limit, and slid to a stop on the concrete pad in front of the barn. She jumped out of her truck and began to shout his name. No answer.

She pulled up the hood of her heavy parka. "He's got to be here somewhere," Eleanor said. She shouted into the wind. The night was as black and frigid as the inside of a closed refrigerator.

If he *hadn't* escaped, he'd have to be in one of the pastures. That meant he was hurt or worse. Something had kept him from returning to the compound.

In another couple of hours the roads would be treacherous, but the sleet had not yet begun to stick to the frozen earth of the pasture. Eleanor opened the pasture gate, drove her truck through, closed it behind her, turned on her halogen headlights and set her floodlight on the dashboard. So far the sleet was light enough that the floodlight penetrated it, instead of bouncing off.

She began to honk her horn in an SOS pattern—three long, three short, three long. That was supposed to be the signal from victim to rescuer, but it was the only Morse code she knew, so it would have to do.

She drove carefully, but still hit bumps and hillocks. She narrowly avoided a half-dozen scrub locust trees that suddenly reared up in front of her where she could have sworn there were no trees before.

The pasture, so familiar in daylight, had taken on a nightmare quality. She couldn't spot even one cow, although she knew they were there somewhere huddled in the hollows, under the trees or in the run-in shed. They were used to bad weather.

She reached the top of the levee that surrounded the stock pond. If Steve had fallen or been pushed into that icy water by one of the cows... She shivered. The pond was shallow, but weighed down with clothes, even a strong man might be pulled under.

She yanked up the hood of her heavy jacket higher, grabbed the spotlight and climbed out of the truck.

"Steve!" she shouted.

Only the wind answered.

"Steve! Where are you?"

For a moment she thought she heard something. She caught her breath. Was it a trick of the wind or a voice? She wove the light from side to side, each time trying to see farther out into the icy water.

"Steve, where are you?" she shouted again.

"South end." The words were faint. The wind tried to rip them away, but she heard them.

Her heart leaped in her throat, and a moment later she drove carefully along the bank.

Her cell phone rang. She'd forgotten to call Selma.

She hit Enter and said, "I've found him." She heard the relief in her voice. "He's at the far end of the pasture. I'll call when I've got him."

"You're sure? You're not just putting me on?"

"No! Damn! I need to concentrate on my driving. I'll call you."

"You now have twenty minutes before I call out the COs."

"I found him, Selma, I told you."

"You say. Unless I hear his voice within twenty minutes, I'm setting off the alarms."

Eleanor heard a dial tone.

Exasperated and with full awareness that she was racing not only the weather but the clock, Eleanor stopped the truck and stepped out to call him again.

This time his voice sounded closer. "About twenty yards in front of you. Be careful. I'm in the pond."

"Oh, my God!" She jumped back in the truck and nearly stalled it.

Then she saw him. He stood up to his knees in water at the edge of the pond. She aimed the floodlight and her headlights at him and climbed out to go to him.

"Are you stuck?"

"No, dammit. There's a cow in the pond. I can't get her out and I think she's trying to calve."

Eleanor pulled her flashlight out of her jacket pocket. Steve had his arms wrapped around the neck of one of the cows. He was obviously pulling, and the animal was just as obviously fighting him.

"What makes you think she's calving?"

"She was hunching and straining with her tail up in the air, and then she came down here. I was my way back to the barn when I saw her and grabbed her. If she's had the calf, it's drowned. I couldn't hold both ends out of the water at the same time."

Eleanor jumped down into the pond. She gasped as the icy water flooded in over the top of her red rubber boots.

"Careful. It's slippery."

She waded to the rear of the cow and stuck her hands into the icy water. She couldn't feel anything. Thank God, the calf's sharp little hooves hadn't broken the birth sac. "The water must have arrested the contractions. We've got to get her out of here fast."

"What do you think I've been trying to do? I've been yelling my lungs out. By the time I got to this stupid cow, I was all alone out here. I thought they'd have the dogs after me by now. This is one time I'd have been glad to see them coming, bloodhounds and all."

"I made Selma hold off reporting you," Eleanor said as she waded back to the bank. "Hang on to her, Steve. If we can get a rope around her head, we can winch her out with the truck."

"Hurry. I can't hang on much longer."

Eleanor positioned the truck so that the winch on the front was generally aligned with the cow's body, slid down the bank beside Steve and slipped the lasso over the cow's head. Every muscle in the animal's body was taut with resistance.

"Stupid cow!" Eleanor said. "Hold her until the line goes taut, then try to keep her from slipping it off."

She kept the lights on Steve and the cow as she tied the line to the steel cable on the winch, engaged it and took up the slack in the line. The instant she felt it come taut, the cow began to low and toss her head as she tried to free herself.

She leaned out the window. "Watch her, Steve, don't let her trample you."

"Don't worry about me. I couldn't feel my feet if she did."

"Come on, you nitwit excuse for a bovine, get your rear end out of that water!"

She felt the truck begin to slip forward down the side of the pond toward the water and jammed on the brakes.

"I've got to move the truck back over the brow of the hill, Steve, otherwise she'll winch me right down into the lake with her."

"Do it fast."

Once the truck was beyond the crest of the hill, she engaged the winch again. The cow began to take one grudging step after another out of the water as the winch forced her forward.

"Get behind her, Steve, and shove her butt out of the water before we have to rescue that calf from a watery grave."

Steve threw her a look, but he went. The moment he put his hands on her flanks, he shouted, "Get her out of here *now*. I feel feet."

Eleanor turned up the winch speed. The cow popped out of the pond like a cork and trotted up the hill until she stood with her nose against the hood of the truck.

From the cow's rump, Steve said, "Eleanor, get back here." His voice was quiet, but there was no mistaking the urgency.

Eleanor jammed on her emergency brake and ran toward him just as the cow gave a great groan and sank onto her chest.

As Eleanor dropped to her knees, the cow's tail came straight up over her back and lashed across Steve's face like a whip.

"Damn!" He grabbed the tail.

"It's coming."

With the floodlight now aimed three feet above their heads, they worked in semidarkness. The sleet had slacked off momentarily, but the wind had picked up. Eleanor's hands were shaking and her teeth were chattering.

But the calf was warm. Or at least it was until it thrust its little front hooves through the sac that covered it and blinked wide brown eyes at the world.

"Get out of the way," Eleanor said, and grabbed Steve's arm just as the cow heaved herself up. They both grabbed for the calf as it slid to the ground.

The cow began to call instantly. The calf lay on the icy ground behind her. The new mother couldn't turn her head because of the line that held her. "We've got to get the line off her."

"We can't leave them out here. The baby'll freeze."

"Can you pick him up?" Eleanor asked.

"This is one time I wish Big were here. Yeah. I can pick him up."

"We'll get him into the back of the truck. You'll have to ride back there with him. I'm sorry, Steve. I promise we'll get warm back at the barn."

"What about the cow?"

"She'll follow us. She won't leave that calf."

Eleanor ran around to the back of the truck to drop the tailgate, then helped Steve get the calf in. She pulled a tarpaulin out of her vet trunk. "Put that over you both."

Steve laughed. A real laugh. "So now we'll stay dry. God, I love your timing, Doctor."

"I have no idea what the mother will do when I turn her loose. She may try to climb into the truck with you."

She hit the release lever on the winch and leaned over the fender of the truck to pull the rope loose from the cow's head.

The cow backed up, and for a terrible moment Eleanor was afraid she'd run back into the water. Eleanor inched around to the front of the truck, ready to toss the rope back over the cow's head. "Cow, don't you dare."

She realized a moment later that the cow saw that truck as the menace keeping her from her calf. She stomped once, made a "humph" sound, and charged.

Eleanor dove for the hood of her truck a nanosecond before the cow hit the radiator grill with full force.

"Eleanor? What's happening up there?"

"Nothing. I'm fine. Stay where you are whatever you do."

This time the cow backed off and simply stood there while steam rose from her body and billowed out of her nostrils.

Eleanor swung to the ground, climbed into the truck, slammed the door and threw it into reverse.

Once Eleanor turned to head back toward the barn, she could watch the cow in her side mirror trotting behind the truck where Steve and the calf huddled together under the tarp.

Eleanor hadn't given a thought to the other cows until she got to the gate. They were all clustered around as though waiting for an opportunity to bolt into the shelter of the barn the moment Eleanor opened the gate.

She drove up to it until her fender touched the bars, then climbed out. "Shoo! Scat! Go find your nice dry shed!" She clapped and shouted. Only the new mama stayed behind.

Eleanor opened the gate, drove through with the cow in tandem, then shut it again quickly before the others could change their minds and charge back. She drove all the way under the overhang and into the foyer of the barn.

Only then did she remember to call Selma. "We're fine," she said.

"You had exactly one minute left. Who's we? Can I talk to Steve?"

"We is me, Steve, a cow of very little brain who is also a new mother, and her calf, which was nearly born under three feet of ice water in the pond. You can't talk to Steve at the moment because he's in the back of the truck with the calf and definitely under siege. Take my word for it. He's there, all right.''

''Huh?''

''Steve was trying to get the stupid cow out of the pond before she had the calf. We managed it, but just barely. We're all four soaked and half-frozen. It'll be a miracle if we don't wind up with pneumonia.''

''I'll come down in the four-wheeler to pick him up.''

''No, you won't! I can't handle the cow and calf by myself, and I can't wait until morning to check them over. Sign Steve out or whatever you do. Ernest already knows there are going to be nights when we have to work late or even around the clock. We've got to get these animals dry and warm, and then we've got to get ourselves the same way. Thank God I had the men bring an extra set of clothes down here. I'll drive Steve up to the compound in the truck after we finish here, assuming I don't have a crushed radiator leaking antifreeze all over.''

''Huh?''

''In the war between cow and radiator, radiator doesn't always win. Don't worry. I'll get Steve back not much the worse for wear.''

''You sure?''

''Absolutely. Selma, thanks for not alerting the COs. I told you Steve wouldn't run off.''

''Not *this* time.''

''Cynic.''

''Experienced cynic. Every time I look at that man I see *flight* written all over him, and I don't usually miss those signals. Be careful, Eleanor. He could still take off, only now he's got your truck to do it in. And a hostage, if he wants one.''

''Won't happen.''

''What won't happen?'' Steve asked as he leaned in the window of the truck.

"I'm trying to convince Selma that you aren't going to steal my truck, take me hostage and escape." She grinned at him, expecting a smile in return.

The startled expression on his face surprised her.

"Steve?" She opened the door and climbed out.

He went quickly back to the calf, who was now bawling lustily and trying to stand. He wasn't getting much purchase on the slick metal bed of the truck, and he was making his mother very nervous.

"Come on, let's bed these two down."

The laughter, the joy she'd heard in his voice earlier was gone.

Despite the cold and wet, they worked side by side until the calf began to nurse and the cow settled down in an empty stall next to the three quarter horses. Eleanor gave both calf and cow shots, checked to be certain the cow was normal, as well, and only then realized how cold and wet she was. Steve must be much worse off, but he'd worked beside her without complaint.

"I've got dry clothes in the truck. I'll go open the footlocker so you can get out your dry set," she said. She tried to sound cheerful because she was still worried. "Go stand in the shower until you warm up, then I'll drive you back up to the compound."

"All right." He turned away from her.

"Steve? You weren't, were you?"

"What?"

"What Selma said."

"No." He touched her cheek with icy fingers. "Not tonight."

CHAPTER FIFTEEN

ELEANOR RAN BACK into the barn from her truck with a change of clothes and a pair of dirty running shoes that she kept for emergencies. She tried to keep them clean, but they tended to give off a faint whiff of cow manure when the wind was right.

She unlocked the footlocker in the storeroom and found the sack marked "Chadwick." She would leave his clothes outside the shower room where he could reach them.

When she got up from her knees and turned around, Steve stood in the doorway behind her with a couple of thin prison towels in his hand. His face and hands were dry, but his clothes were sodden. In the harsh light of the office, his sleek wet hair was the same tawny brown as the cow's pelt.

He'd taken off his jacket, but his shirt was wet through and clung to the muscles of his chest and arms, and his flat abdomen. His soaked jeans were pasted to his lean hips.

Eleanor tried to keep her eyes on his face and not on his body. It wasn't easy. She started to speak, then cleared her throat. "Here," she said, and held the sack of clothes out to him. "You warm up in the shower while I make us a quick pot of coffee. Then I'll shower and drive you back to the compound."

He shook his head. "No."

"No?" Looking at his serious face, she felt that same flutter of disquiet. Had he decided to make a run for it, after all?

He tossed the towels aside and pulled her to him. "There are better ways to warm up. Together."

Now the flutter was no longer disquiet, but excitement. "Steve, we can't. What if Selma comes looking for us?"

"At this point, I don't give a damn." He kissed her softly.

She responded to his kiss, then slid away from him and said with a smile, "You feel like a wet carp."

"So do you. A cold wet carp." He kissed her ear. "We can fix that. The shower room has a lock on the door and plenty of room for two."

"If we're caught..."

"To hell with rules." He ran his hand down her back and up under her sweater. "I want to hold you, touch you, be inside you."

She felt heat welling up from her center. She couldn't resist him. She didn't *want* to resist him. For one night, one small time, she wanted to forget where they were, who they were, and that they might be torn apart tomorrow.

Steve took her hand. He'd turned on the heater in the shower room. The warmth felt wonderful. His hands felt even more wonderful. He locked the door, then turned to her and lifted her sweater over her head.

Her cold fingers unbuttoned his wet shirt and helped him peel it off his shoulders.

Their wet jeans were harder to get off, but finally the things lay on the floor in a sodden heap.

Steve slowly peeled her wet panties down until she could kick them away, then she did the same for him.

He picked her up and carried her with him into the shower. She caught her breath as the warm water began to cascade over and between them.

Her fingertips tingled as full feeling returned. Now she could curl her fingers into the dark hair on his chest, cradle his questing head as he circled her nipple with his tongue.

Her breasts felt swollen, hot, and she knew that she was

ready for him, but he held off, although when she caressed him, she could tell he was more than ready, too.

He sank to his knees in front of her. The moment his tongue touched her, she arched her back and grasped the shower rod to keep from falling. Her body burst from ice to fire in what seemed only an instant.

Then he stood up and braced her against the tile of the shower as he rolled on a condom. He entered her slowly this time. Their bodies flowed together and mingled as sweetly as the warm water that cascaded over them.

The mingling that began softly grew into a torrent, a cataract that beat against her senses until at last she fell over the edge and tumbled headlong into ecstasy.

Shaken, she clung to him and buried her face against his shoulder. She wasn't certain she could stand without his arms to hold her up. Nothing had prepared her for the way he felt inside her. It was glorious.

It was terrifying.

She'd abandoned a part of herself she'd always protected, ever since Jerry. She belonged to Steve now, heart and soul, and if he destroyed them both, there wasn't a thing she could do to prevent it.

Afterward, they dressed in silence and avoided each other's eyes. Eleanor cleaned up the coffee, while Steve straightened the shower room.

Each time they made love, the barriers between them seemed to fall, only to be rebuilt stronger and taller.

Outside, the sleet had stopped, but the black night was still impenetrable. Eleanor drove Steve to the compound, spoke to the CO in charge, saw that he was properly checked in and on his way to his dormitory. She waved cheerfully to the CO as she drove away.

By the time she reached the highway she was shaking, not with cold and not with fatigue, but with fear for Steve. He'd never actually told her he planned to escape, but if he were to really use that gun of Bill Chumley's, he'd have to try to disappear. No, he hadn't told her, but he didn't have to. She'd hoped to hold him back with bonds of love, or at the very least of passion.

He'd turned the tables. She was the one in thrall. She had to break free before he destroyed her. It would be easy to let another disaster, another tragic ending to another love drag her once more into despair.

If he were still intent on murder, she couldn't save him. She could only try to save herself.

SHE WAS HIS NEMESIS, his fate for good or for ill.

He lay on his cot and listened to the men around him in their restless sleep. He was afraid that if he fell asleep, he would groan or call out as he had before. He couldn't afford to talk in his sleep. He was already walking a very thin edge.

But now that he was warm and not only relaxed but drained, he knew he couldn't stay awake long, no matter how much he worried about his future.

There seemed only the tiniest glimmer of hope that there would be a way out that didn't lead to more pain and tragedy. If Steve avenged his wife as he'd planned, he would be no better than Neil. If he let Neil get away scot-free, he was less than a man.

Neither of those Steve Chadwicks would be worthy of Eleanor. After tonight's lovemaking he was afraid that if he asked her to run away with him, she would.

So he must not ask her.

He could only pin his hopes for a happy outcome—his very slim hopes—on Leslie Vickers, the man who'd allowed him to be convicted in the first place, and Charlie Schockley, the man who'd arrested him.

He could only stand and watch. Overwhelmed by the same old feelings of helplessness he'd endured these years in prison, forced to live by someone else's rules, embroiled in a foul culture he barely survived in.

He had to face the fact that he'd fallen in love with

Eleanor. All his good intentions to stay away from her disintegrated the moment she walked into a room.

At first it was her compassion that had attracted him. A different kind of person would have simply done her job and walked away each night without a thought for the people she left behind. But even the first day, Eleanor had treated them all with dignity. She truly wanted to make a difference in their lives. How many people would have seen what a good man Big Little was? Or even bothered to look below the surface of a tattooed career criminal like Gil?

And her tenacity. Even when she was certain he was a killer, she'd fought to understand him. She never treated him like a monster. Now that she believed he was innocent, she was fighting even harder.

Then he loved the way she came into his arms, gave herself to him, wanted him. She had truly become his better self. How in hell could he be worthy of her love and trust when he must betray her?

Steve supposed everybody thought they were in love half a dozen times before the real thing. Until you experienced the real thing, you couldn't recognize the counterfeit. He had loved Chelsea, but even that hadn't had this intensity. His feelings for Eleanor were so different, so overwhelming, that her happiness meant more to him than life. If the only way to preserve her happiness was to thrust her away from him, then that was what he'd have to do.

BY UNSPOKEN CONSENT, Eleanor and Steve tried to avoid each other for the next week. Steve was certain that everyone on the team and at the clinic knew there was something wrong between them, but nobody said anything.

Except Big.

He walked into Mark Scott's office at the clinic one afternoon with Daisy at his heel. "Steve, how come you're mad at Dr. Eleanor? I thought you liked her."

"I'm not mad, Big. And I do like her."

"She's not happy. You're not, either. You have a fight?''

"No. Not a fight. I can't explain, Big. It's something we have to work out.''

Big looked at him in silence, then reached down and scratched Daisy's remaining ear. "It's not right when Dr. Eleanor's not happy.''

"I know.''

"Y'all make up.''

"If we can.''

Big left. He wasn't satisfied.

Steve dropped his head into his hands. He felt as if he was being torn apart from inside. If something didn't happen soon, he'd explode.

TWO WEEKS BEFORE Thanksgiving, Sweet Daddy sought Steve out in the mess hall after supper. "Outside, man. We gotta talk.''

Steve followed reluctantly.

"When you going, man?'' Sweet Daddy whispered. He was shivering. The night was raw.

"Going where?''

"Don't pull that crap on me. I know you're going. I can read the signs. Hell, we all can. You got a plan?''

"If I *were* going, it's no business of yours.''

"I'm going wid' you.''

Steve laughed.

"Nobody laughs at Sweet Daddy. I about had enough of this place. I want out, and I ain't coming back. Man like you, smart, he going, he got a plan, am I right? No three and three, not for Sweet Daddy.''

Three miles away and three hours before they capture you, Steve remembered hearing. He said, "And if I don't take you?''

"Then you don't get no three and three—you get nothing and nothing and lose your good time.''

"You'd snitch?''

"I ain't going, ain't nobody going. I want to eat my own turkey with my own ladies on Thanksgiving day. She helping you, am I right?"

"Wrong. And I'm not going anywhere. You tell the COs that I'm planning to walk off, and you will regret it."

"Don't nobody threaten Sweet Daddy."

"Sure they do. All the time. You snitch on me, and I'll make certain that various groups know about it. You won't last a week."

"I come with you, man, or you don't see your woman."

Before Steve could stop him, he scuttled back into the dormitory.

Steve leaned against the side of the building, suddenly hot despite the chill. That wasn't an idle threat. Steve couldn't take Sweet Daddy along, but neither could he safely leave him behind. He couldn't snitch on him to Gil or any of the others without revealing his own plans. The same for Eleanor.

He'd have to try to move up the timetable. Tomorrow he'd call his man on the outside. The man picking him up outside the prison would bring a weapon for him to use. If he was lucky, the Neil problem would be solved in an hour.

If Eleanor discovered he'd disappeared from the grounds, she'd be frantic. He'd have to trust she'd try to cover for him. Not fair to her, but he didn't dare take her into his confidence.

And Sweet Daddy? He'd think of something.

TONIGHT WAS FINALLY THE NIGHT. Steve thought he'd be nervous, but instead, he felt empty.

At long last Mark Scott had returned from his trip for Buchanan Enterprises. Steve remembered meeting him before the trial, although they'd only been nodding acquaintances.

Mark seemed pleased at the work Steve had done on organizing the clinic's inventory and finances. He suggested that there might be a place for Steve at Buchanan when he was paroled. Steve was flattered but noncommittal. He couldn't think any further than his impending confrontation with Neil.

He'd formed a plan to avoid Sweet Daddy. Unfortunately it involved Lard Ass Newman, but that couldn't be helped. In the end he only had to call in a couple of favors from men he'd helped at Big Mountain before they moved down to the farm.

Newman was now one of the COs on mess duty, which meant he could lounge around while the men ate, then stuff himself with leftovers while the kitchen crew cleaned up.

That night at supper, Sweet Daddy discovered he was sitting surrounded by large genial cons whom he knew only slightly. He couldn't change seats without insulting them. He'd pay for an insult.

Steve sat at the very back of the mess hall nearest the door and watched Elroy craning his scrawny neck trying to locate him.

As everyone was finishing and putting their trays on the conveyor belts to the kitchen, Big Nose Noonan on Sweet Daddy's left took offense at a remark made by Peterman Blake on the other side of Sweet Daddy. The two men argued over Sweet Daddy's head, while the men across the table egged them on.

As Steve figured, Newman waded in to restore order. In the ensuing ruckus, he slipped away into the night and out of the compound.

He kept to the bushes and pine trees that lined the prison road all the way down to the highway. He moved fast, even though he doubted anyone would notice he was gone for some time. This wasn't like the normal prison where a count could be called at any moment. The men were checked in at bedtime and in the morning only. The rest of the day they were all over the farm on their respective teams. Steve had at least half an hour before Selma checked on him—more like an hour, if he was lucky.

The plain dark sedan waited for him in a narrow turnoff under the trees at the highway's edge. Steve vaulted the four-foot perimeter fence and slipped into the front seat.

The driver sped off and turned on his lights only when he was well under way. He didn't speak. Neither did Steve.

CHAPTER SIXTEEN

STEVE LOOKED OUT the car window as they passed the house he'd shared with Chelsea. There were lights on both upstairs and down, and a child's bicycle lay on its side by the front door. For a moment he couldn't breathe. He prayed the people in the house were happy there.

If only he and Chelsea had had children. They'd both wanted them badly, but no matter how hard they tried, she couldn't carry a pregnancy more than three months.

Apparently it was genetic, because her sister, Posey, hadn't been able to conceive, either. Steve thanked God Neil didn't have children. Children would have made what he planned to do even harder.

Steve's driver dropped him in the shadows at the back corner of Neil's yard. Steve had expected Neil to build a high solid perimeter fence, but apparently he hadn't. It was still possible to walk from Neil's yard through the trees to the back of what had been Steve's house.

Neil's house was dark except for a single light in his study. Steve moved closer.

Neil sat at his fine Napoleonic campaign desk under a Tiffany lamp that Steve knew was no modern copy. A fire blazed in the ornate stone fireplace. The heavy raw-silk drapes over the French windows were wide-open, so Steve's view into the room was unobstructed.

He slid his hand under the drooping pot of late mums beside the set of French doors. The key was there as it had always been.

He knew from Schockley that Neil never set the alarm

system until he went up to bed, and that Posey usually took a sleeping pill and went to bed early. Neil generally worked alone until midnight or later. That much hadn't changed. Neil had always been a night owl.

So much for being awake to provide her husband with an alibi, Schockley had said.

Steve slid the key into the French door and, bracing the door handle with his other hand, turned it silently.

Before he stepped into the room, he checked the automatic his driver had provided one last time to make certain there was a full clip and one in the chamber. He eased the slide back into position and stepped into the room.

Neil surged to his feet, gaping at the intruder. Then he shaded his eyes with his hands. "Steve? My God, it *is* you."

Neil's face went gray, but he recovered quickly. "You out on parole already? Man, am I glad to see you." He stuck out his hand.

"Knock it off, Neil, and take your other hand off your desk drawer. This isn't a pipe in my hand."

"I can see that. A gun? Hey, come on, Steve, this is Neil, remember, old friend?"

"Old enemy, you mean. The reason I'm in prison."

"Steve, that's not true and you know it. Why, I tried to convince that jury—"

"You damned me beautifully with every word you said. Just the way you framed me when you killed Chelsea."

Neil spread his hands. "Killed Chelsea? My God, Steve, how can you even think that? I was fond of Chelsea."

"I thought you were *fond* of *me.*"

"I was. I am. You're the closest thing to a brother I've ever had."

"No doubt Cain said the same thing about Abel just before he bashed his head in."

"You know I didn't kill Chelsea. I was home in bed with Posey."

"I've had three years to work out how you did it. I may

be wrong on a couple of points, but overall, I think I know.''

"Fantasy.'' Obviously playing for time, Neil started to sit down behind his desk.

"Don't sit there. And keep your hands where I can see them.''

"Come on, Steve, if this is going to be a long tale, the least you can do is let me sit down. How about like old friends on either side of the fire?''

Steve said nothing.

Neil put his hands palms up in front of his chest and walked carefully around the desk without taking his eyes off Steve. He sat in one of the two armchairs in front of the fire, eased back with a sigh and crossed his legs at the ankles as though perfectly relaxed.

Steve didn't buy his act.

"I'll stand, thank you. Put your hands on the arms of the chair and keep them there.''

"I can't believe you're treating me like this, Steve, after all we've been through.''

"Good one, Neil. What have you been through, precisely? You bought my half of the company for pennies on the dollar because you knew I was in a bind and needed the money for my defense. When I was convicted and couldn't benefit from Chelsea's estate, Posey inherited her money, as well as her life insurance, and now you've sold out to one of the conglomerates for one hell of a lot more money. You'll be a gentleman of leisure in sunny Arizona. The only thing you had to do to get there was to kill my wife and frame me for her murder.''

"I tell you, I didn't kill Chelsea.'' Neil glanced at the fire. "I couldn't kill her. I was in love with her.''

Steve's gun hand wavered momentarily in surprise, but he recovered quickly.

"That's right, Steve. I was in love with her from the minute I met her. I dated her first, remember? But when she laid eyes on you I knew I'd lost her.''

"You said you'd broken up with her. You didn't mind if I dated her. Hell, you were best man at our wedding."

Neil shrugged. "So I lied. You're easy to lie to, you know that?"

"I do now."

"I never stopped loving her. Posey was a poor substitute, but at least it kept me near Chelsea. I could see her, be close to her."

"And the fact that she had inherited the bulk of her father's money didn't mean a thing?"

"Sure it did. She was rich in her own right while Posey only had that trust fund. But I'd have been in love with her even if she'd been some penniless little coed from the Delta. God, she was beautiful."

"If you're going to tell me you had an affair, I won't believe you."

Neil laughed but without mirth. "I wish. God knows I tried. I knew you two were having problems, that the bloom was off the rose. She had her life, you had yours—hell, I saw you every day, heard all your grandiose schemes for making the world a better place to live. I gave Chelsea a shoulder to cry on. I was as much her confidante as I was yours. But then I tried to take it further...."

He looked away to stare into the fire. "She blew up at me. Said I was betraying Posey and you. From that point we never saw each other except when the four of us got together. It tore me apart."

"That's why you killed her? Because she turned you down? And you hated me so much you framed me?"

"I never hated you. Envied you, yes. Envied you your good looks and your easy manners. Envied that you could play polo and tennis and golf well and never care what the score was. I'd have given my right arm to do the things you did."

"The business wouldn't have succeeded without you, Neil. I could do the engineering, but I can't sell snow to a nomad in the desert. You made the business, not me."

"You think I don't know that? But you were always the one who got the kudos. Wonderful idea, Steve, great innovation, Steve. And they *were* great."

"None of this gets to the nitty-gritty. You're a killer. You've got to pay for that."

Neil sounded tired. "Okay, I'm a killer. Just how did I do it when I was home in bed with Posey?"

"You weren't. And I can prove it."

For the first time, Neil sat up and gave Steve his full attention. "Prove it, how?"

"In good time. I'll tell you before I kill you."

"That's what this is all about? Killing me? You'll never get away with it."

"That's what I would have said about you. We were both wrong. So how'd you get the drug into my wine at the restaurant? What was it? Some of Posey's sleeping pills?"

"Who says I did?"

"I say. And into Posey's, as well. You may have made love to her when you got home, Neil, but then she went off to lala-land, while you walked through your backyard and into mine, opened the back door with Posey's key, killed Chelsea, took her jewelry and broke the window. Two minutes, tops. You knew I'd call you the minute I found her. You were there before the police—through our yards again. Any trace of forensic evidence they might have found could be explained by that second trip. Of course Posey said you were in bed with her. What was she going to say? She was blotto and never heard you leave? Then all you had to do was sit tight and make certain the jury convicted me. Would you have let me take a lethal injection?"

"No!" Neil bolted out of his chair. Steve stopped him with the gun. "No, I'd never have let you die. I did everything I could to get you off on a lesser charge. When they sentenced you to six to twelve, I knew you'd be out in three or four years. What's three or four years? You're still a young man.''

"You have no idea how long three or four years can be. So you admit it. You killed her.''

"I don't admit it. And you can't prove it, no matter what you say.''

"Yes, I can. Amazing that evidence still exists. You're not the only one who knows I'm innocent. Ever hear of a cold case investigation, Neil? That's what my lawyer has been running. You made a mistake that would send you to prison if I was to let you live.''

"For God's sake, man, what?''

"The knife that you used to stab Chelsea. It supposedly came from the drawer beside the stove in my kitchen. You identified it. Just like the one you had.''

"Yes, I identified it.''

"Wrong. Chelsea wasn't much of a cook, and definitely not as neat as Posey the perfect homemaker. That night you couldn't take a chance on Chelsea's hearing you open the kitchen drawer and coming to investigate. You took the knife from your set in *your* kitchen to stab her with. Then after she was dead, you took the knife from *our* kitchen and put it in the drawer in your house to replace yours.''

"For the sake of argument, let's say I did that. They were identical. You're not giving me some nonsense about fingerprints, surely, after all this time?''

"Not fingerprints. You didn't know that Chelsea had used that knife to pry open a stuck window in the kitchen. She'd chipped a tiny piece out of the blade, and she'd gotten a couple of flakes of that special white paint lodged between the end of the blade and the hilt.''

Neil's face was a picture. He'd aged a dozen years in five minutes. He no longer paid attention to the gun in Steve's hand. "I don't believe you,'' he whispered.

"I never saw the pictures of the weapon until a few days ago. I knew then it wasn't my knife. You had a telephone repairman yesterday, didn't you? Did Posey bother to tell you?"

"What?"

"He's a private detective hired by my lawyer and my sister. He found the knife in your kitchen. It's not there now. It's in a laboratory under a microscope. The microscopic bits are still there, so is the nick in the blade. The people who own my house now haven't repainted and let us take a sample of paint from that window. Remember how we laughed when Chelsea spent so much time having the paint mixed? White is white. But it's not, Neil. It's one of a kind. And so is the paint on that knife. And only you had access to it."

"That's not enough. Any good lawyer could find a judge who'd rule that inadmissible because of the way you got it."

"Vickers says he'll have no trouble getting it admitted into evidence. Why didn't you dump the jewelry you stole into the river, Neil? It was stupid to keep it all these years."

"I don't know what you're talking about." Neil had gone from confused to frightened. His hands no longer lay on the arms of his chair, but twisted in his lap convulsively.

"That detective is good. He knew what he was looking for and the way most people think when they hide something. The police never even tried to search this place, did they?"

"Why should they?"

"To find Chelsea's jewelry—the things that were taken off her body that night. Granted they were beautiful pieces—that ring her mother left her, the pearls I gave her for our anniversary, the diamond bracelet. But to keep them—stupid, Neil. Truly stupid."

He sounded stupefied. "They found them?"

"Did you think you'd picked such a great hiding place? Wrapped in a piece of oilskin in the back corner of the swimming-pool pump filter? Come on, Neil, what if the pump had broken? The pool man would have been fifty thousand dollars richer.''

"I didn't hide them."

"Oilskin takes fingerprints, old friend. The prints are still readable even after all this time. I don't doubt they'll be your prints. Why keep denying what you did?"

"Because he didn't do it."

Steve whirled, gun raised. Posey stood in the doorway in an old chenille robe and bare feet. The gun in her hand was small, but no less deadly than Steve's.

He didn't think he'd have recognized her. She'd put on at least fifty pounds. Her face sagged. With no makeup, her skin was mottled, the cheeks flushed as though she had a fever.

"Posey, go back to bed," Neil snapped. "I've got this under control."

Posey giggled. "See, Steve, you had it backward. I drugged you and Neil, not the other way around. Neil always thinks he has everything under control. Neil, darling, you don't have anything under control and never did. Put your gun down, Steve, before I shoot it out of your hand. I can do that, you know. I'm a very good shot. One of the few things I could do better than Chelsea. Although I'd really prefer to put a bullet through your damned heart."

"Posey, don't." Neil slid in front of Steve. "Come on, sweetheart. Steve's an old friend."

"Friend? He came here to kill you, Neil. To our home! To destroy my family! Get out of the way. He's an escaped killer, he broke in, he had a gun, I woke up, came downstairs and killed the man who killed my sister. Simple."

"No more killing, Posey!" Neil's cry was anguished.

Steve stood dumbfounded.

"We'll say Steve came over here after he killed Chelsea, changed the knives and hid her jewelry in our pool filter to incriminate you."

"And the fingerprints?" Steve asked.

Posey shrugged. "I'll think of something. I should have noticed the knives were different. That was stupid. But keeping the jewelry wasn't stupid. I certainly wasn't going to throw away Mother's heirloom diamond ring. It's six carats."

"Why did you kill her?" Steve asked. "She was your sister."

"My sister. My beautiful sister, Daddy's girl who inherited the money when little Posey wasn't smart enough to keep it out of the hands of fortune hunters. The sister my husband still loved even after he *settled* for me. The sister who was going to back her dear husband in a brand-new venture so he could walk out on me and Neil and leave us holding the bag. The sister who spent her life trying to advise me on my diet, my clothes, my hair, my makeup, my house, my husband and my life. That sister. Right."

"And you framed me. Why?"

Posey tossed her head. "Who else was there? I certainly didn't owe you any loyalty. Besides, if you were in jail, I got all Chelsea's money. Finally. I should have had it all along. Neil, get out of the way. It's time to end this."

Without taking his eyes off her, he said, "I won't let you. Steve, get out while you can. Run. I promise I won't call the police. Just go."

"You covered up for her?" Steve asked incredulously.

"Of course I covered up for her! Whose fault do you think it was that she hated Chelsea so much? Steve, I'm begging you."

"And the evidence?"

"I don't know. I'll think of something. Just go, for God's sake."

"Not necessary, Mr. Waters." The new voice spoke from the darkness of the hall behind Posey.

She screamed.

Steve saw the spit of fire from the barrel of her pistol as the man knocked her arm upward.

Neil grabbed his left shoulder and fell back against Steve. "Damn," he whispered.

"Neil!" Posey screamed, and tried to run from the strong hands that held her. "Oh, God, I shot him!"

A moment later she was on the floor with her hands cuffed behind her. She kept screaming for Neil.

Steve dropped to his knees and supported Neil's head. "It's just a flesh wound, Neil. You'll be okay."

Neil's eyelids fluttered. "Poor Posey. Poor old Posey...." Then he passed out.

The room was suddenly full of big men. Steve handed over his pistol, pulled his shirt out of the waistband of his jeans and, with a grimace, ripped off the small microphone taped to his belly. "Did you get it all?"

"Every word," Schockley said. "Should be enough to get you off and put them both away for a long time."

"Then it's over?"

"Not quite, but I'd say you're on the downhill swing. Hang in there, Chadwick, just a little longer." He glanced at his watch. "You've been gone over an hour. Time we got you back to the farm. I'll have one of my guys drive you. We'll alert the warden on the way."

Steve dropped his head back the moment he sank into the front seat of the unmarked cruiser. He was exhausted, but for once it was a good kind of tired. He could finally tell Eleanor everything tomorrow. He could come to her clean, not a killer. A man who would soon be free.

And tomorrow he'd take care of Sweet Daddy once and for all. Somehow he'd get him sent back to Big Mountain.

The driver spoke to the prison, then looked at Steve strangely.

"You got a situation at the farm, Chadwick. The cow barn's on fire. They think there may be people inside."

Steve came instantly alert. "People? Now?"

"Yeah."

Eleanor. She'd found out somehow he was gone and had gone looking for him. She could have run into Sweet

Daddy or one of the COs. Like Mike Newman. God, he should have warned her!

"Drive, please! I've got to get there."

The car tore away from the curb.

SWEET DADDY CARRIED an open gasoline can marked "motor pool" in each hand. He dropped them in the aisle in front of the barn office. Some of the liquid splashed onto the concrete. The smell of gasoline rose from the puddle.

"I said he's gone! Bastard run off and left me!"

Eleanor said, "He hasn't run anywhere." She tried to sound certain, but her heart was pounding. Was this why he hadn't spoken to her in days? So that he wouldn't lose his damned *focus?*

"Ain't in the compound, ain't in the mess hall, ain't down here. Damn! I told the man what I'd do he didn't take me with him."

Sweet Daddy stamped his skinny foot in impotent fury.

Eleanor edged backward toward her truck. She'd lost. Sweet Daddy was right. This time she felt in her bones that Steve was not down in the pasture with a cow. She clenched her stomach muscles to keep the fluttering in her insides down.

Why couldn't Steve have hung on? Had her first assessment been right? Had she always been simply a means to an end, to giving him the leeway to escape, to kill Neil and disappear?

She ought to alert the COs immediately so they could go after him, put out an APB or whatever they called it.

She also ought to alert Neil Waters to the danger he was in.

But Steve could be killed if she did. She had to find him and stop him before he committed the final act that would separate him forever from the rest of mankind.

"You ain't goin' nowhere, woman," Sweet Daddy

snarled. "I told Steve. I warned him. I'm not going back. He's out. Now I'm leaving on my own."

"Go on back to the compound before the COs find you're gone."

He moved toward her. She'd never realized how like a snake he was. She kept backing up, waiting for the moment to break and run.

"You think you can outrun Sweet Daddy? Ain't no *female* stop Sweet Daddy." He kept moving forward. His body language became cockier with each step. She hated his smile and the glint of that gold tooth.

Suddenly she bumped into one of the concrete pillars.

In an instant he was on her, twisting her wrist behind her so that she gasped with pain. His cheek was close to hers, his breath in her ear. She smelled the acrid scent of his body.

She ignored the pain and tore at his face with her free hand.

"Ow!" His grip loosened. He put his hand to his cheek. "Bitch! I'm bleeding."

She grabbed the corner of the column and used it as a lever to pull herself around.

Run! She was four inches taller than he was. She ought to be able to outrun him.

She felt his hand twist in her hair.

He yanked her head back, and when she screamed and tried to pull his hands away, he wrapped his free arm across her throat.

She couldn't breathe. She struggled, tried to pull his arm away from her throat, tried to stomp his feet, kick back against his knee, twist around to kick his groin—all the things that were supposed to work against attackers.

But Sweet Daddy was used to battling women. He knew the tricks.

He twisted her away from the front of the barn and threw her facedown against the stacked bales of hay just past the office.

''You through giving orders, bitch. You ain't ever dissin' Sweet Daddy again.''

She rolled over on her back. ''Touch me and they'll hunt you down and kill you. And if they don't, Steve will.''

''Steve's gone, and he couldn't kill squat. Time they dig this place out and find what's left of you, I'll be so far under with my ladies, ain't nobody gonna find me.''

Eleanor froze in horror. His gold tooth flashed in the sudden flicker from the lighted wooden match in his hand. He unbuckled his belt. When he saw her face, he began to laugh.

''Sweet Daddy could teach you some tricks all right, if I had the time, but I gotta get my ass out of here in your truck while they all trying to keep this damn place from burning to the ground. This'll do to tie you up till the fire gets going good.''

''Please, you can't. The animals won't be able to get out.''

''Neither will you, bitch. Get up.''

''Go to hell.''

''You first.''

She realized the thing he pulled from behind his back had once been a long steel blade used to scrape the sweat off horses. Nobody'd noticed it was missing. Now light glinted off the sharpened side, the pointed end. He must have spent hours carefully honing it into a knife.

Sweet Daddy knew how to use a knife.

Eleanor felt her gorge rise. She remembered those pictures of the woman he'd assaulted—the woman who'd testified against him. Sweet Daddy knew how to use a knife, all right.

''You think I won't cut you? You do what I say. Get up.''

She struggled to her feet. Screaming would do no good, for no one would hear. She couldn't reach her truck or her cell phone, or even the panic button on her pager that sat so handily in the front seat of the truck.

He grabbed her hair again and tossed her away from the hay. She stumbled once, recovered, then faked another stumble. If she could somehow get into Marcus's pen, she'd be safe. Sweet Daddy wouldn't dare follow her in there.

She could tell Marcus knew something was wrong. He stamped and snorted nervously as close to the electric wire as he could get without touching it. She could hear the horses at the far end of the barn nervously stamping and kicking in their stalls, too. They sensed danger—maybe smelled Eleanor's fear. She thanked God the cow and her new calf were safely back in the pasture.

"You ain' goin' nowhere," Sweet Daddy snarled.

In her haste to get to Marcus's pen, she tripped over one of the jerry cans and fell on her hands and knees on the concrete. She heard the can tip and the *glug-glug* of the gasoline as it ran out.

She couldn't let Sweet Daddy flick another match now. Even if she could get out, the horses and Marcus couldn't. She needed a weapon, something that would keep that knife from slicing into her.

A towel, a horse blanket, anything that she could wrap around her forearm would help. She looked around and saw nothing that would do. There wasn't even anything to throw at him.

Sweet Daddy grinned at her and kicked over the other can of gasoline. It, too, began to flow out onto the concrete, down the aisle and under the hay.

She was close to Marcus's stall now. If she touched that electric wire, she'd get a jolt, but not nearly so bad as a knife in her throat. She reached behind her, and Sweet Daddy realized what she planned to do.

"No!" He lunged at her.

And slipped in the stream of gasoline.

She felt the pain as the blade sliced through her jacket

and across her forearm. Another lunge and he'd have her.
She grabbed the fence, took the jolt, realized she couldn't
possibly open the gate in time and didn't have the strength
to vault a five-foot fence. She was trapped.

"You gone plumb crazy?" Big loomed up out of the
darkness behind Sweet Daddy.

Sweet Daddy whirled, making circles in front of him
with his knife. "Ain't your business, fool."

"Who spilled gas? That's right dangerous."

"Big, watch out!" Eleanor shouted as Sweet Daddy
lunged at him.

Big swept him aside with one broad arm and ignored
the knife that had come dangerously close to his chest.
"Doc? You all right? Hey, you got blood on you!"

"Big, behind you. Don't let him light a match!"

"Riiight," Sweet Daddy whispered.

The match flickered, then arced through the air to land
in a pool of gasoline between him and Big.

Big turned at the *whomp*. "Oh, Lordy!" He reached
across the flames, grabbed Sweet Daddy by the collar,
dragged him out of the way of the fire, and held him two
feet off the floor while Sweet Daddy struggled to reach
Big's body with the knife. "You shouldna done that."

His voice was quiet, almost apologetic.

"Big, put him down. We've got to put out that fire."
Eleanor held her bleeding arm against her side and reached
for the fire extinguisher beside Marcus's stall.

"Elroy, now I am *mad*."

Big wrenched the knife from Sweet Daddy and tossed
it aside, then he lifted him two-handed over his head.

Sweet Daddy began to scream. He screamed as he flew
through the air into the bull's paddock. Then he stopped
screaming and lay very still.

Eleanor saw the angle of his head and his open mouth
just before Marcus realized that his foe was at his mercy
at long last.

"I got to get him outta there," Big said. "Oh, Lordy."

''The fire, Big, put out the fire!'' Eleanor threw the extinguisher to him and turned on the water hose. She aimed it at Marcus full force to keep him away from Sweet Daddy. She didn't think it mattered now, but she had to try.

Marcus snorted, then reached under Sweet Daddy's limp form with one of his horns and tossed the little man over his shoulder. Sweet Daddy landed like a broken puppet.

Over the hiss and spurt of the extinguisher and the crackle of the flames, came Big's litany of ''Oh, Lordy, Oh, Lordy…''

From the distance she heard sirens.

The gasoline blazed on the concrete, crawled over the bales of hay, and ate at Marcus's enclosure. She heard the snap as the flames hit the electric wire.

Her eyes were burning and tearing. The smoke from the hay billowed thick and acrid. She felt light-headed, but started down the aisle toward the three horses who were screaming and kicking their stalls, desperate to get away from the flames.

From behind she heard the sound of running feet, then someone grabbed her.

''Get her out of here,'' Gil shouted. He pushed her to Robert, who threw her over his shoulder in a fireman's carry and raced out of the barn.

''Robert, put me down!'' She began to cough, and the bouncing made her arm throb. ''Get the horses out.''

He set her on her feet, gave her one look and sprinted back into the barn just as Gil drove the three horses out.

''Where's Big?'' Eleanor shouted.

''He's gone to lock Marcus out into the back paddock.''

''Sweet Daddy's in there. In Marcus's stall.''

''Oh God.'' Gil started back, but Eleanor stopped him. ''Let the firemen bring him out.''

''What you mean, woman?'' Robert shouted. He looked from her face to Gil's. ''He dead?''

Eleanor nodded.

"Marcus got him?"

Eleanor took a deep breath. "Marcus got him."

Gil saw her bloody arm. "You're hurt."

"Superficial."

"Superficial, my ass."

A car screamed up the long driveway from the highway, skidded to a stop, the door opened and Steve jumped out.

"Steve!" Eleanor cried. She forgot her arm, she forgot the fire and Sweet Daddy and everything else.

"Are you all right?" He swept her into his arms.

"Hell, no, man, she's not all right. She's bleeding."

"Eleanor?"

"It's nothing. A little cut. A couple of bandages will take care of it. Oh, Steve, I thought you'd gone. Please tell me you didn't, didn't…"

"Didn't kill Neil?" He shook his head. "Where the hell's the EMT van?"

At that moment Big came around the far side of the barn from Marcus's paddock. He was black with soot and bent double with coughing.

"Big, thank God you're all right," Eleanor said.

"I got Marcus shut out in his pasture. I went back to get Sweet Daddy, but there was too much smoke, and then the firemen wouldn't let me hunt for him." Tears streamed down his face and mixed with the soot from the fire. "Oh, Doc, Lordy, Lordy, I told you I dassen't get mad."

"What's this about Sweet Daddy?" Steve asked.

"You saved us all, Big."

"Not him."

"You tried."

THE FIREMEN WERE PUTTING AWAY their hoses and equipment. The last of the gasoline had been hosed out of the barn, the hay and shavings soaked to avoid the possibility of a flare-up later.

Eleanor leaned against Steve. Her arm throbbed. It felt

like the world's biggest paper cut. "I told you it was just a scratch, Steve. I'm a doctor. I know these things."

"You're a horse doctor. When I think of what could have happened…" He held her even more closely. "This is all my fault. I'm so sorry."

"You couldn't know that Sweet Daddy would try to burn the barn down. I don't think he expected to find me here."

"He would still have killed you."

"He hated me, Steve. *Me*. Not because of you, but because I'm a woman and he couldn't control me."

"I should have warned you about Sweet Daddy. I told Big to watch out for you, but that wasn't enough. I put you in terrible danger, but I was sure I'd be back before either one of you realized I was gone. If Big hadn't come down when he saw Sweet Daddy was missing…"

"But he did. Because you warned him. He saved me and he saved the animals."

"We didn't save Sweet Daddy. Marcus got his revenge."

Eleanor made a sound, hugged herself and turned away from him.

"I know you don't like to think about it, Eleanor, but there's nothing anyone could have done once he was in the stall with Marcus."

"If I tell you something, will you swear no one will else will ever know?"

"Of course. The look on your face…my God, Eleanor, Sweet Daddy, he didn't…?"

She looked startled. "No, oh, no. He said he didn't have time to teach me a lesson." She looked around. Everyone seemed to be busy wrapping up the fire and transporting the remains of Sweet Daddy. Big sat on the running board of the EMT van with an oxygen mask over his face. Gil and the others stood around him in a protective phalanx.

"Nobody must ever, ever, know this. Big couldn't bear it. He caught Sweet Daddy and threw him into Marcus's stall. I don't think he knew where he was aiming—he simply wanted to get Sweet Daddy as far away from that fire and from me as he could."

"I'm sure he knows that."

"I doubt it, but that's not what I'm talking about." She dropped her voice to a whisper. "I saw the way he landed." She looked up at Steve with tears in her eyes. "The fall broke his neck. I think when Marcus Aurelius got to him he was already dead."

Steve closed his eyes for a moment. "Big's no less a hero for that."

"He won't see it that way. He still feels guilty about breaking that punk's arm when he tried to burn that old hound. How do you think he'd feel if he knew he'd killed a man, even a man like Sweet Daddy who'd just tried to kill me and burn down the barn? He's come so far, Steve. He can't ever know."

"Will the autopsy be able to tell?"

She shook her head. "The injuries came too close together. It's even possible that Sweet Daddy was still breathing when Marcus got to him, though I doubt it."

Steve wrapped his arms around her and hugged her close. "No one will ever know from me, my darling."

"Thank you," she whispered.

"Well, Doctor," Ernest Portree said, "I see you're breaking the rules again." But he didn't sound angry.

"Yes, Warden," Steve answered. "So am I."

"You're damn lucky you pulled it off. I should never have agreed."

"What's he talking about?" Eleanor asked.

"This is the first time in my life I've ever let a prisoner of mine loose on purpose. And the last. This night has been hell on my nerves." He patted Eleanor's shoulder. "Sure you're all right?"

"Yes. I hope Big is."

"He's fine. Damned moose." Ernest shook his head. "Guess I'm going to have to move up his parole hearing."

"Parole hearing?" Eleanor pulled away from Steve. "Parole hearing? Ernest Portree, if you don't get on the telephone to the governor first thing tomorrow morning and get that man a pardon, I'll...I don't know what I'll do, but you won't like it."

"Whoa, Doctor, settle down." Portree smiled at her. "I was planning to do just that." He glanced at Steve. "As for you, Chadwick, I want you in my office. Now."

"Yes, Warden."

"Steve?"

"It's going to be all right, Eleanor. Trust me."

He turned away and followed the warden.

"You keep *saying* that!" Eleanor called after him.

She worried about Steve while she and the team bedded Marcus down in his paddock, safely shut away from his charred stall, and saw that the horses were lodged in the spare pasture on the far side of the buffalo. The drenched bales outside the barn hung with icicles.

The inside of the barn stank of wet hay and charred wood. Water ran down the aisles and had already glazed over in spots, but there seemed to be no damage to the new wood on Marcus's stall that a good cleaning and some fresh paint wouldn't cure. The smell would linger, but eventually that, too, would dissipate.

Big kept fighting the EMTs who tried to administer oxygen to him. "I'm just fine, ma'am," he said again and again.

"Why don't you take him back to the compound in your truck?" Gil asked Eleanor quietly. "Then you go home and get some sleep. We'll handle this. Don't worry too much. We all knew the kind of man Sweet Daddy was. We're all responsible."

"No. Sweet Daddy was responsible. Thanks, Gil. Come on, Big, time to go home."

"But—"

"Big, get yourself into my truck."

"Yes'm."

Neither said a word until they were within sight of the compound. Then Eleanor said, "Thank you, Big. You saved my life."

"Didn't save his. I wish…"

"You tried. Will there be other men in the dormitory?"

"Yes'm."

"I probably should have insisted you go to the infirmary, maybe get a sleeping pill."

"I'd rather be with everybody else." As he climbed out of the cab of the truck, he said, "Doc, did I kill him?"

The question Eleanor had been dreading. She tried to sound completely surprised. "No, Big, of course not! Marcus killed him."

"But I throwed him in the pen where Marcus could stomp him. And he couldn't get away. I saw that."

"He wouldn't have been able to get away from Marcus in any case, Big. No, you did not kill him. Put that thought out of your mind. I saw what happened. You did the right thing. You saved my life and Marcus's life and the horses, too."

"Yes'm. If you say so."

"I do."

"Doc, I got *mad* again."

"I know, Big. This time it was right you got mad. If you hadn't been mad, I don't think you could have gotten us all out alive."

"You think so?" He brightened.

"I know so. Now go take a hot shower and go to bed. You're a good man, Bigelow Little, and a hero. Don't you forget that."

CHAPTER SEVENTEEN

SHE DROVE TO the administration building and saw from the parking lot that there were lights in Ernest's office. She might not be welcome, but she intended to see Steve, anyway.

There was no one in the outer office to stop her. She could hear men's voices from inside the office, but they didn't sound angry. She knocked, then opened the door without waiting to be invited in.

A half-dozen men lounged around the room. Ernest sat behind his desk, Steve in front of it, but he didn't look as though he were under any sort of restraint. Through the haze of cigarette smoke she saw Leslie Vickers, the private detective Schockley and a couple of men who had "cop" written all over them.

Steve started to get up, but Ernest stopped him with a hand.

"I thought you'd show up, Eleanor," he said. "We're at the end of our little debriefing."

"What is this all about, please?"

Leslie Vickers came over and took her hand in both of his.

"We now have a confession in Chelsea Chadwick's murder," he said.

She glanced at Steve in horror.

"No, my dear, not Steve."

This time Steve did come to her and put his hands on her arms. "I was after the wrong man. Neil didn't kill Chelsea. Posey did."

"Her sister?"

"Neil knew almost from the beginning," Leslie continued. "He says he had to protect his wife, and in law he
couldn't be forced to testify against her. I think he wanted
the money. If Posey went to prison, the insurance money
and Chelsea's estate would have reverted to Steve." He
smiled at his client. "As it does now, of course. You are
once more a wealthy man, Steve."

"And able to pay your bill, Leslie," Steve said with a
smile.

Leslie laughed. "I had thought of that."

"But—"

"Plenty of time for details later," Leslie said. "At the
moment suffice it to say that Mrs. Waters has confessed
in great detail and on the record, Mr. Waters will probably
go to jail as an accessory after the fact, and as soon as it
can be arranged, Steve's conviction will be vacated."

"Steve? Is it true?"

He nodded.

She clung to him. "Tonight when you weren't there, I
was so afraid you were going to…"

"To kill him? It's all right, Eleanor. It was a setup."

"A setup? And you didn't tell me? You let me think…"

"I couldn't tell you. It had to look like a legitimate
escape. The man driving my 'getaway' car was a cop, and
I had Henry and Charlie over there on me all the time. If
I *had* decided to run, there were so many cops around
Neil's house I wouldn't have had a prayer."

"He was wearing a wire," Leslie said. "I truly thought
Neil was guilty. I seldom make mistakes like that."

"Posey actually confessed?"

"When she thought I was going to kill Neil," Steve
said. "She would have shot me, except that he intervened.
It was close. Neil's in the hospital with a bullet in his
shoulder that was meant for my heart."

"Oh, Steve!"

"This is the first time I have ever aided and abetted a

prison escape, and I'm damned sure it's my last,'' Warden Portree said. He turned to Charlie Schockley. "Charlie, we are now even. No more favors.''

"Yeah, I was right on this one, though, you gotta admit,'' Charlie said. He turned to the assembled detectives. "Ol' Ernie here and me, we go back a long way, back to when Ernie was just a cop like the rest of us.''

"You weren't right the first time,'' the warden said. "Remember *that,* why don't you? Now, since we know Chadwick here isn't going anywhere, may I suggest that we leave the prisoner and the doctor alone and go to the mess hall for some coffee.''

The moment the room was empty, Steve kissed Eleanor. "We both came so damn close to dying tonight.''

"Why didn't you tell me? I feel like an idiot.''

"I didn't dare. You had to seem truly worried when nobody could find me. You're the reason I'm not a killer. Before I met you, I *was* planning to kill Neil. For three long years it's kept me going—until you came along. The more I thought about killing Neil, the more I thought about losing you. You believed in me, Eleanor, when nobody else did.''

"I didn't believe in you, either. Not at first.''

"But you did believe in me eventually. And you fought for my soul. You gave me the strength to make one more try to prove I didn't kill Chelsea.''

She clung to him.

He buried his face in her hair. "Thank God you did. I'd have killed the wrong man. I'll never forget that.''

"Tell me…''

"Later. We'll have all our lives to talk. Right now I just want to kiss you and hold you.'' He smiled down at her. "I don't suppose Warden Portree would be exactly thrilled if we made love on his desk, would he?''

"All our lives?''

"If you'll have me. I don't know what I'll do with my

life, but I do know that I want you to be a part of it forever.''

"Yes, Steve, yes, yes, yes.''

WARDEN PORTREE WAS STUNNED when Steve and Eleanor called on him a week after Steve and Big were pardoned.

At first Steve hadn't wanted to accept a pardon because it implied that he had done something he needed to be pardoned for.

Leslie Vickers told him not to be a fool. It might take a year to get his record completely cleared, and then only if Posey Waters repeated her confession in court. Better to take the pardon, leave prison a free man and start to rebuild his life.

That turned out to be easier than he'd thought possible. Neil officially confessed to being an accessory after the fact of Chelsea's murder. His confession effectively nullified not only Steve's sale of his part of the company to Neil three years earlier, but Neil's sale to the conglomerate.

The members of the conglomerate weren't happy. They upped their offer twice. Steve was perfectly happy to give them a deal on his data engine, but he had no intention of relinquishing control of his company. He'd told Eleanor, "We'll make a deal. It may take a while, but we'll get it done."

She had been astounded when he had her drive him to see Neil in the prison ward at the hospital.

"I nearly let hate destroy me, my darling," he told her. "It very nearly cost me your love, and then I damn near killed the wrong man. Now that he's the one facing prison, he's going to need all the help he can get just to survive. I have to do what I can."

Now Eleanor and Steve sat facing Warden Portree's desk. He sat there shaking his head.

"You want what?'' he asked.

"You are a justice of the peace, aren't you?" Steve asked.

"I have to be, yes."

"So will you marry us, here, in your office?" Eleanor asked. "We were thinking of waiting until late April or early May so the weather will be pretty but not too hot."

"Why on earth would you want that, Chadwick? To come back here after all you've been through?"

"It's the only place where everybody who was on the team can attend—even Slow Rise."

"What about Eleanor's new team members? The ones who replaced Steve and Big—and Elroy?"

"We want them, too, of course, but mostly we want Gil and Robert and Slow Rise and Selma to be able to come," Eleanor answered.

"Gil Jones is due for parole in July."

"I know," Steve said. "He's got a job waiting for him with an old friend of mine who runs a limo service."

"And Robert's already working two days a week for J. K. Saunders," Eleanor said. "But he's not eligible for parole until next Christmas. And of course, Slow Rise…"

"Isn't eligible for parole for years." Portree sighed. "Of course I'll do it. Maybe we can even arrange a little reception afterward in the mess hall if you'll pay the county for the refreshments. No alcohol allowed."

Eleanor asked Precious to be her maid of honor. Sarah Scott fought against what she called "waddling down the aisle like Egg Roll" in her advanced state of pregnancy.

"You're not due until late June or early July. You'll look beautiful."

"I'll look like a beer barrel."

Eventually, however, she was persuaded to act as matron of honor.

Steve had asked Big to be his best man. Big would wear a specially tailored navy blue suit with a specially tailored white shirt and extra long red power tie for the second time in his life. Steve worked hard with his tailor to make sure the suit was large enough.

BIG IN FACT got to wear his special suit a few weeks before the wedding when Gil Jones drove Big, Steve and Eleanor, Robert Dalrymple, Big's dog Daisy, and Selma to Mission, Tennessee. At first the warden had refused to let Robert and Gil leave the prison compound, but Eleanor had persisted. After all, Selma could keep them in line.

"Gilford Jones, do you swear to me this limousine is not hot?" Selma twisted in her seat and frowned at Gil, who had on regular slacks and a polo shirt specially purchased for the expedition, and who drove the white stretch limousine with casual ease.

"Gilford? Your name Gilford?" Robert Dalrymple, who sat on the jump seat behind the driver, guffawed.

"Shut up, Robert," Selma said.

"Yes, Selma, I promise you this limousine is not hot. I borrowed it from the man who's going to hire me when I get out on parole."

"Does he *know* you borrowed it?"

"Yes, Selma," Gil said patiently. "Don't worry. I'm not going to get you busted in a hot limousine."

Eleanor squeezed Steve's hand and whispered, "Just like old times."

Big overflowed the jump seat next to Robert. He had refused to take the rear seat, even though he would have fit much better on that.

From time to time he pulled at the collar of his white shirt. "I ain't never had no nice suit like this," he said again and again. Daisy, the one-eared pit bull, slept at his feet with her brindle head on his shiny new shoes.

Outside the softly purring stretch limo, spring had already begun to ripen into summer. The trees were in full leaf, and thick hedges of wild roses rioted along the verges of the road.

"Steve, you sure this is a good idea?" Big asked. "Me going home like this to see Mama's grave?"

"Absolutely." Steve tucked Eleanor's hand under his arm. He never wanted to let her go again. He'd come so close to losing her, and then, having to endure another two months of prison over Thanksgiving and Christmas before his pardon came through had been worse hell than he could have imagined.

Eleanor and Steve had already driven up to Mission once to oversee setting the tombstone they'd ordered for the grave of Big's mother, Mattie Little. Big had no idea how much the stone had cost, and Eleanor and Steve promised each other he never would.

They hoped he'd like the marble-and-granite headstone. It was simple but impressive.

As the limo drove into Mission shortly before noon, heads turned to follow their progress down the shabby main street. Eleanor saw a few people point fingers and whisper as they recognized Big.

Without telling anyone what she'd done, Eleanor had sent a complete story of Big's heroism and subsequent pardon to the *Mission Weekly Missive.* She'd included Big's story of the nearly burned hound and the mayor's rotten son, but she was certain the paper wouldn't print that part. They didn't.

They did, however, grudgingly print a short squib about Big. The limo pulled up to the small country church with its equally small graveyard, and everyone climbed out.

"Look, there's somebody new buried," Big whispered, and pointed to a large arrangement of spring flowers beside one of the graves.

The others hung back. Steve wrapped his arm around Eleanor's shoulders. She held his hand very tight.

Big walked around the graves, searching for some sign that would identify his mother's plot. Daisy trotted behind him. Finally he stopped in front of the flower arrangement with its tall headstone. He turned to the others with a puzzled expression. "This says it's my mama's grave, flowers and all."

"That's right, Big," Steve said. "We took the liberty of setting the headstone and sending the flowers. I hope it's all right."

"It's beautiful," he said, and began to cry.

Daisy looked up at him and began to whimper.

Eleanor and Selma were the next to dissolve. Gil and Robert and Steve refused to look at one another.

Big snuffled, pulled out a large white handkerchief, blew his nose, and stuffed the handkerchief back into his trouser pocket, but only halfway. It stuck out from under his coat like a flag of surrender.

Eleanor heard the front door of the little church open, and a moment later a man pattered down the steps. "Mr. Little?" He held out his hand to Big. "I'm Reverend Sumner. I've been hoping to meet you." He turned a sunny smile on the rest of the group. "All of you are most welcome, yes, most welcome."

"Thank you, Reverend," Steve said.

"I have a cardboard box of your mother's keepsakes, Mr. Little," Reverend Sumner said. "I brought it out here to the church when I found you were coming today. Would you like to take it with you? It's not much, I'm afraid, but there is a rather lovely old quilt, and some of the finest pine needle bowls I've ever seen. Quite valuable, I'm sure. I kept them back from the sale because I thought they might be family heirlooms."

"My mama made those," Big said proudly.

They had lunch at the same restaurant as before. People looked at Big, but only a few spoke to him, as though they were afraid someone in authority would see them.

As Gil drove them out of town, Big said, "Whew-ee. I don't never want to come back again except to visit my mama's grave."

"Very wise," Steve told him.

"Good thing I got me a good job at the clinic now, and a place to live I can keep Daisy."

"We've needed a watchman on the place at night," Eleanor told the others. "Now that Dr. Weincroft's research building is finally finished, it's going to be even more important. His research is highly sensitive. Lots of pharmaceutical companies would love to steal it."

"Gil, when you and Robert get out, you got to come see me. I got my own little apartment." Big smiled at Steve. "Steve even got me a bed big enough to sleep on."

"Parolees aren't supposed to associate with known criminals," Selma said with a sniff.

"Lighten up, Selma," Steve said. "Nobody in *this* limousine is ever going to be inside a prison looking out again." He leaned forward. "Right, Gil?"

"Yeah, yeah, I guess."

"Right, Robert?"

"Yeah, man. Mr. Saunders's already moved my wife and boy into one of the houses on his place. I ain't never gonna leave them again. I like horses a lot better'n I like drugs." He grinned. "Me and Old Will's just alike. I have finally figured out I *hate* cows."

EPILOGUE

THE WARDEN'S OFFICE WAS SMALL, so only Eleanor's team members, the Creature Comfort veterinarians, and Mary Beth and the Colonel attended.

As Steve's best man, Big shuffled from one foot to the other throughout the ceremony and nearly dropped the rings, but he managed.

The clinic staffers and some of the prison staff joined the others at the reception in the mess hall after the ceremony. Raoul Torres brought his lovely wife and his two children. When he introduced Eleanor to his family, he added, "Hey, even I occasionally miss one. Good thing you didn't listen to me." He raised his cup of punch. "But don't make a habit of it."

"I promise I will not marry any more convicted murderers," Eleanor said.

"I'll hold you to that."

Big actually managed a respectable toast of fruit punch to the happy couple. He blushed like a child when everyone applauded.

Slow Rise kept patting Eleanor's shoulder as the tears ran down his cheeks. She didn't know what to say to him, so she simply hugged him.

"Steve, now that you're married to one of my staffers," Warden Portree said over a large slice of wedding cake, "will you be moving into Eleanor's cottage?"

"Until we can find a house away from the farm to buy," he said. "Frankly I can hardly wait to rub Mike Newman's face in the fact that I'm now his neighbor—his *free* neighbor.''

''Better do it soon. I fired him yesterday. He finally went too far. Put a youngster in the hospital.''

''He's the one ought to be in jail,'' Eleanor said from Steve's side.

''One thing at a time,'' Portree answered. ''He won't be able to get away with anything outside in the world. We may well see him back before too long, but in a prison uniform.''

ON THEIR WEDDING NIGHT, lying in the king-size bed in the bridal suite at the Peabody, content in the afterglow of love, Eleanor lay curled against Steve's shoulder. He kissed the top of her head. ''It's nice making love in a real bed.''

She played with the hair on his chest. ''Desks and showers are fun, too.'' She lifted her face and kissed him under the chin.

''Are you still sure you're doing the right thing?''

Steve nodded. ''Absolutely. It'll take some time to get the kinks worked out, but in the end maybe I can make a difference, even if it's only a small one. I don't have to go to Africa or Brazil. There's plenty of work to be done here.'' He slid up onto the pillows. ''If we can identify the cons who really want to turn their lives around, and if I can give them training and place them with my company or somebody else's when they're paroled...''

''You sound like Raoul Torres.''

''Don't sell old Raoul short. If anyone can tell the bad apples from the good, it's Raoul.''

''He thought you were a bad apple.''

''So he's not perfect.'' He ran his hand down her shoulder and her arm. ''I can't ever be the man I was before.''

''I wish you could talk more about it. Will the nightmares ever go away?''

"With you to hold me, yes. I may never be able to tell you everything that went on in prison, my darling."

"I understand. I just wish I could help more."

"You help more than you can ever know. At least in prison I learned that what I do for the rest of my life has to mean something. Making money alone won't cut it."

"Your father thought you'd stay as far away from what he calls 'those people' as possible. He can't believe we're actually going to live on the prison grounds."

"It's different. I'm free now."

She pulled his face down and kissed him softly. "If I have anything to say about it, you'll never be free. Not of me."

He slid down in bed and turned to take her in his arms. "Free of you? Never's fine with me. For once I'm glad I have a life sentence."

COMING SOON...

AN EXCITING
OPPORTUNITY TO SAVE
ON THE PURCHASE OF
HARLEQUIN AND
SILHOUETTE BOOKS!

*DETAILS TO FOLLOW
IN OCTOBER 2001!*

YOU WON'T WANT TO MISS IT!

PHQ401

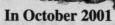

In October 2001
Look for this
New York Times bestselling author

BARBARA DELINSKY

in

Bronze Mystique

The only men in Sasha's life lived between the covers
of her bestselling romances. She wrote about passionate,
loving heroes, but no such man existed...til Doug Donohue
rescued Sasha the night her motorcycle crashed.

AND award-winning Harlequin Intrigue author

GAYLE WILSON

in

Secrets in Silence

This fantastic 2-in-1 collection will be on sale October 2001.

HARLEQUIN®
Makes any time special®

If you enjoyed what you just read,
then we've got an offer you can't resist!

Take 2 bestselling love stories FREE!

Plus get a FREE surprise gift!

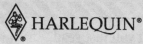

*Harlequin truly does
make any time special. . . .
This year we are celebrating
weddings in style!*

A Walk Down the Aisle
WEDDING CELEBRATION

To help us celebrate, we want you to tell us how wearing the Harlequin wedding gown will make your wedding day special. As the grand prize, Harlequin will offer one lucky bride the chance to **"Walk Down the Aisle" in the Harlequin wedding gown!**

There's more...

For her honeymoon, she and her groom will spend five nights at the **Hyatt Regency Maui.** As part of this five-night honeymoon at the hotel renowned for its romantic attractions, the couple will enjoy a candlelit dinner for two in Swan Court, a sunset sail on the hotel's catamaran, and duet spa treatments.

A HYATT RESORT AND SPA®

MAUI *the Magic Isles*™

Maui • Molokai • Lanai

To enter, please write, in, 250 words or less, how wearing the Harlequin wedding gown will make your wedding day special. The entry will be judged based on its emotionally compelling nature, its originality and creativity, and its sincerity. This contest is open to Canadian and U.S. residents only and to those who are 18 years of age and older. There is no purchase necessary to enter. Void where prohibited. See further contest rules attached. Please send your entry to:

Walk Down the Aisle Contest

In Canada
P.O. Box 637
Fort Erie, Ontario
L2A 5X3

In U.S.A.
P.O. Box 9076
3010 Walden Ave.
Buffalo, NY 14269-9076

You can also enter by visiting www.eHarlequin.com
Win the Harlequin wedding gown and the vacation of a lifetime!
The deadline for entries is October 1, 2001.

HARLEQUIN®
Makes any time special ®

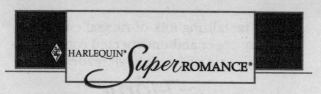